few others and sweep them away to another time and place." —*International Book Award Winner*

"Powerful, magnetic characters... St. Michel is a master at crafting realistic characters who tug at your heartstrings." —*Forward Reviews Bronze Medallion "Book of the Year"*

"*Lord of the Wilderness* is a fresh, unpredictable story with feisty, complex, and complicated characters that magnetize. The author has obviously done a massive amount of research about the American Revolutionary War era and area, and her plot snares you fast, from page one. A raw and rugged story, I was enthralled with Ms. St Michel's writing ~ not your typical, generical romance but one packed with realism and vigor and a love that dares even the threat of death itself. —*New York Times Bestselling Author Parris Afton Bonds*

Surrender to Honor

—*InD'tale's* RONE Award

Surrender the Storm
—Chanticleer International Book Award

in, no emotional stone is left unturned in this romance."
—*InD'tale Magazine*

Sweet Vengeance Reviews:

Sweet Vengeance: Duke of Rutland Series I received the International Book Award. "Elevates historical romance to new heights with an elegance of writing both electric and magnificent...a tangled web of love...deceits and adventures bursting into one fantastic journey across the seas."

Only You: Duke of Rutland Series III Reviews:

Only You: Duke of Rutland Series III won the American Fiction Award and National RONE Finalist. St. Michel's unique voice and talent shine through this exciting tale of loyalty, love and danger." —*American Fiction Award Winner*

"Characters bring unique elements on a lush tropical island with the road to love filled with twists and turns." —*InD'tale Magazine*

Lord of the Wilderness: Duke of Rutland Series IV Reviews:

"An extraordinary writer, a master storyteller, and a superb historian, Elizabeth St. Michel has created a powerful, poignant, and touchingly far-reaching epic of romance and adventure. With vivid characters, arises an evocative love story that is intricately woven in the American Revolution. This extraordinary tale will captivate readers like

On Prevailing Winds

ELIZABETH ST. MICHEL

DEDICATION

*For my daughter-in-law, Evelyn,
a great wife, mother, and the woman my son picked to be my best
friend...*

Chapter One

erlin, Germany 1945

The Third Reich had come to an end. The Age of Darkness that had deceived and easily misled a great nation to heights of power and conquest that Germans had never experienced, had dissolved with a suddenness and disastrous completeness that had few parallels in history.

Truant from the grueling brigades, Sophia and her best friend, Gabrielle raced past blackened ruins. Civilians swept the streets. Hollow-cheeked children sat unusually quiet. Women and men dug around in gardens. People scavenged for wood or coal for fuel from the rubble. Americans with rifles stood at every corner, children begging them for food, chocolate, anything the soldiers might give them.

Sophia wrinkled her nose. "I can still smell the stench of burning, and the decaying bodies beneath mountains of rubble."

Today was Sophia's lucky day, or so Gabrielle had told her with the repetition of a jackhammer. Buried in the rubble, Sophia had found a pack of American cigarettes, and then, a mimeographed scrap of paper glided to her feet on an errant wind—an advertisement for a job as a secretary and interpreter for the Americans.

Sophia gripped her friend's hand. "Luck has a way of evaporating when I lean on it. What if I don't get the job with the dreaded Americans, and then we are fired from the bucket brigade for feigning illness?"

Sophia looked upon the destruction the Fuhrer had abandoned to the women of Berlin, leaving them to push carts loaded with sand, brick, and fire-blackened debris up to the edge and tipping the contents into trenches. Every side street hosted interminable bucket brigades, and in endless backbreaking toil, Sophia Anna Sonderburg-Beck, a Prussian princess far from her ancestral home, had been reduced to a common laborer; suffering dust gummed into her eyes, nose, and mouth, and taunting her amid all manner of cruel cold, icy rain or torrid sun. But not today.

She stared down at her hands. Despite scrubbing them clean, broken nails, callused palms and fingers remained from grueling weeks of lifting rocks, bricks, and debris for a pittance.

"I've just finished a pan of cracklings. No sugar, butter, or meat. Barely bread if we are lucky. How long can we go on living like this?" Gabrielle went on and on painting a black picture of their future.

Sophia didn't care about tomorrow. She just wanted to live as well as she could for now, otherwise she'd collapse like a wet rag, giving in to their horrific existence.

"We can trade the cigarettes for potatoes and have a real meal." Lightheaded from lack of food, Sophia dodged crates, horses on sidewalks, drinking pails, boxes of oats and hay, trampled horse droppings, and cow paddies. Bicycles clattered down the street on bare rims while her wretched, ungrateful stomach beat a demanding tattoo.

On a bombed-out wall, a picture of Hitler saluting hung askew, reminding the miserable German citizenry how they had been duped by criminals.

Gabrielle spat. "No tree is high enough to hang him."

Russian soldiers in quilted jackets crouched around a small fire stoked of broken chairs in an entryway. Then came an endless train of close-cropped hair and well-fed carefree Russians flooding the streets.

"The world is the devil's chamberpot." Sophia said, and shoulder to shoulder with Gabrielle, quickened her pace, her leg muscles tightening as her body prepared to run. "They are not supposed to be in the American quarter. With certainty, they have come to trade all the stolen goods they have pilfered from poor German women who are left to starve."

"Look at them," Gabrielle sneered. "Marched from Moscow to Berlin. So proud of their victory, they're bursting their buttons. Even they are amazed they've made it this far."

"Do svidanya," leered one of the Russian soldiers heavily armed with a sack of chickens as he tipped his hat.

They passed Humboldt University where Sophia had met Dr. Karl Schneider, a young medical resident who had been determined to court her six years before. Karl, for whom Sophia had felt a warm friendship and nothing else, did not take long to propose to her, an offer Sophia had refused and kept on refusing. Sophia didn't want to hurt him. She had dodged him in the library, laboratories, and gatherings with their friends. The doctor had brushed aside her refusals, stayed on the offensive as strong as the Third Reich that rolled over Poland. He had invited her to dances, to elegant restaurants, operas, to the cinema or to take a stroll in Tiergarten Park. Being alone in Berlin, Sophia had found it difficult to resist his enthusiasm, his company, and his devotion. She had to only look at Karl to know that she would never be able to love him. Not the way she dreamed she would love somebody one day.

Toward the end of the war, news of her family's death had shocked her. They had been arrested and executed for acts against the Third Reich. With certainty, her last name would ring alarm bells. The Nazis would hunt her down, arrest her and send her to a detention camp to be executed.

Gabrielle pressed her with urgency. "You must marry Karl."

Gabrielle was the only person in the world Sophia had told of her royal lineage. When she had first enrolled at Humboldt University, she preferred her anonymity to avoid people bowing and scraping. With her parents' treason, her silence regarding her heritage might save her life.

"You must change your last name." Gabrielle had warned. "Karl loves you and will protect you. He is from a powerful banking family and a high-ranking Nazi."

And so, through need and weakness, Sophia had encouraged the doctor's advances and said yes to his next proposal. Never had she seen a happier man. For survival, she had married Karl, hoping one day she'd find a way to love him for his kindness and devotion.

Six months ago, Karl had left for the front, a more devout and dedicated servant of Hitler she'd never seen. That part of him Sophia hated for what the Nazis had done to her family and was glad she'd never told him of her heritage and about their executions.

Her chest tightened as she stared off in the distance where someone played an ironically cheerful tune on an accordion. She never had to learn to love Karl. He'd never returned.

The two women entered the black market, bustling with activity. The crowd had a life of its own, moving like a shoal of fish. The haggling between sellers and buyers amplified in irritating crescendo. Horse scent wafted through flapping cardboard. German pistols, medals and war regalia were selling to the American soldiers for a fortune. She wished she had Karl's medals. You couldn't eat medals, but she could trade them for potatoes, maybe even some eggs.

Sophia stopped at a farmer's cart laden with fresh eggs and potatoes. She flashed the valuable pack of cigarettes. "Give me three dozen eggs and four pounds of potatoes.

The farmer let Sophia simmer a few moments longer while he examined a broken fingernail. He waved her off. "You crazy."

His yellow nervous fingers rubbed together. He was addicted.

Sophia looked down her nose, pulling herself up into an aristocratic posture she hoped would inspire a sense of subservience. "Too bad. They are American." Sophia walked away. The farmer dogged her heels.

"I thought so." She retraced her steps and waited while the farmer counted out her eggs and potatoes. He grabbed for the cigarettes. She snatched them back. "I said four pounds not three."

His leathery face puckered as he heaved a sigh through rotted teeth. When he added the correct poundage, she handed the cigarettes to the farmer who stuffed them in his coat pocket like a dormouse stowing seeds in his cheeks.

"You are a ruthless negotiator," Gabrielle whispered.

"With certainty, he'll make a neat little profit and you'll be making a wonderful meal," Sophia said, her spirits lifting. She was drawn to an old gypsy woman with a tray in front of her supported by a leather strap around her neck. From high above on a rooftop, a crow swooped then settled on the woman's shoulder.

Sophia dragged Gabrielle to the woman. The gypsy nodded her head, her all-seeing rheumy blue eyes regarding them.

Gabrielle pointed to the crow and hissed in Sophia's ear. "That's a bad omen."

"Nonsense. Crows are messengers from the gods. A bird of prophecy and it gives advice to heroes in Slavic epics."

"You're a lunatic and my mother said to stay away from gypsies."

"More gibberish. I grew up with the gypsies. My father let them camp in our forests. My brother, sister and I played with them." Sophia's heart panged remembering her siblings that no longer existed. The old gypsy standing in front of them was so like Granny Roma from back in her village who'd treated her like a daughter. She prayed Granny Roma and their tribe had gone deep in the woods and survived.

The old woman stepped toward them, her tattered plaid skirt swishing about her clunky boots. "For a pfennig, I can show you your future husband." Her numerous brass bracelets clinked as she waved her hand over her tray.

"I don't have money, but I do have potatoes to share," offered Sophia.

Gabrielle clutched the bag of potatoes to her chest. "You are not giving up our precious potatoes."

"We have been lucky with our bounty and must share. Gypsies were taken to concentration camps and suffered as bad as the Jews."

Thick iron-gray coils bounced beneath a maroon diklo, a head scarf, knotted at her nape as the gypsy's deft fingers shuffled a deck of photos, placing them face down.

Coal-black feathers lifted as the crow moved its head from side to side, eyeing Sophia, and studying her overlong. Small hairs stirred on the back of her neck.

The crow hopped down on the tray, pecking at different photos, stopped, and picked one with its beak. With gnarled fingers the gypsy woman flipped it over and presented the photo to Sophia.

"My God," said Gabrielle. "This photo is an exact image of Karl. I don't believe it. This is a cruel trick. Karl is dead."

The gypsy lifted her hunched shoulders. "The crow picks at his will."

The crow waddled across the tray again, tapping with his beak, and then chose another photo. This time, the crow presented the photo.

Gabrielle meant to take it, but the crow veered away and pushed it toward Sophia.

The gypsy woman's craggy face broke into a genuine smile. "You are a lucky one, Fraulein. You will have the love to two men."

Sophia flinched. Why the terrible sense of foreboding? Granny Roma had told her crows were sometimes premonitions for disaster. Hands shaking, she hesitated. For a moment, there was no sound from the market. People were moving and talking but Sophia remained in a bubble of frozen silence.

A twinge of caution erupted in her chest with the crow's scrutiny, yet something intangible nagged at her, warned her of the future, and the potential heavy price she might pay. A wind swept over the market, swirling a tendril of her hair, and whipped it against her face. The gypsy woman splayed her hands on the photos to keep them from blowing away. As quickly as the prevailing wind arrived, it vanished.

Sophia shook those feelings aside.

The crow gave an adamant nudge against her trembling fingers, and at the bird's insistence, she took the photo, arranging Karl's image beneath. She frowned. The man was indeed handsome but of a different lineage she could not name. Unlike her late husband, he had dark hair and she could not determine the color of his eyes in the black and white photo. What caught her attention was his bearing, spurning the world like the Greek god of war Ares overlooking a battlefield ready to fight to satiate his lust of blood to win a noble cause. A knot grew in her throat. What would it mean to be in the company of such a man?

"Ridiculous," Sophia said.

With shrewd eyes, the gypsy gauged Sophia's reaction, closing her blue-veined hand over Sophia's wrist. "This man...rare are those who have a love so powerful and out of control. Your souls were intertwined in the stars long ago."

Gabrielle rolled her eyes. "This is the most absurd prediction I've heard since the Third Reich promised us streets paved with gold."

The gypsy woman gave her one last squeeze before releasing Sophia. "You have been blessed by the gypsies and know what I say is true."

Rattled from her encounter with the gypsy, Sophia with Gabrielle hurried from the marketplace toward Berlin-Zehlendorf where the United States military command was headquartered. Storm clouds rolled in threatening the sky's floodgates to open.

Sophia stopped at the front entrance and gripped her friend's hand like a drowning woman to a life rope. "I'm scared. I do hope fortune shines and I get the job, but my fate of late has been bleak. If not for bad luck, I'd have no luck at all."

"You can ensnare any man with those blue eyes of yours," Gabrielle said, hugging her, and then pushing her on. "You never know what your worse luck is until your bad luck has saved you. Make sure nothing happens to my last pair of precious stockings."

Chapter Two

Exhausted and late, Sophia waited in line, wishing the guard would hurry.

Her throat was parched, and she prayed the rain would hold off, so she'd look her best for her interview. She checked her old wool skirt she'd bought before the privations of war, when she was a student, and the world was full of possibilities. The skirt now was as worn as she was. The moth hole she'd stitched did not show. She exhaled. Well-scrubbed and pressed clean, her blouse gleamed white despite its age. A stray blonde hair flew across her face, and she tucked it behind her ear, summoning the aura of confidence nurtured on royal estates a lifetime ago.

She presented her papers to a guard whose upper teeth protruded over improbable lips. He leaned forward to inspect the documents. "State your business."

"I'm here to apply for a job," Sophia said in flawless English."

"Who with?" he said gruffly, and Sophia sensed he was weighing the danger level of admitting her.

In the wake of war, Sophia had become accustomed to the fake smiles and flat tones of voice that conveyed the distrust of the different militaries that had divided up Berlin into four sectors by the major superpowers. Russia. America. France and Great Britain. "Colonel Robert Pratt."

He made a note and jerked his head, signaling her to enter the American military compound. Pressing her valuable papers to her bosom, she passed several brick buildings of the former Luftwaffe district headquarters now occupied by their conquerors. The place was vast with cars zooming past her. Why hadn't she asked the guard for the way to the office?

Now she was tardy. The man she'd hoped to impress might even refuse to see her because of her lack of punctuality. She stopped a soldier and asked for directions. He pointed and she ran, rounding a corner and smacking into a brick wall. A *human* brick wall.

Down she went, her papers scattering across the sidewalk just as the skies opened with a torrential deluge. She cried out, scrambling on hands and knees to retrieve her papers. Mud and whatever unmentionable slicks of dark grime soiled her smart white blouse. Her skirt had not fared better.

Strong hands grasped her upper arms and began to pull her up. "No!" She violently protested, placing her hand on his chest, trying to ignore how the warmth of his skin felt against her palm despite the rain. A passing car honked its horn, startling her. She jumped, propelling the man back on the curve's edge. He lost his footing, flailed, and grabbed her, falling, and taking her down on top of him.

Sea green eyes, as light as a sunlit forest stared back at her. Sophia felt a flush race from the bottom of her toes to the roots of her hair. Their anatomies lined up, her breasts pushed into his steely chest, her hips into his manhood.

Beneath her, he felt carved out of marble like an unsung Roman warrior. A torso to rival the neoclassical masterpiece sculpted of Ares she'd viewed on Brandenburg Gate before the bombings. A blur of soldiers marched by. Cars honked for them to get out of the way. Pigeons swarmed up and scattered in all directions.

The muted daylight was... was what? Watchful? Expectant? Or was she being dramatic? A heat skittered across her skin that had nothing to do with the unseasonable late-spring warmth. His gaze touched her. It peered past the art and artifice she'd tucked around herself, through the skin and sinew of her, to the cold and lonely darkness beneath. Dear God. This was the man who matched the photo the crow had chosen. She shoved the thought away. Absurd.

Still, she felt, in that moment, like a diary opened to a stranger, and yet she had no reason to do so. Were they somehow connected? No. Never could she be linked with her enemy, the conquering army that had brought a tidal wave of destruction over Germany.

Filthy water sluiced around him to a storm drain drenching his uniform. She could feel his erection stirring.

"The endeavor could be illuminating." His voice dropped low, aloof, and confident.

Sophia shivered at the rich, masculine tone of his depraved proposal. The intimation swept over her like a caress. "There are some things best not learned."

"Are you able to stand?"

She felt his hands on the sides of her hips. How fiendishly strong. How vulnerable she'd be against that strength. No doubt, well-fed while Germans starved. Nostrils flaring, she kicked as though to free an insect that had crawled on her leg. "Unhand me."

She scrambled off him. What a mess she was. Her hair fell into her face, torn from her neat chignon. She pushed it back. How was she to go to her interview looking like this? Especially now that she was even later because of this halfwit.

And he stood, towering over her, like a swarthy Leshy, the mythical forest king of her childhood fairy tales who controlled the animals and threw wild parties that uprooted trees.

Sophia blinked once. And again. "Leshy?" she said, unsuccessfully attempting to tear her gaze from his mouth. Lips so supple absolutely didn't conform to a face as chiseled as his. The discordance was jarring, and both confused and compelled her.

He wiped at his uniform, an exercise in futility since the rain soaked through everything, changing what must have been khaki into a deep raw umber. "I should be angry with you pushing me into the street. I've an important meeting today," he said tersely.

She ground her teeth with his ridiculous accusation. "I did not push you into the street. But, if I had, I would have made certain the storm drain swallowed you up."

He looked lower and she glanced down to where his concentration lay. Her skirt had ridden up exposing her garters and the soiled corpses of Gabrielle's stockings. She yanked the woolen folds down. "Such boorish behavior is exactly what I'd expect from a mongrel American whose ancestry comes from dubious lower animal species."

And then he threw back his head and roared with laughter, making her think he'd suffered a grievous bump to his head on the pavement, and had lost his sanity.

A gust of wind blew and her carefully crafted resume was snared in a whirlwind. She snatched at the winging papers. The top sheet floated higher, and then descended into a puddle.

Sober now, the man retrieved the errant document and presented it to her dripping wet. "I apologize—"

Of course, his apology did not carry any remorse. Nerves raw, her temper snapped. No longer could she curb her tongue and cursed him in five different languages. "I need this job." To tell him this job was between her and starvation would be beyond his intellectual capacity.

He put up his hands to ward her off.

"You oaf." She continued her tirade in German. "You should have looked where you were going. Now, I'm late. Of course, you wouldn't realize how important this day is to me." She threw everything she had at him, including calling him a donkey's rear, stating he must have been dropped on his head at birth to disparaging the legitimacy of his ancestry. She raised her chin and stalked off in the other direction, having no idea where she was going as long as it wasn't anywhere near the barbaric American.

Chapter Three

"This way, Miss."

On the fifth floor, a khaki-uniformed officer led her to a private office away from a pool of soldiers with sky-high files flung on their desks, allowing the incessant tapping of typewriters and murmurings of male voices to drum in her ears.

The door was left open. A foregone conclusion was they considered her the enemy and not to be left unsupervised in an American army office.

In her reflection in the window, she rose a hand to tidy her hair. Every bone and muscle throbbed with tension and her toe ached from a blister from the five-mile walk that sapped what little energy she had left. What a mess she must be. What would her interviewer think of her pathetic appearance? Her hopes for the position were dashed before her appointment was even started.

She steadied her shaking hands and twisted in her chair. She leaned over and squinted through a crack in the door jamb to see if the man who was to interview her had arrived. At least he was late as well.

Like a clap of thunder, one voice rose from the tumult, commanding the rapt attention of the men. Chairs screeched back and men stood, saluting. "Good morning, Colonel Pratt," they echoed.

Sophia tried to identify the man named Colonel Pratt with the distinctly masculine voice. There'd been a resonance to it. Sonorous and commanding. A voice that reverberated through her, rough, deep and with arrogant dominion. A voice whiskey smooth, sending shivers up her spine, and...so familiar. It couldn't be—

Drat. A soldier stood at attention in front of the fractured window, blocking her view. Brisk footsteps followed, and then paused.

"A candidate for your secretarial position is in your office, sir."

"Hell, this early. I told you not until noon."

Sophia's stomach flipped over. If St. Patrick had such a voice, he'd not need a staff to drive the snakes from Ireland. The reptiles would have heard him coming and fled into the ocean.

"I hope this one is not as bad as the other ones I had to throw out of my office."

Sophia took a quick intake of breath. *Throw out of his office?*

His wasn't the voice of a saint, nor anything resembling what belonged to the heavenly hosts. The timbre carried too many shadows.

The kind that enticed. Tempted. The sort of shadow which shielded ruthlessness and hidden needs.

The kind she evaded in the most vigorous way conceivable.

"Yes, sir," said the soldier, saluting again. "If I may say so, sir, looks like you tangled with a badger in a mud bath."

"A badger with claws and sharp teeth. The encounter has put me in a bad mood and my tolerance for idiots is at an end. I have an appointment with General Hazard at two and I need you to go to my apartment and get a fresh uniform. Also, get me directions to where he wants to meet. You can set me down in the heart of Africa and I can find my way home better than I can find my way around Berlin."

"Yes, sir."

"And quit saying, 'yes, sir'. It's getting on my nerves."

"Yes, sir. I mean, sorry, sir."

The officer named Colonel Pratt growled. "Some days should come with a warning label." He stepped into the office, kicked the door shut with the heel of his shoe. With his back to her, he shuffled through his mail. He'd not looked at Sophia once. He stripped off his sopping coat and tossed it on the back of his chair. His wet shirt clung to his broad shoulders and his pants stretched across his firm backside. Had she ever in her life noticed such a thing?

He turned and she blanched at being caught admiring him. *Dear God.* Her mouth went dry. This was the man she'd crashed in to less than an hour ago. Was this some cruel, cosmic joke? This was who she was going to interview with?

He stared at her. The strong line of his jaw tightened, and a dark brow lifted as he recognized her as well. His eyes snared hers, holding them against her will. He wasn't smiling. He wasn't not smiling either. She cleared her throat, trying to make sense of his expression. Guarded? Censure? Amusement?

She squirmed inwardly at the unnatural silence yet straightened her spine. She was from nobility after all. Years of posture and bearing were bred into her, and she must live up to her ancestry. He continued to stare at her and said nothing. What was he thinking of her after bumping in to her and—her terse, unsatisfactory chastising of him? After all, her clothes were just as dirty as his. Yet he made no reference to the incident as if it had never happened.

"You speak English very well," he said, his tone accusatory as if being of Germanic descent did not give license to speak the language of the lion.

Mostly, she had learned English on the university level. She had also practiced with Gabrielle to affect more of an American accent. "I watch a lot of American movies."

She took the time to study him more. He had a harsh-hewn

face and a commanding brow in contrast with his mud-smeared uniform. His nose was bold rather than broad, and she stared at his mouth again. It shouldn't have tempted her. Not as hard as it was.

Hard like his gaze.

He was a man all over. Extraordinarily fit, tall, bred to stand out in a crowd.

She swallowed hard, painfully aware of the condition of her own clothes despite her efforts to hastily clean them before her interview. Mud and dark grime from the street covered her skirt, splattered her white blouse, and there was nothing she could do about her torn stockings. The pair of stockings she'd sworn to Gabrielle to protect with her life.

The phone on his desk rang and he picked up the receiver, listened. "Tell General Taylor I'll attend to his requests after I get the shipment. No, I do not have horses arriving, and why the hell does he need a horse?" He scanned a sheaf of papers. "Tell General Taylor his horse arrives in two weeks."

Colonel Pratt put down the receiver and spoke to her. "The ruse is not to let the horse know he is smarter than General Taylor."

She laughed at his jest and the phone rang again. "Colonel Pratt, speaking. Yes, sir. I can't promise your shipment to be on time. All right. You can indulge in your righteous rage, but it won't get you anywhere." He slammed down the receiver. "I can get away with hanging up on peers but not generals. The trick is to inspire your own policy, that's the best efficiency one can achieve."

"Yes, Colonel Pratt," she said, taking the effort to make herself agreeable. She'd been indoctrinated to hate the Americans and had seen them as the enemy during the war years. Moreso as cities were bombed to rubble and people left to starve.

While maintaining a sense of cool professionalism, she noted the bronze of his skin, the perfection of his slick, dark hair, and the impeccable grace of his bearing that seemed incompatible with the rest of him. Like he'd once been a wild thing only recently tamed. An athlete, perhaps?

"When I joined the army, I believed in the war. But this peacetime in Berlin is going to kill me with ridiculous requests."

Her thoughts raced, half her brain screaming to be wary, yet the other disobedient half attempting to find a word to describe him. *Breathtaking.*

"You have typing skills?"

She straightened. "Very good skills, Colonel Pratt."

"How fast can you type?"

"One hundred and thirty words per minute and with ninety-nine percent accuracy."

Everything about him bespoke domination. Power. Unequivocal strength.

Something deep, deep within Sophia trembled. Not with fear, per se. It was more feminine than that. More primitive. This strange feeling was one that she'd never experienced with Karl.

He asked another question. So taken, she didn't know how she was able to respond, remaining on memorized verse. She dropped one of her papers and fished for it. Damn him.

No doubt the man could smell her weakness, and now that weakness began in her knees and worked its way into all sorts of alarming places.

"Sergeant Armani attempts to type my letters, but he is at war with the typewriter and a butcher to English grammar which is an irony since it's his first language"

Her frayed nerves and the long walk had sapped her strength. No fat in her diet exacted a collective toll. For the past week, her diet had been boiled nettles she had picked from abandoned gardens behind her apartment. A wavy mist appeared in front of her eyes.

He rose from his chair, stood close, too close, "Are you all right?" His query was more of a command, and she resented it.

Awareness of his proximity threatened to overwhelm her. A

floating sensation came over her as if she were getting lighter and lighter. So low on energy. She started to sway. *Do not swoon.* Black spots danced in her vision.

His arms snaked out with amazing speed and caught her, holding her in place so she wouldn't fall from the chair and end up on the floor. Faint strings of rapid, angry conversation permeated a fog.

"Sergeant Armani, get me coffee and food, pronto."

A soldier appeared laden with food, and hot steaming coffee, setting the tray on the table. He stared.

"Don't you have work to do?" Robert kicked the door shut on the gawking soldier.

Consciousness threatened to desert Sophia. She tried to clear her head. The weight of his hands on her shoulders pinning her to the chair, drawing from her a breath of protest.

He passed her the coffee, pressing the cup into her shaky hands. "Here drink this," he ordered harshly with a fury imperceptible to most anyone, but not to her.

During the war years she had trained herself to listen; first to the Nazis, and later the Russians, a skill that had helped secure her survival in a highly volatile world. To understand the flow of vibrations underneath scheming subtleties and pointed fallacies.

Underneath his sharp authority prowled an inexplicable desolation...and an amassed intensity that might sear through her muddied clothing and set afire the flesh beneath.

She drank deeply of the sugared coffee. Real coffee. She thought she'd swoon again.

Sea green eyes narrowed beneath satirical brows. "When was the last time you ate?"

She laughed. He blamed her for not eating.

"Berlin seems the only city in the world where starving to death is considered an art."

She took another drink of coffee, and then coughed.

"Slowly," he commanded, handing her a plate piled with

pastries. "Eat this danish. Eat three danishes, and I'm staying right here until you do."

Struggling to eat a bite at a time, she grew resentful that so many were starving while the Americans snapped their fingers and had a feast. She suffered his attentions which seemed a bit too long, and responded to his commands which she rarely did. However, her lack of response was an involuntary mutism caused by her current physical weakness—and his voice that came smooth and dangerous and beautiful, like molten ore hardening into weaponized steel.

Savoring the sweet confection so plentiful during her child-hood but had been nonexistent in the past two years was an elixir for her growling stomach. It felt odd having someone stand over her and forcing her to eat. After two danishes, she put her hand up. Her stomach could handle no more. The nourishment restored her.

"I'm quite well." She looked at where his hands held her, shifted ungracefully until he reluctantly withdrew.

She took the napkin he proffered and dabbed her lips. "Thank you. I'm sure it's not protocol for a potential employee to faint. I hope this won't deter your decision to hire me."

He returned to his desk and scanned her resume. "Proficient in six languages."

"Yes, sir. I read and write German, Prussian, French, English, Italian, and Russian."

"That's quite an accomplishment. Says here you have a doctorate in zoology. You are overqualified, nor do I need an animal *doctor*."

The dark and wicked light in his eyes jangled her nerves, but a touch of impish charm emerged, enough to convince her she might still be in the running for the job.

Her awareness of Colonel Pratt had nothing to do with desperation. She adopted a demeanor of nonchalance to cover his effect on her. "By definition of the job requirement, you need an assistant who can translate and write letters for you in different languages. My knowledge of grammar, spelling, linguistics, semantics and syntax are perfect."

Her every interaction had been calculated. She doubled her efforts, throwing in a few spikes, hazards, and bon mots to entice him. At least he'd not thrown her out of his office yet. "I'm able to use the rules and constraints of different languages so the listener or reader will understand the context and overcome any ambiguity since meaning relies on the manner, time and place of the written word or utterance. Many of those who do not exercise these skills tend to make mistakes. The kind of mistranslations, misunderstandings and misconceptions that can start a war."

This American wielded a smile that would disarm the most protected of hearts. These Americans. They certainly did breed a specific sort of man. Sensual and arrogant. Bold to the point of impertinent. Maybe he wasn't the inferior beast she'd been led to believe.

"You are very confident for a woman. I like confidence," he said.

She lifted her chin a notch. "I am not most women."

"No, you are not."

A shift in his voice made it impossible for her to look up just then. Some strange meaning as rich and thick as cream. "Do I have the job?"

"You had the job when you cursed mein six languages, I assume."

Her mouth dropped open, and she prayed he couldn't translate all the insults she'd heaped on him. "I want to apologize—"

"No apologies needed. I should have looked where I was going. I need a secretary. A good one. I've gone through a dozen soldiers and have not found one that can speak let alone write in more than two languages. Most of them Spanish and, that, I don't need."

Her heart beat a thundering tattoo, unable to believe her good fortune. To be relieved of dreaded and arduous long lines of removing rubble and to be able to work in an office? She cleared her throat. "When do I begin?"

"Right now. I have a huge backlog that needs attending. I expect you to work long hours. Is that agreeable?"

How would she manage walking to and from work with long hours? "Yes, Colonel Pratt."

"The United States Army pays well. Fifty dollars per week."

That was a fortune and forty-five dollars more than the rock lines. "Thank you. I won't disappoint you."

Sophia rose. The man was a hurricane. He opened the door for her. "Your desk is right outside my office. Sergeant Armani will brief you on your duties. If you require anything, ask him."

She had been so starved and exhausted when she entered his office that she'd nearly fainted. Instead, she extended her hand, so thankful to have the job. He shook twice, the calluses on his palms catching on her skin as his hand glided away. Small jolts scraped at her as though every minor edge on his fingertips were wired with sensation.

"One more thing."

"Yes, Colonel Pratt."

"My ancestry is legitimate."

She widened her eyes in mortification. He'd understood everything she had hurled at him in German. "If you would forgive—"

His grin was both boyish and roguish. Of course, he was teasing her.

She felt a mischievous smile tug at her lips. "And I'm not a badger with teeth and claws."

Chapter Four

Robert studied her. For two weeks, her desk showcased neatness and order. The pencils were sharpened and perfectly lined up. The papers and folders were arranged and placed in three even rows. He liked order and noted how his personal office had been kept in the same shape since her arrival.

Framed with thick, dark lashes were her captivating blue eyes that mirrored the color of the sky, and burned with brilliant vitality, and a hint of mischief. Despite her worn and out of fashion attire, she was immaculate and carried herself with the refinement of an aristocrat. Above all, she dazzled him, like one of those women out of the movies when they materialized out of the mist of a train station, enveloped in halos of improbable light. Untouchable. Unreachable.

Robert's hand fisted as Corporal Thomas sat on the edge of her desk. He'd been like a tick on a mule's tail with his fascination of Sophia.

"You're a little ray of sunshine." Thomas took a drag on his cigarette and blew smoke rings across her desk. "You work too hard, Sophia. Work isn't everything."

Thomas' nasally voice grated on Robert's nerves like sandpaper across shards of glass. Maybe he should slam his fist through the corporal's nose and end the man's communication altogether.

With a stack of papers, Sophia blocked the obnoxious corporal. "I have much work to do. If you don't mind."

"You must enjoy yourself while you are still young. Why don't we make the most of it? In fact, may I suggest—"

Sophia slammed the carriage of her typewriter to the right and commenced typing. "As a matter of fact, you do suggest something. To me you suggest a baboon. I'm sorry I said that. It isn't fair to baboons."

Robert chuckled. Sophia could take care of herself. Despite the corporal's pompous façade, the man could smell good prey the way a wolf scents blood. Robert had little tolerance for men like Corporal Thomas.

"I've heard one night with you is incomparable," Thomas murmured boldly, coughed, and then blew smoke circles. "Let me see," he said, feigning interest, yet leaning over to look down her blouse. "What have we here?"

"You have nothing here," Robert said, towering over him with menace. "There are twenty boxes of files that need your attention."

"That is slave work. It will take me six months," Corporal Thomas grumbled.

"Now." Pratt dismissed him with cutting negligence.

The soldier saluted and stormed off, muttering bureaucratic bullshit.

Robert glanced at her, met her serene gaze, then glared at the other men in a way that said, *keep off* if any of them thought to make advances toward her, and then returned to his office with the door open.

He exhaled. The men were like dogs after the butcher's cart with her. He worked through a mountain of papers, trying to ignore her. Wasn't he as bad as his men?

He felt like a fool, reduced to a schoolboy in short pants as he caught himself staring at her from behind. He tried to distract himself by looking at her desk, her books, and the collection of lined up pencils.

Sophia Anna Sonderburg. Sounded lyrical, more Danish than German, even royal, and attached to a mystifying female. Was he becoming fanciful?

His gaze fell on the elegant curve of her long neck and firm rounded buttocks. Maybe too thin.

Just sensible, businesslike, and womanly flesh.

Yet his disobedient hand twitched each time he recalled the time they'd collided in the street, and then again when she'd nearly passed out in his office. He could exactly recall the flare of her waist. The quirk of her lip. The weight of her own palm against his. The delicate structure of her frame, down to her finely boned wrists, and the flawless features of her skin.

Refined and formal. Sweet and sensual.

A perplexing contradiction of mystery and clarity, a baffling dichotomy of mischief and sophistication.

He was afraid if he blinked, the vision would vanish. He remained there, paralyzed, breathlessly viewing the mirage, unable to tamp down a latent yearning for a captivating woman to return his desires.

She sensed him and turned to look in his direction. The beauty of that face seemed painful, unsustainable. Was there a hint of a smile on her lips?

"Did you need something?"

How he needed something. He needed to lock himself in a cold shower for a week. He was hard enough to hammer through granite. His blood simmered with the want of her, with an anticipation he'd not felt since he'd been a lusty lad seeing a naked picture of a woman for the first time.

"Nothing," he said at last, and then he glared out his office window into the unrelenting storm that spread across the American-occupied complex. Tanks and trucks parked at the border of the main gate. Soldiers hurried and jeeps raced along a boulevard. After his father's death, he had inherited the largest automotive industry in the world. Against his mother's wishes, he had handed the reins of the company to his board of directors, allowing him to continue fighting the Germans. That part of his life seemed so far away. The war had distorted his world like hot iron being stretched and wound and twisted out of shape. Triggers like little mental explosions crashed through internal barriers he'd built, evaded trauma rapidly, unpredictably, flashing back into consciousness.

The Battle at Hürtgen Forest spelled suicide. Maneuver the right southern flank. German artillery kicked up mud and billowing clouds of snow. Impossible to hide. In front, Hitler's last desperate efforts came at them with no warning. Panzer tanks, tank destroyers, assault guns charged. Murderous numbers.

Töten! Töte den feind! Keine gnade! Kill! Kill the enemy! No mercy!

Trapped.

Guns roared. Overhead, Luftwaffe aircraft sounded like angry mosquitos, pelting the ground with bullets and bombs. Men swept away. White, deep snow drifts ran scarlet with blood. So cold. Cries of his men crushed by tanks. So many men fell. His men. Thousands of them...in wicked contortions...agonizing cries, shouting for help... praying to God to end their agony.

Jaws of death.

The mouth of hell.

His hands shook. How he'd worked on ways of protecting himself, of burying emotions until the dam burst and the weight of guilt and regret dragged him under. How that weight branded him. To admit he had a problem was weakness and would not work well in his future plans.

On the tenth ring, he answered his phone and gazed at Sophia

Sonderburg. He grunted out a hot breath, testing the syllables of her name in his mind as he had a hundred times in the last hundred minutes—a necessary addiction to distract him from battle fatigue.

Chapter Five

A few days later, Sophia rose from straightening her desk and closed the window against the gathering night. With her work completed she could begin the long arduous and hazardous walk home.

"You don't like me very much."

Sophia jumped. How stealthily Colonel Pratt had come up beside her.

"You keep me long hours," she said. "You're stoic, and your indifference leads me to believe you are vain and proud." Her hand flew to her mouth. "Please accept my apology. My exhaustion has caused me to voice words I normally would not have said."

She caught it then, a flash of uncertainty—no, something else—something stronger. Anger perhaps? Men didn't like to be criticized by a woman, no less insulted. One he thought was a German woman and his former enemy, no less. Most especially a high-ranking officer and her conqueror.

The instantaneous flare of emotion smoothed back into a more pleasant expression of interest and charming curiosity.

A façade, to be sure. Sophia had donned enough of her own to recognize one. So, what did the intrepid Colonel Pratt think now. Would he fire her?

Colonel Pratt burst out laughing. "You are the only one with courage enough to say it to my face. I like that." He looked at his watch. "I've been a boor and have kept you late many times. I'll drive you home."

"No," she protested. German hostilities still simmered, and a lone American might find it fatal.

"I insist."

"It is too dangerous for you to enter my quarter."

He nodded his head. "How about I drop you near where you live? Give me ten more minutes."

He went back in his office. Sophia used the time to package up what food remained on trays on the buffet table and stow the parcels in an overlarge bag she'd brought. She glanced over her shoulder. Good. He was busy. Every day the food had been discarded. Working late offered her the opportunity take the food home to the other occupants of the apartment building. Nana Grimm was so thin, and with the food she brought home, Nana's granddaughter was starting to lose the paleness in her cheeks. Gabrielle delighted in the danishes and everyone craved the sliced meat and cheeses.

"What are you doing?"

Sophia swung around; her fingers pressed down on her breastbone. "Every day the food is thrown out. Many of my friends are starving. To waste good food—"

He said nothing and walked back into his office. Sophia exhaled. Doubtless, he did not want her to take the food to feed Germans. A contemptuous man, bristling with prejudice and motivated by pride. Everyone hated the Germans. No one saw how the women and children starved and suffered during and after the war. The defeated were invisible. She returned the food to the table.

He plunked a large US military canvas duffel on the table and immediately started putting food in. "Put the food back in your bag. No sense wasting good food."

She fidgeted with one of the packages. "Why would you feed Germans?"

"I believe the greatest failure of mankind is war, and more than an end to war, I want an end to the beginnings of all wars."

Sophia stood completely still. "I don't understand."

"If we do not care for those less fortunate, then we will never have peace."

Awed by his words, she allowed the warmth of his benevolence to seep into her bones. "You are unexpected."

"Why? Compassion is a necessity, not a luxury. Without it, humanity cannot survive."

"You have given me a different view—" *Of you.* She had been mentally trying to find reasons to dislike him but could not.

"Are we not all members of this world? Shouldn't we focus more on brotherly regard? No one wants peace more than I do."

Sophia blinked, unable to take it all in. "A man of peace? And you are representative of all Americans?" she asked, yearning for the assurance of a greater future.

"Unfortunately, no."

She gave a frustrated shake of her head. "At least small steps toward bridging a peace can come from you."

She could feel the weight of his burning gaze on her skin as he said, "The war has defined me in both good ways and bad. In the wake of misery, destruction, suffering and death, what remains in me is a stirring desire for mankind to banish the temptation of violence and war...to gain harmonious reconciliation, and hope of a new era, an era of peace. I can't feed a whole populace, but I can certainly feed a few."

They finished packing the food, and he guided her out the back of the building and opened the door of a jeep. He couldn't be more polite and treated her like a lady.

"I moved Corporal Thomas to the second floor. You won't have any more problems with him."

"Thank you," she said, still mystified by his revelations, and the fact that he removed the horrid man from her surroundings.

"He's as droll as that new French author, Claude Nasal Passages."

Sophia laughed with his description of Corporal Thomas. She needed to laugh like the desert needed rain. "Corporal Thomas will cough away his life smoking Lucky Strikes."

"May I ask who Leshy is?"

Sophia's cheeks burned with his recollection of what she had called him that day when they'd collided. "You are very bad to remind me of that indiscretion."

"I insist."

Startled, she clutched the bag of food. The man was domineering to a fault which precipitated a demon of mischievousness in Sophia. She felt the corners of her lips turn up and said, "Leshy is from a Prussian fairytale, compared to the forest god of earth, waters, livestock and the underworld. Often, he is portrayed with horns and surrounded by packs of wolves and bears."

He broke out laughing. Sophia could not get over how devastatingly handsome he was when he truly smiled. His body was lean from months on the march, and with certainty, this rugged, vital man doubtless was drowning in women who'd swarm him like locusts. She must be cautious.

"May I inquire your destination, Fraulein Sonderburg? Or is it Frau?" Something smoothed the gravel from his voice, as though he'd drizzled honey over shards of rock.

"Fraulein," she told him. Karl was dead. Her marital status didn't matter anymore.

She had come from a world so hard and unmerciful. Colonel Pratt was a brilliant splash of color and kindness. When the degenerate Corporal Thomas had made lewd remarks and advances to her, Colonel Pratt's dangerous tone sent the man slinking away. In fact, many men would have departed under his glacial stare. Not Sophia. She would not retreat. She had survived the war and the Russians. She could survive anything.

"You are not from Berlin," Colonel Pratt said. "You have a slight difference in your accent. German yet not German. Less guttural. Reminds me of a Polish woman back home."

It was a statement, not a question. He was quick to seize on a discrepancy.

Her accent was as the land she was born into, whispering of gentle forests and rising toward the clouds. "I am from Prussia."

"There is a difference?"

A foregone conclusion. Many of the Prussians had united with Germany, and many of the high command were Prussian aristocrats, including many of her cousins. "I come from northeast Prussia. My parents were against the Third Reich and all it stood for. They helped subvert the Nazis by blowing up bridges, trains and helping Jews, Gypsies and Poles escape from being sent to the death camps."

"Very hazardous activities."

Her voice caught confessing the sorrowful part of her past where senseless violence and evil had won. "For their great courage, my mother, father, little sister and brother were executed by Hitler's forces."

He braked the jeep to a stop. "I'm sorry. I know those words won't give you much solace—"

There was comfort in feeling the goodness of Colonel Pratt. Her vision blurred and she stared out the window into the darkness.

"Know you can unload on me or not say a word. Sometimes the night is enough to reveal our troubled thoughts."

The night hid many a sin. "I do not wish to talk about my family. Too many painful memories."

He moved the jeep back onto the road, passing a muddle of bombed out buildings.

"How have you survived?" he asked quietly.

There were many times she had pondered the same question. Was it the darkness or the gentleness in his voice that prompted her to speak of things she'd tried to bury? "Near the end of the war, there was no electricity, gas or water. What was worse was the dearth of information. Absence of newspapers, radio, telephones. Rumor was the sole source of news and sadly deplorable with the wickedness of bad omens that mirrored the horror really occurring."

"Go on," he encouraged, but his voice hardened. Then he spoke more temperately, and she shoved away the self-protective caution she hid behind.

"At first, we heard a distant rumble as the war rolled to Berlin. Then it became a constant roar. I drowned in the din. My ears were deafened to all but the heaviest guns with the incessant bombings. We hid in the subways, emerging to the charred ruins of apartment houses. Berlin was completely encircled. All the outlying districts occupied.

"Despite desertions of the immoral culprits who created the great lie, the people remained. At first dazed and bleeding and hungry, and when winter came, shivering in their rags in the hovels which the bombings had made of their homes; a vast wasteland of rubble."

Like a faucet turned on, Sophia poured out the horrors. "There came the unspeakable atrocities of Russian soldiers."

"I heard," Robert said.

She looked at him with terror in her eyes. "Do you know a bomb was a gift?"

His head reared back. "How so?"

"After one of the bombings, I emerged from the subway. Russian soldiers chased me. I passed through a maze of alleyways, losing them. At my street, soldiers were listening to a speech by their commander. With their attention drawn, I dashed across, ran up the steps to my apartment and stopped. A bomb rested in the wreckage on the third story. The bizarre occurrence should have blown up the entire building. The landings on the upper three stories were gone, leaving the skeletal frame of the steps to the right intact, yet creating an impossible gap to the apartments linked to the left.

"Light from the opened roof poured over me. I scrambled over the rubble and up the remaining three flights, stared at the gaping hole to my apartment. The Russians were moving about the street. Their commander's speech had ended. Soon, they'd be in my apartment building.

"There remained an eight-foot jump to the six inches of floor edging in front of my door. If I jumped, I'd risk falling three flights and onto the bomb. My life would be over, and all I wanted to do was to crawl beneath the covers of my bed and never come out again.

"The sun fell brighter through the dust and illuminated a plank against the wall on the side of the bomb. I descended, and with my bare hands heaved off plaster and rubble, wiggling the timber, knowing at any moment the missile might explode. I didn't care. I jerked and tugged.

"Russian soldiers shouted outside my apartment building. I climbed higher, wrenching the trapped board and fell backward. My arm sockets ached. The voices were getting closer. I yanked one more time, freeing the board from its nesting place, and then prayed it was long enough to bridge the divide. I dragged the timber up the remaining flights and slid it over the gap.

"The Russians entered the foyer, intending to loot or find a woman to rape. I put one foot in front of the other, crossed quickly, and unlocked my door. I could see the Russians coming up the stairwell. Unseen, I pulled the board into my apartment, closing the door and locking it. Ridiculous. A locked door would not keep them out

"Breathing hard, I listened. Russians ran up the steps and stopped at the bomb. There was much discussion. They left the building. The bomb that had been an impediment would protect me."

"Do you realize how dangerous an unexploded bomb is?"

Seeing the vein twitch in his neck, she shrugged. "Gabrielle, my roommate was delighted for the Russians never came into the building again. I realize it is like living on borrowed time, yet so far, fortune has favored us."

"The situation with the bomb will have to be rectified." His tone held an air of unequivocal authority.

"I'm happy with my apartment. Right here. You can let me out right here. For your own safety, I don't want you to go beyond this point."

"Good God, Sophia. We've traveled over five miles. The hell with it." He drove farther and she pointed to her block of build-ings. He braked the jeep, jumped out, and then circled to open the door for her. He held out his hand and she placed her palm in his. The warmth radiating from him was electrifying, like her hand belonged there for all eternity. His lips parted and, inhaling, he hesitated for several seconds, surprised by the gesture as much as she.

A world of complexities pulled her heart away from the gloom of war and its aftermath. His nearness, after so much loneliness, was like pulling her out of the quicksand and into the wild rich-ness of air.

"I'm not happy my valuable secretary has to walk the distance from this dangerous slum so she's half-dead with exhaustion before she begins her day," he reprimanded, and then released her.

"You don't have to worry—"

"I insist on finding you transportation to and from work."

The heavily populated working-class streets appeared shut off from the world. No sound. Nothing but an oppressive silence broken by the jeep's engine. One would think the ten thousand people that lived there had emigrated or died.

She could feel eyes upon her. Those who no doubt watched

from the apartments above, their tongues wagging and skewering her with horrible slurs for being in the company of an American officer, yet they'd be first in line to take the food she brought home.

"Good night," she said crisply, picking up the bags of food. On two accounts, she reminded herself not to encourage any attraction. Such an attraction to the handsome colonel might be fatal to her job, especially if he tired of her. Considering how impulsive Americans were, it was best to keep matters impersonal.

In the glow thrown by the jeep's high beams, she walked to her doorway, and then stopped in a triangle of light. She turned, caught the sight of his retreating shoulders as he sauntered toward the driver's side of the jeep. As though sensing her gaze upon him, he paused, his foot resting on the running board and glanced over his shoulder. He nodded, and so did she.

For the first time in a long time, she felt protected. *Safe.*

Chapter Six

Outside his office, Robert listened to the roar of Remington typewriters, file drawers opening and closing, phones ringing. Chaos. He welcomed the busyness.

Over the crescendo, he heard his good friend, Captain Van Smith, enter and greet the men.

"Fighting a war to fix something works about as good as going to a whorehouse to get rid of the clap," said Van. "Sorry, Ma'am."

Van had noticed Sophia.

"Where's Colonel Pratt?" Van insisted. "I must see him immediately."

Sophia opened the door a crack to ask but when she turned to get his name, Van barged past her.

"Thank you, Sophia," Colonel Pratt said.

As soon as the door closed, Van said, "You devil, you have been hiding your treasure under a bushel. What a woman. Would stop traffic. And such class. You can tell she's attended the finest schools and—wow! The fire in her eyes!"

Robert crossed his feet up on his desk. "Meaning?"

Van whistled. "Holy Smoley, Pratt. Did you rob a palace? You must be deaf and blind. She is the most stunning creature I've ever laid eyes on."

"She's my new secretary."

"How do you get any work done? I'd be looking at her and dreaming all day. I think I'll introduce myself."

"Don't even try. Next time, I'll have you cool your heels until you rot. Is this an actual assignment or purely social? Because right now I'm aggravated enough to plant my fist through someone's face. Sophia's fan club is a hindrance."

Van raised his hands and gave a hoot of laughter. "You are downhill all the way for this dame."

"And you are an expert?"

Suddenly, a hailstorm of bellowing erupted in the outer office. "Now what?" Robert swung his legs down and stalked to the door.

With wild theatrical gestures, a disheveled forty-year-old man with a worn felt hat in hand, shabby trousers and a dog-eared shirt shouted at Sophia. In return, Sophia yelled at the man in a language Robert didn't understand. The petite man numbered several offenses on his fingers.

"Silence," ordered Robert. Both turned and glared at him for interrupting, and then returned to their heated dispute.

"Is there a problem?" Robert intervened once more to execute his authority.

With her fists plunked on her hips, Sophia turned to Robert. "Pigs!"

Perplexed, he let the dispute go on for another minute. Sophia pointed to Robert. The Polish man nodded his head, smiled, saluted, donned his hat, and then departed.

"Do you mind telling me what that was about?" asked Robert.

"I told him his problem will be solved and that if he carries on anymore, I'd roll him up in a pierogi and feed him to the pigs."

"I imagine he took that well."

"Only when I told him you'd requisition three pigs to replace the ones that the Germans stole from him."

"Great. Now I have to find three pigs."

"Three pigs are better than starting a full-blown war."

Robert dragged his fingers through his hair. "You are a pearl of diplomacy."

From behind him, Van cleared his throat with exaggerated abandon. Robert had forgotten him. "Sophia, this is Captain Van Smith. He was just leaving."

With flamboyant execution, Van snapped his heels together, leaned over and kissed the back of her hand. Overlong.

"It's nice to make your acquaintance," said Sophia, smiling.

"No, it's not." Robert gritted his teeth at Van's outrageous gesture.

Van sighed, purposefully ignoring Robert, and keeping his eyes on Sophia. "I should always take my cue from your impeccable manners, Colonel Pratt, sharing in your good mood and hospitality. You always were a clever devil. Never could outwit you at the University of Michigan, which, by the way, calls me to reflect on our school days. Perhaps we should regale Sophia with some of our exploits."

"Hardly. Don't you have some important assignment to accomplish?"

Van put his hands palms up as if in worshipful supplication. "Ah, Sophia, military intelligence. What a contradiction in terms. With all humility, I will tell you—" He paused and with dramatic flourish placed his hand over his heart. "My importance to the world is relatively small. On the other hand, my importance to myself is tremendous."

"I'm charmed by your honesty," Sophia laughed.

Robert snorted. "Van, you forgot the exit is over there." Robert gripped his friend's arm and dragged him to the door.

Van blinked at Robert as if noticing him for the first time. "I never forget a face, Pratt, but in your case, I'll be glad to make an exception."

At the door, Van tipped his cap to Sophia. "This isn't the last you'll see of me."

Robert dragged him outside the office and slammed the door. "You are like gum on the bottom of my shoe, Van. Be forewarned you are meddling in forbidden territory. My new secretary is not to be trifled with."

Van chuckled. "Your wit underwhelms me."

Robert released him, dusting his hands. "You may look like an idiot, talk like an idiot, but I never let that fool me, because you are an idiot. So, next time I see you, remind me not to talk to you."

Van whistled. "Oh, you got it bad. I'm going to have so much fun."

Chapter Seven

Sophia worked on a pile of correspondence for Colonel Pratt while typewriters rattled on soldiers' desks, the din of the keys creating a rhythm of universal music. As promised by Colonel Pratt, and for the last two weeks, Sergeant Armani had waited outside her apartment bright and early. Not having to walk five miles back and forth to work had been a luxury. She had been delivered early enough to eat from the generous buffet of scrambled eggs, sausages, and sweetbreads. With a cup on her desk brimming with steaming coffee, sugar, and rich cream, she was as close to heaven as she could imagine.

Nothing was inferred by Colonel Pratt from when he'd driven her home that first night, and neither had he taken her home again, leaving the duty to the efficient Sergeant Armani.

As far as she was concerned, that was for the best. To prevent forfeiture of her job, a reserved and professional persona saved her from emotional entanglements. Sophia tapped her lip somewhat hurt and betrayed, yet chalked Colonel Pratt's detachment up to mandates by the US Army meant to prevent socialization between Americans and Germans—especially women. Battle-hardened Colonel Pratt followed these orders verbatim.

The door opened behind her. "Sophia, could you come in and take a dictation?" he asked.

With a pad and pen in hand, she rose and followed him into his office, taking the chair opposite his desk. He looked tired. Of course, he worked long hours and his job was demanding. His phone rang and he picked it up. "Yes, General Stimson. I'll be right over."

"Sophia, dictation will come later. I need you to accompany me to Leipzig. There is a dispute my superior is having with a problematic Russian who seems to want to rewrite the Potsdam Agreement. Again, you do speak Russian?" he asked, obviously needing to make sure of her qualifications. She had grown up next to Russia's border and spoke the language fluently.

"Perfectly."

Robert guided her to a jeep and opened the door for her. "General Stimson wants me to pick up a few correspondences before we set out."

Sophia nodded her head, happy to be getting out of the office. The sun was scorching, and her wool skirt chafed against her thighs. The jeep's windows were open, and she felt relief as the wind cooled her heated skin.

Up the Wilhelmstrasse, they passed the Adlon Hotel where she had spent her honeymoon with Karl—a honeymoon nothing like a young bride might dream of. Karl had kissed her once. Not the passionate, romantic kiss she'd seen in the cinema. More a peck on the lips with no soul-stirring reaction. She peered in the rearview mirror and watched the hotel disappear in the distance. She experienced no passion, no nostalgia, nothing, left clean and as emotionless as a copper pot.

She couldn't remember what the weather had been like that day. She did remember the wind. The kind of dominant wind that would blow your words in the farthest direction, so they'd never be heard.

"Hitler's bunker," Robert said as he angled his head as they passed the bombed out and unrecognizable remains of the Reich Chancellery where Hitler lived his last days in a luxurious bunker fifty feet below that could house twelve thousand of his loyal followers. Soviet flags fluttered over the wreck of the Reichstag and on the Brandenburg Gate. Hitler had taken the coward's way out and committed suicide with his new bride, Eva Braun. General Goebbels, his loyal follower to the end, injected his six children with poison, and then shot his wife and himself.

Colonel Pratt wanted her thoughts. Sophia looked into Robert's eyes. Oh, how she'd been thinking of him more as Robert and felt like she was standing alone on the edge of the world...on a windswept ocean precipice. She could hear the roar of soft waves hitting against the cliffs.

"None of this conflict was of my choosing, but, in spite of that, I have inherited the shame and sorrow of the aftermath. See what is left of that beautiful fountain?" She pointed. "All that is left of the Roman god Neptune drawing his net is his shot-up body. Once he was surrounded by four beautiful maidens representing the four rivers of Prussia. They are decapitated and crumbled. I cannot hear the water tinkling anymore."

"Sophia, the saddest people I've met are the ones who don't care deeply about anything. If it is any consolation, you are made for better things. I can imagine life has become a torture for you where you've expected to endure, surviving, not living. Yet you have risen from the ashes. You are a strong woman and I admire you."

Sophia straightened with his compliment. Colonel Pratt possessed the power to arrest her attention. His smile was open, but his eyes were as mercurial as the cosmos, and possibly just as fathomless. She began to compare him with Karl. Robert was taller, more muscular and she sensed, more benevolent. Karl had a wrestler's build, a gladiator's shoulders, and a steely, penetrating gaze. Karl had chosen to delete their wedding night because he didn't want to leave her with child—in case something happened to him. The train he was traveling on was bombed by the Allies. No one survived.

Being alone with Robert rose much different than in the office environment and the comfort and ease of his offered friendship compelled her to continue. "I remember the fearsome goosesteps smacking against the brick, every echo turning my stomach into rock. I remember the fervor and cheer of Hitler's army, saluting their Fuhrer with idolized adoration. I had beat my pillow with my fists then, and cried tears of rage. To send young men to march off to a calculated battle where roads would soon be laid across their bones. No small voice could turn the tide. The masses rose, intoxicated with the lie."

"Man makes his errors over and over again. God laughs."

Sophia tucked a loose tendril of hair behind her ear, and she looked at the cemetery in Hasenheide Park. Oh, to free an unfettered scream. Long, uniform rows of graves stretched endlessly in the yellow sand from the last big air raid in March. The park remained desolate. The German army had felled all the trees to have a clear field for shooting and later by Berliners needing wood to keep their fires going in the winter. The ground was scored with trenches strewn with rags, bottles, cans, wires, and ammunition.

"I don't care for God's humor," she said.

At the edge of the Schöneberg district, debris had been left by the troops—gutted cars, burned-out tanks, battered gun carriages. Two rickety old ladies, their hands gnarled, stood in front of a pile of rubble so huge it towered over them. They scratched at refuse with a coal shovel, loading it onto a little cart. She offered a quick prayer to be saved from the bucket brigades.

Robert took off his cap and rubbed a hand over his damp hair. "We've learned how to destroy, but not to create; how to waste, but not to build; how to kill men, but not how to save them; how to die, but seldom how to live."

There seemed not to be enough air, but Sophia was breathing. "Things can change. They must." Sophia shook her head. "If I were an artist, I'd paint the world with color...and so many colors... soft pinks and purples of spring, summer blues, dazzling reds, and golds of autumn, and lastly the hypnotic cloak of pure white snow in winter. With colors, I'd drown the stark grays and terrifying blacks of arrogant destruction."

Robert lifted his hands up and then let them fall on the steering wheel. "The mistake of arrogance is always learned in hindsight."

The bridges were unblocked. Below the railroad embankment, a jumble of tracks were pockmarked with craters a yard deep. Pieces of rail wrenched high above the ground, upholstery and scraps of fabric streamed out of bombed sleepers and dining cars. The heat was stifling. The lingering smell of fire hung over the tracks. All around was continued desolation, a wasteland, not a breath of life...the carcass of Berlin.

"There is so much to do," she began. "I tell myself to rebuild is important, to have courage for whatever comes in life—everything depends on that. The only thing left for those who've survived is to start doing what's necessary. Then do what's possible. And finally, do the impossible."

"We need dreamers like you, Sophia. Dreamers are the world's last hope."

Soon, they were out of Berlin and zipping through suburbs and into the rural areas that had escaped relatively unscathed. The hills remained covered with aromatic pine forests. Clear bubbling streams cascaded into wide lovely valleys and rekindled her spirit.

"What, exactly, will be my responsibility today?"

"To translate for General Stimson."

Sophia had heard of the famous American general. "Doesn't he have his own interpreter?"

"Came down with pneumonia. Stimson needed someone good, and I'm delivering."

Sophia gave him a sidelong glance. "What is to be discussed?"

"With certainty the Potsdam Agreement negotiated by the Allies, governing the initial terms set up to govern Germany. This meeting's purpose is to keep tempers cool and not give in to petty Russian demands. The last thing we need is to go to war with Russia."

A zillion butterflies erupted in her stomach. She touched her head, her blouse. "My clothes. My hair. I'm not prepared for such a meeting." Sophia backpedaled, and then she stared at him. "You have that much confidence in me?"

He flashed her that killer smile of his. "I saw how you handled the Polish farmer and his absent pigs."

Sophia's voice caught in her throat on a horrified whisper. "That's a far cry from chief diplomatic circles."

"There's not much difference," he laughed, and then looked her over from head to toe. "You'll do fine. And you look perfect."

~

Soon, they arrived at a former palace General Stimson had confiscated for his headquarters.

An officer leaped to his feet when they entered, saluting, and then bowing as if at a dance lesson, greeting them individually.

"You are late," the soldier informed them, "and General Stimson loathes delay."

They were led to an elegant dining room, and a heaviness grew in Sophia's chest. Four enormous crystal chandeliers scintillated in the afternoon light. The vaulted ceiling was painted a summer sky blue with a host of smiling cherubs, reminding her of a dining room in one of her family's castles. Beneath the peaceful and saintly landscape sat several American and Russian officers, the hard-bitten combatants flanking a long, gleaming cherry table. They stood when Sophia entered.

Distant, formal, and flawlessly polite, General Stimson made introductions and instructed Sophia to sit next to General Ivanov, announcing she would be acting as an interpreter.

General Ivanov stood resplendent in his blue-lapis tunic with gold epaulets and matching breeches. A bold red sash crossed his front. He wore the mandated knee-high black calvary boots that made her shudder. How they reminded her of the click of bootheels on the streets when Russian soldiers flooded Berlin.

He addressed her in sophisticated Russian. Well-educated. Sophia translated the greeting. Robert seated her and sat to her right. He gave her hand a reassuring squeeze. She straightened bolstered by his strong callused hand and with that hand she could move mountains.

Stimson folded his arms across his chest. "Miss Sonderburg, tell General Ivanov that we welcome him and his officers."

Sophia translated, switching back and forth from Russian to English.

For some odd reason, the Russian general glowered. Was it a perpetual frown or because he had a woman translator? He fluttered his flaccid fingers in unconcerned consent for his host to continue. Sophia gritted her teeth, her immediate contempt for the Russian general filling her with revulsion. How she wanted to scream at him for the thousands of Russian soldiers who had committed their foul deeds on the vulnerable German populace and raping helpless German women.

"We need to hammer out additional points on the peace agreement." General Ivanov flicked his eyes over the Americans. Clearly, he considered them his inferiors.

General Stimson's mouth tightened, his version of a sardonic smile. He shook out his napkin, leaned over the table to give a personal tone to the watchful eyes and said, "All points were mandated in the Potsdam Agreement."

Sophia leaned over and spoke with a quiet intensity, her eyes meeting Robert's. "With certainty, General Stimson is pitting the legality of Western philosophies against Russia's. I have a distinct feeling the consequences of the 'German Question' will remain a deepening conflict between the United States and Russia in the years to come."

Robert leaned toward her. "You are very astute. Just do your best."

Sophia sucked in a shallow breath, jerked her gaze away, and then turned back to General Ivanov. There was a faint trembling at the corners of the Russian's mouth followed by a flush of anger on his cheeks. "We all know the agreement is not satisfactory. The Germans need to have their proud spirit crushed under the boots of their conquerors."

Arrogance hung in the air.

"Stalin, your leader, approved it," General Stimson clarified.

The Russian frowned like a priest hearing a vulgar confession. "Not good enough."

General Stimson sat fuming. He'd had enough.

Robert intervened, lifting his hands, palms up. "Is it not useful to maintain a peaceful settlement unifying Germany?"

There was a silence broken by alarmed squawks of pigeons on the terrace and the sharp cry of an eagle, strong and threatening.

"Whatever is necessary." The Russian general's hard blue eyes peered down the table, as if studying his prey.

Sophia felt it was a giant power grab by Stalin, quibbling over the agreement in making sure the German military power never rose again as an excuse to gain additional claims for Russia.

Robert cultivated a pose of well-bred indifference and pinned his regard on the Russian. "May I compliment you on securing the northeast border. No doubt, your brilliant action is seen as exemplary in Stalin's favor," said Robert.

Sophia translated. Robert's comment, grudgingly politic and masking his disgust, was both complimentary and slur. The allies had forced the Russians to draw back after the general had conquered Berlin.

Yet wasn't diplomacy to do and say the nastiest things in the nicest way? Sophia cleared her throat and plunged in, softening her translation to the irascible Russian general.

General Ivanov beamed with pride and pleasure, drawing in everyone to share the news. "Of course, one must earn greatness. For me, it appears to be consistent. I suppose it depends in part upon the myth-making creativity of humanity. The person who achieves greatness must have a feeling for the mythology he plays a part in. He must reflect what is thrust upon him."

Nauseated, Sophia watched as all eyes turned to her, and then to Robert and General Stimson to see their reaction.

General Stimson's lips flattened. He looked ready to physically throttle the Russian, but he made no return comment, allowing Robert to continue to speak for him—no doubt to prevent a diplomatic faux pas.

Robert leaned over the table. "Indeed, those are admirable and serious reflections."

Sophia could tell Robert's compliment was forced, yet an ounce of flattery went far.

The egomaniacal Russian did not see how he was being played. He waved to a servant to refill his glass with more wine. "My reflections? I bask in the knowledge that Mother Russia, like its generals, does not aspire to become extraordinary. But seemingly without effort, adding happenstance and burning desire has made our history extraordinary."

"I appreciate your honesty," said Robert. "To think fate has blessed you."

"With certainty." General Ivanov smiled oblivious to the mockery.

Pleased, General Stimson nodded to soldier-servants who brought plates of food for the table. Puffed pastries of piroshki, crispy roast duck with apples, creamy beef stroganoff, golubtsy or stuffed cabbage rolls, dressed herring, dark brown sourdough bread with fresh butter, even a sturgeon loaf filled with caviar. The Americans had presented Russian foods to gratify their ally. Many of the dishes had been prepared for Sophia's family by their chefs. Her mouth watered at the sight of the elegant fare for she had been denied such luxuries for a long time.

General Ivanov raised his wine glass, held it aloft where the lights shot beams of reflection off it. "As Commander of the Russian Forces in Berlin, I give a toast to the Americans and the return to civilization."

Sophia raised her glass with the others, all eyes focused on the Russian general. In the sudden stillness, a breeze moved shrubbery outside the French doors and threw shadows across his drooping face.

There was an abortive movement of glasses toward mouths—stopped as the Russian lifted his glass higher. "The die is cast. The inferior Huns must submit, the criminal enterprise of their war must be accounted for. We cannot allow Germany to rise again."

"Perhaps introduce a single currency?" General Stimson dared. The Allies wanted the new Germany to be an economic whole. The Russians did not.

She translated, and then inhaled. Those were fighting words.

"No!" The Russian general pounded his fist on the table. The dinnerware jumped. "If this comes, we will resist. We will block all rail, roads, and canal access to the city."

Robert intervened. "But the people will have no access to food, medicine, fuel, electricity and other basic goods."

Sophia knew Stalin as well as his subordinate's agenda was to punish Germany economically, forcing the country to pay reparations.

General Stimson gave a hard smile. "We Americans differ in philosophy. We see Germany's economic recovery as crucial."

Sophia's mouth went dry. A grand chess game was in play by

the Allies to preserve a democratic buffer to communism. The Russian general met the coup de gras like a capped volcano.

Speaking quickly, Stimson said, "I understand an award is going to be presented to you."

Sophia offered a flash of a smile in her translation. Push and pull, a principle of diplomacy to abate ruffled feathers.

"An award you say?" the Russian general pressed.

He already had enough brilliant medals on his chest to topple him over. To find room for another medal would take a miracle from his tailor.

"You haven't heard?" said Robert who sat back in his chair mystified.

Sophia exaggerated the honor. With certainty, an elegant lie. "An award from General Eisenhower for your role in the war. It is the highest of all recognition from the Americans."

She whispered to Robert in English with a benign expression, and he tipped his head, acknowledging her cleverness.

For dessert, Praga cake was served. Rich layers of sponge sealed with chocolate custard buttercream.

Before Sophia plunged her fork into the delectable sweet, the Russian general spoke to her. "So, you're Danish."

"I am not. I am Prussian."

"Good God," ranted the Russian, clattering his fork to his plate. "You allow a German to eat with us?"

Russian and American officers cleared their throats. Some shifted awkwardly looking over their shoulders. The war was over, but hatreds remained.

Enraged, Sophia gripped her fork. She was proud of her heritage and would not let anyone speak to her like that anymore. "I am Prussian. Some of us were against the Third Reich, including my family who assisted Russian soldiers in blowing up German trains and supply chains. When Russian soldiers were caught by the Nazis, my mother and father helped them to escape. For their sacrifice, my family was executed by Hitler's forces."

Sophia clenched her fist around her fork and waved it in the air. All reason fled. "You ungrateful ape, horns of Satan, donkey's rear..." She hurled insults and carried on with all kinds of threats upon the Russian general's person. She could not stop and didn't care what Ivanov thought.

The Russian officers uncomfortable with the rapid and heated words of exchange glanced worried looks to one another. Her shoulders sank with Robert's and General Stimson's eyes boring holes through her. Had she created World War III?

Wide-eyed, the Russian general did something that took everyone by surprise. He slapped the table, threw back his head and howled with laughter.

Sophia sat speechless.

"What a woman," said General Ivanov. "We should have had you in Stalingrad. The Germans would only have had to hear of you and would have run back to Berlin." Beneath a tangle of brows, the general hiccupped into full-blown belly laughter completely unsettling her and making her question his mental soundness.

The Russian soldiers stopped staring and laughed uproariously. General Stimson pointed to soldiers who carried trays with shots of vodka to be served.

General Ivanov downed several shots, saluting her, then stood, clanking his glasses to his comrades and everyone about the table. He howled again, slapping his hand up and down almost involuntarily. He could barely breathe, his laughter flowing over the room.

Sophia frowned from their hilarity. General Stimson shrugged. Robert shook his head, laughing, and thoroughly enjoying himself.

She wanted to kick him.

After dinner, formal goodbyes and shakes of hands were exchanged with General Ivanov inviting General Stimson, Robert and, of course, the lovely Sophia to his headquarters for dinner. After the Russians departed, General Stimson and Robert cornered her.

"Good God, what did you say to him?" they both chorused.

"I insulted him a hundredfold, and then told him I'd skewer him with my fork."

Stimson laughed. "I've never seen the like. You have an unusual aptitude for diplomacy, and I thank you for getting me through this headache."

"What cemented his understanding was when I told him if he carried on anymore, I'd shoot him myself. He was pleased with that."

Robert whistled. "What a minefield this part of the world is."

General Stimson adjusted his cap. "Welcome to the world of international relations. By the way, General Taylor stored the horse you procured for him in the stables and has been trying to ride him. The brute is a monster and needs to be put down."

"Let me look at him. I may be able to help," offered Sophia. "I have knowledge of horses."

The general looked her up and down, and then shook his head. "You are like thistledown, Ma'am. That horse will eat you alive, but if you have any advice to keep General Taylor from breaking his neck, I'm inclined to listen. In fact, I'll take a much-needed break and show you to the stables."

They passed a lake that reflected blues and greens. The willing canvas of earth and sky brought its own artistic watercolor effect to the daytime. Her heart panged thinking of her home.

Upon approach of the corral, Sophia saw the largest stallion she'd had ever seen, leaping and bucking with alarming grace and speed. The whites of his eyes gleamed wildly, and his ears were pinned all the way back.

"He's too unsettled," said a soldier keeping tension on a rope. On the other side, another soldier cautiously tugged until it ran out of slack, and then wrapped the rope several times around his forearm and wrist before locking it in his grip. Obviously not a skilled horseman. Another man, she presumed to be General Taylor, launched himself onto the saddle. With certainty, the general was at war with stupidity.

Pandemonium erupted as the obsidian-black Arabian reared on his hind legs, striking out at whoever was unlucky enough to be in his path. The two men holding the ropes went down. It all happened so quickly, she couldn't tell if they'd fallen, been kicked, or merely dove out of the way.

As she approached the gate, Sophia gasped as the soldier snagged in the rope he'd wound around his arm was dragged like a sack of potatoes through the dust. His head barely avoided the horse's churning hooves. He worked vigorously and finally unwound himself, springing free from the beast.

The girth securing the general's saddle slipped, and so did his hold on the reins, his foot trapped in the stirrup on the other side of the animal as he rode beneath the horse. The metal horseshoes clattered like hammers against a concrete abutment. The general was unconscious.

She opened the gate and rushed inside and leaped toward one of the long ropes trailing behind the beast.

Seizing it in her hands, she set her feet and leaned her hips back, putting all her weight into yanking the horse's lead around.

The stallion's head jerked to the side, and with a recalcitrant neigh, his monstrous body followed.

There was no time to think.

Until the whites disappeared from the stallion's eyes, she had to keep him off balance. She darted toward him, tucking her body next to his long middle as she tugged his lead forcefully around with her, compelling him to turn in a continuous circle with the general still dangling in the stirrup.

Her first thought was to free the general. She saw a soldier move toward the other tether. "Slowly," she warned him.

Sophia kept moving the beast in circles, keeping her eyes

locked with the breathtaking creature, her breath keeping time with the deep pants of his flaring nostrils.

"You sweet beast," she crooned, maintaining the circles, but slowing the pace. "You've had a bad day. We must find out what is the matter, my dear friend."

The stallion snorted his displeasure.

"You're right, my dear brave boy," she commiserated. "You didn't ask to be dragged here and ridden when you didn't want to. I'm guessing you desire a cool stall with golden oats and plenty of fresh green hay. How about some nice mash for a chaser? You'll get whatever your heart desires. I promise," she cooed to him.

When he began to settle, she breathed out a sigh, and resumed murmuring nonsensical banalities to the stallion. Dim sounds from outside permeated their odd little universe. Colonel Pratt swearing and General Stimson's praises.

She glanced down. General Taylor had no signs of a head-wound. No doubt, he had the wind knocked out of him. She signaled to the soldier to grab the freed tether. When the stallion was secured from the other side, she reached up, and carefully unbuckled the girth that had slipped from the thousand pounds of horseflesh. A soldier dragged the general out of harm's way.

Sophia hung on to the horse, calming the massive beast with her voice. She smoothed her hands over his flanks until the beast became putty in her hands. With her toe, she kicked over the saddle, and then bent to run her hand over it. Her palm caught on something sharp, a protruding sharp screw, due to a cheap manufacturer. She cursed beneath her breath.

"No wonder you wanted no one atop that saddle. We will throw that horrid contraption away. I promise, my dear friend." She went to the front of the horse and pulled his head down and placed her forehead against his, all the while stroking his cheeks, taking the animal's stresses into herself. "I love you, but you know that. From now on, you will be a good boy."

She drew the stallion to a riding block, and then mounted him bareback.

"No!" she heard Robert call out and she smiled at him. She was in full control.

Slowly, she urged the stallion into a canter around the paddock, loosened the reins, letting the horse have its head. She held her arms out. It had been so long since she had ridden, and the freedom made her want to shout with joy.

She heard General Stimson say, "That is one heck of a woman."

Sophia came to stop in front of them, patted the horse's withers, and dismounted as gracefully as she could with her skirts hiked high. She handed the reins to one of the soldiers. "No way does this magnificent animal need to be put down. Give him extra rations of oats and mash and burn the saddle. He deserves to be rewarded. There was a screw poking into him every time General Taylor rode him. That was the problem."

As the soldier guided the horse toward the barn, the stallion craned his neck to look back at Sophia and whinnied, upset at being led away from her. She laughed.

"Well, I'll be dammed," General Stimson said. "Can you imagine Taylor went through a whole war without a scratch but was nearly left immobile by a damned equine? We certainly don't want that bit of information circulating."

A soldier helped General Taylor to his feet. Unsteadily, he said, "No, I'd rather not suffer that humiliation. I've ridden horses for years. To think I've been outclassed by a woman. And thank you for saving me from injury."

Feet planted apart, a vein throbbing above his eyebrow, and his hands clenched at his sides, Robert glared at Sophia. "That foolhardiness could have broken your neck," he snapped.

Sophia smiled, delighted at his concern. "I have restrained a pig owner, disciplined a Russian general, and tamed a beast. You don't scare me, Colonel Pratt."

Chapter Eight

No matter how much Robert scrubbed at himself, he couldn't wash away the imprint of Sophia Sonderburg. Not from his nostrils, his hands. His skin.

She lingered all over him. Stayed with him in every imaginable way. Her fragrance remained long after she'd gone. Flowery. Lavender. A powerful serene scent. It negated the fiercer scents of the city in favor of her lovely one.

The woman with the blonde hair, a thousand shades of gold that made new mosaics each moment in the warm sun.

A voice so all-encompassing, so wry, with devilish mischief, and not often found in a female. As if he should immediately assume she were of royal lineage and be duty-bound to genuflect.

And then there was the feel of her. Not that he'd sampled enough of that to know. Just sitting beside her was enough. Light as a fairy, as if she'd been born upon the winds. To touch her had electrified him. He needed her like the desert needed rain.

She was an enigma. The way she handled the Russian general —even the best of seasoned diplomats could not have done what she'd accomplished. Bar none, her experience with horses reigned unequal. Her education and poise, remarkable. Her dreams to rebuild Germany and make it a better place was extraordinary. Perhaps women should run the world.

Every time she appeared smiles never faded. She was a siren leading everyone to sudden happiness—including him.

He shrugged and scrubbed his face. He had a girl back home of impeccable pedigree. Beautiful. Wealthy. Finishing school. Perfect debutante. Her family owned a company that would enhance his automotive enterprises. Their notoriety, wealth and political influence would enhance his bid for the Senate.

With his family's dynasty behind him, and imminent expectations of becoming a United States Senator, he had potential to secure the United States Presidency.

No time to foolishly dally with fräuleins, a scandal that might reach the ears of voters back home and muddy his future. No. He'd have to control his urges.

He could do it. He could turn back the Rhine River and drive it to its mouth. Mouth? Lush full lips beckoned him. What did she taste like?

The question walloped him with such longing, such brazen hunger. He let cold water beat on him. He pressed slick, soapy fingers over his chest, cresting the ridges of his ribs and angling to where his cock pulsed, swearing for the hundredth time at the very thought of her. He was a colonel. Had commanded a platoon of hard-bitten men, drove them through torrid combat across a continent in the most brutal war mankind had ever waged. He certainly could control himself.

A piece of his anatomy said otherwise, and he tried to mentally talk himself out of his attraction. The woman possessed all the sexual characteristics attributed to a seductress. Despite her thinness she exhibited curves in all the right places with long supple limbs.

She was neither demure nor submissive but dignified with a hint of rebelliousness. Her smile lit the heavens, her jaw determined, and her gaze assessing. She spoke with the conviction, and unrestrained, forthright confidence of someone who had experienced profound events at a young age. No doubt from surviving the war.

He had caught her eye a couple of times. That is, he'd caught her looking. At him.

As if she existed as the sun, and she already knew he was suffocated in darkness, and in the offing to be yanked into her orbit. Yearning for a touch of her warmth.

He banished the thought. No way should he have hired her. His men had colossal testosterone buildup from the war. With no access to women, they crowded around her desk laughing like a choir of hyenas at something witty she said.

That was his conundrum. Fluent, six-language speaking American soldiers were not a dime a dozen. If such a scholar did exist, the top brass confiscated them. She was his most valuable asset.

He was a war hero. The notion left a sour taste in his mouth. Eradicating an evil had taken its toll on him and left scars. There were days when his brain became a cold fire, more like a panic. He struggled to sleep. To breathe. He blended into this mad world, but people disappointed him. He told himself he could live his dreams, yet he was—alone. He shrugged off the dismal thought. There were sacrifices he must make to obtain his goals after all.

Another part of him, the biggest part of him wished that, one day, he'd be able to process and rid himself of all the trauma and nightmares. Every day, he fought through the headaches, fatigue, depression, anxiety, and apathy. No one knew the weaknesses he kept hidden. He drew a steadying breath. There were two kinds of wounds. The exterior ones, and then the worst ones, buried deep inside.

Sophia. She had woven her magic around him. Made him feel again. Made him feel alive.

Chapter Nine

Robert shifted gears on the jeep. "I'm still having heart palpitations over what you did at the stables yesterday. Don't ever try it again, or I'll wring your neck. That said, what a remarkable gift you have working with horses. That comes from years of experience," Robert said, shifting gears on the jeep again. He had stunned her, picking her up at her apartment instead of sending Armani.

"Growing up, I learned many tricks from gypsies who are savvy with horses, Colonel Pratt," Sophia said.

"When we are out of the office, you can call me, Robert." To hell with the breech in professional etiquette as her boss and a former enemy soldier.

She said nothing. *Damn*. The professional persona remained in place. He gripped the steering wheel.

A slow smile played about her lips. "Robert." She nervously whispered his name, unaware of how her tantalizingly sweet and maddeningly sexy voice feathered along his nerve endings.

"You must tell me some time of your knowledge of horses, but for now, I have a surprise for you." He braked the jeep, hopped out and opened her door.

Momentarily puzzled, she followed. He tucked her hand in the crook of his arm and he guided her down a long block of quaint buildings, a perfectly preserved neighborhood spared of bombings. He ushered her to the second floor of one of the buildings, fished for keys in his pocket, and then opened the door to an apartment. "Go in and look around."

She walked through the rooms, exploring a fully furnished kitchen, living room, dining room and two bedrooms, all meagerly furnished but a royal palace compared to her present situation. "I don't understand."

"It's for you and your roommate, Gabrielle. I don't want you traveling the dangerous distance to and from work." To avoid any misunderstanding of his intentions, he made sure he included her friend to avoid any rejection.

"I cannot possibly accept."

"You will accept on the grounds that I cannot lose a valuable secretary and interpreter. General Stimson insists and so does the United States Army."

She saluted him.

Grinning, he said, "I won't risk you to a bomb or vagrant. This apartment is in the American quarter and two blocks from work."

Sophia played with the locket about her neck. "I'm convinced that you've taken on fretting over my safety as your second occupation."

Out of his own pocket, Robert had paid for the lease, knowing the apartment would be the answer to all her problems. For a moment, he thought she'd walk into his arms. On the verge of tears, she went into the kitchen, opening a drawer, staring at the contents. He knew rejection was coming and cursed her stubborn independence.

"I still cannot accept."

"Sophia. So proud. Think about it overnight."

Chapter Ten

Sophia rounded the corner of her apartment building and froze. Helga Schneider, Karl's sister, stood in front. Sophia had been living at the family estate until they'd received notification of Karl's death. Then Helga had thrown her out. What was she doing here? Gloating? She wanted no part of the hatchet-faced woman with the cruel-looking mouth.

How much Helga had aged. Her braided hair, drawn low over the top of her ears, was gray; deep hollows almost like eggcups curved beneath her icy eyes. Her chin hairs were gray, matching the wiry gray hairs that bristled in her ears. The flaccid skin beneath her jaw sagged like a plucked fowl.

Next to her was the landlady, Ursula, doubtless filling her sister-in-law's head with gossip about Sophia's comings and goings with the Americans. Sophia hitched up her bag of food.

"Here comes the whore of Berlin, working late, on her back," spat Ursula, her face garishly painted to hide her warts. And this was from the woman who pigged down the food Sophia brought home every night.

Helga caught her arm. "I've heard of your unseemly behavior. You are a traitor to your race. Karl is rolling in his grave."

Sophia narrowed her eyes on Helga's hand where she dared to detain her. "I must support myself since Karl has left me nothing, and you have chosen to cast me out of the family. I have a job that keeps me from starvation."

"I never understood what my brother saw in you. You are a worthless fortune seeker. It was good I threw you out."

Sophia tore from Helga's grip. "I do not wish to speak to you."

"I'm doubling your rent," Ursula screeched up the stairway. "You work for the Americans; you can pay it!"

"There is a bomb in this building. I should back charge you."

Sophia walked across the plank to her one-room apartment. The door opened with a rusty groan, and she slammed it shut, looking around her. Two small beds with musty quilts, a chest of drawers with a chipped ceramic bowl on top for washing. Sophia had the three bottom drawers and Gabrielle had the top three. A wardrobe stood against the wall.

Sophia sat on her bed, pulled a table into the center of the room. After tugging out two planks from a wall, she pulled out a porcelain enameled music box with gold filigree and silver gilt with pearl and ruby insets. A treasured piece her father had given her on her twelfth birthday. Despite starvation, she'd not part with it. Not because of its great value, but because of the music box's sentiment.

She wound the piece. A little bird popped out as it tinkled *Clair de Lune* and magically transferred her to her ancestral home. For a moment, she could inhale the piney smells of gentle forests, rising toward the heavens. The happy mornings watching the swallows elegantly gliding over the gardens to the river and down to the farmworkers' cottages. She could hear the laymen sharpening their scythes, or the trumpet-like calls of the mating cranes that lived in the marshland between the forest and the lake.

Her finger tripped open the secret compartment and her hand closed around pictures of her father, Prince Albert Philip of Konigsberg-Holstein Sonderburg-Beck, and her mother, Princess

Magdelena, and her sweet brother and sister. Her heart panged. How she'd love to have one last walk through the forests with her father as he explained the rudiments of forestry to her. "The forest is your spare treasure chest. If needed, it can yield profits that can be comfortably utilized. Save it, for harder times." He had made her familiar with crop rotation so important for productive farming. The hours spent together learning the management of the estate were precious to her and brought a deep love of Zachwyt, named by Spanish Crusaders oddly placed there by the Catholic Church many centuries before. Zachwyt meant enchantment and had been in her family for five generations The fifty-seven-thousand-acre estate hosting three grand castles was her birthright, and always passed down to the eldest daughter. Knowing that she'd spend her life there filled her with love for everything that was connected to Zachwyt, the people, the animals and the land and lake.

What was it like there now? The word she'd received was that everything had been confiscated after her parents' conviction as traitors. Her vision blurred. What had happened to the people there?

She tucked the precious last picture in the drawer and snapped it shut. All her former life had been snuffed as easily as the melody played out. She had lived a life of privilege, and nothing had prepared her for this reality. Survival was her only priority; dreams were a thing of the past.

Sophia stared at the broken windowpanes as shattered as her hopes, the empty space now blocked with cardboard. A tiny needle of hazy light bored through the darkness. She shivered, remembering the ice-cold air of winter that blew through the cardboard windows. No coal for heat. No gas stoves, heating plates, central heating, or water. A candle affixed to a saucer provided flickering light.

Dazed from her encounter with Helga and Ursula, she could see the apartment more clearly. The roof leaked, for many of the tiles had been shattered or blown away. Efforts to patch the roof with salvaged lumber had been a pointless exercise, as evidenced by buckets on the floor, ready for the next rainfall.

She looked at her books and pictures, few clothes, and meager belongings. The apartment belonged to Gabrielle, her best friend who offered her shelter when thrown out of her husband's ancestral home, a mansion endowed to her late husband, the inheritor of a wealthy banking fortune. Yet Karl had not updated his will, and his death had brought out the dark side of his sister who wasted no time in locking the gates and placing Sophia's things at the curb for thieves to take. What little she could carry in two suitcases were all the possessions Sophia had left.

She rose, struck a match to light the tallow candle of a Hindenburg lamp. A tiny flame flickered, casting overlarge shadows on the ceiling. A tattered tablecloth looking more like a shroud covered a shabby table. Two chairs held a symbolic wake, together with a couple of cabinets that guarded dishes, glasses, and a tea set. An armchair with a long, threadbare cover was next to the door. Beside it, a coffee table on which rested a stack of precious books. The inside of the apartment was full of cracks, the wallpaper in tatters. The lone rare luxury—wildflowers Gabrielle had gathered and stood proudly in a vase.

Sophia stripped her clothes off and, for a moment she was naked in the soft light of the lamp. Reflected in the mirror, her high, full breasts were very white, and the nipples stood disobediently erect. Below was a pale triangle, dangerously outlined against the pale swell of her thighs.

Sophia turned to the side, wondering how Robert would view her. She ran her hands down the sides of her rounded breasts, patting her small flat waist then smoothed her palms over the back of her firm hips. He had never called her beautiful, but he had with his eyes. And now he had insisted on her calling him "Robert", a big step in familiarity that she was unsure of.

Karl had not touched her on their wedding night, and she had no idea what it would feel like to be with a man. The war years had crawled at a snail's pace, and she felt robbed of her youth and the romance that should come with life.

Part of her yearned for Robert to kiss her, his lips hot and hungry against her mouth, his eyes gleaming. More kisses, then hands on her breasts, legs, and hips, everywhere testing, touching, and teasing, bringing forth a kind of hidden awareness and womanly boldness instilled from birth.

Running up the steps, Gabrielle called to her. Sophia scanned the room, throwing on a robe as her friend entered.

"You look tired, Sophia."

If only she could sleep. No matter how long she laid awake thinking about Robert, she could not sort out her fears. Fear of initiating a relationship, and then fear of being humiliated when he tired of her. Followed by fear of pregnancy. Fear of the scorn. Fear of intimacy and sex and love. Then came the fear of being alone forever.

Perhaps she was entirely wrong about his attraction to her. Self-doubt decreased her confidence. Had she misread a romantic situation when none existed?

"I was offered a two-bedroom apartment for the both of us in the American quarter."

Gabrielle reared her head back. "Really! Is there electric with hot and cold running water?"

Sophia smiled. "There is even a bathroom that we don't have to share with the other residents in the building."

Gabrielle dug through the bag of food Sophia had brought and selected two danishes. "Paradise. I'm sick of looking for a crust of bread, watery porridge, old people eating grass like animals, foraging for nettles."

"I turned it down."

"What! We live on a bomb, Sophia."

Gabrielle's eyes, riveted in their intensity, rested on Sophia too long for comfort. "There'll be a price tag."

They stared at each other in the ringing silence.

"Robert is not that way."

"It's Robert now. What happened to Colonel Pratt?"

Chapter Eleven

Breathless, Sophia hurried up to Colonel Pratt outside of their office building. Her knees almost buckled, thinking he might have rescinded his offer. "If the apartment is still available, I'd like to take it. What are the leasing fees?"

"Already taken care of, courtesy of General Stimson. He was so pleased with your mediation the other day that he insisted, especially when I told him about the bomb."

Sophia frowned. Not for one minute did she believe a word he said.

His sexy, arrogant mouth curved into a smile. "You'll get the keys on one condition."

Sophia swallowed, thinking of Gabrielle's warning. The price she must pay.

Sea green eyes sparkled with mischief. "You must go out for an early lunch with me."

Sophia tilted her head to the side. "That, I can do. When?"

"Lunch first, and then you can take the day off. I'll have someone help you move your belongings. I want you out of that place."

Sophia was dizzy with the rapid changes. Colonel Pratt was a whirlwind. He escorted her out of the compound and two blocks away. Unlike the Russian quarter, the American sector bled optimism. Representing progress came the clamor of beating rugs, scrubbing, and hammering, an isolated train, and people in bucket brigades cleaning rubble. He parked the jeep in front of a restaurant that had returned for business. It was full of customers.

The maître-d, a scrawny fellow with the face of a scalawag and wearing a white apron guided them to a booth by a window and handed them menus. "May I suggest our sauerbraten, a delicious hearty stew marinated in tenderizing vinegar and spices. It is served with red cabbage and potato dumplings. We also have Wiener Schnitzel with green salad and potato pancakes."

"We'll take two of each and an appetizer of Butterkase with pretzels. And two steins of pale lager."

"Right away, sir." Happy with the double sale, the German owner all but rubbed his hands with glee before hurrying off to the kitchen. American money was better than the bankrupt German mark.

"I cannot possibly eat that much food," Sophia protested.

"You'll eat to your heart's content. You can take the rest back to your apartment and feed Gabrielle while you are packing."

"What am I going to do with you?" she said.

"You will enjoy the food. It will be like going to heaven, but without dying."

Sophia placed her worn purse next to her, and then turned to him. "What do you do in America? And don't tell me you make a living playing the accordion in a restaurant surrounded by beautiful women of easy virtue."

"I have a little farm in Michigan."

A lopsided grin appeared that she found endearing. Her curiosity caught the best of her, and she blurted, "Do you have horses?"

"A few. You like horses, don't you?"

"I don't just like them, I love them. I love all animals."

"Thus, your zoology degree?"

With her hands spread around the cold glass of beer, she warmed to her favorite topic, and smiling, said, "Since I was a child, morning was my favorite time of the day. I'd hear the birds' calls from the lake and could hardly wait to run outside and greet my favorites, be it the old pigsty keeper, Mateusz, or the ring-necked duck that lived in the chicken yard. All of them loved me and the feeling was mutual. There was Tracnen Stables, the greatest stud farm in Europe and Asia where I always tried to help when one of the animals was sick or had a wound that needed cleansing. I'd fetch a bucket of soapy water from the farm kitchen and wash the infected wound. Soon, I was allowed to watch a mare giving birth to a foal or a cow to a calf. I spent hours in the stables and became a sort of messenger and confidante of the workers.

"When the vet arrived, I stuck to him like glue. The chief milker, the coachman and the pig keeper would allow me to watch over an animal in labor while they went for a warm meal or a schnapps. Through such early experiences I became familiar with many natural occurrences and the treatment of diseases."

She felt her face grow flush from the beer. The conversation in the rest of the restaurant seemed to have receded and came to her ears now in a steady, soothing rhythm, like the sound of far-off surf.

"For me, horses have my complete affection, and I spent a lot of time by myself with them. Horses give unconditional love. I dream of having my own horse farm someday. But that is just a dream."

A pit of hopelessness opened in her stomach thinking of Tracnen Stables, her family's celebrated jewel. Accommodating five hundred horses of renown bloodlines, the unique two-story stables possessed one of its kind elevators. The day the Nazis took away the horses for the war, she had been inconsolable grasping their demise.

"I have a fondness for animals, too," said Robert, "but my real love is automobiles, and the faster the better."

"Mechanical skills are good to have because you can fix the tractor on your farm and be self-sufficient. Do you have cows and chickens, ducks? Do you keep bees? How do you manage your land? Do you rotate your crops? Do you have any forests?"

Robert put up his hands. "There might be a few cows or ducks."

"With certainty you are being modest." She chewed on her lip. "Somehow I can't picture you in muddied overhauls and boots, tilling the rich earth."

He reared back. "How do you picture me?"

"Like a king, overseeing his kingdom."

He lifted his mug of beer and saluted her. "King of my farm. Has a nice ring to it."

A restless awareness plagued Sophia as she glanced toward the simple curtained window now stripped of blackout drapery. Her intuition told her Colonel Pratt was a master of deflection and what he told her didn't ring true. He *might* have a few cows and ducks? Wouldn't he know what livestock he had? What was he hiding? Outside, an explosion reverberated the building. Sophia shut her eyes tight and pressed her hands over her ears.

Sweat beaded up around her hairline, then bored straight through her spine. Her throat closed and her mouth went dry as she felt herself sucked back into the past, the oily drone of Russian airplanes, bombs dropped, howling like wolves, and shrieking and wailing so loud they nearly broke her eardrums. Bundles of flaming streaks left trails of fire across the sulfur-yellow sky. She stood in line at the water well. Could not move.

Hurry! Go dig out people buried in the rubble.

Robert pulled her hands to the table and squeezed. "Sophia, it was a car backfiring."

She snapped opened her eyes and breathed. "I'm sorry. My reaction is..."

"Is normal for what you've been through."

"During the bombings, we hid in an underground tunnel beneath a subway and wondered if it would be our mass grave. We called it our cave, underworld, catacomb of fear, mass grave, seeking safety and shelter from the air raids, artillery fire, looters— and ultimately rape from victorious Russians in repayment of Hitler's attacks on Stalingrad.

"We were a disparate group of discards, unwanted at the front, rejected by the Volkssturm, the civil defense, and inspiring pity and lack of hope.

"There were three elderly sisters, widowed by the war and huddled like a big black pudding. A high-explosive bomb had buried itself in their neighbor's garden and had demolished their home. The pig they'd been fattening up was flung all the way up to the rafters." Sophia took a ragged breath, knew she was prattling on, but Robert held her hands and let her talk.

"Fraulein Hunte was a brash and disapproving spinster with a heaving chest who lived to nit-pick her late husband interred in France, and then trumpeted Germany's ultimate victory. Whenever she spoke, we'd exchange meaningful glances. Who wanted to argue with a madwoman?

"Against everyone's protests, Fraulein Hunte had gone to rescue her parakeet. A bomb hit the courtyard near her building. Upon her return, her hair was gray with plaster dust and her face was streaked with blood. 'But I got, Pookie,' she'd said. Pookie lay in the bottom of the cage dead from shell shock. No one had the heart to tell her Pookie was in another world.

"Then there was a scrawny bookseller and his wife, who were always lugging around an artificial leg made of nickel, leather, and wood, hoping that their one-legged son was alive somewhere.

"A hunchbacked pharmacist nicknamed 'Herr Limburger' by virtue of the peculiar aroma he exuded, despite the bath of eau de cologne he marinated in. He was a man with refined tastes and possessed a firm and militant conviction that pork knuckles and sow's stomach provided a miracle cure for his gout. Notwithstanding his peculiarities, he hoarded his food, and complained about everything ad infinitum.

"Then there was sweet seventeen-year-old Domino. He went out to get bread and stepped on a live grenade. He triggered it somehow. Shrapnel went through his flesh; his leg need to be amputated. No way to get him to the hospital. He bled to death."

Robert was silent and so was she. There were no words, and she knew he had buried his own wounds deeply. Weren't they a mirror of each other? "Why have you done all of this for me? Given me a job? Got me the apartment?" she asked. "I've done nothing for you."

"You have been my friend," Robert said softly. "That is an incredible thing."

Robert wished she would never stop speaking, that her voice would wrap itself around him forever, that Berlin and the war would never rush back in to break the spell of this moment that belonged to him.

He released her hand, took a drink of beer, and wiped the foam from his lips. "I survived a waging war across the entire continent of Europe. It was impossible not to think of my own mortality, that it was pure accident that I survived to face the next threat, even if tomorrow came."

A piano player started in the corner accompanied by an accordionist. He listened to the lively music, happy to see Sophia relax. "Do you play the piano?"

She shook her head. "My talents are sorely lacking. My father forbade me to play Bach, saying what I did to him was sacrilege."

"The only Bach I knew was a gaunt professor of chemistry with a tendency to flatulence."

Sophia laughed.

Her comforting scent of lavender entwined him. It was

uncanny, this potent magnetism between them. And the bond...a bond fashioned of fascination, admiration, and, yes, contentment —something that had been missing in his life. "There is so much to admire about you, Sophia. You have a compassion for those who are vulnerable, and despite everything, you've held on to the best part of yourself, and pushed onward. You are refreshing, Sophia."

At home, as an automobile magnate, Robert was fed up to his back teeth with being feared and flattered by everyone, with having people throw themselves on the ground like doormats as he went by. He despised ass lickers, cowards, and anyone who showed any sort of weakness, be it physical, mental, or moral. He had been pestered by sycophants and boot lickers all his life.

He didn't want Sophia to have to pretend with him. Maintaining his anonymity remained paramount. He rolled a toothpick in his mouth. Telling her the truth might change their relationship and that was the last thing he wanted.

He paid the check with a handsome tip, and they departed with the maître d oohing and aahing for their return, and Sophia shaming Robert for his lack of economy.

Outside, he loosened his tie. Sophia possessed a knowledge of farming he didn't have which seemed far beyond her feudal existence. He chalked it up to her rabid love of nature. Still, he must tread lightly to keep up his charade of a rustic farmer. She possessed an expertise far beyond his realm of experience.

In the bright light of day, she walked side by side with him, and then took his hand as if it were the most natural thing to do. She stroked his palm in silence, as if she wanted to read the lines on his skin. For a second, his hand shook like a schoolboy, and it annoyed him. Her eyes met his, and she sensed that he was lonely like she was.

"I feel freer speaking to you—a stranger—than to people I know. Why is that?"

Robert sighed and put on his most Socratic expression. "Probably because a stranger sees us the way we are, not as he wishes to think we are."

"Is that from a famous philosopher?" she asked.

"No, I've just made that up to impress you."

She glanced up at him. "And how do you see me?"

"Like a mystery."

She raised a fine feathery brow. "That is a strange compliment."

"It's not a compliment. It's a threat."

"What do you mean?"

Holding her hand was like holding an enchanting butterfly. Or a heartbeat. "Mysteries must be solved; one must find out what they hide."

"You might be disappointed when you see what's inside."

He loved the way her hand felt, warm and soft. "I might be surprised. And you, too."

"I'm surprised you have so much cheek. I suppose it comes with being an American."

"Maybe—what little energy I have for cheeky exchanges, I save entirely for you."

That stopped her. "Why?"

Because I'm afraid of you. He looked at her for a few moments without saying anything. He thought about how much he wanted to lose himself in those evasive eyes. He thought about the loneliness that would take hold of him that night when he said goodbye to her. He thought of all the things he could offer her, and how much he wanted from her, and it stunned him.

Chapter Twelve

Squirrels scampered across the lawns, chattering, and rustling through pink flowering bushes. The park was a sanctuary in these challenging times with its bounty of clover and sun-strengthened grass where each strand moved in a summer breeze. The lake met the sun with such grace that day, and Sophia and Robert were so enchanted by this eternal dance that they barely noticed the ruins of Berlin. The two of them walked down meandering paths, the sunshine bringing out a childlike lightheartedness in her, and she reveled in bursts of golden laughter that radiated a warmth that went to his soul.

"How does Gabrielle like the new apartment?"

"Like? To have such luxury? She is in love with the apartment and thinks you walk on water. A real stove and refrigerator. Our own bathroom. You cannot imagine the indulgence of hot and cold running water. Not having to wait in line at a pump well, and then worry the handle might break. Not having to be anxious about a bomb blowing us up as we carry buckets of water up four flights of steps to wash. I can list dozens of things we are grateful for."

Her enthusiasm for what he took for granted was infectious and he'd pay a thousand dollars for every one of her smiles.

Her voluminous golden hair was caught up in pins, threatening to come tumbling from their confines at any moment. The effect was marvelous, as he wanted to pluck out every pin to make it do just that.

"Oh, look, it is my gypsy friend. I met her before you hired me for my job. And now, she is selling lavender." Sophia ran ahead of him, leaned over, and inhaled the lovely scent. "Lavender reminds me of home," she said wistfully.

Robert pulled out his wallet and paid for a bouquet and a small bag of grain among the wares spread out before her. Perched on the old woman's shoulder, a crow lifted coal black feathers and squawked its approval.

"You didn't have to do that," Sophia protested, holding her bouquet like it was made of gold.

He could see she was overwhelmed with the simple gift and would have bought the whole tray for her if she allowed. He tipped the gypsy well.

With Sophia, the simple things were wonderful. What a contrast to his fiancée in Michigan who nagged about having the latest and most expensive fashions, horses, jewels, and vacations.

"I see you found your young man," the gypsy woman said as she returned Sophia's gimlet gaze with a confident one of her own.

Sophia blushed and silenced the woman with a gesture that seemed made for a teachers' meeting.

The old woman's bracelets jingled as she stroked the bird's feathers. "The crow is never wrong. Be it said, the universe has faith in you, even if you don't."

When Sophia lifted the bouquet for Robert to smell, he asked, "What did she mean found your fine young man?"

As they continued down a path to the lake's edge, Sophia said, "She had a stack of photos. On a lark, I gave her a fee, and the crow picked out a photo of my intended."

"And—"

Sophia gave a quick shake of her head. "The photo was an exact replica of you. The gypsy claimed we were star-crossed lovers which is superstitious nonsense. Gypsies are devoted to spinning all sorts of stories incorporating legends, myths, and fairy tales with grand exaggeration. They are clever at hooking you with their predictions so your will come back."

Robert rather liked the growing blush across her face. "Of course, if you roll the dice enough, you get the numbers you want, but I've I heard gypsies were accurate with their fortune telling."

"Granny Roma from my home province was always true to me. Her tribe camped in nearby forests, and we always traded with them."

A flock of ducks crowded on the shore, and Sophia delighted in tossing grain to them.

The effect on her face was more than staggering. The smile came unhurriedly, emerging in her eyes until they completely sparkled, then drifting to her generous lips softening them at the corners until they separated, permitting a glimpse of flawless white teeth, and a pair of dimples that peeked at him from the corners of her delicate mouth.

"At home, one of my favorite activities was feeding the swans. There is a sapphire lake filled with lilies that meets the sun each day with such grace that one could not help but be caught up by the endless shimmering. I think that is why sapphire blue is my favorite color."

Robert stored that information away, and then looked back at the gypsy woman who fed the crow grain from her pocket. "Do you think there is a thread of truth in what she said, even though we don't see the whole picture quite yet?"

Sophia snapped her concentration to him to divine his intentions. He leaned over and, for a moment, she thought he was going to kiss her. There emerged a feeling in her heart that said "yes" but another in her gut that said, "no".

She held her breath, as the beats in her heart echoed as loud as a cannon blast. Sunlight danced off the broad angles of his face, and oh, damn. The air was suddenly too close. Too thick and full of—him. Someone cleared his throat behind them. Captain Van Smith toted a picnic basket over one arm and a folded blanket over the other. "I see I came just in time."

Robert groaned. "Your timing always was impeccable.

Van grinned. "I think the only way to be properly intrusive is to be punctual. If you are on time, you have a chance to be entertained, and I have yet to be amused. Do you like to play cards, Sophia?"

"Never let Van lure you into a poker game. You can lay your cards on the table with Van, and when he finishes with you, you have neither cards nor the table."

"Here," the blond Adonis smiled, thrusting the picnic basket and blanket into Robert's arms. "I suppose the colonel has told you how famous I am for eating small children for lunch and virgins for dinner."

Sophia laughed. "Do you farm as well?"

A look of comical surprise lit Van's face. He arched an eyebrow to Robert, and then looked to Sophia. "Farming? Is that what he told you? Yes, an agreeable pastime, but not for me. I'm in the automotive industry."

"What company do you work for?" Sophia asked.

"Oh, a little company you never heard of. Of little significance." He laughed, and Robert glared holes into him. "About Colonel Pratt's farming, now that is a fascinating trade. What has he told you?"

"That he has a few acres and has a small number of horses."

"All that? A few horses and some acreage." Van rolled his thumbs under his lapels, imitating the concept of suspenders. "A noble and humble profession. Why, Robert gets up at the crack of dawn to milk the cows, feed the chickens and steal their eggs. He hitches up the plow to his horse and carves out forty acres before noon. Then he—"

"That's enough, Van. She gets the picture."

Van lifted the lid on the picnic basket, snatched a bite-sized streusel and popped it in his mouth. "Aren't you going to tell her how you pick up hay bales on your shoulder and toss them into the upper loft without an elevator?"

"I don't want to bore, Sophia. Don't you have something to do, like drill a hole in yourself and let the sap run out."

"That bad?" Van feigned a wounded look as if someone had shot his dog. "I thought I'd pal around with you today."

"Over your dead body," Robert promised.

Van rolled up to the tip of his toes, then heels down, said, "Sophia would love my charming company."

A muscle flicked in Robert's jaw. "She'd love a toothache, too."

Van sighed heavily. "I came over here to be nice, and what do I get? Nothing. Not even ice cream."

Sophia laughed and extended her hand. "It is nice to meet you again."

Van pouted. "To think I gave you my kidney, Pratt."

"Don't believe him, Sophia. He still has his First Holy Communion money."

"You should admire my thrift," said Van, thoroughly enjoying annoying his friend.

"Admiring your generosity is like placing a lion in the house to keep a mouse out."

Robert placed his arm around her shoulders and swung her away.

"You were awfully rude to your friend," she chastised.

"Van understands me. We have been friends since childhood. Besides, it is a lovely day, and I don't want to share you with anyone else."

Sophia waited while Robert spread the blanket, and then they sat. The lake presented a calmness from its core to the ripples that danced and reflected the blue sky as the sincerest of smiles. Both dined on slices of jagdwurst, katenspeck and Black Forest ham, rich Butterkäse cheese and crispy baguette with glasses of fruity white wine.

She gave him a soft warm smile. "The men in your office admire you for your bravery. They talk about you in worshipful reverence."

Sophia instantly recognized a weariness about him. No. A wariness.

Something familiar reflected from eyes as green as an emerald and as fierce as a storm at sea. Something tired and wounded. How many times had she seen hints of it before?

"I'm not a hero at all," he said.

When the tip of his tongue had tested his upper lip, the uncertainty of the motion had stimulated something tender within her. An emotion deeper than pity, softer than curiosity. It had tugged at her and, for an incredible moment, she thought of him, among all else, like everyone else, easily torn and not easily mended. She took a deep breath and plunged in, hoping he might be prompted to reveal why he said he wasn't brave. "Vulnerability is truth and is also courage. Truth and courage aren't always easy, but they are never to be mistaken for weakness."

"Then I am weak." He leaned down, his eyes touching every detail of her face as though memorizing it, and then he stared off into space. "Beyond the beaches of Normandy, beyond St. Lo lay the blood bucket of Hürtgen Forest. Through thick and trackless forest terrain, we were surprised with blistering artillery, mortar, machine gun and rifle fire that pinned us in a valley. Machine gun fire mowed our men down. More pops. More shrieks. More maimed boys. Dead men from a whole division littered the forest, bullet holes in their field jackets like blood-ringed grommets.

"I remember the cold. Deep snow. Sleet. Then more snow. Soon we lost our scruples and stripped footwear from the dead to avoid trench foot.

"In addition to the foul weather, there existed the shortages and delay of two more divisions that forced an excellent plan of attack to splinter. Lowering clouds had grounded Allied pilots. We were hemmed in on three sides by enemy forces, and by the time reinforcements came, we'd be dead.

"I'd had enough. Under cover of darkness, I crawled through the underbrush alone. I reached one sleeping German machine gunner and killed him. With freezing sleet burning down my back and neck, I crawled across a ridge and disabled two more machine gunners. At dawn, a huge detachment of Germans raged up a hill toward me. I turned the machine gun on them. More advanced and my ammo was low. I waited, laying still. When they got close, I threw a grenade causing many more casualties. The sun came out and that's when I heard our planes."

Robert's voice caught. "I saw my men coming toward me, calling me a hero. I looked down the slope. Hundreds of German boys lay dead. All by my hand. They were my enemy. Would have killed me if they'd had the chance. Even so, I was ashamed."

"Guilt can become shackles to your feet. Like rust upon iron, guilt consumes until it eats out the heart of the metal. You are not responsible for the madness. You saved your men."

"I'm haunted by those German boys all the time. I hallucinate the dead and their families."

"Moving on from the past can only come with forgiveness and the most important person to forgive is yourself."

"Why?" he asked.

So much was packed in his one-word question, his eyes filled with the futility of war.

Sophia answered softly. "That is the eternal question."

Chapter Thirteen

Rain ended their picnic and soaking wet from the deluge, they went up to his apartment. He disappeared momentarily, leaving Sophia time to scan the interior. His dynamic presence lingered in every corner of the masculine apartment. She could smell it in the pungent notes of cigar smoke clinging to the plush olive-green mohair sofa, flanked with matching side chairs upholstered in gold frieze, and facing a fireplace.

Toweling his thick crop of dark hair, Robert returned. He handed her a fresh towel as well, and then clicked on a pair of elegant brass and marble table lamps with orange-yellow fringed shades, casting the room in warm amber light. He loosened his tie and unbuttoned his collar and Sophia could feel a hot blush rise to her face. She cleared her throat and wandered to his bookshelves, and said, "A room without books is a body without soul."

"Cicero."

"I'm impressed." she said over her shoulder. "I've always imagined this side of heaven is a library. During the last dark days of the Third Reich, and then after the bombings, I hid myself in my apartment absorbing books. They helped me maintain a remnant of my sanity in a world of havoc when the simplest rules of human decency were shattering."

With reverence, Sophia ran her fingers along the spines of his books, and then turned to him. "I feel, in some magical way, that you absorb the wisdom contained in these volumes through your skin, without even opening them."

Robert placed a blanket around her to warm her. "If only man were smart enough to accept the wisdom of the ages."

Solemnly, Sophia nodded her head and settled on the couch beside him. "If only people, and especially Germans, had read more, perhaps they would have had better judgment. Maybe there would not have been a great war that made women widows and children, a sea of orphans.

But no, the tsunami of black and white moral absolutism robbed the soul of the people with no one escaping its share of responsibility for the abandonment of the democratic principles, and precipitating Hitler's power."

Robert tossed his damp towel on a coffee table and combed his fingers through his hair. "No doubt, the fundamental error of the Germans who opposed Nazism was their failure to unite and fight against an evil."

Sophia lifted a shoulder. "It began with the lies through cleverly contrived propaganda offering millions a way out of their misery. Like the Pied Piper, they were drawn to the hope that Germany would be made strong again, would be able to refuse paying reparations, repudiate the Versailles Treaty, stamp out corruption, bring the money barons to heel—especially if they were Jews, and then see to it that every German had a job and food. In the end there existed no conquerors and no conquests, only the rubble wasteland of cities and charred remains of the dead."

She plucked a book off the shelf, studied the copyright page and publisher. "Mark Twain, the famous nineteenth century American humorist and an original." She stroked the paper as if it were a rare silk, and then returned the tome to the shelf.

He retrieved the book and placed it in her hands. "This is a gift."

Sophia could feel a smile grow on her face and a slow, silent tear fall down her cheek. "This is far too valuable."

"Rather than collecting dust on the shelf, I prefer someone to have it who will appreciate the work." He ushered her to the sofa, sat down beside her and poured two glasses of wine, offering one to her. "I love to read, too. Fills the lonely time in between hours."

Sophia paused in lifting her wine glass to her lips. "Really. You don't seem at all lonely to me."

"Because..." he said quietly, "I'm not when you are with me."

Her heartbeat raced at the unexpected admission, and she placed her glass on the table. Oh, to have his solid presence beside her, fingertips light on the nape of the neck, and whispers entangling hers in the night. Someone who'd smile at her like a million rainbows when he saw her coming. Who'd dance with her beneath a starlit night, share promises and know her secrets, and make a little world with just the two of them.

"I find that, too," she said. But a part of her resisted. Would he offer marriage and a chance for a family, or would he just have a fling with a German fraulein, using her for his amusement before going stateside like so many other soldiers had done. No. Robert was not like other men. He was noble and honorable, wasn't he?

Her emotions swung like a wild pendulum. "For the longest time, I've felt like tissue paper in the rain with the sky holding nothing but more storms. All I wanted was a hand to hold or an arm about my shoulders, but none came. The world had become cold and empty, a slow poison for my soul." She gazed into his eyes for an answer.

He set his glass down. "I think the most terrible poverty is loneliness and feeling unloved."

The magnitude of his statement touched her heart as if the sun had poured into it, and with it, the unexpected tenderness that his eyes conveyed making her breath hitch.

He moved his arm around her. Her pulse beat wildly.

Her blanket slipped to the sofa, and in the golden light, the colonel's eyes fixed upon her. She had not the slightest wish to embrace that threat, or to cultivate it. "You won't."

He caught her chin in his hand and stroked the curve of her jaw with his thumb. Her skin grew hot, her mouth went dry. She was unable to breathe. Steady now. He lowered his head, his lips hovering above her. Was he going to kiss her? She had never been really kissed before. Karl had given her a peck on the cheek on occasion and nothing more. What would it feel like? To be really kissed. Luscious anticipation and the slow burn of curiosity and desire curled through her.

He took her in his arms, crushed his mouth to hers, kissed her longingly and deeply, igniting a bone-melting fire that spread through her blood, consuming her. His fingers splayed through her hair, making her scalp tingle. Unable to halt the overwhelming stirrings ensnaring her heart, she moaned into his mouth.

From the time she'd clapped her eyes on him, her fascination for him knew no bounds. And touching him now, she was incapable of resisting the fierce attraction between them.

His fingers slipped beneath the soft cotton of her blouse and undid the buttons, one at a time, then eased off the garment from her shoulders.

She trembled beneath his hands, and he put his arms around her. She had dreamed of this, touching him, and he, touching her. Tentatively, she placed her arms around his neck, breathing in the bay rum scent of him. He captured her mouth again in a light-teasing kiss, deepening the forceful demand of his mouth every bit as raw and unapologetic as it was seductive. His hands explored farther. Images flashed. Hairy, dirty Russian hands ripping her dress, scraping over her skin, pinching her nipples, clawing in between her legs.

"No. I-I cannot do this." She thrust him away from her. Hands trembling, she yanked her blouse closed and curled her legs beneath her. How could she explain her strange behavior when she hurt so much that she could scarcely breathe?

He drew a ragged breath, straightened, and gave her distance. "I want you to know that you are a beautiful and bright young woman. I'd never take advantage of you."

Silence loomed like a heavy mist, broken only by the ticking clock on the mantel. "I did not tell you what happened before the bomb was lodged in my apartment." Bile rose in her throat, and she plunged onward with her story.

"The bombs were dropping heavily, and we had gone to our cave. As I mentioned before, we were a motley collection of societal outcasts. There was a young man with gray trousers and horn-rimmed glasses who on closer inspection turned out to be a woman. She was saved from rape and so was the woman with eczema all over her face. The Russians feared syphilis.

"Elisa and Gertrude were the baker's two seventeen-year-old daughters. Both girls had been injured from falling debris and their heads were wrapped in gauze."

"Go on," Robert encouraged, his deep voice even and infinitely patient, but she felt him stiffen beside her.

A smothering nausea overtook her. Sophia wanted to crawl out of her skin to escape them. She needed to be back in the office, shuffling paperwork and making ordered sense out of chaos. Pretending she had no time for emotion, for grief, for guilt, only responsibility and an endless list of things to do to keep the dissonance of her thoughts occupied.

"Then there was Ilsa. She was beautiful and always stood apart from the rest of us. I gave her a cut of my bread. The pudding sisters scorned Ilsa. 'Do not go near her. She is a bad woman.' What was a bad woman? Ilsa was so nice. Growing up, I led a sheltered life and was innocent of the intrigues of women who provided for men. I ignored the pudding sisters, and both Gabrielle and I shared our blanket with Ilsa, pressing together to share our body warmth.

"There was an oil lamp that smoked away on the beams above us. Bombs made the walls shake, and then suddenly everything stopped. Footsteps hammered toward us. The Russians had found the labyrinth of passageways. The baker put out the lantern and we pushed to the back of our cave. I shoved Gabrielle up into the ventilation shaft. The staccato of their booted feet drew nearer. Staggering from one support beam to the next, the soldiers shined their flashlights on our faces. All forty of us together, pausing each time they came to a woman, letting the pool of light flicker for several seconds on our faces.

"Everyone in the ventilation shaft froze. No one moved. No one said a word. I could hear the forced breathing, including my own. The spotlight settled on the twins; their heads swathed in bandages."

"How old?" demanded a Russian.

"I stepped forward and answered in Russian. 'They have suffered grievous head wounds. They are not here. Bomb.' I pointed to their heads and made a circle as if they were daft. He was surprised I spoke Russian. He pointed at me. The other soldiers grunted. I knew they'd chosen me...my God it would be gang rape."

She couldn't look at Robert anymore. Couldn't see the wrath piercing at her with a machine gunner's precision. Couldn't face him with her shame.

"I glanced behind me. Gabrielle had crawled farther into the ventilation shaft. She could not be seen. Impatient, the soldier with the black eyes grabbed my wrist and jerked me along the corridor. Another soldier put his hand on my throat, squeezing my windpipe. They both dragged me, tearing me away. I hit the floor. My breath whooshed out of me. I could feel the damp tiles slide beneath me; my head on a concrete step. High above, the door to the street was ajar where a soldier kept watch."

Sophia clamped a hand over her mouth as her lunch churned in her stomach and crawled up her throat with an acid burn. "The

Russian tore at my clothes, pawed at my flesh, I kicked and hit them. Everything happened so fast. I-I couldn't stop it. Then I heard a sultry voice. Ilsa. She fluttered her hands in erotic gestures, mesmerizing them. She lifted her skirts, gaining their attention, luring the men away like a siren. They went for her. She continued her soft, seductive invitation, speaking in German of which the country brutes did not understand."

"You have given me a kindness," she said to Sophia. "I'm a prostitute and accustomed to such activity. Run."

Sophia's composure finally broke, swallowing frantic gulps of emotion. He started to reach for her, stopped, as if sensing a touch would break her.

"I pushed from the floor and scrambled to my feet, ran up the steps. I don't remember how I got past the guard, but I rushed through a web of alleyways and gardens to the safety of my apartment."

"You've braved so much," he said.

Sophia lifted her chin. Her head barely reached the knot in his tie, so she had to crane her neck to look at him. "You talked about the guilt of killing so many. If I'd had a gun, I'd have killed the Russian who dared to touch me. I would have killed every Russian that defiled an old nun of seventy, twenty-four times. I would have killed the Russians who caused a woman to jump out of her fourth-story window to evade them, and then the ten Russians who raped a sixteen-year-old girl with an amputated leg."

Tears spilled over her lashes and washed down her cheeks, causing her breath to tremble in her chest and rattle through her lips. "Gabrielle and I found Ilsa torn and bludgeoned to death. We buried her in a garden behind some gooseberry bushes using an old broom closet for her coffin. Out of two boards ripped from a door, we wired a cross together."

Robert clenched and unclenched his hands.

"Ilsa gave me the greatest gift. I know what women in her profession do, but do you think God will allow her into heaven?"

"Damn it! I think she has earned the highest place for her sacrifice." He bellowed in a voice that Sophia swore rattled the windows.

She cringed away from him in fear, but he reached out and held her hand, and she said, "I saved myself, left Ilsa to those monsters. And when all those women suffered, I felt utterly powerless, and that is my prison."

"None of this is your fault."

"Robert, isn't the chronic remorse you carry from turning the machine guns on those German boys illogical as well? Would they have shown the same mercy toward you? Toward your men? No. If I'd had a machine gun, I'd have killed those Russians a thousand times for murdering Ilsa. Are we not a reflection of each other?"

Robert produced a handkerchief and passed it to her. Between clenched teeth, he said, "We'll not insult either of our intelligences by lying to each other."

She wiped her eyes. "I thought with time the grief and crushing guilt would fade, but it hasn't. It was my fault. I should have stayed and, together, we could have fought them."

His hands fisted, and he said, "Two women up against heavily armed men?"

"You don't understand. I didn't even try. I ran. And because of my cowardice, Ilsa died."

Robert's face hardened and he looked like he wanted to shake her. "There was no cowardice on your part, Sophia. You must rid yourself of that notion."

Blinded by tears, she said tremulously, "The two of us—it is like being in a boat with holes and we are sinking. We have a choice to clear out the water by dipping and throwing it over the side to survive. The difference is that you bailed. I did not."

"You have no blame, Sophia," he said darkly, his eyes swirling with the intensity of a storm at sea.

"And you have no blame, either, Robert. In fact, your men were right. What you did was heroic. I was a coward."

She dabbed her eyes again, dampening his handkerchief. "Please forgive my weakness, it does not bring out my best qualities. Could you just hold me?"

"You are far from weak." He moved closer. A butterfly's wing wouldn't have survived in the space between them, and she could feel the sensation of him through every inch of her skin. He slid his arm around her and tucked her head beneath his chin.

His body was coiled as tight as a bowstring, and he said nothing more. Yet to her, he offered a tenderness, conveyed in his caring touch as they entwined their fingers. The shape of his hand fit hers, every joint and solid tendon and hard muscle designed for perfect alignment. Beating in the pulses of their wrists came strength, comfort, and hope. She would remember the feel of his hand around hers for the rest of her life.

Chapter Fourteen

Robert chafed like a penned bull and gazed out his office window at the former Luftwaffe headquarters, one of the few complexes that had not experienced the terror of bombings. Built of flax-colored stone blocks, the grouping of rectangular buildings possessed an imposing façade. Decorative corbels embellished the first and second stories, the only ornamentation the Germans allowed. Everything was built with sharp angles and perfect symmetry like the goose step marches of the Nazis.

An American flag flapped in the breeze, and he squinted at the sun in the late afternoon light, sweating with the heat. He lifted his collar away from his neck, listening to Sophia typing away outside his door.

Two weeks had passed since they had been to Robert's apartment. Daily, they had gone for walks together. Just being with her and doing nothing was perfection. He'd kissed her, and in that instant of passion, a million loving thoughts came to him.

The gypsy's uncanny foretelling came to mind. Was it possible that unseen powers had brought them together, that two bodies could be composed of a single soul? He anchored his hand on his hip. There could be a million stars in the universe, and he'd pick the one that was Sophia every time.

On rainy days, they went to her apartment and played cards with Gabrielle. Robert had procured a desk job for Gabrielle, getting her away from the brigades. Her roommate was head over heels with praises and not afraid to voice her opinion.

"So handsome. So manly. So urbane and such a gentleman."

He liked the blush that stole up Sophia's cheeks as she admonished Gabrielle for her over-the-top adulation.

The office environment proved problematic. In his thirty years, he had never felt an unbearable need for someone…just to be in the same proximity as Sophia. Even now, he longed to take her in his arms and kiss her. He wouldn't call his musings dishonorable, more along the order of wicked, with absolutely, delicious sensual imaginings. Not altogether wise, considering kissing her senseless had lust exploding through his veins and roaring through his ears.

Thinking back to that day in his apartment, the scent of her had unleashed something primal in him, drugged his mind. The thrill of something timeless had brushed against them as he had circled his arms about her and pressed his lips to hers. The kiss had started slow and thoughtful. Her lips had softened willingly, her arms had trembled as she circled them around his neck. Her warmth and the fierce thudding of her heart had sent his own heart racing. Her soft full breasts had flattened against his chest and had nearly undone him.

The latent attraction erupted with such force, and Robert had taken full control. He had reached down and pulled her tight to his body, thrusting his tongue deeper into her mouth to fire her passion. He breathed her, tasted her, tasted the sweet echo of the wine she sipped lingering in her mouth as he savored her. His kisses, gentle at first, became more forceful. His hunger suddenly released, he thrust his tongue again and again…like a branding iron, searing her, having her.

Suddenly, the danger of what they were doing hit him like a

blast of cold air. Breathing hard, they had stared at each other. Her lips were swollen from his kisses, and she had scuttled away from him to the far side of the sofa. To Robert, her behavior had seemed incongruous from moments before, and then came her explanation. My God, she'd almost been raped...

Robert swore. He'd been a complete fool.

Since then, he'd taken things slowly, letting her decide.

He wanted to sweep her far away where there would be no lingering memories, but what could he offer her long-term? Pain knifed through him. He would be sent stateside soon. To a different life. He'd resume his place at the head of Pratt Motors and cultivate his bid for the US Senate.

A mind-numbing disgust rose inside him. He didn't deserve Sophia. He should break things off, put an end to their growing attraction.

Out on the street, two GIs were arguing over which way to fix a flat tire. Two to one odds, the altercation would lead to a fist fight. With testosterone levels high from battle, it would be a long time before men would return to more peaceful solutions. He'd seen fights break out over a pack of cigarettes. He opened the window. "Is there a problem, soldiers?"

Both men looked up, saw his insignia, stood to attention, and saluted. Rank worked every time. "No problem, Colonel," Both men chorused, then went back to work.

The war in its infinite idiocy had raked up death and ruin and madness everywhere. No one was unaffected. His thoughts drifted to Sophia and what she had suffered. Rage tore through him like shards of glass, slicing at his soul. How'd he'd like to kill the Russians who had dared to touch her. He thought of a million painful ways to make their deaths meaningful, to exact a perfect revenge.

Sophia had been attacked and the trauma remained stamped on her mind. She had been spared by a friend who had been bludgeoned to death. The guilt from that alone would have made most people fold.

To Robert, Sophia seemed innocent to the sort of passion he'd experienced with her and seemed inconsistent with someone her age. *Could you just hold me?* Her voice had sounded small, helpless, and childlike. Her lush ocean blue eyes had shone with tears. How many years had she been alone?

Most remarkable, she had suffered a sense of powerlessness yet had risen. She was a fighter, and with that, he reflected on the many wonderful and fascinating aspects of Sophia. How she cared for a prostitute despite the scorn of others. How she shared her food with her starving neighbors. How she stepped forward, braving the Russian soldiers to protect the people in the tunnel. How she lived with a bomb that might have gone off at any second. Most importantly, how she managed to forge on despite the crushing weight of the knowledge that her family had been wiped out by Nazis.

She'd survived because of her serenity to accept the things she could not alter, her courage to amend the things she could, and her insight to know the difference.

Her benevolence did not only extend to strangers but to him. Hadn't she exonerated him from his guilt? He had resided in the darkest of places, like being in the bottom of a deep well with no rope to pull him up. She had given him a light when all the other lights had seemed to have gone out. Despite her tribulations, Sophia, in her infinite, generous and unselfish nature, had given him a gift. With her, he'd heal.

Further mystifying him was the essential need he felt to make her happy. How he'd love to buy her cars, jewels, everything life could offer. Yet, he had the distinct impression that luxuries didn't mean one whit to her. Her joy in that simple lavender nosegay purchased from the gypsy had said it all.

Sophia walked into his office. He didn't have to look behind to know it was her. "I have these papers for you to sign, Colonel."

To hell with signatures. Robert turned and fiddled with the objects on his desk, a paper opener, an old-fashioned inkstand, and a tape dispenser, anything to keep from taking her in his arms and devouring her with a kiss.

"Sophia…" He cleared his throat. "There is an important cocktail hour at the American Consulate. If I must navigate diplomatic worlds, I need someone like you to mitigate their idiocy. Would you accompany me?"

"Of course. But there is one problem. I do not have a dress for such a function. There are no stores available in Berlin yet—"

"I work miracles." He dropped a pink box with a black bow on his desk. "Open it."

Her pale brows knitted together as she carefully untied the bow. Moving aside the tissue paper, she gasped, and then smoothed her hands over the black velvet. "Oh, to wear something soft and feminine." She held the dress against her, as if embracing the Crown Jewels. "This is the most beautiful dress I've ever seen."

She placed the garment in the box, and threw her arms around him and kissed him, then pushed away, checking behind her to see if anyone in the office had seen her indiscretion. His lips twitched in amusement.

"Where did you get it?" she said, picking up the dress again and smoothing her hands over the rich material. Her eyes dipped to the engraving on the cover. "Chanel! This cost a fortune. I cannot possibly accept."

"You will accept. You are working for the United States government."

"How did you know my size?" she accused, her eyes crinkling mirthfully.

He spanned his hands. "Gabrielle."

The pleasure on her face was priceless. He'd procured a special courier to obtain the dress from the famous French designer in Paris. Being head of logistics for the army earned him benefits, and the small fortune he paid was worth every penny. So infectious was her excitement, he entertained the idea of buying her a complete wardrobe. But then she'd wonder where all the money came from. He didn't want to risk ruining their relationship by telling her of his family's wealth. No, best to keep things simple.

Chapter Fifteen

In the lobby of the American Consulate, Robert drew her coat from her and whistled. "You scare me."

She twirled, making the skirt flare out. "I feel quite daring." she said. "I almost feel naked."

He looked her up and down, a wicked, feral smile curving his lips. An incredible vision in black velvet, she was too exquisite to be flesh and blood; too regal and aloof to have ever let him touch her. He suddenly realized he'd been holding his breath. He filled his lungs and smiled. "The dress is designed perfectly for you. Every man will want to take you out of it."

"Including you?"

Robert's nostrils flared. He enjoyed the advantage of his height that offered him an alluring display of smooth flesh, exposed by the neckline of her gown. Gone was the practical chignon she preferred for the day's work. She had let her hair down so that it swirled around her shoulders and his hands itched to grasp the riotous waves cascading down her back. He flexed his hand, and then grimaced. "A dozen officers will come up to you tonight and ask for your telephone number," he said.

"Shall I give it to them?"

"Upon pain of death," Robert said with a mixture of tenderness and lethal determination.

More and more, he was thinking of having her come stateside, but his mother, Judith, had set her cap for him to marry Cynthia Roessler whose father was a powerful industrialist. Cynthia was an exceptional match—beautiful, wealthy, sophisticated, and he liked her. He weighed the pros and cons thinking of how his mother had made it her mission to see his future secured, the company thrive, and her ambitions for her son to be president. He'd thought that's what he wanted, too. Until Sophia made him see the world differently.

Judith would not react well. She'd do everything in her power to destroy Sophia. Not only would Judith tag her as a Nazi, everyone else he knew in the US would also see her as the embodiment of the enemy.

He lifted his arm and Sophia placed her hand there. The heat from her fingers struck fire, as if she were always meant for her to be by his side. He marveled at the sudden tug of emotion, as if they were one soul and that whatever door they came to, they'd open it together.

With undisguised pride, he led her into the main room jam-packed with officers, diplomats, and their wives. Captain Van Smith lowered his glass, a sardonic smile twisting his lips. "And I see sparks in your eyes, Colonel. Like a bonfire on Midsummer Night. That's what I call finding a rose in a field of rubble. I envy you, Colonel. If you hadn't found Sophia first, I would snatch her away from you."

Robert gave a noncommittal grunt. "I think we're going to have to find you a woman."

"Ah, women. The world's mystery. Nobody knows much about women, especially Freud. Not even women know themselves. But it's like electricity: you don't have to know how it works to get a shock on the fingers." Van swiveled. "Oh, there's Janine Daniels. She's such a great conversationalist."

Robert saw Van's eyes dip to the swell of Janine's miraculous bosom with an enraptured smile. An American and secretary for one of the American diplomats, she was startlingly made up, with colored eyeshadow and a brilliantly lipsticked mouth.

Van peeled off his bar stool. "With women, the best part is discovery. You don't know what life is until you undress a woman. A button at a time. Sorry, Sophia. I react before I think."

"You're a mockup for an American soldier, Van. Sometimes you look as though you have a thought in your head, and then other times..."

"Ouch. That bad," Van sighed. "Personally, my ambition is to get my time as a cockroach shortened for good behavior and be promoted to general. It's not much of a step up but I am humble."

Sophia smiled.

Van picked up two drinks. "But if I did not pursue...the hypocrisy would be a canker in the soul of my red-hot American ancestry, wouldn't it?" He winked, then left them for the brunette.

Officers and foreign diplomats surrounded them; their eyes acquisitive, thoughtful. Robert liked to think it was because Sophia could converse with them in their languages, but he knew different. She had charmed and entranced all of them. As the evening wore on, and he watched her laughing with her audience, listening to the compliments they lavished on her, he noted that while he found diplomatic occasions tedious and boring, Sophia thrived in the setting. She belonged here, he realized. This was the world, the setting where Sophia glowed and sparkled and reigned like a young queen. It was the world she obviously loved.

He'd seen her glance his way several times in a muted appeal to ask him how she was doing. He lifted his glass, and made a subtle toast to her, and a soft knowing smile touched her lips as a string quartet started up in the corner.

A group of old army officer buddies swept him away, prattling on about the peace agreements and Nuremburg trials. "Good lord," Lieutenant Warner breathed, turning clear around, and staring at Sophia. "She cannot possibly be real."

"Exactly my thoughts, when I first saw her," Colonel Ambrose averred walking up behind them. "I'm besotted like half the males in here. I'd like an introduction." He handed his glass to Warner instead of the waiter and went off toward Sophia.

It took a physical effort on Robert's part not to go after him. Instead, he glared holes in Warner's back. He wanted Sophia to enjoy her evening.

Van came up alongside Robert with his captured female. "That's a lot for you to handle," he said tipping his head toward Sophia, scrutinizing Robert's face and annoyed eyes. "In my august opinion, you are doing a great job resisting your claim on her."

"Am I?" Robert gritted his teeth. He was thinking of a million tortures he could devise for any man who dared to ogle her.

Van choked on his cocktail. "This exercise in diplomacy is like a tango: absurd and pure suffocation. You must save Sophia. It is the price you must pay for being able to piss standing up."

Sophia's hand curled tightly around the stem of her wine glass as the Russians shouted, *"Vypit nado!"* every time they put their glasses to their lips and celebrated each swallow as if it were indeed worthy of distinction. She was tempted to go on stage, grab the microphone and state all the atrocities committed by Russian soldiers.

Robert moved up beside her and whispered, "You will break your glass if you hold it any tighter."

She sent him a startled glance. Fragments of memories from the Russian invasion of Berlin haunted her. In the past few weeks with Robert, she had come back into herself like someone returning from a long voyage, resentful of the rape, not only of bodies, but of spirits, that had taken place during the occupation.

"I don't like them either," Robert said, his voice coming chilly and precise.

A strange awareness had flooded her. A shocking sense of something she distantly identified as...refuge? Security? His body beside her was rock-hard and powerful. It didn't seem ludicrous to imagine that he was invulnerable, a fortification in opposition to all that would do her harm.

And for an instant she'd felt as though she could have taken sanctuary in his strength forever. *Protected.*

An orchestra started up with a Russian accompanying them, playing wildly and full of fire on a harmonica, no doubt a plundered German Hohner. Guests were pushed aside to clear a broad circle. Three low-ranking, Russian officers in their soft leather boots danced a vigorous Cossack dance, squatting down with their arms folded and making a flurry of kicks with first one leg then the other, celebrating a victory for the glorious Mother Russia. The Russians hand-clapped to the lively entertainment. The American and British audience were less enthusiastic. Would they be fighting one another soon?

General Ivanov crossed the room, parting the crowd like Moses did the Red Sea. He stopped in front of her and saluted. Everyone turned from the frenzied dancers, focusing on the spectacle.

"I've talked to many of my Russian soldiers who were saved by your parents. I want to extend my deepest condolences for your loss and appreciation for their bravery." He lifted his glass of vodka and threw the entire contents down. "You are welcome at the Russian Embassy anytime. Just say my name. The doors will swing open."

Sophia thanked him, he saluted again, and left to talk to other diplomats. "What a hurricane," said Sophia to Robert.

"You have the world at your feet," Robert whispered beside her, his grin both boyish and roguish.

The music ended and a man in civilian dress shouldered his way through the crowd to get to her. She took a step back. He possessed a mouse-colored toupee and penciled mustache, blade-like nose, elf-like eyes, and his skin crinkled up into odd little grimaces on his face. Before he spoke, she knew he was French.

With a haranguing rant, he complained about everything from the lack of caviar and civilized behavior to the status of the Germans.

Robert leaned over. "If phrases were pennies, I'd have a battle-ship full by now."

With the smallest curve of her lips, she responded in English. "The man's oratory could kill flies in midair, but if I'm to find out anything, I need to stay on good terms with him." She offered the French diplomat her most saintly smile in delight at his French outpourings.

The crowd around her seemed to be expanding. Apparently, they had heard she could converse in several languages, and they couldn't resist being heard. Hubris was in the air.

A very tall and wiry man with pale skin, and black eyes, sunk so deep back that they appeared as if they were staring out of caves at her. He possessed a Czech-sounding name but spoke with a Russian accent. He stretched out his hand, took hers and kissed it with the composure of a Knight Templar. Then he delivered a magisterial lecture on the many mysteries of his country's geography that Sophia rapidly translated.

Robert groaned beside her. "This guy should earn a kidney stone for every arrogant word he utters."

She turned to Robert, warning him with her eyes, and then, smiling, turned back to the Czech.

Another diplomat broached their circle. He was from Poland, his tone pitched to a low, rasping hum devoid of vowels, somewhat like Russian but more bestial. Like a maestro, he made grand gestures, whisking his hands through the air to emphasize the most exciting historical events his people played in the war. Sophia responded graciously.

Robert stifled a yawn. "His people fought German Panzer

tanks on horseback, admirable but if I have to listen to anything more, I'll be wishing for a kidney stone."

Sophia turned to him. "You are too much of a pessimist."

"I have to be. I listen to too many optimists. General Stimson just arrived, and I must go and meet him. As you know, he's a stone-faced pillar of contempt but don't be put off. He's a genius of a commander and his men come first."

Sophia was left alone and took another glass of wine from a proffered tray. An officer with leathery skin, protuberant eyes, clad in dress whites, boasting an ocean of medals hovered nearby. Clearly, he was hoping to get into a conversation with her.

"I'm Commodore McAffee," he said with magnanimous inflection.

Should she genuflect?

In the light of the chandelier, the senior level naval officer made her think of a weasel as he looked her up and down. His rat-like, glistening eyes paused on her breasts. He was drunk, she realized, his voice came loud and sloppy as he pushed into her space.

Turning, she used a sip from her wine glass as an excuse to scan the teeming, smartly dressed men in various uniforms decked with so many medals it was a wonder they didn't tip over from the weight. Where was Robert?

The commodore peppered her with lewd remarks accompanied by his oily, putrid smile, a smile full of disdain for her because he presumed her to be a Nazi.

Sophia took a step back. Each time she stepped away, he filled her space. His face wasn't the kind to inspire deference from subordinates, and no doubt he doubled aggressiveness to push himself on her. "Forget Pratt, come and work for me. Why not tonight?"

He grabbed her arm and brushed her breast. How dare he manhandle her in public.

She broke free and slapped him. "I can see where some men prove Darwin's claim that you evolved from apes."

And just like that, in an overheated room over-filled with

people, she saw a fist connect in a teeth-jarring blow with the commodore's jaw.

Sophia blinked. The commodore dropped to the floor.

The man was knocked out cold.

In disbelief, she stared mutely at the man looming above her, his eyes slits of rage and his teeth bared. Robert stood, a study in strength and ruthless control, yet his frightening visage chilled the subtle warmth stealing into her chest. What would it mean to ever defy such a man?

Yet, he had championed her from unwanted advances. Seized by a sudden need to ease the situation, she wanted to smooth out the tension in his shoulders. To warm the sheen of frost from his stare. To soften the rigid mask of his features.

Van burst up beside them. "I'll bet that felt good. Of course, it might mean losing your stripes, years in the military brig, all kinds of humiliations and punishments for striking an officer."

Sophia clutched Robert's arm, feeling responsible for the damage she had caused for his career in front of so many witnesses. His superior officer, General Stimson appeared assessing the situation, as did General Ivanov. Her heart sank.

Stimson's face was screwed around an unlit Cohiba cigar which he savagely chewed into submission. "Poor bastard. Tripped on his shoelace. Eminently and certifiably drunk."

That produced a dark sound from deep in Robert's throat.

"Bring him to the Russian sector. I shoot him. No one ask questions." said General Ivanov.

Sophia's mouth went dry. *And start another world war?*

Van curled his lip in disgust. "He even had the nerve to come up to me and ask whether I knew the etymology of the word 'prick'. All he had to do was look in a mirror for edification."

"We'll take care of this," said General Stimson to the Russian general, and then clapped a hand on Robert's back. "The war is not over yet. There are still a lot of idiots waiting to be killed. Lucky he was Navy. If he was Army, matters would be different.

Men, pick him up and deliver him home. He'll have a hell of a headache tomorrow. Colonel Pratt, perhaps you should escort your secretary home."

Robert guided Sophia to the door, putting two fingers up for their coats. In minutes, they were out of the building and heading down the street. "Men have been devouring you with their eyes all night. For attachés and officers that pride themselves on matters of diplomacy, they sure as hell go too far in admiring beautiful women."

That startled a smile from Sophia. She hauled him to a stop and lifted her eyes to his and said, "Robert, have you ever wanted something very badly—something that was in your grasp—and yet you were afraid to reach out for it?"

Taken aback by her solemn question, Robert's face hardened, no doubt attempting to ignore his impulsive reaction moments before. "No," he said scrupulously, attempting to keep the curtness from his voice as he gazed down at her. "Why do you ask? Is there something you want?"

Her gaze fell from his, and she nodded at the medals on his chest.

"What is it you want?"

"You."

He froze. "What did you just say?"

She raised her eyes to his again. "I said I want you, only I'm afraid that I—"

His fingers dug reflexively into her back, starting to pull her to him.

"Sophia," he said in a strained voice, glancing a little wildly at the curious people they passed. "You don't know what you are saying."

Chapter Sixteen

Sophia barely remembered how he grabbed her hand, rushed her into a car and home to his apartment.

He closed the door behind them. Trembling, Sophia stood with her hands at her sides in front of the fireplace. A small part of her screamed to flee his apartment, almost drowning out the part of her that wanted him.

He pulled her to him. "Just for tonight, Sophia, let's put away all our damning shadows, all our haunting pasts. Just for tonight, let it be you and me and to hell with the rest of the world."

The air between them sizzled in a wordless clash of far-reaching desires and fears, carrying them beyond friendship, beyond human bond and any other passion they'd ever felt. That missing part of her life seemed to be within reach at last, that isolated part of her that desperately needed and begged for her soul to become one with a soulmate. Even if it was only for this night.

"I thought we might..." She couldn't finish, not with his fathomless green eyes with bursts of gold fastened on her while his deep, husky voice caressed her, pulling her further under his spell.

He loosened his tie and tossed it aside. "You talk too much."

. . .

Robert noted the shaking of her fingers as she moved them to the shoulder of her dress. He could see that she was affected by his nearness, an awareness that stole the nimbleness from her movements. Despite her nervousness, she strove to keep his gaze locked on her intriguing eyes, but Robert couldn't stop from visually devouring every hint of skin. The slender column of her throat. The smooth expanse of chest and collarbones, so full of nerve endings.

Impatience ruled him.

Yet he held himself back, remembering how close she'd come to brutal rape, how the experience had wounded her. He'd not push her. He was not a monster.

She shivered slightly, allowing her black velvet dress to pool at her feet, followed by a lacy slip that glided down her body until the garment joined the dress in a pool of silk.

The soft yellow light from the Bohemian lamp kissed her pale golden hair and her creamy ivory skin with amber until she stood in her bra and garters and stockings. He cursed. How he wanted to touch her and keep on touching her! How he'd dreamed of this moment for weeks.

Guilt tried to pull at him, to stir the reality buried down deep beneath the layers of ambition, arrogance, selfishness, and dishonorableness he walled within that solid exterior of ice.

This was Sophia. Should he trivialize her like this?

She slowly unhooked her bra, and her breasts were bared to him for the first time. High, rounded breasts tipped with tight dusky nipples.

She stood proud and erect. He swallowed.

The question was: could he stop himself?

Robert suffered the intoxicating, almost elemental mixture of thrill and shame he imagined had tortured men from the time of Delilah. All his senses were involved with her, creating a need so deep he burned for her, even though he'd hate himself in the morning because of the complicated question of bringing her to

Michigan—or not. Yet the deepest part of him insisted that they were destined to be together. How could he fight the fates?

Tentatively, she reached up and, with delicate fingers, began to unbutton his shirt. In slow agonizing silence, her fingers brushed his heated skin and he flinched with the release of each button. All coherent thought dissipated like the mist before the sun's rays, and everything around him receded except for her. Despite the self-control he prided himself on, words failed him. For once, he couldn't speak.

Sophia found it extraordinary, that the more she revealed, the bolder she became. Perhaps it had something to do with the way Robert groaned when she'd allowed her dress, then her slip, to cascade to the floor. Or the flare of his nostrils as she had reached to remove her bra and stand boldly before him clad only in her garter and stockings.

She felt powerful, daring. Her insides knotted at the same time her most feminine parts turned warm and liquid, pulsing with an answering ache. She was overwhelmed with feelings. Never had she felt this way with anyone, including her husband.

She wanted Robert more than anything.

Trapped in a whirlwind of heady arousal, she watched, intrigued as he shed out of his shirt, reveling in the lean muscularity of his chest, arms, and shoulders. Lower down on his abdomen, his navel was circled with dark hair, muscles flexing and relaxing with the flow of his movements.

Waves of sandalwood scent enveloped her, and she longed to run her hands across his skin, to glide her fingers over every muscle and sinew of him.

He picked her up, crossed the living room and laid her on the bed, his gaze sweeping over her nakedness.

Sophia moistened her lips with the tip of her tongue. He watched her with hunger in his eyes. A slight sheen lit his body, sleek and strong. There was no mistaking the hungry, sensual growl in his throat as he unpinned one of her stockings, teasing the silk over her calf, then ankle. She shivered when he slowly unrolled the other stocking, stroking, his callused fingers lingering a warm, rough texture against her skin.

He finished shedding his trousers, and her eyes widened, her gaze riveted to his manhood...impressed and even a little frightened.

"You are truly lovely," he said, his voice slipping over her like crushed velvet, and a strange, delicious tension scorched below as he devoured her with his eyes, touching her everywhere. He lay next to her, the heat of his body running down the entire length of her, and keenly evident—his manhood pressed against her thigh, and the barely controlled power wound in his body. Sophia closed her eyes not quite sure...how would they fit? Of course, she'd seen stallions in her stables at Tracnen, even enabled the breeding...but this was something else.

He drew Sophia up beside him and stopped. She opened her eyes.

Robert took her hand and placed it on his chest, the strong pulse of his heart drumming beneath her palm.

"Sophia, I promise I will care for you. It is not a careless pledge." Her heart raced at the rich timbre of his voice.

To be cared for. She melted. Oh, to trust his words! She placed a finger on his lips and shook her head. No. She'd not deceive herself. But her caution was lost when he used his thumb to circle her nipple. She raised her fingertips to trace his jaw and trailed them down his neck, entranced by the sensual feel of his firm skin and silky texture of his hair. She memorized everything about him, sensing his vulnerability and reached up to stroke his cheek.

Unable to resist, she kissed his throat and then his shoulder.

Robert shuddered. "How many times have I created this in my mind?" He pulled her body until her breasts pressed firmly against his chest, and her thighs tangled with his own. His hand wandered down her waist, drawing intricate patterns, moving downward to stroke her thighs. She trembled beneath his caresses.

Her curiosity regarding him was just as searching. Her finger followed across his belly where his muscles rippled, hard and lean. She had dreamed of this, touching him, absorbing the beauty of his body with her fingertips, lightly tracing the dark furring of hair spanning his chest, and running down to where his maleness lay. She circled around it, never touching him there and heard his intake of breath every time her exploring fingertips drew close. She reveled in the power she had over him and raised her eyes to his. They were a darker shade of green now, darkened with passion, hard and penetrating.

"You are playing with fire," he growled against the curve of her shoulder, but his words were lost as he took her mouth with his, and then seared a trail down her throat and shoulder. A warm hand closed over her breast, caressing in circles then capturing a nipple and squeezing it between his fingers before trailing to her next breast.

He crushed her to him, his hands exploring the hollows of her back and down over her hips. Automatically, she curled into the curve of his body, her breasts tingling against the muscles of his chest. His hands and lips were everywhere, the gentle massage sending currents of desire through her. His mouth moved to her breast; his tongue caressed her sensitive, swollen nipple.

"Do you like that?"

"Yes." She arched toward him.

His hand seared a path down her abdomen and onto her thigh. He stroked there, and she groaned, pushing her hips into his hand. His palm sought the warmth of her woman's mound, circling her wet cleft. She jerked.

"I love the way you respond." He did it again. She writhed.

Urging her thighs farther apart, he slid his fingers deep into her. Again, and again came the probing of his fingers, the pleasure pure and explosive. She breathed in deep soul-drenching draughts.

He kissed her, parting her lips, and setting her nerves ablaze with a slow search for her tongue. Sophia's hands crept around his neck, her breath labored, her body turning light and hot. When he dragged his mouth from hers, she kept her arms around him, her head spinning.

"So moist and hot and silky."

"Yes, yes." Sophia gasped in sweet agony, not wanting him to stop. He rolled on top of her, separating her thighs with deliberate pressure of his own. He continued to stroke her with his fingers, and Sophia thought she'd spiral off the ends of the earth.

"Look at me."

She opened her eyes, saw the unleashed power of his manhood. He thrust into her body, filling her completely. A sharp, unexpected pain slashed through her. Sophia cried out, shoved against his shoulders.

"Sophia!" His face was taut with emotion.

The pain vanished, and she didn't want him to stop the lush, exquisite sensations she was experiencing. She moved beneath him then, adjusting her body to his, welcoming him into hers, melting against him, and the world filled with him. To have more of him. She gasped with pleasure. She wriggled. He fit well. Very well.

He grabbed her shoulders to still her movement beneath him. "Why didn't you tell me you were a—"

"It doesn't matter."

"It does matter!"

"Robert." She took his face in her hands. "Why are you angry with me?"

"I'm not angry with you." He almost shouted, and because she squirmed beneath him, he moved against her. She wrapped her arms around his neck, offering him her parted lips, matching the erotic rhythm as he moved inside her, tenderly drawing upward, and thrusting deeper and deeper. Sophia responded with each demanding stroke of his body. Passion radiated from the core of her being until he freed her in a bursting of sensations, flooding her with hot pleasure. She wrapped her legs around him as Robert made one final thrust, his body jerking convulsively again as his warmth spilled into her.

Sophia felt Robert move onto his side, carrying her with him. Her breath came in long moans of surrender, and her eyes unsteadily opened and focused on the patterns of light dancing across his face from flickering streetlights.

She reached up, outlining his chest with her fingertips then raised her head and nipped at his nipples. He groaned and grabbed a fistful of her hair, holding her in place. He stared at her with startling intensity, his green eyes penetrating, his wide, muscular shoulders filling the entire scope of her vision.

A look passed between them more eloquent than words. "I need you, Sophia. I love you. I want you to come to the States."

"How you fill my mind with fanciful dreams."

"To be near me."

"What would I do there?" *Be your wife?* She had dreamed of a home, a husband, and children.

"I'll get you a job. You like working with horses."

No promises. Her eyes clouded and she looked away, speaking to the cheerless flowered wallpaper. "Horses? What kind of job?"

He pulled her face to him, and his laughter came warmly and richly, strumming down her spine. "I know a very wealthy man. He's difficult, controlling, stubborn and reckless to a fault. You may not like him. Most can't get along with him at all. Some imply he is a beast with teeth and claws looking to shred to pieces anyone who gets near him."

She widened her eyes. "Will I be able to work with such a boss?"

The faintest trace of humor lit his eyes. "I have the distinct feeling you could hold your own with him. He owns the largest state-of-the-art horse stables in the Midwest. He owes me a favor and could use someone with your talent."

What was left in Berlin? She could have a fresh start. "Do you live nearby? Will I see you?" She couldn't think of going someplace foreign without knowing someone or not seeing Robert again.

"My little farm is in the vicinity," he chuckled, taking her in his arms.

"Hm-m-m." She snuggled up to him. She wanted to hear that he'd be there for her.

"I need you, Sophia."

Her breath caught and her palm immediately cradled his cheek with caressing care. "I need you."

His chest expanded with short, rapid breaths as he held himself straight and taut as a marble statue. His jaw, however, leaned slightly into her hand, searching for comfort.

"You were so wonderful with me...so gentle."

"Not gentle enough. I had no idea you were a virgin."

She massaged a finger over the frown between his eyes. "You were perfect. We were perfect."

She wriggled beneath him, her breasts pressed into his chest, her body molding to his. "I do not regret giving myself to you... having you...does that make me unforgivably wicked in your eyes?"

"No."

She sensed the tempest in him, the battle of his honorable nature. His characteristic vocation to protect and safeguard those he thought vulnerable.

"Is it possible—" she asked.

"You've turned into a seductress."

"You didn't answer my question. Are you able to—"

"Damn right, I am."

Chapter Seventeen

Summer dissolved into autumn, and then to winter. Robert luxuriated in nights filled with long leisurely lovemaking, exploring each other's bodies with wicked and tantalizing innovations. Gabrielle had taken off to visit friends farther south for the past two weeks, so they had stayed in Sophia's apartment.

Robert's plaguing nightmares from the war slowly dissipated. When they did occur, Sophia wrapped her arms around him and soothed away all the horror. Of late, he'd slept uninterrupted until her hand warmed the rebellious part of his anatomy and pulled her to him.

"Wake up, sleepy head." Robert's lazy chuckle brought Sophia awake. "It is a glorious morning," he told her as she rolled onto her back and smiled languorously at him. "A day made for loving and now," he kissed her cheek, "eating."

He surprised her with a steaming cup of coffee and laid a tray of eggs, toast and sausages on her lap.

She rose on her elbow and brushed his cheek with her lips. Her hair smelled of lavender.

"Sophia, I love you."

She shook her head but said nothing, sealing his lips with her fingers as if his words were upsetting her.

He placed her tray aside, wiping toast crumbs from her face. Her hand reached out for him, carefully. The touch of love, cherishing him, an act apart from all other acts, profoundly apart.

With the windows draped to obscure the sun, he took her sweetly, gently.

By the time he had to arise, she'd drifted off to sleep again. He groaned and rose, reluctant to leave their bed. He smoothed the pale golden hair from her face. Like an angel she lay, her sleeping form drawing him back to her. He was in love with her smile, her voice, her body, her laugh, her eyes. "I am in love with you, Sophia," he whispered.

Even though it was his day off, General Stimson needed him for a special assignment. He'd not wake her and would return as soon as possible.

Chapter Eighteen

Robert was gone. Six weeks of plodding through work, knowing he was not at his desk. She should have known better than to believe his words of love. This was just another frolic by an American soldier with his fraulein. She grabbed her coat and escaped into the street where not a soul would know her.

Part of her wished she'd never met him. No need to desire him. No need for crying over him. No need for pain and tears and heartbreak. No need for loving him.

Hardest to comprehend were the broken promises and everything he'd done to make her feel like a nobody. She had gone back to his apartment. Everything had been packed up and sent stateside the landlord had informed her. She had asked other officers where he was, but they wouldn't tell her anything. Even Van had disappeared.

Not a word. No message. Nothing.

She gave herself up to the streets that seemed to bleed in the freezing rain. Going nowhere in particular, she walked with her eyes downcast, dragging with her the image of Robert, then burying it. Soaked through, she sought the security of her apartment. At least the lease had been paid out for the remainder of the year.

Gabrielle rushed to her. "Where have you been? I've been so worried."

Shivering, Sophia stood dumbly, and allowed her friend to divest her of her clothing.

A knock reverberated at the door, and Gabrielle helped her into a warm robe that still smelled of Robert.

"Are you expecting someone?" Gabrielle asked.

Sophia shook her head. "No one."

With her fingers, Sophia combed out the tangles in her hair while Gabrielle answered the door.

"I've finally had a chance to look for you, Sophia." A much thinner Van rushed in. "A month and a half have passed! I'm so sorry. I have an envelope Robert gave me for you but was unable to deliver for I had been sent to France on a mission. Then I had an emergency appendectomy, became septic and almost died. On my return to my office there were dozens of telegrams from Robert. I discovered the envelope I was to give to you stuffed in my coat pocket. Forgive the lateness. It was totally unintended. Now delivered, I have a million things at the office to catch up on for I'm being transferred to England. You know the army." Van kissed her cheek and left as quickly as he came.

Under Gabrielle's rubbernecking curiosity, Sophia fingered the envelope with Robert's refined scrawl.

"Open it," Gabrielle commanded.

Sophia tore it open. Several hundred dollar bills fell on the sofa. It was dated six weeks prior, the morning he'd left her. Her breath caught. Was he guilty about leaving and paying her off like a prostitute? Fingers trembling, she unfolded the letter.

My darling...

Via telegram, I have been called home on an emergency. My mother had a massive heart-attack and is dying. There's no time to contact you as I must catch the last Red Cross flight home. I lost my father during the war and was not able to say goodbye. I know you will understand.

Please find enclosed fifteen hundred dollars for travel to the States and to buy a wardrobe. Have Van secure you necessary documents, a passport and make travel arrangements. There will be a job for you in America. Come as soon as possible. I miss you already.

Love,

Robert

Tears filled her eyes and joy filled her soul. She handed the letter to Gabrielle. "All these weeks and Robert's disappearance has been a chain of communication mishaps."

Gabrielle finished reading the letter. "Sophia, you have a chance to leave Berlin."

"To leave Europe? Everything that is so familiar to me?"

"I know this is painful for you to hear but your family is gone. The forests are gone. Your castles are gone. You have no ties here."

Gabrielle was right. She'd lost everything, been kept a prisoner of the past, and the last few years, she'd been trapped in a labyrinth, thinking about how she'd escape one day, and how amazing that would be. Imagining that future had kept her going. Sophia's voice came out small and childlike. "So far from you."

"Don't be ridiculous and don't remain a rat in the rubble for the rest of your life. Be the architect of your future. Seize this opportunity. Germany is decades from restoration, and you are drifting with no goal to anchor you."

"What if I get there and people hate me because of my accent. There is much hatred after the war."

Gabrielle waved the letter through the air. "The world is full of 'what-ifs', Sophia. Go! Besides, he loves you. Loves you madly."

She wanted to believe. Hoped for it but would not let it control her. Life had been so full of disappointments. More and more, Gabriele's urgings sounded like lines lifted from an idealistic movie or romance, but her heart urged her to go.

Chapter Nineteen

etroit, Michigan, spring 1946

Sophia hurried through throngs of energetic people in the busy Michigan Central Railroad Depot in Detroit. Everything in America was so different. Peaceful and alive, fresh and new, spirited and exciting.

She wended her way to the foggy outside where a man approached. "Excuse me, are you Miss Sophia Sonderburg?"

She nodded.

"I was instructed to take you to your job interview."

Her shoulders sank. Robert had not come to greet her.

When the man opened the door of a limousine, she stared wide-eyed for a full two seconds. Was this conveyance traditional for a new hire?

Her heart trip-hammered, remembering what Robert had told her about her potential employer...a boorish man with beastly manners. Her throat tightened. After hours of travel and wrinkled clothes, she looked a mess. How could she possibly have an interview without the opportunity to freshen up?

She sank into the comfortable leather squabs as the car passed quickly through a bustling city alive with postwar building, then into the green rolling countryside. She took out her resume and rehearsed for the tenth time what she'd say, and then looked up and saw a sign that read, Dearborn, Michigan.

Overhead, the road was hugged by great oaks that stretched long arms of newly budded green on hamlets, hills, and mysterious places of wealth and legend. Peering over the ivy-covered walls and gardens of castle-like mansions, she imagined all sorts of statues, fountains, stables, tennis courts, and swimming pools. The fortunes of American industrialists had flourished from remarkable decades of inventiveness and ingenuity. Her heart beat harder. Did Robert work at one of these mansions or just on his farm? Oh, how she missed him.

The driver turned, and they went through a wide entrance gate where a large gold letter "P" flashed. The entrance led onto a long serpentine driveway, meandering through sculpted woodlands, well-hidden from the road and prying eyes. Expansive meadows and gardens made up the larger landscape with naturalistic plantings of flowers. For a long time, she craned her neck to get a glimpse of the dwelling and was impressed when a large, majestic home with three floors emerged out of the mist. Ivy ran over the spectacular fortress, as if to defend it against knights in armor and dips in the market.

The driver left her at the front door. Should she walk to the back entrance as a potential employee would do in Germany? Maybe they did things differently in America. She shrugged, rang the doorbell, and then tilted her head back. The home was two to three times bigger than all the other imposing estates she'd peeked at on the way. A uniformed maid, wearing a white cap and expressionless look of a soldier, opened the door for her with theatrical servility.

"I'm here to see to see Mr. MacDonald for an interview."

The maid glared at her as if she inquired about the sex of seraphim. "Servants are to come to the rear. I'm the head house-keeper. Follow me."

The housekeeper affected a ceremonial tone that could not conceal a disapproving Scottish accent thick enough to spread on toast. She motioned with a sweep of her hand for Sophia to enter the main foyer paved with hypnotic chessboard tiling. The space was awash in powdery light that spilled down from third-story transoms and illuminated the enormous double marble stairway. With pomp and grimness and a quick pace, the older woman led Sophia to the right wing of the mansion as if Sophia's status as a servant entering the front door was an affront to the whole household. As they wove through a myriad of halls, Sophia glanced right and left passing a billiards room, library, various salons, and a ballroom. The exquisite paintings on the walls were every bit the equal of the flair and apti-tude in her Prussian castles. There were statues, marble busts, and great vases filled with fresh flowers. Golden light filtered through the glass panes of a conservatory overflowing with foliage and tropical species, and the languid scent of roses spiraled through the air. Every-where, an army of servants was engaged in cleaning and polishing with the efficiency and submissiveness of a body of well-trained ants.

Spirited tones from a piano hovered in the air. Mozart. There was a great sense of rhythm to the playing, flawless, no mistake on half notes, a serenade of liquid heaven. With certainty, years of study were involved to become an accomplished master pianist of this quality.

Sophia was annoyed as the maid's heels tapping a quick stac-cato across marble floors interfered with the recital. But Sophia was happy to be led nearer to the music and hoping to get a glimpse of the gifted musician. She pictured a gray-bearded man hunched over his piano.

Two French doors opened into a grand room of rich oak wainscoting and cork floors. For a moment, Sophia stopped, stunned by a young slender blonde girl playing at the piano. She was sitting up straight at the keyboard with a half-smile, her eyes closed, and her head tilted to one side in rapture. Sophia's mouth dropped open.

The maid looked disapprovingly behind her miming, *keep up, eyes ahead.* The young girl was not to be disturbed.

"This is Mr. MacDonald's office," the head housekeeper announced, then rapped three times, and opened the door. Sophia entered a large, dark-paneled room with mahogany trimmings. A large desk stacked with papers was a study in effective tidiness. Books lined the shelves.

A man with vulturine features framed by thick gray hair rose and gave her a ghost of a bow. His impenetrable gaze rested on her while he affixed an unlit pipe to his mouth, the pipe's contents infusing the room with the aroma of a Persian market. "You may go, Mrs. Stitt. I'll take things from here."

"Remember next time, servants must be delivered to the back door." With a crisp snap, Mrs. Stitt shut the door.

"Haughty old bitch," MacDonald said. "Would love to draw and quarter her, but my employer might frown on it."

Sophia widened her eyes. She couldn't agree more and handed Mr. MacDonald her resume.

He motioned for her to take a seat, and then leaned back in his chair, humming on his pipe as he read. "A doctorate in zoology. Impressive. Worked at Tracnen Stables."

"If I might say, I did more than work at the stables. I possess a great knowledge of veterinary care, including birthing and improving the well-being of the horses. I can maintain barn records including financial accounts and supervise employees, order supplies and feed, make sure the horses are well-shod and provide riding lessons if needed. My foremost skills are in breeding to produce strong bloodlines."

He studied her over and her resume. "Impressive. Colonel Pratt recommended you and I can see why."

Was he referring to her looks or qualifications?

As a woman and of German lineage she had two strikes against her. What if MacDonald didn't think she was fit despite Robert's recommendation? What if he harbored prejudices? What if they had already filled the position or had a man in mind? Where else would she work? A million what-ifs played in her mind. How stupid she was to give up the job in Berlin.

Thank providence, she'd spent little of the money Robert had provided for her wardrobe and travel expenses. At least she had a fortune tucked away to live on for a little while. How wasteful Robert was giving her all that cash. She must admonish him to be thriftier.

"May I ask, what does your employer do?" How she wished she'd asked Robert for her prospective boss' name.

"He makes automobiles. In fact, he is the largest automobile manufacturer in the world. Didn't Colonel Pratt inform you?"

Sophia's hand flew to her chest. "No, he must have forgotten to mention it."

MacDonald's bushy eyebrow rose high enough to create a bridge of bare skin.

Sophia concentrated on the three books on his desk, Charles Dickens, *A Tale of Two Cities*, Ayn Rand's *The Fountainhead*, and poetry by Robert Burns.

"Are you familiar with the bard?"

Sophia smiled. "One of my favorites. '*Upon that night when fairies light...*'"

"*Or owre the lays, in splendid blaze...*" MacDonald's eyes twinkled. "I believe I'm the last of the romantics and have direct lineage to Robert Burns." For the next fifteen minutes, MacDonald boasted an elephantine memory allied to the rigid adherence to the traditional rules of the English language that matched his demeanor and the melody of his voice.

"Go ahead and take the Dickens novel," he offered. "I envy you. To read this volume when one has a young heart and a blank soul. The bard I could never part with. The other, by Ayn Rand, I hold in contempt and would not recommend to anyone. It's the ostentatious and futile erudition of a narcissist with egoist depravity."

The manager became distracted, probably with an errant literary genre. Every nerve in Sophia's body shrieked to know if she'd be hired. Clearing her throat, she tugged him back from his academic woolgathering. "Mr. MacDonald, might I be in running for the position?"

He laid her resume on his desk. "You had the job before you walked in here."

Chapter Twenty

No sooner than the scholarly Mr. MacDonald whisked her to where she'd be working, he was called away, leaving her to peruse the stables on her own. She became immediately enchanted. The building was painted a cheerful yellow that was capable of charming God and was strikingly trimmed with green. She halted at the mouth of the barn where a main corridor, laid with flagstone, stretched endlessly between regular stalls and box stalls. The familiar scent of sweet-smelling timothy, manure, and then the echoing whinnies of horses swishing their tails beckoned her.

Farther down were offices, a tack room, a walk-in bathtub and shower room for horse grooming, and a birthing room. Sophia held her arms up and twirled. To work in such a place where no expense was spared.

What was most remarkable were the stunning bloodlines of the horses. She greeted each one with a pat on the forehead, while the horses nodded their heads as if in genuflection. One fine black stallion nudged her, and she laughed. "You want to be spoiled, don't you, dear boy?"

Suddenly Sophia was picked up and swung around.

Back on her feet, she turned. "Robert! What are you doing here?"

"I've come to steal some kisses." He flattened her against the wall and captured her lips in a kiss that made her head reel. His mouth all but consumed her in a rush of frantic kisses, clouding her mind. She kissed him back with all the pent-up stress and loneliness over the past three months, and an explosion of pleasure went off inside her.

Breathing hard, reality set in and she pushed him away. "Robert, you make me forget myself. How is your mother?"

"She's doing great. Miraculous recovery. It was like she was never sick." He scrubbed a hand over his jaw, then lowered his head to kiss her.

She held him away. "I'm so happy to hear she is doing well, but I don't think you are allowed on the property unless you work on the estate. How is it you're here?"

He pushed her into an empty stall and his gaze met hers with a force that licked through her body. He traced a tortuous trail along her jaw line with his tongue and nibbling teeth, his hands plunged into her hair. His warm breath whispered over her neck.

"I have my ways."

"I've missed you," Sophia said breathlessly, wrapping her arms around his neck.

Robert gave a low growl of approval. "I've missed you, too."

He kissed her like he wanted to devour her. She pushed him away at arm's length. "Robert, we can't be doing this here. I could meet you on Saturday, my day off."

"I'm not waiting until Saturday. I will not spend another day or moment without you."

"But my job. I don't want to lose this job. It is my dream job. My new employer was generous enough to give me a little house of my own."

He lifted his head. "Is that all? He should have been more generous than that, the greedy buffoon."

She pressed her fingers to his lips. "You will not speak of my new employer that way. Nor will I let your attentions get me fired."

"Have you met your new employer yet?"

"No."

"He's a brutal man, a lecher."

With his hand, slowly, lingeringly, he traced a path from her bottom to her breasts.

She sighed. "I will deal with him." What was she saying? She couldn't even control what Robert was doing to her.

Over her blouse, he scraped his palms over her nipples. "People say he eats young maidens with doctoral degrees in zoology for his breakfast. Hm-m-m, that sounds like a very good idea."

She pushed hard on his chest but could not move him. "Robert, we must stop. What if the owner were to—"

He deepened the pressure with his strong, hard lips, pulled back and laughed.

"Shouldn't you be milking your cows or plowing fields?" she castigated him, trying to bring her body's sensual response under control, despite the delicious things he was doing to her.

Like a philosopher, he tilted his head to consider. "Ah, yes. My farm. I can't wait to show you all of it."

"One more thing," Sophia scolded. "You were foolish to leave me with all that money. You'll need it for your farm. Very unwise of you to be throwing around your meager earnings. I bought a couple of outfits suitable for work in the stables and will return the rest to you."

"You only bought a couple of outfits!"

"Your spendthrift ways are a recipe for disaster. Mama Zeilinski told me she had to sell five thousand eggs to earn fifty dollars!"

"Why that's robbery. I would have given Mama Zeilinski three hundred dollars for her eggs."

She widened her eyes in horror. "You exercise poor economy. Someone needs to take you in hand."

Robert shook his head and bent his head to kiss her. "I am lacking. Do you think you could help with my paltry accounts?"

With one great thrust, she pushed him away. "I have a bone to pick with you. Why didn't you tell me my employer sold cars?"

"A car salesman, you say. Would it have made a difference?"

She folded her arms in front of her when he tried to kiss her again.

"Mr. MacDonald said he is the largest automobile manufacturer in the world. How could you forget a detail like that?"

"Sophia, are you here?" Mr. MacDonald called for her.

Her brain seized. Her saliva turned to sawdust. "That is the manager. How will I explain your presence?" She took in a deep breath against rising panic. "Stay here."

Sophia pushed him to the corner of the stall to hide him, patted her hair and walked into the main corridor. "I'm here, Mr. MacDonald."

She'd lose her job if he discovered Robert. Where would she go? Damn Robert for coming at a time like this.

She felt Robert behind her, turned, and flashed daggers at him. "I told you to stay put. Now I'm going to be fired." How was she going to explain Robert on the premises?

Mr. MacDonald's mouth fell open. "Didn't expect to see—"

Sophia was so upset she didn't see Robert waving his arms behind her. "I can explain," she said. "This is an old friend, and he has a farm near here. He is just leaving. I promise."

Robert placed his arm around her shoulder and gave her a tight squeeze. "We were discussing the terrible owner of this place and his worship for strong, blonde-haired women who can speak several languages and act as goddesses in scandalous pagan rites."

Sophia felt a hot blush creep over her neck. Was he trying to get her fired before she started? She resisted the urge to kick him. "I never said such a thing, Mr. MacDonald."

MacDonald dipped his pipe in a tobacco pouch. "Truth be

told, the owner does have a penchant for hoodwinking people." He laughed.

Sophia didn't think it was a bit funny talking about their boss in this manner. MacDonald would have been terminated for such disloyalty if he had worked for her father. "Mr. MacDonald, Colonel Pratt is leaving." She dismissed Robert with a warning flash of her eyes.

MacDonald's lips twitched. "As a matter of fact, the owner is fine man. One of the finest I know. I think you'd like him."

"What does the word 'hoodwinking' mean?" Sophia asked, her eyes narrowing and attempting to push Robert from the barn. He was like moving a stone wall. He wouldn't budge.

"Hoodwinking is like bamboozling," provided MacDonald who rocked up to the tip of his toes, and then heels down, pontificated his knowledge like Socrates.

Robert scoffed. "MacDonald affects literary airs and sometimes becomes the hero of the story. Boasts of being able to recite *Beowulf* in a perfect Anglo-Saxon accent, and no doubt will tell you he can swim across the sea carrying thirty coats of armor."

Oh, how'd she like to wipe that arrogant grin off Robert's face. Why wouldn't he leave? Frowning, she said, "Bamboozling? I'm afraid I don't understand the word."

"We should discuss more the terrible traits of the owner, MacDonald. I hear he is a terrible bore, sleeps until noon, possesses a horrible temper."

Sophia placed her hands on Robert's mouth. "Please don't listen to Colonel Pratt, Mr. MacDonald. He was hit by a grenade during the war and hasn't been quite right since." She hoped to get a vote of sympathy for an injured veteran and explain Robert's disrespectful behavior.

Sophia saw MacDonald's mouth tighten, then a slight upward tilt of his lips. The manager cracked a smile and winked at Robert before bursting into a full-blown grin. Soon, both men were roaring with laughter. Robert slapped MacDonald on the back.

Sophia's eyes widened with Robert's inappropriate familiarity. She set her teeth. Their mirth bordered on insanity, and she was about to tell them so when a small black groom arrived with a hay bale on his shoulder.

"Good morning, Boss. Haven't seen you in a while," he said dropping the hay bale and patting a stallion. "Mr. Robert, what horse will you be riding today?"

"Boss?" Sophia echoed. Every muscle in her body froze, and the blood drained from her face.

"Yes, Ma'am. Colonel Pratt, he's the boss man," said the little black man with a thick unidentifiable French accent.

Sophia's wits washed blank. Her brain cogs wouldn't turn. Going completely still, she counted on her fingers. "The large 'P' on the front gate. Pratt begins with a 'P'. Robert is Mr. Pratt. Robert is the owner of the largest automobile company in the world?" The shock shattered her like glass.

"Oh, how you think to make fun of me." She jabbed her finger in Robert's chest, and in a shaky, disbelieving voice, said, "And how you deceived me. Little farm. Help you manage your paltry accounts. I should have known when you were so free with money. What a fool I've been. I thought you were my prince. Instead, I find out you've lied to me from the beginning. I'm just some part of a big joke." On and on she went, cursing him in six different languages.

Unshed tears blurred her vision. Her watery gaze wavered to MacDonald who suddenly studied his shoelaces, to the little black man with a sympathetic expression.

She swallowed hard, and unable to let anyone see her misery, she turned and ran. She ran and ran not knowing where she was going. How cruel life could be. She came to a river with no place to cross and leaned against a tree, sobbing. Robert came up behind her.

She held her hand up. "You are the last person I want to see."

"I didn't know what you'd think of me if I told you the truth. I have women falling all over me, but they are fake. How would you have reacted if you'd known how wealthy I was? Would you have let me walk you home, let alone take me into your bed? For once in my life, I wanted a real relationship where someone accepted me for who I truly am. Is that so difficult to understand?"

"So, this house, the stables, even the limousine that picked me up belong to you?"

He combed his fingers through his hair. "I didn't want to taint our relationship with my wealth."

"I should have guessed. The Chanel dress. The way you spent exorbitant prices on meals and extravagant tips. My dream job working with horses. I'll bet you paid for my apartment in Berlin," she said reproachfully.

He took his handkerchief and wiped the tears from her cheeks. "I planned to tell you over a leisurely dinner tonight, but Diruvert let the cat out of the bag. Do you forgive me?"

"I should make you suffer."

"You made me suffer enough. How many weeks have I waited for you to arrive?"

"Van was terribly sick and there were mishaps in getting your message to me."

"So, I found out from the dozens of unanswered telegrams I sent."

"Does Van know about you?"

"Van is a vice president of Pratt Motors, at least he was before he left for the war and will be again when he returns stateside. I swore him to secrecy."

"It seems like I'm the only one who didn't know. I would have been happy sharing your little farm."

He laughed and took her in his arms, resting his chin on her head. "Could you be happy sharing a bigger farm?"

Chapter Twenty-One

"What are you going to show me today?" Sophia asked.

"A number of things," Robert said, clasping his hands behind his back. They had made love several times, but she'd been exhausted from her long trip, and he'd been content just to hold her by his side while she slept. On top of that, she took her job seriously, working long hard hours despite him ordering otherwise. Strong-willed as she was, she refused preferential treatment.

She tilted her head and smiled, the way a child did when they've been promised a riddle or a conjuror's trick. "I have Saturday and Sunday off. After all, my boss is a terrible boor and has a horrible temper."

Robert laughed. Sophia made him laugh and that is what he liked about her. Letting go with her was among the most wonderful experiences he had, and he wanted to make the most of every prized moment.

He'd been sick with worry, wondering if she had refused to come stateside. Those weeks of not hearing from her or Van had been hell. The nightmares had returned, and he'd suffered little sleep. With Sophia, the night terrors had been wiped away.

"Shall I give you the sophisticated or the mundane tour?" he asked.

"I'm all ears for the sophisticated tour. Yet, try as you might, I doubt it will be refined."

"You think so." He walked backward and swooped a hand over the terrain. Pulling his chin up, he spoke with the haughty discourse of a university professor. "Our landscape architect added thousands of native shrubs. The lawn spreads wide and is a path, highlighting the summer solstice, the longest day of the year. The magic of the sun sets in the notch of A tree over the lake at the far end of the meadow and reminds us of nature's rhythm. The floral diversity designed into the landscape ensures the idealized setting will endure."

He watched her as she looked out over the terrain where dazzling colors swathed the countryside. Columbine, lupines, pansies, violas, daffodils, hyacinths, forsythia, zillions of vivid tulips, and bright blooming dogwood covered the landscape.

"I'm enchanted."

Like a pope in his pulpit, Robert pontificated more. "In addition, there are thirteen hundred acres, one hundred of which are daily manicured. Extensive garages that house many kinds of cars feature an upper-level laboratory where I work on new designs, and a boathouse built in stonework cliffs that allows the family to travel on the Rouge River. The estate also boasts its own electrical station and shares power with the nearby town. In the house, there is an indoor pool and bowling alley."

What he wanted to show her the most was his private laboratory and workshop. "The car has become an article of dress without which we feel uncertain, unclad, and incomplete in the modern sphere." Robert took her hand, explaining amazing innovations as he guided her through a maze of old and new cars in the state of being torn apart or completely put together.

"This is amazing. You are going too quickly. I cannot possibly take it all in."

"This garage is my mistress and where I work out my stress, hashing out future ideas and designs. You have the distinct privilege of being one of the few I have allowed to visit these hallowed halls."

She dipped in a deep and teasing curtsey. "Then you must show me what you are currently working on."

Robert complied, dizzying her with technological aspects of a new carburetor. Her eyes widened, seizing bits and pieces of his discussion.

"I can hardly fathom the depth of your mechanical genius." She shook her head. "Amidst this perfect chaos of fan belts, engine parts, grease, and shiny bumpers, I sense this is where you live and breathe. This world of cars makes you alive and passionate, and I'm electrified to be in your company. I'm awed by this vital part of you that you have shared."

Her gaze locked with his, and, in that moment, the winds of heaven danced between them.

"You understand me, Sophia."

"I do."

Sophia followed Robert along a serpentine path through arches, passing a fountain with a magnificent angel passing its judgment with a sword, all under the leaves of a myriad of oak trees that shimmered, its leaves like tears of silver. He showed her his tree-house in the woods, and then stopped at a beech tree by the river and produced a penknife. The sheen of his dark hair rivaled the brilliance of his arrogant grin as he carved a heart with his and Sophia's initials into the tree trunk.

He checked his watch and drew her to the house. "Built of limestone, this formidable edifice I call home is a cross between a classic 'Prairie style' of architect Frank Lloyd Wright and an English manor home."

Sophia frowned. "I think the architect was a bit confused."

Robert chuckled. "He was at that. My mother had decided on one fashion and, after the home was half-built, decided on the latter after a European trip. One can easily see the alterations. Like putting a stripe with a plaid."

"The home is beautiful, nonetheless. Will I meet your mother?" Sophia asked.

Robert's lips pressed together in a slight grimace. "She has gone to Chicago for the weekend to shop and take in the theatre."

What was his disapproval concerning his mother? Sophia was confused, thinking he should have been relieved his mother had lived, but then, people had strange reactions to grief. She didn't think of it anymore for he clasped her hand, tugging her along, delighting in showing her every nook and cranny of his home, from the tunnel in the basement, to all kinds of hiding places that no one knew or remembered anymore. They were his secret world and his refuge. A few minutes later, he swung open a giant oak door, and switched on a chandelier, illuminating an enormous room, lined with books, emitting the delicious smell of leather and learning.

"Bound sets. Voltaire. Kipling. Help yourself to decadent poets, dead languages, and neglected masterpieces," he said closing the door.

Sophia walked along the shelves of books. Her ancestral libraries had included one of the most comprehensive private collections in Europe, the shelves reaching three stories high. She ran her fingers across the gold-embossed leather and sighed.

"What's the matter? I thought you'd be happy with my library."

"I am, but I was thinking of the time spent reading long hours with my family."

"I'm sorry for your loss, Sophia. They must have been very important to you."

"They were. The most significant lesson my father taught me was to know the pleasure of reading—of exploring the recesses of the soul, of letting myself be carried away by imagination, beauty, and the mystery of fiction and language like a fugitive riding on the spine of a book, eager to escape into worlds of fiction and second-hand dreams. Can you imagine Hitler burned books and desired to rewrite history? So much was lost during the war."

Robert placed his hands on her shoulders. "Hitler is a history we need to forget, Sophia. To linger anymore is a drill in pointlessness."

"What haunts me is that Hitler and many of his high-ranking followers somehow survived. They were too smart to be defeated. The fear that skulks in my mind is that Germany lost but Hitler won."

She frowned as he leaned over, one hand cupping her neck, and pulling her to him. His smooth lips tasted of strawberries, energy, and torrid masculinity. Gradually, she melted into him, slipping her arms beneath his jacket, and encircling his waist. Her breasts pressed against his solid chest as he slanted his mouth over hers and parted her lips in a rough, sighing moan.

She pushed him back. "I must get back to my job before my ogre of a boss dismisses me."

He moved toward her again and she thrust her hand up, laying her palm flat on his chest, his skin warm beneath his shirt.

"Your ogre of a boss longs to take you away from the stables and drag you into an unstoppable spiral of lust and sin."

"That bad?"

"It's a mathematical certainty."

The door slammed open with a shot. Sophia jumped and stepped back from him. The young blonde girl who Sophia had seen playing the piano days before halted. "What is a mathematical certainty?"

Robert grunted at the interruption. "What are you doing here, squirt?"

The girl raised a condemning feathered brow. "Am I not part of this household? If you need to know, I came to fetch a book.

Perhaps your friend can suggest a novel to read. That is, if you care to introduce me first."

Robert flourished an exaggerated hand in the air. "Miss Sophia Sonderburg, our new stablemaster, this is my precocious little sister, Caroline. She can slice and dice you with her wit."

A boy about seven years old skidded on the slippery marble, knocking Caroline flat on the floor.

"Careful, knucklehead," Caroline scolded, then stood and dusted off her pants. "We have company."

Robert pulled the blushing boy up, and then ruffled his dark hair. "And this scamp is my younger brother, Liam."

Like a military officer in full review, Caroline strolled into the room, examining Sophia like an unknown species. Her eyes, so like Robert's, were astute and discerning. "I saw you the other day while I was practicing."

"I didn't think you noticed me; you were so involved with your music. You play exceptionally and are gifted for one so young," said Sophia.

"I have two loves—music and horses." Caroline heaved the sigh of a ten-year-old martyr. "I'm not so good at Latin and Greek or mathematics, or the rest of my studies. Mother keeps threatening that unless I improve my grades, she'll sell my mare."

Robert crossed his arms in front of him. "I will not allow Mother to sell your mare, but you must try harder in your studies."

"I would if I had a better tutor than old Belette." She raised her chin and effecting a proper moue with her lips, blew imaginary smoke from an imaginary cigarette.

Robert laughed. "You did an excellent impression of him."

Like a shadow, Liam stood behind his older sister. She anchored her arm around him. "My little brother is very smart, but he doesn't like to talk. He gets embarrassed because he can't stop stuttering."

Sophia stooped in front of Liam. "I can help if you like. My younger brother stuttered, too. I rallied round him and by the time he was eight, he spoke like a Greek orator."

The boy brightened.

"He thanks you, Sophia." Caroline said, assumed proxy for her brother. "Liam and I will walk with you to the stables. I'll show you my mare, Rosie."

"Who invited you?" Robert protested.

"I wonder...might mother find it peculiar you taking so much time off work? And since when do you show the library to the stablemaster?" Caroline blinked her eyes innocently. "Don't worry. I won't tell."

Robert loosened his collar. "You are a blackmailing little rascal, Caroline."

"I know, but you love me for it."

Sophia laughed, enjoying the camaraderie of Robert's much younger siblings. For a moment, grief stung, the pair so reminded her of Louisa and Stefan, her sister and brother. When Caroline and Liam flanked her, taking her hands, and pulling her toward the stables, her heart leaped, hoping that she might one day, again, belong to a family.

Chapter Twenty-Two

Sophia loved her job, working with the horses. While soaping and rinsing one of the stallions with the little black groom, she asked, "Diruvert, how did you come to work for Mr. Pratt?"

Diruvert Tiday, the gap-toothed groom, leaned on his broom in the manner of Rodin's *The Thinker*. "I am from Haiti," he said in halting English with a musical Creole accent. "I go fishing. Big storm. Blow faraway in sea. No water for me to drink. No food. Then, my boat fill with water. Sharks all around, waiting to eat me. A squall in the distance. Mr. Robert ordered his yacht to stop. I t'ink he felt sorry for me. He took me aboard, fed me, sailed to big city...New York, I t'ink. He got me papers. I'm a United States citizen," he pressed his shoulders backward. "Then Mr. Robert say, 'You like horses?' I say, 'I dunno, they are very big.' Mr. Robert laughs. 'You come work for me,' he says. I'm very grateful to Mr. Robert."

"That is quite a story," Sophia said, reorganizing the tack on a wall. How generous of heart Robert was, showing kindness and infinite compassion toward others less fortunate. Hadn't Robert rescued her?

"Liam and Caroline, Mr. Robert's siblings, are adorable." Sophia said, smiling on how she was picking up Diruvert's reference of "Mr. Robert". "I've yet to meet Mr. Robert's mother."

"Yes, Mr. Liam, Miss Caroline, Mr. Robert very good. Mother, well, I not say."

Sophia raised a brow. In other words, Diruvert did not think much of Robert's mother.

Caroline skipped in and they ceased their conversation. Sophia finished rinsing and allowed Diruvert to take the stallion back to his stall. Caroline followed Sophia into the tack room and helped her untangle the bridles, reins, and halters. "No school today?" Sophia asked.

Caroline fingered the fringe on a saddle. "My tutor, Mr. Belette, is ill." Caroline leaned over, and then whispered confidentially, "Too much cognac. He canceled our lessons. He pretends to be French because Mother thinks it's chic. I know different. He's not French."

Liam came in and sat down on the stables' floor next to where Sophia and Caroline were working. He drew a calico cat onto his lap.

"How do you know he is not French?" Sophia asked, above the din of Diruvert spilling grain into a trough.

"He doesn't know the first thing about conjugating verbs. He even makes up French words that don't exist, and he is demanding and mean."

At the reference to the tutor, the calico's ears pulled back and its tail flicked. What was most remarkable was Liam's reaction. The boy tucked his chin down like a turtle would hide in its shell. Sophia frowned at Liam's reaction at the mention of his tutor. "Have you discussed your discovery with your mother?"

"Are you kidding? Mother is too absorbed in her country club, shopping, and charities to be concerned about something as insignificant as that."

"I see." With the tack room in order, Sophia moved to the

stalls, checking on the condition of each animal. Caroline trailed after her, and Liam picked up the cat and followed.

"With Mother, it is all about Robert. Robert this, Robert that. I just wish—oh well, I love Robert. I wish I could see him more."

The mother was absent.

Sophia's mother had always been her quiet strength, gently encouraging her to do more and had always been available for a hug. A hand to hold when things didn't go well. Infinite love had been showered on all her children. Yet her mother was gone now, and by her choice. Her mother must have known that what she was doing was dangerous. Sometimes, Sophia resented the sacrifice that left her an orphan.

Liam and Caroline's case was different. Albeit alive, their mother appeared emotionally unavailable and unattuned to their needs. Why?

Sophia made a mental note to tell Robert to spend more of his time with his siblings. They desperately needed an adult in their lives and not servants.

For Sophia, there was joy in Caroline and Liam's daily visits. They laughed, and when chores were finished, they enjoyed riding the many trails in the woods together. A lightness settled on Sophia. Diruvert, Caroline, Liam and Robert had become her family, diminishing the horrors of war, and giving her hope and new purpose.

As promised, Sophia took Liam into her office and worked with him to correct his stuttering. "Slow down and pronounce one syllable at a time." With her reassurance, he soon verbalized whole sentences, and then paragraphs with confidence.

While she brushed down the horses, Liam settled in a pile of hay in the corner of the stall to read aloud while the calico purred on his lap. Sophia smiled. Liam read with flawless accuracy. Nonjudgmental, the cat proved a safe environment that freed him from any censure.

Liam's enthusiasm grew with the books he read aloud, and they discussed at length what he was reading. Liam did not realize he didn't stutter anymore.

Chapter Twenty-Three

In the birthing room, Sophia ran her hands over the mare's shuddering stomach muscles. Milk dripped over her forearm from the horse's teat. The mare had been in labor for hours and now it had stalled due to a breech presentation.

Diruvert threw up his hands. "I do not know what to do."

Caroline and Liam sat wide-eyed on the stall wall. "You must help her," wailed Caroline.

Sophia exhaled. Despite experiencing several births, breech births took expertise and strength. A veterinarian had always been available at Tracnen to perform the complicated procedure. Sophia doubted she and Diruvert had the wherewithal to perform such a task. A back hoof projected out of the birth canal. Without immediate attention, the mare and foal would die.

Appearing out of nowhere, Robert walked in. "I thought I'd find you here. What happened to our dinner date?"

"The mare is in trouble, and I cannot leave her. Hand me that pail of hot water," Sophia ordered, tying her hair up in a topknot. The horse danced in front of her. "Easy, girl, you're going to have some pain, but you and your baby are going to make it through."

"Why haven't you called the veterinarian?" Robert demanded.

"I have," Sophia huffed. "Several times. He said he'd be here hours ago. Something must have happened. We can wait no longer."

"Have you done this before?"

Never a breech. "Wisdom is knowing what to do next." She answered with a vague platitude. She needed to believe and act as if there were no chance she'd fail.

Sophia took a sponge and soaked hot water around the horse's cervix. "To help expand and make the birth easier," she explained. "She can't deliver without help. The foal may die and take the mother with her. I'll need your help."

Robert tore off his suitcoat and silk tie, throwing them to Caroline, and then rolled up his snowy-white shirtsleeves. Frowning, he said, "I've never done this before. What do you want me to do?"

The contractions heaved in the mare's abdomen. Sophia refused to give in to despair. Rubbing her hands and arms up to her shoulders with lubricant, she said a silent prayer of thanks that Robert had agreed to help her, for she required his strength. She glanced to Caroline and a sleepy Liam still wide awake from the late-night hours and expectant of her.

She scuffed through the straw and curved her hand over the extended hoof so it wouldn't cut the mare's uterus as she pushed it back in.

Please. Please. Let this work.

Blindly, she felt for the tailhead, found it, and then sliding her hand down the side of the foal, located the middle joint of the other hind limb. Sweat beaded her forehead as she rotated, reached farther, and then located the other hoof. She cupped the hoof with her hand, gently pulled it out, and then succeeded with the other hoof.

The sac broke, soaking her. The horse attempted to kneel. "Keep her standing, Diruvert," she ordered the little Haitian.

With shaky hands, Sophia tied a padded rope to the fetlock

joints. "We have only minutes to get her out, Robert. When the next contraction comes, we are going to pull with all our power."

The mare snorted with her next contraction.

Gripping hard, they pulled. The hips emerged. "Keep a steady tension. Don't let up."

The foal slipped out and Robert caught her. The foal lay unconscious on the straw.

"Is it dead?" Liam whispered.

No. With a suction bulb, Sophia cleared mucus from the nostrils. The baby still did not respond. No doubt from lack of oxygen through the prolonged labor. Heart racing, Sophia took a piece of straw and tickled the inside of the nostrils. "An old gypsy trick to encourage breathing."

The foal coughed and sneezed, its lungs swelled, its barrel worked in and out.

Sophia had almost forgotten to breathe, her entire body steeped with the most powerful and intense sensation she'd ever known. It was something like a frenzied hunger, and something like fulfillment. It was wonder and awe and yearning and fear captured in a bold new world. There were no words, only joy in having Robert at her side at the dawn of a new life.

She threw her hands into the air and cried out. "Oh, Robert, you are magnificent. Do you realize what you have just accomplished?"

"We," he emphasized, and she loved the ring of that. "We have brought life into the world."

Diruvert took the halter off the mare. She licked her baby. On trembling legs, the foal stumbled to stand; on the third try the foal succeeded and searching for the udder, commenced nursing.

Caroline and Liam hugged each other. Diruvert smiled broadly and suddenly they were all laughing. Heady, like wine for the soul, their laughter poured soft and loud and deep, a carefree declaration of pure joy.

In that cherished moment, Sophia felt an unshakeable bonding between all of them. In the humble setting of the stables, they were cradled in love, beauty, and solitude, both fierce and permanent.

His good silk shirt plastered to his chest with sweat, Robert reached out one long arm and caught Sophia to him. "If you don't want me to fall in love with you, you're going to have to stop making miracles happen."

"Miracles?" hissed a haughty voice from the dark shadows of the stables.

Sophia pushed away from Robert. An older woman approached the stall, the click of her heels like an accusation.

"Mother," said Robert. "What brings you to the stables at this hour?"

Robert's mother glowered in indignation. Her highly arched eyebrows, plucked to a fine pencil line, gave her a look of doll-like surprise. "I couldn't believe my ears when Mrs. Stitt announced Caroline and Liam had not been in their beds all night."

Robert rubbed the back of his neck, checked his watch. "Five o'clock in the morning. I take full responsibility. I wanted them to witness the foal's birth."

"Robert you are a mess. Why are you doing menial labor that the help has been hired to do?" She gazed at Sophia like the queen of the jungle might gaze upon an assembly of rabbits.

"Mother, I have been remiss. May I introduce you to our new stablemaster, Miss Sophia Sonderburg, and Sophia, this is my mother, Mrs. Judith Pratt."

"I see." That was all the woman allowed, which spoke volumes.

If money could buy youth, Sophia could see Robert's mother had gladly paid the price. Yet age could not be defied, evidenced by the crow's feet feathering out from her green eyes—Robert's eyes. A chic black dress draped a seamless figure, enhanced by flawless skin, and a perfectly coiffured, dyed blonde hair, makeup precise, despite the late hour. She possessed a smile that was permanently in conflict with some inner stricture against humor.

What a time to be introduced to Robert's mother! Sophia

started to raise her hand to shake but her skin was streaked with blood and afterbirth. Her cheeks flushed, and she lowered her hands to her sides. "It's nice to meet you."

Robert's mother turned her back on her. Despite Judith's ageless appearance and sophistication, Sophia thought her a bit papery, like a paid receipt that was tucked away for countless years, brittle and yellowed and flaking at the edges.

"Consorting with the help in the stables is not an appropriate place or activity for Caroline and Liam. Back to your beds. Now."

"But-but-Mo-Moth-er," Liam stuttered.

"You heard me," Judith ordered.

"Ple-please, Mo-Mother," Liam begged, and Sophia's heart broke to see him stuttering again when he had been doing so well.

Heads down, the children trudged out. Sophia ached for them, and her hands fisted around a rake as she scraped up the musky placenta and laid down fresh straw, the chaff floating in the air and stinging her nostrils. How could Robert's mother take such a glorious experience and trample it with her feet?

Diruvert picked up feed buckets and left to tend the other horses. Sophia focused on a spider spinning a web across a post.

"Robert, this kind of activity for Liam is not good for him. It's so upsetting, and out of the ordinary and will make his stuttering worse." The emotion emitted in her voice came incongruous, like the screeching from a rusty filing cabinet drawer opening. With dramatic flourish, Judith pressed both hands to her temples. "That terrible stuttering is an anathema. To listen to him churn out his words gives me a headache."

"That's unfair, Mother."

"I have been helping him and he is improving," Sophia said.

Judith scoffed and skewered Sophia from head to toe with her glare. Obviously, she'd seen Robert holding Sophia in his arms moments before. *The help*, as she'd so scornfully labeled her. Sophia could see from the flash in the older woman's eyes that

Judith Pratt relished the prospect of crushing Sophia beneath her heel.

Chapter Twenty-Four

It was Sophia's day off and looking forward to the solitude of a hike around the property, she skirted the back of the house. Like a gaggle of geese, Judith held court over her adoring followers at a luncheon she was hosting in the courtyard.

With her back to Sophia, Judith sat stiffly on one of the blue-and-white striped satin chairs. A silver service and lovely china gleamed upon tables spread with white linen and decorated with flower arrangements, the guests shaded by giant blue umbrellas to spare them from the torrid sun.

Judith tapped her crystal glass with her fork to get the women's attention. "Let's all be seated."

Sophia saw Robert enter, his mother motioning to him. He bent down so she could offer her porcelain cheek.

"Hello, darling," said Judith. "You're looking wonderful, as usual. Do say hello to my esteemed ladies of the Detroit Horticultural Society."

Sophia ducked behind a giant oak.

"Ladies," Robert bowed in their direction. The excited women in their fifties appeared extremely youthful but beneath the gleam and polish of the gilded façades, they seemed like show dogs, silly and inbred despite their grooming. When the excited buzz of women chorusing their oohs and aahs over Robert's entrance faded, Judith continued.

"I feel so good when Robert is here." Judith snapped out her napkin and smoothed it over her lap. "That dratted war kept him away from me. To think I might have expired, and he'd not have been at my bedside to see me off."

"Mother, you have a number of years before you'll let that cloven-hoofed fellow take you."

Judith circled his wrist with her perfectly manicured fingers. "As you know, my handsome son will be running for senator of our beloved state of Michigan. When people hear of his heroic feats during the war, he'll be a shoo-in for the presidency after that. To think, I'll be First Mother of the White House."

Sophia's mouth dropped open. Running for senator? How had Robert failed to mention that plan to her? What was more appalling was how his mother sought ways to improve her status by promoting her son.

"Robert is so principled, aren't you, darling. Unfortunately, he doesn't yet understand that he must view the world as us and them. There will always be the haves and the have-nots."

Like bees, the women droned their agreement.

Robert pulled loose from Judith's grip and straightened. "Excuse me, ladies. What my mother fails to recognize is that my goal is to work for the people, *all* the people."

"Yes. Yes. Yes. Those are noble dreams, and you are so noble, although if not a bit naïve. You will understand what I'm talking about in time." She narrowed her eyes on him for contradicting her, and then smiled at the ladies. "All my charming friends are here to donate to your campaign even before your formal announcement and—most generously."

A tick pulsed in his jaw. "I've seen war and what it does. I want to work for the greater good," he said, his voice ringing out loud and powerful. He was not to be upstaged by his mother, and Sophia was proud of him.

"I have business to attend and shall take my leave, ladies. Enjoy your day."

Judith rose and kissed him again. Robert hurried through the French doors and disappeared.

How affectionate Judith was with her eldest son. The few times Sophia had seen the woman since the time in the stables, she had not seen the woman give any affection to her younger children. How sad. Caroline and Liam were exceptional and thirsted for their mother's love.

At that moment, Caroline sidled up to Judith and placed her hand on her mother's shoulder. Judith flicked it off, mortified at the public display of affection in front of her friends. "My daughter can be so cloying." She tittered. Her friends made moues of their mouths, and then laughed at Caroline.

Caroline's face reddened and she pinched her lips tight to keep them from trembling. Head down, she cast her mother a long-pained look, and then hurried away from the crowd of small-minded women. Sophia balled her hands into fists. How Sophia would love to haul Judith over hot coals.

Sophia went in search of Caroline and found her exactly where she knew the girl would be—pouring her tender heart out to her mare. "I'm dying and Mother shuns me." Caroline sobbed; her silky blonde head leaning on her mare. "You are the only one I have in this world, Rosie"

"I care," said Sophia. "And what makes you think you are dying?"

Caroline swiped at the tears streaming down her face. "I'm dying from a dreadful disease."

The girl looked a picture of health. "What ailment to you think you have?"

"I suffer horrendous pains in my lower belly...and I-I'm bleeding." Caroline buried her face into her horse's withers.

Sophia pulled Caroline into her arms and stroked her silky hair while the girl dampened her shirt with tears. Sophia laid a million different curses on Judith's person, furious that this beautiful young, talented, and intelligent girl suffered from fear of death had endured public humiliation by her mother when she needed her the most.

"You are not dying," Sophia soothed.

"I am. The blood comes out, and then it stops, and then weeks later it starts all over again."

Sophia placed her hands on the sides of Caroline's face. "You have become a woman. It is a part of maturing into the fine young lady that you are. All women have the same monthly flow every month. It's what makes us so special."

"You have it, too?"

Sophia ruffled her hair. "Of course."

Caroline started with a fresh wave of tears. "On top of that, my tutor, Mr. Belette complained I was not attentive enough and must be punished. Mother is selling my Rosie to teach me a lesson. You know her value as a prized thoroughbred. A buyer is coming in three days to take her. I cannot lose her. I'd rather die."

Hot fury rushed through Sophia's body. How cruel of Judith and the tutor. Sophia's first thought was to tell Robert. Then she realized Caroline's mother might still have the last say. She didn't dare risk it. "Your mare will not be sold. Sometimes a little subterfuge and chicanery is in order and the quickest way to achieve one's goals."

Caroline let out a snort of defeat and examined Sophia carefully, like a suspicious yet hopeful policeman. "I don't understand."

"Promise to keep a secret?"

"Scout's honor."

Sophia clipped three long horsehairs from the tail. "Thank you, Mademoiselle Rosie." Sophia wrapped the hairs tightly around the top of the mare's back hoof. "This will reduce the circulation but not harm the horse. Now dry your eyes, Caroline, and let nature do its trick.”

Caroline hugged her and Sophia wrapped her arms around the girl with the spontaneous affection. “How do know about this?”

“How do I know? I will tell you a story,” Sophia said, staring wistfully off into space. “Once upon a time, there was a princess. She had a wonderful father and mother, a prince and a princess who doted on her, and a younger brother and sister she deeply loved. They lived together on a vast estate of thousands of acres and boasting three castles. One of the castles perched behind a dazzling sapphire blue lake where graceful snow-white swans glided...”

To Caroline’s rapt attention, Sophia finished her story. “I learned the trick from an old gypsy woman when the Nazis came to my family’s stables to take our horses. Like you, I couldn’t part with my beloved mare.”

Three days later, Sophia heard the familiar staccato clicking of high heels on polished slate. Taking her time, Sophia finished pulling a curry comb over the curve of the stallion’s back, and then swiped dust and chaff from her clothes and hair. She slipped out the door and slid the latch back into place, then headed to Rosie’s stall.

She could hear the sudden thumps of hooves draw heavy as agitated horses danced in their stalls, sensing the negative aura of the visitors. Farther down, Judith stood with a striking young woman and a gentleman.

Judith pivoted. “Miss Cynthia Roessler, *Robert’s fiancée,* is here to purchase Caroline’s horse. She has brought her stablemaster.”

Fiancée? “Miss Roessler.” The words clogged in Sophia’s throat as she cast a sidelong glance at the heiress with a cigarette dangling from her fingertips. Robert had never mentioned a fiancée. Sophia froze momentarily, reeling from what she'd been told, then straightened. Feasibly, it might be one of Judith's machinations.

The woman's eyes stared vacantly back at her. The skin on her face and arms was almost translucent. Her features were well-defined, drawn with solid strokes and framed by a chestnut head of hair that gleamed like moist stone.

She seemed almost ageless or trapped in a state of perpetual youth reserved for mannequins in shop windows. Sophia strained to catch any sign of a pulse under her swan's neck. Could Robert marry such a woman?

A fist closed around her heart. He'd been gone for three days, and she'd had no opportunity to question him about his senatorial bid, let alone the fact that he had a fiancée.

Sophia snapped open the stall door. No way would she play the part of the other woman.

With jerky movements, Rosie shied away, favoring her one leg. Did the horse know its peril and exaggerate its injury?

The stablemaster made a quick assessment, settling on the right rear hoof that Sophia knew he'd pick up on. She checked earlier in the morning to make sure the strands of hair were invisible. She suppressed a smile.

He shook his head, and frowned, put off that the mare was flawed. "I'm sorry, Miss Roessler. This horse is lame. I do not advise buying it."

"Lame?" Judith stepped back with a high-pitched squeak and stepped in fresh manure. "Drat. Why aren't these stables attended to?" She wheeled on Sophia. "And above all, why have you not cared for this horse? You are responsible and made a fool of me."

Sophia picked up the mare's hoof and made a show of examining the injury. "It must have happened overnight. Definitely swollen. I'll make a poultice."

"The horse is lame and should be taken out and shot. It's no good. I've seen animals with less injuries that had to be put down."

Cynthia's voice was hard crystal, transparent and so brittle Sophia feared that her words would break if she dared to interrupt her.

Sophia possessed the distinct idea Cynthia would relish putting Rosie down. She reminded Sophia of a Prussian cousin who'd taught her it was best to remain a respectful distance from femme fatales like Cynthia. They tended to be vindictive.

Sophia let the horse's hoof slide to the ground, and then with her arms folded in front of her, stood in front of Rosie. "The horse will not be shot. It can heal and will remain here."

Judith narrowed her eyes on Sophia as if she'd just seen a pack of dynamite sticks alight at her feet. "You must think me an *idiot* not to believe your neglect caused this horse's lameness."

I'm beginning to come to terms with it.

Judith stood with a grim stare that would have made most anyone uncomfortable enough to flee her presence. No doubt it worked on her sorority of matronly companions. Her staff feared her sharp tongue and considered her a member of another species. Sophia did not.

Her nature was not to retreat. She straightened and looked innocently into Judith's eyes. Sophia drew on her royal lineage and proud ancestry far superior to Judith's own.

The brunette also stared at her for a long time, without a word, studying her with the sour expression of a woman who is being offered a financial statement with fudged numbers. Her eyes gave off an air of bravado and arrogance, disdain, and sugary politeness. Sophia smiled at her openly, reading insecurity, fear, and emptiness under that shell of vanity and complacency.

"Where are you from?" snapped Cynthia.

"Northeastern Prussia."

"Oh!"

So much said in the simple exclamation. Sophia refused to bite.

"What are your qualifications if I may ask?"

"I'd like to know the same," Judith insisted. "How do we know you are not a fraud?"

Judith possessed a gift—using clever arguments in which she displayed both ingenuity and a poisonous bite.

Diruvert scraped a shovel across the floor in a discordant shriek.

Judith jumped. "Stop that! Why my son hired that illiterate, I'll never know."

Diruvert's throat bobbed, and he left the barn.

Sophia glowered at Judith. "You will not speak to Diruvert like that. He is a hard worker."

"And who are you to tell me—"

Drawing in a slow, steadying breath, Sophia said, "As long as I'm the stablemaster, I'll make sure those in my employ are treated with respect."

Judith's eyes gleamed daggers. "You're supposed to have proficiency in working with horses. Considering your neglect of an expensive thoroughbred, you should be fired. We Pratts insist on superior talent."

The only talent Sophia saw in Judith was an unrestrained mean streak.

Sophia ignored her and addressed Cynthia. "I have a doctorate in zoology and have worked at the finest horse stables in all of Europe and Asia." She didn't tell her that her family owned the stables and had bred prized Arabians for over three hundred years.

Sophia winced as Cynthia let her ashes drop onto the floor of the stall and grind the stub of her cigarette with her heel. The woman was a fool. Didn't she know how flammable straw was?

"What is the name of the horse stables?"

Cynthia thought to one-up her. "Tracnen Stables."

"Even I have heard of that. You could be making it up and lying about your credentials as I'm certain many of *your kind* have, considering where you've come from. I suppose we'll never know."

"The Geneva Convention stipulates that when captured, a prisoner of war must only reveal his name, rank, and serial number." Robert said, coming up behind them. "I can vouch for Miss Sonderburg. In fact, she is overqualified, and we are very lucky to have her. Mother, let it be known I concur with Miss Sonderburg. All our employees are to be treated with respect."

"Oh, Robert," Cynthia swiveled and pouted. "I came to purchase this mare, but the animal is flawed with a terrible limp."

"Isn't this Caroline's mare?" Robert asked. A muscle ticked in his jaw.

Judith gave a crisp nod. "Yes, I'm disciplining Caroline for not being attentive to her studies."

"Dammit!" With a sharp wave of his hand, he directed them out of the stall, barely restraining himself from slamming the door shut behind them. "You'll never sell her mare, Mother. I won't allow it."

"If you say so." Judith protested, peering at her jeweled wristwatch.

"I'm afraid the beast won't be sold to anyone." Cynthia tsked and touched Robert's arm, clearly staking her claim on him. "The poor thing must be put down because your stablemaster did not perform her job well. You must remove her."

Robert looked down to where Cynthia's hand rested on his arm. Robert shrugged off the placating gesture. "Mother, your bridge club members are waiting for you." It was a tacit command for them to leave.

"I forgot completely. Come, Cynthia, I want to introduce you to them."

In a huff, Judith left the stables, wiping her shoes on the grass outside. She had lost this round, but Sophia knew, as in the game of chess, queens were the most dangerous.

"Thank you," mouthed Sophia.

"Nothing like going through the Inquisition," Robert said, shaking his head. "They're ruthless, and I'm sorry you had to go through that."

"I've faced Hitler, the Russians and—"

"I should feel sorry for my mother. Anyone who took on General Ivanov—"

"I have my own Inquisition. How is it you failed to mention your run for senator? And your fiancée?"

Robert scratched his throat. "Yes and no. Up until the other day, I'd only been thinking of running for the US Senate. Now that bid is in motion."

Sophia folded her arms in front of her. "I see, and the rest?"

"To tell you the truth, Cynthia and Mother concocted the notion of the fiancée...that was before I met you."

Sophia rubbed her forearms up and down. "Are you sure she is not your fiancée?"

"Absolutely positive."

"I-I couldn't bear it if there was someone else..."

"Sophia, you should know by now, you are the only one for me."

She could hear the truth in the sincerity of his voice, see it in his eyes, and the defenses she had put up collapsed.

Robert pulled her into her arms and brushed his firm, full, sexy lips back and forth over hers. He stroked a need that began to consume her like a flame sucking up oxygen. All the tension from his mother and Cynthia evaporated as a low moan passed through her lips.

A shower of straw fell on their heads. Caroline wriggled out of the hayloft and scrambled down the rough wooden ladder. She jumped to the floor and clapped her hands together. "Sophia, it worked."

Growling soft and low in his throat, Robert dragged his mouth away. "Hm-m. Do I detect a bit of collusion?"

Sophia reached for scissors she'd left hanging on a splintery beam, and then snipped the constricted horsehairs from above the swollen hoof. She massaged the circulation back into the animal's leg. "We are in agreement not to say a word of this to your mother?" She looked to Caroline.

"Don't worry, I'll be like the Sphinx." After a few probing nuzzles at Caroline's pockets to make sure all the carrots were gone, Rosie rested her chin on the girl's shoulder. "No one is going to separate us, ever," reassured Caroline, and then on impulse, turned and threw her arms around Robert. "Thank you for protecting me and Rosie!"

Robert stood, surprised, not knowing quite what to do. He lifted his arms, slowly lowered them, and then held her tight. Sophia's heart sang at the beauty of his sister's affection, Robert's love and loyalty reflected back to him.

Sophia saddled Rosie. Robert made a nest of his hands and boosted Caroline atop her mare. "Now, off with you."

Caroline took the reins and smiling, saluted. "To outwit Mother, our tutor and to have their plotting go belly-up? You must be cunning and wicked in this world. Robert, were you aware Mother faked her heart-attack to get you home from Germany?"

"I guessed."

"And Sophia," Caroline continued, "don't worry about all the gobbledygook about Cynthia. She may have her peepers out for Robert but she's a cold fish and Mother cooked up the whole fiancée thing."

"Don't go all Tolstoy on me." Sophia beamed, and watched Caroline trot her mare from the barn, looking as delighted as a hound who'd cornered a fox.

Sophia sighed. "You really need to spend more time with your younger siblings. They need you."

Robert nodded. "I'll give it some thought, my Sophia with the great big heart. Don't think I haven't heard of how you helped Liam to lessen his stuttering. The only problem is he is so confident in his speaking ability, he doesn't shut up. And Caroline. The girl idolizes you. Thank you for being there for her. My mother is less—"

He referred to the advent of his sister's womanhood.

"You do not need to say another word." Sophia protested. "I'd do anything for her. Which brings me to another point. I need to mention your siblings have brought some alarming concerns about their tutor. I know most kids hate their tutors, but I have suspicions that Mr. Belette's methods are cruel, considering Liam's reaction when the instructor's name is mentioned, and—how Belette insisted Caroline's mare be sold."

Outside, Caroline tugged the reins to halt the prancing, Rosie. "Robert, quit whistling Dixie and have Sophia show you her cottage. I hear it is very nice."

Sophia flushed. Robert's younger sister was incorrigible.

Robert pulled Sophia tight to his side. "The little rascal has a great idea."

Chapter Twenty-Five

Wide-eyed, Diruvert ran breathless up to the fence of the back paddock where Sophia trained a new stallion. "Miss Sophia, you must stop the tutor."

"What is it?"

"Mr. Liam. He needs your help."

Sophia unhooked the lead rope. She ran from the corral and alongside Diruvert, remembering Liam's response when the tutor's name was mentioned.

She'd only seen the tutor once. He was a gaunt, mean-spirited little man, hard to tell if he was asleep or awake, because he breathed like most people snore. He'd been well-dressed in a white suit and flamboyant tie more suited for the tropics, and affected a fake French accent, doubtless to impress his employer.

In between the house and the stables, the tutor stood over Liam with a stick. Liam covered his head.

"You stupid boy. Stutter more," shouted the tutor. Beneath his pointed nose, his mouth was glued to a half-smoked cigarette that seemed to grow out of his tiny mustache.

"What did you say?" Belette demanded

"Pl-please st-st-op," begged the boy.

"It is because you are an idiot. Discipline is what you need."

Down came the stick on Liam's crossed arms. The boy whimpered.

Anger poured through Sophia, boiling her blood, and clouding her brain. "Stop, you rat-faced dummkopf." She wrested the whip away and brought the stick down, thrashing the tutor. "Don't you ever hit that boy again or touch Caroline or you'll have to deal with me."

The maggot of a tutor's face went pink with distress at being caught. The hands that had wielded his hickory cane were shaking.

Sophia broke his whip over her knee, glaring at Belette. His little slit eyes moved from side to side like a nervous weasel. "What a cruel little man you are. I thought we were rid of the Hitlers."

A crowd of groundskeepers had gathered. Maids from the house inched across the backyard, craning their necks over the garden wall to observe the bitter altercation brewing.

"I'm going to report you for interfering," Belette bit out, puffing a curl of blue smoke from his cigarette.

Sophia wrinkled her nose. The sugary sweet Brylcreem pomade flattening his hair did not cover the whiskey fumes.

She pointed the broken switch at him. "I'm going to report you for drinking."

Emboldened by his drink, he lifted to his full five-foot, four-inch scrawny frame on grasshopper-bowed legs. "I have Mrs. Pratt's full backing."

Sophia had the distinct idea Mrs. Pratt would continue supporting the tutor regardless of his dereliction and mistreatment. No way would she take Sophia's word.

Belette sniggered. "A whore has no power over me. Everyone knows you spread your legs for the owner."

The man staggered. Surprising her by his quickness and strength, he grabbed the broken stick from her. He raised the splintery rod to strike her. Panic seized Sophia, enough that she had to fight little spots of darkness in her periphery. She ducked the wild blow.

Sophia saw a blur out of the corner of her eye. Robert leaped forward, grabbing the stick, and then spun the tutor around, dealing a vicious blow to Belette's nose. Sophia heard the bone crack beneath Robert's knuckles. She took a step back, stared wide-eyed for a full two seconds. Belette tottered and fell backward, blood gushing from his nose, his white suit sprayed with scarlet.

She glanced around. No one moved. Blank stares, open mouths. Blood drained from her face to her toes. Everyone had heard what the tutor had called her. They would hate her.

Suddenly, a roar of applause drowned them. The normally stoic Diruvert grinned and cheered, Liam ran to Robert and hugged him. The maids waved. The gardeners pumped their rakes and shovels up and down in salute.

Sophia gaped.

"Well done, sir," spat one of the groundskeepers. "The man is worthless and should be beaten to a pulp."

"Well done, Miss Sophia. Never liked the cur dog," said another. "I heard he beat Mr. Liam on several of occasions. Today, I saw the bastard do it with my own eyes, until Miss Sophia intervened."

"Get him out of here." Robert's voice edged with deadly calm.

Belette was yanked up. Speaking through a bloodied handkerchief held tight to his nose, he said, "I'm here to tell you that whatever steps I take to educate your younger siblings are necessary."

Robert took a step toward him, and the tutor put his hand up.

"Nothing would give me greater pleasure than beating the shit out of you," Robert grated. "Today, I'm in a good mood. Pack up and leave within the hour. You're fired."

Two men flanked the tutor. As Belette was dragged away, he

turned, his eyes burning with hatred and pinned on Sophia. "I will get even with you, bitch. I don't know how yet but give me time. A day will come when you think yourself safe and happy, and suddenly your joy will turn to ashes."

Chapter Twenty-Six

Sophia watched Robert shift the car with ease. Two thousand pounds of steel, paint, and chrome, and through him, the car seemed to breathe and take on energy. Even her own heart raced with the speed and adrenaline, the warm blacktop leading into the horizon of tall buildings, gave an untarnished sense of freedom.

"I'm testing out this never-before-seen Pratt original direct from our research and development lab. I named the sportscar *Zeus*, and it will rival the *Jaguar* in speed, style, and luxury with its twin side-draft SU carburetors, and a straight 6XK engine that can run up to one hundred and thirty-five miles per hour."

Robert shifted again, and the air that made its way through the filters was meadow-sweet, the world outside like some choreographed dance of green fields and warm sunshine. "I love fast cars and going fast. If everything seems under control, you're not going fast enough."

No doubt, they had reached the one hundred and thirty-five mile per hour mark. Her chest hitched, overwhelmed with his pride in his new creation as she hung on to the sides of her seat for dear life. "I see why you named the car *Zeus* after the God of the

Sky. I feel like I'm in the clouds. Knowing two speeds—fast and faster—how do you get around without killing yourself?"

Robert eased up on the pedal. "There can be a lot of stress in running an automobile company, but once you get in the car, it all goes out the window."

At a reduced speed, Sophia blew a sigh of relief, feeling safe enough to brush her hair into order, using the rearview mirror. She was conscious of Robert watching her while he drove up Michigan Avenue.

"One of the nicest things a man can see in this life," he said, "is a beautiful woman with her arms up, brushing her hair. I believe that's why so many artists have painted it." He turned on the radio and Benny Goodman blared out *Paper Doll,* playing his trumpet like silver lace.

"I have something special in store for you today."

"And what might that be?"

"You'll have to be patient. That's Briggs Stadium over there, home of the Detroit Tigers," he angled his handsome head. He caught her studying him and an inarticulate sound vibrated from somewhere deep within him, quickening her heart and rushing the blood through her veins with an injection of heat.

She surged closer, her fingers gripping his collar as a kiss deepened of its own accord. In this moment, they had their own language. One that was as lilting and lyrical as any that exists.

A car horn blared in front of them. Robert swerved sharply and, with immediate expertise, returned the car to right side of the highway. He released her, and the tempting spicy scent of him invaded her head and left her breathless.

"You are dangerous and distracting, Sophia. Could have totaled a five-million-dollar prototype." His eyes drilled into her with that dizzying change they made from sobriety to amusement. "You've never experienced anything more American unless you've seen a baseball game with a hotdog in your hand. Maybe the Tigers will win the World Series again this year."

"Without seeing the Tigers play, I already have a good concept of America. Everyone uses Listerine, people celebrate Christmas, birthdays, weddings, anniversaries, and Mother's Day. On television, I laugh at *Jack Benny* and am led to believe everyone acts like the *Three Stooges*. Church on Sundays and Winston tastes good like a cigarette should."

Robert grimaced. "You have a skewed view of America." The traffic was denser as he turned onto Woodward Avenue. "Over there was where my grandfather developed Pratt's first assembly plant and rolled off cars one by one," he said proudly.

A few blocks up, Robert parked the car and opened the door for her. Sophia craned her neck to look up at the seven-story edifice.

"Hudson's Department Store. The tallest department store in the world. I'm sure you'll find something to wear here, especially since you didn't spend the money I sent you in Germany"

He tugged her along, grinning at her continuous exclamations and refusals.

The store resembled an ambitious Beaux Arts classical palace with a noble ionic façade rising above plate glass windows. Surrounding the entire city block were fantastic window displays, each one with their own elaborate theme.

Through revolving doors, thousands of people milled through hundreds of departments where no expense was spared in the brass, wood veneer and colored lights to encourage every consumer to fling open their pocketbook. She lost count of the elegant elevators and the myriad of busy escalators carrying frenetic shoppers up and down. She darted her eyes at the fashionable women and felt woefully inadequate.

At last, Robert dragged her to a well-dressed woman and stopped.

"Good morning, Mr. Pratt. I'm Gigi and I'm a specialized consultant for Hudson's VIPs." She extended her hand to Robert, and then to Sophia. "I was told to outfit you with everything. We must hurry for we've a lot of ground to cover. And as you indicated before, Mr. Pratt," she nodded to Robert with efficiency, "we will leave you here, and then meet up at three o'clock sharp. This is going to be so much fun!"

Wandering up and down thirty floors of merchandise was exhausting. Sophia couldn't stop looking at all the departments and the endless variety. Each area specialized in a vast array of clothing, cosmetics, hats, books, perfumes, stationary, sheets, and furniture.

Sophia halted in front of a baby department with cribs featuring frilly laced canopies, polished wooden highchairs, and cuddly teddy bears. Her heart caught. To have Robert's children would be the most wonderful thing in the world. They had been careful in their countless nights of lovemaking. Even so, in their eagerness, they had made mistakes, yet nothing had come to fruition despite the slip-ups. What if she was one of those women who were unable to have children?

Yet Robert had made no sign of offering for her. Even though she felt his love, was their relationship only for the time being, to become no more than a blip in his memories? Would their we-composite disintegrate if he found another—especially Cynthia who seemed a good fit for his senatorial run? To be loved—but not know the future—was comforting but superficial. Swallowing hard, she pushed the notion away, refusing to let his lack of commitment to distress her. Underneath, she had every faith he would propose.

The ever-patient Miss Gigi escorted her to the most luxurious departments.

Sophia doted on a dyed-blue alligator pocketbook. "I can't possibly—"

Gigi leaned low and whispered conspiratorially, "Mr. Pratt said no expense was to be spared! I can tell you he's never brought a woman here. You must be very special."

They ended up in the custom dress department where she was

taken to a special fitting room and a modiste took her measurements.

Outside, pandemonium flamed. "I'm your biggest fan," Sophia heard one woman gush.

"Three generations of my family have worked for your company, Mr. Pratt."

"You are so handsome," babbled another.

Sophia dressed and returned to the main lounge where Robert waited.

All the sales ladies oohed and aahed over the handsome automobile magnate. "Enjoying your fan club?" Sophia laughed, seeing his discomfiture with all the female adulation.

He flicked her a tortured glance and narrowed his eyes. "Rescue me." He patted the seat beside him. "Most importantly, are you having fun?"

"Too much, Robert." Sophia protested.

"It's repayment for all you've done for Caroline and Liam. And for standing up to Mother, I should buy the entire store for you."

Gigi clapped her hands. Dozens of designer dresses were brought out for Sophia to view. The ever-industrious sales ladies had snapped up matching purses, shoes, scarves and coats to complete every ensemble and, of course, to make an exorbitant commission.

"Miss Sophia is so beautiful and magnificent to dress," averred Miss Gigi.

"We'll take one of each," Robert ordered. "Put the blue dress on," he told Sophia. "It'll be perfect for the other activities I have scheduled for today." To the sales consultant, he said in his baritone as dark, deep, and smooth as moonlight over marble, "Box everything else up, and if you can send it to this address in the next twenty-four hours, you and your staff can collect an extra twenty percent gratuity."

"Right away, Mr. Pratt," Gigi said with the efficiency of a general, rounding up her sales staff.

Robert pressed his hand to Sophia's back, and soon they were in his car, careening up the street in his characteristic heart-in-her-throat flying fashion. Still reeling from the shopping trip, she realized life with Robert would be a whirlwind and never dull. He turned past a sign with elegant gold letters that read *Pratt Motors*.

He escorted her past a myriad of offices where vice presidents tripped over themselves to leave their desks and converse with the president. For the first time, Sophia saw Robert in his true element.

Robert Pratt demanded the full attention of any room he entered.

It was as if he claimed every plot of ground he tread upon and dared someone to take it from him.

Sophia told herself that her heart only leaped because of the setting.

Not the man. Nor the sight of him in his double-breasted suit, his shoulders straight and jaw sharp.

No man could have been more devilishly handsome nor shrewd and toughminded than he, striding at the head of a handful of men who were near nipping at his heels, as if his word, alone, divined their significance.

In a fleeting moment, a twinge of fear pawed at her breast. Something intangible nagged at her, warned her of the future. Sophia held the distinct idea that Robert, if crossed, would be an unforgiving and ruthless antagonist. She shook the feeling aside.

On the top floor, he introduced her to his three secretaries and propelled her into his office with a panoramic view of the city.

"Breathtaking," Sophia said.

"I agree."

He was looking right at her.

"I thought I heard familiar voices. Welcome to Pratt Motors," said Van.

Sophia swiveled. "I have a bone to pick with you."

Van threw up his hands. "To be fair, I was sworn to secrecy. Please forgive—"

"All forgiven," Sophia smiled.

"That said," Van rubbed his hands together, "since I'm Vice President of Manufacturing, a tour is in order. Follow me."

For the next hour, they walked through a seemingly endless assembly plant, Robert explaining to Sophia the entire process of how all the parts and mini-assemblies came together at the exact time to keep the final production lines going. Her insides vibrated with the deafening noise, the majesty of machinery, the people all working in a vast synchronicity under a seemingly invisible genius. How could all of this happen?

Robert stopped, strode swiftly to where workmen collected in a tool and die room, and spoke to them over the clamor. With micrometers in hand, those who'd been measuring a steel block got up at once and went over to him. When he extended his arm to point at something, they scurried at once to carry out his wishes.

He returned and put his arm around her. "We exercise maximum efficiency and maintain the best quality. That's why everyone wants a Pratt car."

Sophia sent him a level look from beneath the robin's egg blue of her new hat and veil. "You are the maestro."

Robert checked his watch. "I don't know about you, but all this sightseeing has made me hungry. Can you join us later when you're finished, Van?"

Chapter Twenty-Seven

Robert drove out of the city and pulled up to a restaurant. "It's not much to look at but they have the best Italian food."

Once inside, a man flew from the kitchen and smiled in a flare of unconvincing dentures. "Mr. Pratt, what a surprise, I'm so happy you can join us this evening. Mademoiselle, I am Vito Romano, proprietor."

They followed the almost hunchbacked owner with thick, silver-rimmed glasses into one of the dining rooms. Ten tables were occupied. A few officers in full regalia. Other sporty couples. There were flowers on red-checkered cloth covered tables.

The conversation in the room died as they followed the owner to a small table at the window, overlooking a park and river below. She felt the young officers regarding her and the jealous looks of elderly matrons. She touched her hair.

Suddenly, a woman screamed from across the restaurant and flew to Sophia, her husband, and another couple in tow. Speaking rapidly in Polish, they cried, "It's Princess Sophia, it must be. You look just like your mother."

The couple knelt in front of her, kissing her hand. Sophia flushed from her toes to the roots of her hair.

In brisk Polish, they charged on with their praises and wonderment. "How is it you're here? How are your parents and family? We escaped because of your parents. They guided us through the woods, and we departed at Gdansk, making our way to the United States. We survived because of your parents and now live with our relatives in Detroit. We have good jobs working for an automobile company."

They turned to their family members and told them everything. They, too, knelt in front of Sophia. "How are your parents? Are they here? We wish to thank them."

Sophia's voice quaked and her vision wavered with unshed tears. In a broken whisper, she answered them in Polish. "My parents didn't make it. They were captured and executed by German soldiers." Her heart breaking, she saw the living proof of her parents' heroics.

The group looked to each other, shaking their heads. They began to wail loudly.

"This cannot be. Their bravery and sacrifice will always remain legendary in our hearts. We extend our belated sympathy. How we wish the outcome had been different."

"So do I," said Sophia. Tears burned her cheeks.

"What's going on, Sophia?" Robert asked, mystified by the excessive attention they were receiving and the fact that Sophia was unable to stop crying.

Sophia looked to Robert, Mr. Romano, and the other people in the restaurant. With her nerves raw, she could not deal with the attention.

She tugged her hand away and ordered them to rise. "Please, do not tell anyone of my royal lineage."

Sophia swiped at the tears beneath her veil. They hugged her and kept on hugging her like a lifeline, and she drowned in their gratitude, holding on to it like a lifeline. "Because of your parents, my wife is expecting. A new life will be born. That is sacred."

"What is going on?" demanded Robert again.

At last, they released her, and it took all her power to stop sobbing when all she wanted to do was to draw up into a ball. "These people were saved from the Nazis by my parents. They are thankful."

Robert combed his fingers through his hair, the gravity dawning on him.

The people looked at her expectantly. Drawing on years of dignified heritage, she took Robert's proffered handkerchief, dried her eyes, and composed herself. This time, she spoke in English. "May I ask at which automobile company you are employed?"

Shoulders back, the men straightened, and struck their chests with their fists. In broken English they said, "We are the Grabowski brothers, and we work for Pratt Motors. We make the finest automobiles in the world."

Sophia gave them a tremulous smile and waved her hand to Robert. "May I introduce you to the owner, Mr. Robert Pratt?"

They fell to their knees again, holding Robert's hand. "We are so proud to work for you, Mr. Pratt. What an honor to meet you."

On and on they went, with effusive adorations until Robert, having more than enough, hauled them to their feet. They said their goodbyes, walking backward, and bowing continuously as they exited the restaurant.

Wide-eyed at the wondrous adulations and felicitations, the patrons and Mr. Romano chattered.

Robert seated her. "If you want to leave—"

Sophia shook her head and took off her hat, placing it on the seat beside her blue alligator pocketbook. "And ruin a perfect day?"

Mr. Romano, in his red checkered apron, coughed beside them. Struggling to keep the emotion out of his voice, he said, "Any drinks for you and the lady?"

"Let's try something sweet. For the lady," Robert said. "A nice daiquiri, made in your incomparable manner."

The owner snapped his fingers. "On the house."

From across the room, Sophia watched the bartender squeeze the limes and toss in the ice and shake the drink with expert, manicured hands. The frothy drink was tangy, and she drank it like lemonade. Robert watched her, one eyebrow raised, as the drink disappeared.

"I've never had anything so delicious, and I'm thirsty from the day's activities." Her voice caught in her throat on a horrified whisper.

Robert held up his hand. "Bartender, another."

Her past had caught up to her. What if she told Robert she was a princess? At this point in her life, the truth would sound vain and impractical. That part of her life was gone forever with the Soviet takeover of her country and the seizure of her estate. Her title was hollow and no longer existed. She took a sip out of the next glass. If she didn't leave her past in the past, it would complicate her future, bringing her further pain.

"I'm sorry," Robert said. "I know thinking of your parents must be painful."

"We live for what today has to offer, not for what yesterday has taken away." She took another sip and let the alcohol settle in. "For a long time, I have been selfish in my anger with my parents for forfeiting their lives. They could easily have saved themselves by staying neutral yet chose to sacrifice for others. Unfortunately, the penalty spelled death for my younger brother and sister. Sometimes, when I was in my crude apartment in Berlin, I'd talk to my family in the darkness. Laying on my hard cot, I'd tell them of what I'd seen that day, or what I'd learned. I couldn't hear them respond or feel their touch, but their radiance and warmth haunted every corner of my dwelling.

"I have conflicting emotions regarding my father and mother's sacrificing the safety of my innocent siblings and me for their cause. I have packed and unpacked my nightmares in a box, to learn what were lies and what was truth. My parents were supposed to be with me forever and protect me. My siblings were always to be there. The safety was an illusion spun from my clever mind and my bitter heart. When I have children," Sophia said emphatically, "I will not make the same mistake. I will do everything, and I mean everything in my power to protect them."

Robert stirred his martini. "Greif never ends, but it changes. It's a passage, not a place to stay. What you once cherished, you can never lose. It's the price of love."

The rueful note to his words railed at the unfairness, yet despite her loss, she'd made her way forward to a life full of promise and, for that, her spirits soared.

"There will be another generation growing here in America," Sophia said. "You can't imagine how much satisfaction that gives me. The Grabrowskis are expecting their first child."

"You like children, don't you?"

Sophia sighed. "Someday I want to have children. Lots of children."

Your children, Robert, if you offer for me.

Robert's strength surrounded her, and her mouth trembled as she reached up to touch his face with her tentative fingers. "Thank you for everything. Thank you for being you." She took a deep breath and dropped her hands. "Let's start the evening anew. Did I tell you how I enjoyed the tour of your offices and assembly plant? It has left an indelible mark on me—all of it built with your talent and genius."

"Sophia, I could be offered gifts of gold and I've heard fancier words, but none of that holds a candle to your praise. You are the real thing, the one who loves without measure. You are my rock."

Sophia became weepy again and stared out across the park. An old couple lingered, arm in arm, their lovely affections implicit. Pigeons and doves clustered and swirled around them, flying in a great white cloud as the elderly couple spread crumbs. Sophia sighed. How sweet it would be to grow old with Robert at her side and share the same simple activity.

He looked at her as if reading her mind. He reached across the table and took her hand. "As we grow old together, I will always keep falling in love with you."

They were interrupted by a woman's loud, abrasive singing from across the restaurant. Sophia stared at the woman, clad in the lush, licentious costume of a diva.

"What do you think?" he asked.

"Italian opera meets Big Band?"

"You are too polite. She belts out *Chattanooga Choo Choo* with a hurricane force wind capable of stunning sparrows out of the trees and sending them spiraling to the ground."

Robert put his hand up. Mr. Romano, ever attentive, took the hundred dollar bill, Robert proffered, and secreted it into his pocket. "She is my wife's niece. You know the embarrassing and demanding requirements of family." He then hurried over to whisper in the diva's ear.

She gave Mr. Romano a dirty look and stopped.

Robert chuckled. "They have good food here, but I don't want my ears to bleed."

Van scooted into a chair next to them. He saluted Robert with his typical irreverence. "To the only man I know who trades in his Prattilac when the ashtrays are full."

When Mr. Romano extended the menus, Van picked up a conversation with the proprietor about the gangster, Capone, who'd been locked up in Alcatraz for tax evasion and who was the owner's dubious spiritual influence and hero.

"There have been three impressive figures in history: best actor ever, Bogart, baseball legend, DiMaggio and Al Capone," the owner proclaimed, a bit lofty, even evangelical, persuading the canonization for sainthood, the legendary and murderous criminal figure.

Strains of the Andrew Sisters' *Ferryboat Serenade* beamed

from a juke box. Nibbling on her fried calamari appetizer, Sophia listened to Van encourage Mr. Romano's prattle, who at intervals punctuated his emotive biography of the underworld's leader with matters of doubtful historic accuracy.

With mock appeal, Van slapped his hand on the table. "I've heard Capone had been suffering badly from prostate trouble ever since he swallowed a peach pit, and now he can only pee if someone hums *Sicilian Heart* for him."

At that, the Italian owner's hands flew, his mouth juggling a toothpick, which he twisted and turned through his teeth with acrobatic agility. "Pure myth," the waiter scoffed. "The man pees like a bull. The Mississippi River would envy such a flow. Did I mention Capone was here? I was a down and out mechanic. His car broke down and I fixed it, and then I fed him my pasta. He loved it. I told him I was saving for a restaurant, but that dream would be years in the future. The next week, I found five thousand dollars in the mail. I know Capone was my benefactor."

Sophia laughed and then felt Robert's hand squeeze her thigh. She looked up at him and he smiled, thoroughly enjoying himself, yet his caress held promises of the night ahead.

Chapter Twenty-Eight

French door windows that welcomed the passage of light flooded the dining room with the vibrant hues of midday. Robert had spent a splendid night of lovemaking with Sophia and waking up to her ever-present smile was the key that fit in the lock of his heart. How her face turned rapturous when her joy bubbled over was infectious to everyone around her. Sophia loved unconditionally, without selfish intent, and without concern for personal gain.

He drank his heavy dark roasted coffee and ate the rest of his cheese omelet, dreaming of Sophia sitting across the table from him every morning for the rest of his life. Then he imagined having their children around the table.

In the stables, Sophia had knitted together a little family calling it her home...Diruvert, Caroline, Liam, and himself, and through her irresistible benevolence, had healed and unearthed a haven for them.

He'd taken Sophia's advice and spent more time with Caroline and Liam and never had he enjoyed himself more. There had been such a huge age gap in the Pratt siblings. He was basically an only child until Caroline was born when he was around twenty years of age. He was off to college, full of his own importance, having little to do with them, and now regretted that time lost.

Thinking back, he realized the tragedy where his whole childhood had been robbed. His father had been too busy with the workings of the company, and his mother with her charitable causes. With absent parents, what brief family events they managed to cobble together proved artificial and left him isolated and empty.

With the numerous imaginative and simple activities Sophia created, he could experience everything he'd missed. Kite flying, scavenger hunts, building twig sailboats to sail on the river, card playing, stargazing, and croquet, and even entertainments with Diruvert's magic tricks. The hilarity they shared making cookies in her cottage had become a raucous event with flour flung in the air, and the sweetness of sugar, butter, and cinnamon wafting from the oven.

Robert took everyone to the zoo where he found himself laughing with his siblings at the antics of the penguins. Another trip took them across the Mackinac Bridge to the Upper Peninsula for flyfishing, and then sailing on Lake Michigan.

Despite his contempt, Sophia dragged them to the Ford Museum, yet he had to admit, he enjoyed the day watching Liam and Caroline run about, carefree and full of whimsy. By means of her magic wand, Sophia made him aware of the randomness of birdsong and gusts of wind, cutting through the quietness within him, bringing happiness with everything she touched.

Yesterday had been perfect. Her wonder at the department store made him come alive, like seeing the excitement through the innocent eyes of a child. He liked buying things for her and wanted to keep buying things for her.

Her avid enthusiasm and genuine enchantment made him delight in showing her Pratt Motors, marveling at her gift for making the sun seem to shine on everything he did. She believed in his dreams, encouraged his ideas, supported his ambitions, brought out the best in him, making him feel magnificent in every feat he accomplished.

The one time he'd taken Cynthia on a tour of the assembly lines had been a disaster. Agitated her shoes would get dirty or that soot might soil her new dress, her shrill exclamations over the ear-splitting machinery aborted the excursion before they'd traveled an eighth of the way.

He cut through his hickory-smoked slab of bacon and thought about the Polish people in the restaurant the day before. His hands tightened around his fork as he remembered the way Sophia had broken down, and his anger toward the Grabowskis for making her cry. When he'd learned the reason for her sorrow, he'd been stunned at how quickly she'd composed herself despite the onslaught of emotions. Like a princess she was.

From outside the courtyard, an advancing cloud blocked the sun, dimming the room into ashen light. It was as if the room dropped ten degrees.

"I'll have the usual, Karen," said his mother. "Except yesterday, my soft-boiled egg was a little overcooked and my toast was hard. Tell the cook to be attentive."

Robert lowered his paper and raised a brow. Dressed in iridescent watered black silk, his mother looked as if she stepped out of a scene of a gothic horror as she settled in the chair across from him.

"Going to a funeral, Mother?"

"Of course, you'd find some way to mock me." She lifted her chin and fluttered her hands over the table, settling like a vulture stretching its neck and spreading its wings. "To tell you the truth, it is your funeral, Robert. You don't know much about women, and the stablemaster is playing with you like a cat with a canary."

How many times had his mother harangued him about Sophia? His hands briefly clenched the newspaper as he creased it in sharp folds and ditched it on the table. "Mother, I fought a war. I run the largest automobile company in the world. I feel I'm adult enough to decide who I want to spend my life with."

"That Nazi! You must be crazy. No one will vote for you."

"She's not a Nazi. In fact, her parents were executed by Hitler's men. She suffered a lot during the war and should be admired."

Judith scoffed. "No doubt, she's had plenty of time to come up with that lie. All the former members of the Third Reich have come up with the same persecuted narrative, and to think my intelligent son has fallen for that claptrap."

"You know, Mother, how do I tell if someone's not good for me? You, being yourself, is a great example."

His fork halfway to his mouth, Robert hesitated. He didn't understand the Polish spoken the in the restaurant, yet might there have been deeper communications? Did Sophia have a hidden story? He stuffed the salty bacon in his mouth with vehemence, his temper snapping in the wake of Judith's skill at casting seeds of suspicion.

"I'm warning you. Leave Sophia alone."

"I've barely spoken to the woman."

"Mother, what is it like being wrong about everything?" Robert snarled. "What's it like—demeaning, criticizing, and denigrating everyone around you? What's it like having to be the center of attention, infantile and petty? The yoke must get heavy."

Robert braced himself as his mother pulled herself up and adopted the tone of a sermon. Precise came her sculpted sentences, measuring them out with a cadence that seemed to promise an ultimate moral that never emerged.

"And to think, I had to care for Liam and Caroline while you were away," Judith said, implementing years of practice that had affected an edifying tone of someone used to being in control and fawned over. "I had Caroline in my forties, for God's sake, and it is a wonder she wasn't born an idiot, although she fawns over that horse of hers like one. And Liam! He is as stupid as he looks, stuttering like a fool. Imagine a woman at my age being saddled with children." Her words fell like knives, her scorn for Liam and Caroline sickening Robert. "If not for them, your father would never have strayed."

"My nanny, Mrs. Green, told me that there were no monsters under my bed, or hidden inside my closet," Robert said. "But she failed to warn me that sometimes monsters come dressed as people that claim to love you more than the sun loves the moon. At least if Father were alive, he'd checkmate your bitter malice and cruel taunts, especially to your own children."

"To think all I've sacrificed for you—"

"Do you have the capacity to love me, or am I your show pony?" Robert leaned back and folded his arms in front of him. "You may want to take a page out of Sophia's playbook and learn how to love freely."

"That Nazi is possessed by the devil. She has totally taken over Caroline's and Liam's minds. They were never so rebellious before her arrival." She dug orange marmalade out of a crystal compote and attacked her croissant.

"Definitely evil," Robert said. "A clear sign of possession, the positive improvements in my brother and sister because of Sophia's tender loving and—motherly care."

"I suppose you are going to tell me that whore you are parading around the countryside can do a better job parenting. I've heard about the escapades at the plant, and then dozens of packages arrived yesterday. I'm mortified by the astronomical bills coming from Hudson's. Oh, yes, the rumors of your goings-on with the Nazi have fallen on me like an avalanche. What humiliation I've had to suffer. My son with the hired help." Judith sniffed, dabbing the corners of her eyes with her linen napkin.

The muscles in Robert's neck corded and he could almost forgive his father for having a mistress.

"Mother, I regard it as a matter of self-respect to spit on your insufferable vanity, and of your petty following."

Judith toyed with her diamond brooch as if the light reflecting from it divined her power. "I can take your insults, but my 'petty following' is throwing out huge sums of money to support your campaign."

Carefully controlling his voice, he said, "No more will you wield that nasty tongue against Sophia or fling anymore vile slurs against Liam or Caroline. You are toxic, Mother, contaminating and polluting everything around you. No doubt from some deep underlying issue in your life. If I hear one more word...I'll have you moved out in a heartbeat. Father left the care of the entire estate to me."

"How dare you threaten me. Your own mother!"

"Whatever must be done to curve your maliciousness, I'll do. No more deep pockets. No more social events or charities. Your allowance, everything, will be cut off. Think about how that will play with your friends."

"I'll bide my time until you see the light. You will apologize to me then. For now, I will tell my informers that you are just sowing your oats and will toss her out when you get tired."

"Enough!" Robert pounded the table. The china rattled. The silverware jumped. He shot to his feet, his chair toppling over and slamming to the floor. Glaring at his smiling mother, he threw down his napkin. "That's my last warning," he snapped and stalked out.

Chapter Twenty-Nine

Outside Sophia's little house, the winds howled, swooping down from Canada, stealing over the Great Lakes and across the land. The colors of autumn had disappeared and, subsequently, Michigan froze into a long arctic winter and christened the landscape with a late April snowstorm so like her homeland in northeast Prussia.

Sophia had built a cheery fire. Liam snored quietly on the couch as she pulled a fragrant loaf of homemade bread out of the oven.

A familiar tinkling chimed in her bedroom. Caroline had discovered her music box.

Sophia let out a slow, controlled breath and attempted to loosen her tense body. She gave her shoulders a wiggle and forced her stride into to a casual pace as she walked to her bedroom. It was a decent effort, enough to fool Caroline about her unease, and for Sophia to prepare herself to be hammered with a myriad of forthcoming questions

"Where did you get this?" Caroline asked, winding the piece again, mesmerized by the little bird that popped out. "Is this made of real gold and silver, and are these real rubies and pearls?"

"My parents gave it to me for my twelfth birthday." Best to cloak her response with as little as information as possible.

"I love the sweet melody. *Claire de Lune* is it not?"

Sophia nodded. "The melody is about the soul filled with music, and where birds are inspired to sing by the sad and beautiful light of the moon."

"Did you ever have a boyfriend before Robert?"

"What a question!"

"Did you?"

The girl was far too precocious.

Sophia sat on the bed beside Caroline. For too long, Sophia had been carrying the guilt of not telling Robert about her former husband. Karl was dead and gone, his body never found. The Allied bombings had disintegrated the train and hundreds of men were never unearthed. Why complicate things with affairs that happened thousands of miles away and seemingly eons ago?

A twinge of remorse pawed at her breast because of her secrecy. At the same time, something intangible nagged at her, warned her of the future, the price of a secret. She shook that feeling aside.

"There was no time for romance," Sophia said, choosing not to talk about her complicated life. "I was working on my doctorate, and then there was the war."

Caroline popped open the secret door revealing a photo. "Is this your family?"

Sophia's muscles tensed. She had kept that part of her life hidden, too. The past drifted, it gathered. If she was not careful, it would entomb her. The cure was to clean-sweep the past and all its pain. "Yes."

"Tell me about them."

"They are no longer with me." Tucking a wisp of hair behind her ear, Sophia stared out a darkened frosted window. After a weighty silence, she sought to rekindle her fondest memories. "Between my father and me, many experiences outdoors formed a special bond. In the early morning hours, we met and shared a deep love for the many different plants, insects, birds, fish, and other animals, and a never-tiring interest in their growth and behavior. A proud, warm feeling would flood through me when I could tell him the whereabouts of a nest that he'd long been searching for.

"My mother was spirited, intelligent and excitable, like a child at Christmas. She'd react with sheer delight over the golden-yellow swamp flowers along the grassy trenches and could never see enough of the velvety brown gypsy women who begged at our door.

"She liked to paint, and the gypsy women posed for her. During that time, the gypsies lived to tell me the latest scandals and romances of neighboring farmers. They used the knowledge to their advantage when they read the future in their clients' palms or laid their cards to tell their fortunes. Of course, the clients were mystified at such accuracy and compensated the gypsies well.

"What I remember most about my mother was how she trained my eyes to see the great beauty surrounding me. We rode together through endless fairy tale forests and were happy to see the first lemon-colored butterfly that fluttered like a spring messenger out of brown foliage of the previous year to the tender, green-budded birch trees. Often, we'd dismount and rest in the deep purple heather.

"My brother, Stefan, and my sister, Louisa, liked to ride horses like you." Sophia replaced the fragile box in a wooden case and slid it back under the bed.

"You are sad, Sophia. I can tell."

Sophia tousled Caroline's golden hair. "I'm not sad. I have you."

Caroline threw her arms around Sophia and hugged her. "I was so hoping you'd say you were my sister."

~

Robert had his driver pull up in front of Sophia's house, the snow as thick as whipped cream, forming little peaks like gnomes' caps on the lighted posts.

Inside, Caroline ran and hugged him. Liam slumbered with his socks dangling. Robert gently scooted his little brother's coat onto the sleeping child him and shrugged him into his boots, the boy grumbling drowsily with annoyance.

"Liam sleeps with a Napoleonic talent. There's no waking my brother in his unconquerable sleep." Robert handed his siblings off to the driver to take home.

When the children had left, Robert turned to her. "Liam is smitten with you. My Sophia, the sort that breaks a man's heart by just walking into a room."

"I am proud of Liam. He doesn't stutter anymore and is doing well with his new tutor and reading books beyond his age level."

"Liam blushes so hotly to your praises he could set a cigar alight a foot away. I'll tread carefully and make sure to never insult you."

"If you did, I'd tell Liam, and he'd pull your head off like a stopper."

Sophia set a tray of hot, aromatic bread and a triangle of cheese on the table. Robert inhaled the bread's yeasty aroma and cut a slice of hard crust from the loaf. The pillowy bread melted in his mouth.

Sophia knelt by the hearth and, with a poker, stirred the logs with confidence, conjuring up a crown of flames. He imagined Cynthia attempting to do the same simple task and failing.

He uncorked the wine and poured.

Sophia joined him on the couch and ruffled his hair. "You look much better with your hair mussed." Inhaling the aroma of the wine in her glass, she took a sip. "Hm-m. It tastes of exotic cherries and summers in Prussia."

"Read me the novel you are reading," Robert said.

"I thought you hated Hemmingway."

"I do, but I like it when you read."

He watched as she positioned herself to read, sitting half in shadow, because the one lamp that was lit threw its light obliquely from the side. She was fragile, vulnerable. He'd always protect her.

"Are you sure you like my reading? Like Liam, when I young, I was always a terrible student. I wiggled too much. My brain pinged from one thing to the next until my thoughts threatened to tumble everywhere like a litter of unruly kittens."

"I find that hard to believe."

Sophia commenced, becoming immersed in the narrative, unearthing cadences and turns of a phrase that flowed like harmonious themes, prose made of timbre and pauses that her accent enriched. Entirely captivated, he felt the tension of the day melt away. He could be with her for an eternity and simply listen.

Three logs crackled on the heavy andirons. One fell, and a rush of red cinders spiraled up the chimney, then surrendered to an evening light. Robert was happy here—in this little cottage. He could be happy in such surroundings for the rest of his life. If Sophia was with him.

"Are you content, Sophia?"

"I've never been happier," she told him, putting down the book.

The lights from the fireplace played across her lovely face. She leaned over and brushed his cheek with her lips. Her hair smelled of lavender, and he allowed his gaze to wander over her with an indolent appreciation.

"I sometimes forget..." he murmured as he thought to himself.

"Forget what?"

"How beautiful you are." He placed his glass on the table. "Then I see you and realize that memory cannot compare to reality. I'm left as breathless as the first time we met."

He took off his sweater and undid the top buttons of his shirt. "I want to talk about my senatorial campaign."

He felt her suck in a breath and saw her jerk her gaze away.

"I cannot see how it might work the way things are now," she said. "The war was long and bloody with many bad memories. People will not forget. I would sink your chances to win. And I know you could win without me."

Tender concern slipped into his mind. The unselfish Sophia would never interfere with his life. He clasped her chin and pulled her to face him. "I could not do anything without you in my life." The desperation in his voice came out of its own accord.

"Robert."

Her seductive whisper stroked over him with the effect of a soft warm kiss.

Her full breasts flattened on his chest and anticipation thickened the air in his lungs. He tightened his arms around her as she slipped her arms around his neck. Her lips parted, and he claimed her mouth fully.

Growling soft and low in his throat, he dragged his mouth away and picked her up and carried her to the bedroom. Impatient, he drew her cashmere sweater over her head. She had worn no bra and her breasts rose and fell with each shuddering, uneven breath. He swallowed.

"Did I ever tell you that you have the most magnificent breasts?"

She unzipped her skirt, letting it slide to the floor. No panties. Just the soft light hairs of her womanhood. Desire pulsed through his rigid flesh.

"You will pay for such wickedness," he warned her.

She quirked an eyebrow at him. "Is that a threat?"

"A promise."

She tugged at his shirt, worked her sensual hands beneath it. Restless, he shrugged out of his clothes and, one by one, tossed his shoes, shirt, and pants on the floor. She pushed him back on the bed and climbed astride him.

He arched a brow. "My bold Sophia."

"Of course," she laughed. "I am in charge."

She leaned forward and, in one smooth movement, covered his mouth with her own. Their mouths meshed in a fiery web of passion, their faces so close, the sight of her blurred into flesh and flashes of eyes. He drank pleasure from her mouth and returned it in generous, overwhelming increments, worshipping her.

His lips wandered across her soft cheekbones, her eyelids, her chin, nuzzling her ear. His chilly fingers grazed the warmth of her neck before threading through golden strands as sultry as silk.

Some astounding part of Robert suddenly refused to move. Desiring, instead, to revel in her devilishly fearless exploration of him. Her hands curved down his arms, outlining veins corded beneath his skin by contracted muscle. Delicate fingers delighted in skimming down his ribs and robbed him of his control.

Her hands hesitated at his hips and they both ceased to breathe. Her blue gaze wavered, warring with seductive curiosity and the power she held over him.

If she squirmed one more time, he'd lose himself. An instinctive fear became a swelling of satisfaction as her thighs parted wider for him, and his nostrils flared, inhaling the scent of lavender and her feminine heat coating his hardness. No longer could he not touch her. Gently, he outlined the circle of her breast, holding it firm, his head bent. His tongue caressing her sensitive, swollen nipple, drawing it in his mouth, sucking and teasing, the touch and taste of her filling him with emotions and sensations. When he tore his mouth from her breast. She gasped.

He touched pleasure points, allowing his fingers to sample every curve, every line of her delectable body. He moved his hands to her waist and held her against his rock-hard length, his skin sizzling where he pressed against her, and getting heady pleasure from her delightful moans. Allowing her to take the lead, he stroked her back, finding the deep curve that gave rise to her firm, tight bottom.

She groaned beneath her breath, adjusted herself, leisurely, accepting the thick fullness of him. Hot. Wet. The temptress lifted, dared to move slowly, agonizingly against him, allowing only the head of his cock to bathe in her heat.

"Sophia, the games you play," he growled.

She laughed, continuing her slow torture. With her hands braced on his chest, he felt his heart pounding wildly against her fingers. No longer would he allow her to toy with him. Cupping his hand beneath her bottom, and holding her hips, he yanked her down, sheathing his cock to the hilt, and began a hot matching rhythm.

She kissed him again, her mouth sweet and damp, a wicked temptation.

He could not get enough of her. His restraint broke and he flipped her over on her back, wanting to bury himself inside her as deeply as he could and not pull out until he got his fill. Her long, smooth legs wrapped around his hips. He plunged into her, his cock parting her soft folds, filling her completely.

He bent toward her, surrounding her with his strength, hoping to lend it to her. Sorry for all the bad memories she had of her past, the loss of her family and the war. Wishing he could kiss it away somehow or take it upon himself the way she'd ridden him of his nightmares.

Flecks of silver shone in her blue irises, and he answered her pleas, her hot, wet flesh closing in on him, drawing him inside, inviting him to fill his seed into her womb. It was beyond heaven.

This was about giving her a memory that she'd remember far into the future. He could feel her ultra-soft pink flesh swelling with excitement, her body milking him. She gyrated her hips, rhythmically, edging around his, twitching, and rolling her body and sending him spiraling out of control. Her gasps stroked not just his body but gave him a sense of pure male satisfaction.

She clawed his backside, grasping for an elusive flame. In answer, he plunged with long, slow, deep strokes. He held back his impending release until her head pressed back into the pillows, then began to turn from side to side, and a tremor inside her vibrated with liquid fire around his cock.

She hauled him with her into a shimmering place. One made of gasps and wavering moans. Time merged with the flickers of swirling firelight embers, piercing the shadows, stunning them as its complement lanced through their joined bodies. The pleasure just as scorching and blazing. The rapture just as dazzling. And the desires as vital as a promise one secures with irrefutable fate.

At last, Robert lifted his head, drew in a ragged breath, and rolled to his side, carrying her with him.

He held her head against his chest, his breathing unsteady and his heart stumbling to find its rhythm. His eyes felt heavy as she snuggled against him, and he let them slide closed, feeling warm and more content than he could ever remember.

"You are a rare find, Sophia," he murmured, and nuzzled her breast, the musky air scented with their lovemaking.

"How's that?" she asked, disentangling him, and rising—no doubt swimming in a sensual haze since he'd kept her up all night.

She ascended like an immortal goddess, dragging the sheet like a wedding train, and granting divinity to measly mortals. His breath caught.

He knew this wanting of her would never grow old; his body would always be hers. She returned to their bed and snuggled up to him, her hand splayed across his chest.

She looked him directly in the eyes. "You want to look to the future and create something good. In your run for the US Senate, I believe you will make the world a better place."

He slid his finger beneath her chin, tilted her head up until their gazes met...held.

"Sophia, I love you."

"I love you, too, Robert."

"I want you to be my wife."

"All I need to make me secure is your love. I'd love to be your wife, but—"

"My US Senate bid. It will work."

"I cannot hold you back."

Whenever he opened his mouth to speak about his run, he felt her withdraw, the dread of her retreat wrapping icy fingers around his throat. "You know me by now. I'll put the right spin on it. I'll make it work."

Her fingers stroked his cheekbones. "If anyone can make things right, it'd be you, Robert."

"So, yes?"

Her face turned rapturous, and as long as he lived, he'd never forget her joy.

"I promise to love you forever, Robert. Every single day of forever."

He grinned. "With you, Sophia, I can conquer the world. I can walk on water."

She plucked one of his chest hairs. "You are being arrogant. I suppose it is a commonplace American male pretense."

"Commonplace." He sucked in a ragged breath and rolled her beneath him, claiming her lips in a kiss that promised forever. "I'll show you commonplace."

Chapter Thirty

A square of late spring light progressed from Robert's window, inching across his rosewood desk and onto the electric-blue carpet, which lay untacked on the African blackwood floor. Robert took the papers Van handed to him.

"I'm confused." Van said. "Your mother is telling everyone that you are marrying Cynthia. The irony is you spend all your time with Sophia. Am I missing something?"

Robert shifted in his chair. "You should be familiar with my mother's machinations by now."

"Look, Robert. Women—with remarkable exceptions like Sophia—are more intelligent than we are, or at least more honest with themselves in what they want and don't want. Life is lot like pork: there's loin steak and there's bologna. Each has its own place and function. Which is it, Robert, steak or bologna?"

"Don't worry, Van."

"Make her yours. Sophia is the best thing that has ever happened to you. If you let her go, you will be making the biggest mistake of your life."

"I'm taking Sophia to the jewelers in a few days to browse."

Van whistled. "It's about time."

"Keep it under your lid. I don't want anything to get back to my mother. Speaking of my mother, she's arranged a dinner party." He glanced at his watch. "I'm already late. Important guests. Big doners. I can't wait for it to be over. It's like having a tooth pulled."

He didn't realize the disaster until he showed up for dinner. The important guests that demanded his presence were Cynthia and her family.

Cynthia preceded him, her perfume overpowering. She walked peevishly into the dining room, her high heels making brittle, impatient sounds on the marble floor.

"I understand you've been quite busy—" she said, dripping with sarcasm.

So, she had heard of him with Sophia. Good. Perhaps she'd drop her schemes of matrimony and save them both from embarrassment.

Dinnertime turned into a battleground of silences and hostile glances. How could he get out of this one?

Robert excused himself and asked MacDonald to interrupt in thirty minutes, and say it was important business. He wanted to be with Sophia, not the ice queen. No matter how much maneuvering his mother did, he'd outmaneuver her scheming. He had to be careful because the ice queen's parents owned a tire company that could shut off his supply of excellent quality and best-priced tires if offended.

Caroline, his sister and comrade in arms, sat beside him. He whispered in her ear, "This should be a lot of fun."

Caroline fluttered her eyelashes at him and muttered, "With Cynthia? I would rather watch a cat massacre."

Robert howled.

Judith, wearing a lot of jewelry that glittered in the reflection of mirrors, shot the two of them with a reproving glance. "To think the likes of Nazis and other rabble arriving from across the ocean are ruining the moral fiber of the country."

Robert gripped his fork with the innuendo aimed at Sophia. His contempt for his mother grew. A vain and spoiled socialite, his mother reigned the epitome of an overcontrolling mother and had set her cap for him to marry Cynthia Roessler. With vehemence, she'd never upset his supposed fiancée's powerful industrialist father.

"What an embarrassment and denigration for America," Cynthia concurred.

Denigration? A big word for Cynthia. Of course, Cynthia and his mother were a team.

"I just finished an interesting book," said Robert.

"Do tell." Cynthia made a pout of her mouth.

"It was about a man's relation, playing games. He had warned the individual not to mistake the fact that he could make their life a misery. The relative still challenged him. So, he threw the offender out the window...and he didn't open the window first." Robert nodded to his mother. His tone was not threatening but jovial, as if he were offering her a cup of tea.

"How beastly. What a dreadful story," purred Cynthia.

Robert sighed. "It had a terrible end. But we're all like that, aren't we? We're all barbarians at our core. Savage, brutal beasts when pressed. I know I am."

Robert lifted his glass for the waiter to pour more wine, looked at the clock and tamped down a yawn. The evening was an exercise in patience and idiocy. Adam Roessler, Cynthia's father was a braggart, incessant name dropper, and had grown up with a silver spoon in his mouth, inheriting Roessler Corporation. It was a wonder the company hadn't been run to the ground.

Robert scorned Adam Roessler who rose as head of his company through nepotism. Robert had also inherited his company, and his rise to head of Pratt Motors was so different than Cynthia's father who hadn't ever had a fresh idea in his life. Robert redefined Pratt Motors with his innovations and had taken the company farther than even his father could.

As superficial as her father, Cynthia ruffled her shoulders irritably under her silver fox stole. "Honestly, darling," she continued, "prying you away from that automobile plant of yours is like wrestling Heathcliff from the deathbed of the proverbial Catherine. I swear, I often wonder what you'd do if you didn't have that business to rush to every day."

Aggressive.

"That's easy," said her father. "He makes money by performing an honest living. Every car he rolls out comes with four tires from my company, almost enough to pay for furs and jewelry for you and your mother."

Robert picked up the *Detroit News*. The Tigers had won the day before.

"Bored?" Cynthia accused. "What are you thinking about?" she purred, toying with a double rope of perfectly matched pearls. She leaned low enough for him to get a glimpse down her low-cut dress.

He looked around the paper at Caroline, and then Liam, slumped in his chair, the children bored out of their minds and trapped.

"He's thinking about a new design for a carburetor," Caroline said breezily.

That subject caught the old man's ears. "Really, what kind?"

Nothing you'd understand since you won your seat by nepotism. "A Dual Jet," Robert furnished. "It's still in the design stage. Nothing to remark upon."

Liam started tapping an annoying rhythm on his glass with his fork.

"Stop that," Judith said. "You're giving me a headache."

"Sorry," Liam said, then muttered beneath his breath, "I'll take up the saxophone for my next concert."

"I swear, it's too much to ask this family to be polite for even one day!" Judith snapped, her stiff posture smacking a dramatic pose of persecution.

"Excuse me, Mr. Pratt," MacDonald interrupted per instruction. "You have an important phone call, sir." Robert jumped from his chair. Liam and Caroline narrowed their eyes on him, as if he were leaving them on the sinking Titanic.

He stopped, scratching the back of his head in an exaggerated gesture. "It completely escaped me. I bought box tickets to the Tigers game for Caroline and Liam." He checked his watch. "They must leave now if they are to make it on time. MacDonald, there's a third ticket, can you manage escorting them to the game?"

"Yes, sir."

"Oh, God. Can't it wait, Robert? We have guests. I demand you stay," Judith said, her eyes blazing.

"Can't you stay?" Cynthia pouted. "Your mother and I wanted to go over ideas for your campaign. We have been working night and day. Father is eager to finance—"

There it was in a nutshell, like a witch's brew. Cynthia, and his mother's secret assignation to entrap him. Robert raised his wine glass. "I'm sure, Mother, you can manage without me. Just be that well-known ornament of Detroit society...the Pratt society. I bid my adieu."

Chapter Thirty-One

Judith snapped the doors shut to her private office. "What information do you have that is supposedly of vital importance to my family, Mr. Belette?" What a day for the former tutor to show up, yet something about the eagerness in the man's expression nagged at her.

"Information that, if not acted on, will be a great scandal to your family—and cost your son his senate bid."

The former tutor examined his nails overlong. "It involves his whore of a stablemaster."

Judith fidgeted with a paperweight on her desk. She had heard that he'd purchased the Nazi a vulgarly expensive engagement ring the day before but, thank God, he hadn't given it to her yet. Was it possible she could stop this madness? "How much?"

"As you know, I've fallen on unfortunate times..."

He referred to his dismissal. "I don't have time for nonsense. Name your price."

"A hundred thousand dollars."

"You must have a head injury."

"Sofia Sonderburg is really Sophia Schneider, married to a former high-level Nazi lieutenant."

Her body temperature rose. The bastard had her hooked. Like a shark on a blood scent, she said, "I don't believe you have such evidence."

"I can produce her husband."

"Now you have my attention."

On her knees, Sophia hung her head over the toilet in her office in the stables. For six weeks, her stomach had been in rebellion, an epic journey in vomit and sickness that went on all morning until it lifted at noon. She wretched three times more, then wiped her mouth.

"Are you sick?" asked Caroline.

Sophia moaned and pushed away from the toilet. Standing on trembling legs, she washed her face over a sink basin. "I must have had something that didn't agree with me last night," she lied.

"You are coming to the bar-b-que?" Caroline insisted.

"I wouldn't miss it for the world. I have some duties here then I'll dress and be there. Save me some chicken, and please don't mention this incident to anyone. Our secret?"

Since Robert spent his nights with her, keeping her sickness from him had been tricky. Sophia had managed to rise early, dress quickly and leave for the stables, giving her just enough time to throw-up in the bushes.

Caroline hesitated, noncommittal in her answer. Horses snorted in the outer stalls. Less distant, the scrape of a shovel twanged against the flagstone floor where Diruvert cleaned away soiled straw.

"Scout's honor," Caroline finally said. She saluted and skipped off.

Sophia stood at the window, the light streaming in feeling all the warmer as she placed her palm over her flat belly. As confirmed by her doctor, a new life had started. Joy blossomed inside her, her reality shifting upon its axis at the thought of welcoming a sacred and sentient being into her heart and soul. She smiled. With certainty, the baby was conceived that night in April during the snowstorm.

She glanced repeatedly at the clock. After the bar-b-que she was going to tell Robert the happy news. He'd be delighted. More than once, he'd told her how he'd love to have children more than anything else in the world. Their children.

Karl. To tell Robert about her late husband? Her throat constricted. She knew she'd been avoiding it, but with the baby coming, and the marriage, she didn't want any further secrets between them. She'd tell Robert about Karl.

Robert had taken her to a jeweler the day before and had her fitted for a ring, looking over diamonds and asking her preference. He'd hinted at a very special surprise after the bar-b-que.

Sophia finished her chores and took a long bath. Checking the time, she dressed quickly in a new Dior creation Robert had procured for her. Opulent was the word describing the elegant dress that accented her tiny waist and underlined her curves with a crisscross, semi-off-the-shoulder bodice, and long-flaring skirt. Turning in front of her mirror, she smoothed her fingers over the mint green taffeta so unapologetically feminine. She slipped on her wide-brimmed matching green hat and gloves and shoes.

She walked to the main house, and her hand flew to her chest. A great number of people milled about with fluted glasses of champagne in their hands. Caterers struggled to set up a grand buffet. Streamers and bright-colored lights spangled the air while maids in crisp uniforms carried trays of canapes through the crowd. The pleasant smell of woodsmoke wafted in the air from the chicken and ribs grilled over an old-fashioned bar-b-que pit.

Judith stepped between a bevy of servants, caught Sophia's eye, and waved. Dressed in a Chanel polka-dot dress, Judith looked more upholstered than dressed. Her unexpected friendly gesture caught Sophia off guard. Had Robert told her about their engagement? Had Judith consented and approved?

A light bulb went off in Sophia's head, but she couldn't read the Morse code. Boiling with uncertainties, her mind bubbled like a kettle about to overflow.

Camouflage was a game Judith played over what she concealed. Loose ends dangled; inconsistencies abounded.

Warning bells clanged in Sophia's head. No. Judith would never change. Not for one minute would the harridan allow anyone near her eldest son that she considered inferior, nor relinquish her hold on him. Sophia posed a threat. Judith would stop at nothing to destroy what she considered a menace.

Judith looked up again, to make sure Sophia was still there. The smugness of her smile rattled the nerves up Sophia's spine.

Sophia placed her hand protectively on her stomach and waved her feelings aside. No. She'd not let Judith destroy the best day of her life. Instead, she concentrated on a canopied crib, cute little booties, and stuffed rabbits.

A hushed murmur rose, growing into a cacophony as the Pratt family took the stage. Liam and Caroline waved. Robert winked at her. Hope welled up inside her. She celebrated how the world was good and that good would prevail over everything. Nothing or no one could dim the light that shined within her. This was a new beginning for them and her heart burst with happiness.

Several dignitaries crowded the stage, including Mr. Roessler and his daughter, Cynthia, the woman his mother hoped he'd marry. Sophia frowned. Doners had earned center stage. Judith stared straight at Sophia like a cat that grabbed the cream.

Out of the corner of her eye, Sophia spied Mr. Belette, the tutor, in his white suit. She frowned. What was he doing here? He curved his finger along his mustache and smiled benignly, like he'd fed her rat poison and was waiting for her to die. Her breath hitched.

Sophia stared at Robert. No doubt, she was being fanciful.

Upon his introduction, Robert went to the lectern and formally announced his bid for the United States Senate race. Applause and cheering broke out. He gave a formal speech, all the while keeping his eyes on Sophia, telling the audience that with the conclusion of war, how he planned to make the world better and brighter. This was his time, and she was so proud of him. Later, he'd take her in his arms and quell all her fears. She'd be safe. She'd be truthful about Karl, and then give him the good news of their impending child.

Judith crossed to the podium, put her hand up to silence the crowd. Of course, the woman must have her moment in the spotlight. "There is more good news to share today." She waved a reluctant Cynthia forward, the woman feigning proper embarrassment from being made the focus.

Judith placed her arm around Cynthia, and then looked directly at Sophia. "I'm proud to announce the engagement of my son, Robert, to Miss Cynthia Roessler."

The crowd gave a thunderous applause. Fireworks went off. The air whooshed out of Sophia like she'd been sucker punched. She looked at the smiling Cynthia, the smugness of Judith, and the tutor chinking a champagne glass with a stranger. Glaring at his mother, Robert received backslapping and hearty congratulations.

Caroline looked appalled.

Cynthia surged upon him, wrapped her arms around his neck, kissing him with a full open-mouthed kiss. The crowd cheered. Robert pushed Cynthia away. With a grim expression, he took the microphone and looked at Sophia. "Let's not get ahead of ourselves, Mother. There's lots to do with my campaign before nuptials are announced."

Sophia fought the nausea rising into her throat, knowing she'd been fooled twice. She had believed in Robert's love, and then been deceived about his fiancée. Robert had never loved her. He had used her.

Knees buckling, a pain sharp and jabbing, like an icicle, lodged in her stomach.

Blindly, she reached behind her, stumbling from chair to chair. Was everyone staring at her? *Escape.* Her vision blurred. She shuffled back until her shoulders hit an ivy-covered wall. Holding on to the partition for support, she inched, the vines tearing at her dress.

Run. Now. Make your feet move. Clenching her teeth together against a wave of hopeless bitter grief, she picked up speed and ran to the darkness of the stables.

In the musty-smelling hay of Rosie's stall, she collapsed against the horse's neck and sobbed uncontrollably.

"Sophia," came an accented voice. A German voice. She snapped her head around. It was as if her heart had stopped beating and all her blood had run down to her feet.

"Karl?"

She staggered backward against the prancing mare, her mind swirling, her breaths shallow until the world went black.

Beneath his calm, rage rolled off Robert in waves. After his speech and galvanized into action, guests rushed him. He greeted the tsunami of well-wishers, tolerating the hand shakings, backslapping, and ingratiating remarks of a conquering hero. He did not want the trumpet blast—hated it. Stamped on his mind was the ravaged look on Sophia's face. She'd be at her house. Inconsolable. He had to get to her.

A crimson haze surrounded his vision from the vicious carnage his wicked mother had wreaked. It was almost as if he could hear her cloven hoofs clatter up the drive after him.

Robert barreled through a group of local politicians. They stopped him and he looked over their heads to get a glimpse of Sophia. "Could I be your campaign manager?" This was from a man who had inflicted havoc with bizarre zoning requirements on

Pratt enterprises. Did he have the gall to smile? Robert wanted to smash his fist into his simian face.

Robert approached the new state assemblyman. "Have you seen a young woman in a Chanel dress go this way?" Robert remained cryptic.

"Who would this woman be?"

Equally cryptic. Robert's muscles tightened. How long would it take to pull off limb by limb to get the answers he wanted?

The man put up his hands. "I've not seen her."

"Congratulations, Mr. Pratt."

Belette? The tutor. Something didn't ring right. "What are you doing here?"

"Whatever do you mean?"

"You are whatever way the wind blows that benefits you. You're a complete opportunist. I don't like playing games."

"What kind of games?"

"The kind of games where I count to three, and if I don't get the answers I want, it gets interesting."

"What do you mean interesting?" the tutor dared to taunt him.

"The kind where I drag your carcass down to the river and drown you."

"Now see here!" The tutor poked his finger in Robert's chest.

Robert looked down at the man's bony finger. "What I see is that if you don't remove your hand, I'll be obliged to remove it from your wrist." He glared at the little man until he turned away. He smelled an alliance between his mother and the tutor. He'd deal with them later.

After searching for Sophia at her house, he headed to the stables. He reached into his pocket, felt the box with her diamond engagement ring tucked inside. She'd know of his love then.

He heard Sophia's moan. She was with Rosie. The horses were a balm for her. He rounded the stall. Sophia was on the floor.

Unconscious. A man hovered over her, moving his scarred hands on her. Molesting her.

Blood pounded in Robert's ears. Bitter bile clogged his throat. Like a fire, it burned and raged. "Get away from her."

He tore the man from Sophia and threw a punch, connecting with the man's jaw. He'd kill the man for touching her.

The stranger swung his left fist from the left to right. Robert dodged, but the next blows came from his foe's right and knocked Robert to the floor. Robert scrambled to his feet and planted his fist in the man's midsection. The momentum knocked him to the floor. The man rolled and came to his feet. Wiry bastard. Rosie whinnied and shied to the far side of the stall.

"Robert! Stop!" Sophia tugged his arm. He turned. "Please, Robert," she pleaded.

The man landed another punch on the side of his head. Robert shook it off. He deserved that for getting distracted. He gave the man an upper cut. The man tottered and then went down. Robert continued to pummel him.

Sobbing, Sophia pushed him away, planted herself between the two men.

He couldn't fathom why she'd protect a man who meant her harm.

Breathing hard, he pulled out the box and showed her the engagement ring wreathed in diamonds. "I've come to undo my mother's wicked lie. I'm proposing to you, Sophia. You are the one. I love you with all my heart. The one who I want to have children with, to cherish and spend the rest of my life with."

Closing the box, Sophia shook her head. "I'm sorry."

"Sorry?"

"Well, isn't this touching?" droned Judith, appearing from the dark recesses of the corridor. "I don't think we've had this much excitement in a long time. But—I think we need to straighten this matter out."

MacDonald, Belette, Diruvert, Adam Roessler, and Cynthia grouped behind his mother. Why were all of them in the stables?

Judith raised an eyebrow. "I told you that you'd eventually apologize to me."

The tutor smacked his lips with relish. "Touché."

Cynthia appraised Robert with the speculation of a hawk. Diruvert shrugged. Adam Roessler stared daggers at Robert.

"Miss Sonderburg, I think you have some explaining to do," purred Judith. "or should I address you as Mrs. Schneider?"

Breathing hard, Robert stared at Sophia. Her chin trembled ever so slightly, her face etched with misery. He wanted to do nothing but place his arms around her and soothe her. With pleading eyes, Sophia looked to him, and then to the half-conscious stranger, then back to him.

"What's going on?" Robert demanded.

"He's my husband."

"You're married?" Blood pounded Robert's temples as he absorbed the stunning news.

With tears running down her cheeks, Sophia nodded her head. "I'm so sorry, Robert."

"Sorry you're married?" The words exploded from him. "When did you plan on telling me?"

Sophia's chin quivered. "I-I love you, Robert. I thought Karl was dead in the war."

Hands clenching and unclenching, he wanted to hurt someone. He wanted to see blood. "You never said a word about the marriage. I don't want to hear anymore lies, and no more useless words of explanation."

"I always knew she was scheming," Judith hissed. "What a mess, Robert. Pray this scandal never reaches a reporter's ear. From now on, you will listen to me."

Robert's eyes clouded, grappling with a myriad of emotions—anger, hate, bitterness, heaving resentments, bewilderment—all emotional famines.

He burst from the stables, collided with Van.

"What is the matter with you? Your face is a white as a nun's buttocks."

"Out of my way." His first instinct had been to punch Van in the face. Anyone in the face. He needed a place to come apart. The rage surging through his veins could only be released by destruction. He wanted to break something. There was a whole house of windows if he desired. No. He wanted to dismantle all of Detroit, burn it to the ground.

And it was from that instinct that he fled, just as much as anything else, away from the revelers who gorged on Pratt champagne and food.

He circumvented the house and headed for the river. He needed a place to exhaust the need of destructive violence. He came upon the tree where he'd carved their initials. He punched the tree, and kept punching, until he stopped, exhausted, his knuckles a bloody pulp. He thought about chopping down the whole damn tree...but somehow that seemed sacrilege.

Gasping for breath and his heart torn in two, he returned to the house, going through the back servants' entrance to his room. He didn't want to see anyone. He needed to clear a new path, far from Sophia's betrayal. To completely eradicate her from all thought. To never trust anyone to get that close to him again.

In his Italian onyx bathroom, he ran cold water over his bloody hands. What a fool he'd been. He had planned to run off with her and get married. How would that have played with the papers? Automobile magnate and senatorial hopeful commits bigamy with Nazi woman.

There were scars that he'd hide. Scars that numbed him. Scars that rid him of the capacity to ever feel again. Easy to harden his heart.

~

Pinpoints of heat seared her inner lids as Sophia packed her suitcases and lugged them to the cottage door. Karl stood stiffly outside, his black eye swollen. He'd barely said a word to her, wouldn't tell her their destination or where he'd been for the past year and a half.

They had a train to catch. For a moment, she paused in the doorway, taking in all the memories. The charming fireplace and warmth of the home where she and Robert had made endless love, now as cold as the ashes lying in the hearth.

The scene in the stables replayed in her head nonstop. Robert vanishing from the barn, the angry sound of his footsteps receding like a poisoned tide and leaving behind it a residue of despair. He'd abandoned her when she needed him the most. She'd almost died of grief and guilt at that moment. To know he'd found out the worst way possible.

She picked up her bags and struggled to get them over the threshold. Karl refused to assist her. The taxi driver gave Karl a dirty look, picked up her luggage and placed it in the trunk. She locked the door.

"I need to stop at the house to drop off the key," she told the cabbie.

Karl remained in shadows. Waves of anger flowed off him. She'd be punished. The well-ingrained German psyche of strictly adhering to the rules had been broken *Ordnung muss sein."* There must be order, Hitler's useful aphorism shouted in the silence.

Later. She'd deal with one thing at a time. For now, her emotions were too raw.

The cabbie let her out at the front door. She passed the fountain, noticed the statue, the figure of an avenging angel. The hand of that fiery angel emerged from the water, an accusing finger, as sharp as a sword, thrust toward her, and seemed to condemn her, "I know you are a whore."

She ran up the steps and entered the great hall, hoping she'd run into Caroline and give her the letter she'd written to give to Robert.

Sophia stopped dead in her tracks. He was there. All of them were.

She saw how terribly he'd suffered, a deadly quiver, nothing more. His hands were bandaged, and her heart went out to him.

Judith stood wreathed in smoke, and for a moment, Sophia hesitated, wondering how a woman who possessed everything could embody perfect hatred.

Cynthia looped her arm in Robert's. Her slender fingers played with a ring. Sophia's heart clenched. The engagement ring Robert had picked out for her.

Cynthia leaned her head slightly to one side and touched Robert's shoulder, a clear demonstration of staking her territory.

Sophia took a tentative step toward Robert. His handsome jaw was taut, his mouth drawn into a ruthless, forbidding line. "Robert, if I may have a word?" Sophia said.

Let me explain...

He dropped Cynthia's arm and stalked off to the library.

Sophia followed. His implacable expression did not falter. At least he was allowing her to speak to him.

He snapped the doors shut. He just stood there, his hands fisted at his sides, and let his silence unravel what little composure she had.

Why didn't he say something? Do something. Throttle her. Murder her. She didn't care at this point. "I want you to know, I love you."

His very presence laid her bare, raw, stripped her of everything, even her pride.

"If there's nothing else, there's that—" she said on the verge of tears again.

He advanced on her and, for one terrible moment she thought he'd put his hands around her throat and strangle her. "I will expel my thoughts if they think of you again, and I will rip my tongue out if it says your name once more. There are no words except I never want to see your face again."

The hard ire in his voice echoed off the walls and battered her with fractals of rejection. She took a step toward him. "Robert, please let me explain—"

In two steps, he swept his arm across the desk. Papers scattered. A glass paperweight shattered in a thunderous blast, glass skittering in all directions across the hard marble floor. "Liars don't explain. You're dead to me."

Blood drained from her face as she placed a letter for him on the table, the envelope damp from her tears. This should have been the happiest day of her life. The day she would tell Robert of their coming child. "I hope when you are thinking clearer...it is not what you think. If you can bring yourself to read my letter..."

"Get out!"

Sophia gripped her hands together to keep them from shaking. "In my heart, I wish things were different—"

"I thought...love was honesty, but apparently that was something you and I never had. Trust, once broken, can never be regained. Now leave, before I have you thrown out."

Sophia walked to him and placed her trembling fingers on his arm. "Regardless, I will always cherish our time together and take with me a part of you."

"Shut the hell up." He flung her hand away, ripped open a desk drawer, signed a slip of paper, and threw it at her. "Payment for services—of a whore."

He walked around her.

"If I might say goodbye to Caroline and Liam before I leave—"

"Stay away from them." He slammed the door behind him.

Sophia stared at the oak grain and counted the lines. She had opened her heart to experience a love and joy she'd never dreamed possible, and it had been shoved away like so much refuse.

She had cast the die and lost.

With a small cry, she buried her face in her hands, recognizing once again where she was—once again at a crossroads. It was dark and she could not see her way. Where was the resourceful Sophia? Where was that infallible sense of logic, that strength on which she prided herself? She searched frantically, despairingly, and she could not locate either of them.

Tears stung her eyes, but she refused to shed them, refused to let Robert, his mother and his fiancée have the satisfaction of witnessing her anguish at his rejection of her.

She wiped her face and straightened. She was a Sonderburg.

She'd been so close to Caroline and Liam. They were nowhere. She regretted that she didn't have a chance to say goodbye.

The sun was just setting and the shadows on the roads were violet and indigo when Sophia and the taciturn Karl drove away. She thought of the horses she cared for and loved. She thought of the memories of Caroline jumping a fence on Rosie, Liam chasing his kitten, and Robert striding toward her with love in his eyes.

She looked back for a second, caught the once bright golden "P" on the entry gate, tarnished brass in the declining day. The river slid by like wet steel, with a smell like a deep, cool crypt in chalky ground. The streetlamps went on, their flickering lights mocking the coming darkness hostile to any bright spark to call back a rainbow with all its hues. She said goodbye to every tree, bush, and building, wondering if the illusions of time could ever erase the pain of loss.

Don't look back. Don't think.

Chapter Thirty-Two

Sophia lost count of how many trains they had changed, Karl refusing to tell her their destination and leaving her anxious.

She looked out the window, reading the many billboards that blurred by—*Richmond, Virginia, Drink Delicious Coca Cola, More Doctors Smoke Camels, Go to Church Next Sunday, Buy a Buick.* On one hand, Sophia could count the words spoken to her by Karl. His silence was a punishment.

The clackety-clack of the train wheels mocked the heavily weighed heartbreak of Robert. Souls entwined. Star-kissed by destiny. The gypsy's foretelling, wildly flawed.

The memory of Robert and that last day stung like a reopened wound. His mother smirking. Karl furious. And then, Robert— the vibrant force he'd radiated stripped away, his sharpened face fixed in such finality that she'd been frozen in mortal terror and engulfed by abysmal despair.

She darted a glance at Karl. She pitied her husband for the scars he endured, the terrible pain he must have suffered from the explosion and subsequent fires. For his inner scars, she pitied him the most. The war had left him without feeling.

Karl, once handsome, had been reduced to cold ash. He'd lost the status of his rank, his family's great wealth, and the great future of the Third Reich that now lay interred in rubble. What remained was a shell of a man with little pride and no prospects of great conquests.

He was her husband and she had married him for the protection his name had given her. No matter what, she must live with the consequences. They were survivors and she had a duty to honor and obey. She owed him that. Duty to be a good wife. Even if their lives were not perfect.

Nerves danced in her stomach as she again attempted to broach the silence. "Where have you been the last eighteen months?"

He turned his glacial gaze on her for daring to speak. "I should have had you before the American. But no. On our wedding night, I was too much of a gentleman to leave you a widow with a child. Except I didn't die, did I?"

She fought the nausea that climbed up in her throat. "I don't know what you are talking about."

"You don't? Your unfaithfulness was as plain as day. How short a time it was before you jumped into Robert's bed—especially after I pursued you for so long with no results before the war."

She sucked in a breath, combating the urge to bolt. "You did not answer my question. Where have you been? I was told you were dead. They told your sister, Helga, you were dead, and she threw me out."

Through gritted teeth, he said, "I suffered months of pain, endured horrendous rehabilitation, not knowing if I could get to you, and then—to find greater pain—your infidelity."

"You are deluded." She bit the inside of her mouth surprised by the coppery taste of blood. No matter how difficult, she had to convince Karl that he was the father of her child. To enact a lie so enormous it laid her bare to that soul-eating degradation. Then came the terror of being thrown out on the streets if she could not convince Karl that the baby she carried was his.

Why not tell him the truth?

She'd tried. So often during their sojourn, she'd opened her mouth to tell him.

And something stopped her. Karl stopped her and so, too, did the ugly black, spidery arms of the swastika floating in front of her eyes. The angry goosestep marches and worshipping calls and salutes of adoration owed to that symbol of greater Germany. Karl was part of that world. Reared on propaganda. Indoctrinated as the superior race. Above all indiscretions. Especially when it came to his wife.

She enumerated to herself the many logical reasons to maintain the deception.

When men were hurt or deceived, they tended to become angry. An angry man was generally an unpredictable creature. Often cruel. She'd seen that cruelty with the Russian soldiers raping the women of Berlin in revenge for Stalingrad. While a part of her was afraid of Karl's rage, she was more afraid of the costs. To be tossed out and unable to care for her baby?

"How did you find me?" she asked.

"Helga had learned from your former landlady who knew how free you were with the Americans."

Ursula, the horrible woman with the viper's tongue. "I was not free with the Americans, nor do I appreciate being denigrated. I had to get a job to support myself. You left me with nothing. Do you hear me. You left me with nothing. I had nowhere to live. I was on the verge of starvation."

He rose as if he couldn't stand the sight of her and left. No doubt he coughed his lungs out in the men's smoking car.

Chapter Thirty-Three

B ahamas 1947

Sophia had gathered no one would hire an ex-Nazi in Europe, let alone the rest of the world. The only position that was inclined to hire Karl was a branch of the International Paper Company in a lumber camp in the bitter end of the world—and that was out of desperation.

From an amphibious airplane, Sophia followed Karl and stepped into a dinghy that took her, and their luggage to a dock built far into the shallow water of the western shore of a remote island in the Bahamas.

She boarded with their luggage onto a strange vehicle on rails, or "popshot," that drove through a marshy, flat landscape to the eastern part of the island. Tropical heat flickered above the rails. The sun burned mercilessly on her head. A slender black man sat in a yoga position, steering the crude conveyance without uttering a word. The rails were as crooked as if a child had drawn them, with the vehicle wobbling and threatening to run off the track. Dark buzzards hovered and circled over stands of mangroves that extended far and wide into the sulphureous shallow water that covered the strange landscape. Soon, the swamp gave way to dry and rocky ground, revealing the heart of a lumber camp where several machines, a locomotive with flat trailers, and a blaring sawmill sat amidst numerous rough, tin-roofed shacks. Her shoulders dropped. Her new home was a touch between a coal miner's village and slave quarters.

"Greetings," a portly man called from his seat on the porch. "I'm Mr. Walnut, the manager of this lumber camp."

They climbed the steps to where he sat like a fat spider on his frayed wicker throne. Without rising, he shook hands with Karl, then looked Sophia up and down, unable to hide the lust in his eyes. When Karl said nothing to thwart the man's rudeness, her spirits sank further.

The shade offered by the porch was the first respite she'd had from the sun and delivered her from a menacing sunstroke. Sophia fought to stay awake. To place toothpicks in her eyes to keep them open seemed like a good idea. To lay down and sleep, better. The men droned on and on, Mr. Walnut keeping her awake by tapping his cane to emphasize every boorish point he made.

Mr. Walnut gave a final loud knock on the floor with his cane. Sophia jumped. Several large black men understood the sign and moved Sophia and Karl's suitcases ahead, signaling they should follow. Sophia stepped up a rickety wood plank stairway into a two-room shack. The men deposited their luggage and departed. Under the tremendously hot flat roof, Sophia took an inventory of their humble dwelling: an ancient double bed, thin walls riddled with rat holes, a dirty couch, a cracked mirror on the wall, and three rusty coat hangers in the closet. She didn't even want to think about unpacking. Where would she place their clothes?

Karl grunted and jerked his head. One of the black men waited to guide them to the clinic where her husband, contracted for the next five years, would begin his practice.

The clinic was nothing but a chicken coop. The outer room contained benches for patients. The second room had a splintery wooden examination table, a shelf lined with a few salve jars, bottles of alcohol and iodine. To get ventilation in the room, Sophia pushed out window shutters at the lower end and supported them with sticks. The openings let in light, but heat and flies streamed in as well.

Sophia walked out onto the porch to savor the cooling breezes.

Strange how memories stirred in fleeting moments. She had felt the love of her mother, father, and siblings, known the joy of their holiday gatherings, the fun of shoving each other into the lake, racing their horses along the deep blue river. Felt the soul-deep love of her mother when she kissed her cheek and her father's deep, abiding love delivered with a hug. Even now, she could hear the echoes of the words her parents had spoken every night before retiring to bed… *"I love you."*

Sophia wanted the affections of a family more than anything. To be cherished, protected, and loved. She placed her hand protectively on her stomach. "I will always be there for you, little one. To hold you, guide you, protect you, and love you with all my heart. Not just when you need it the most, but every day of your life. From your first breath until my last."

She tried to have faith that, someday, she could heal Karl's wounds and have a semblance of family life together. Filled with a dull melancholy, practical problems grew into mountains. Where could she cook or do laundry? What would she cook? Would they have to walk far to native settlements for supplies? Who would pay for them? The most vital pressing question was how to make a decent home for her child with the pitiful roof over their heads.

Outside the clinic, a large native woman possessing one blue and one black eye lingered with unconcealed curiosity. She began a conversation in strange English. Sophia strained to understand the combination of Old English accented with a heavy island inflection.

"My name's Queenie. If you all need help, I'm here to help. The nurse who was here before you left cause Mr. Walnut forced her to live in a pig sty. She'd been a good, helpful woman, but Mr. Walnut loathed her. He refused to get her medical supplies."

Queenie lifted her hand and gestured for Sophia to follow her. "You can leave your husband at the clinic and let him settle in while we make a tour of your new home."

Hesitant at first, Sophia looked behind at her husband who pointedly ignored her and remained transfixed on the lack of medical supplies.

"Come along, Miss." The woman laughed warmly and richly, drawing Sophia's attention, and arresting a strong desire for her to get to know the black woman.

Sophia bit her lip.

Sophia caught the strange blue eye, and before she could turn away in shyness, she was captured with a genuine grin spreading across the woman's face, turning it from ordinary into divine. In that moment, Sophia felt her body wrapped in a warm quilt. She heard Karl's harsh curse inside. Sophia stepped off the porch.

She wanted the woman with the warm smile.

Queenie was built like Renoir's *Bather Gazing at Herself in the Water,* with tiny ankles and curving calves expanding upward to a billowing overabundance of flesh. As she moved, she resembled an unmolded aspic, quivering and midnight black as soil.

Dizziness swept over Sophia, and she swayed, a hand going to her head. Queenie caught her, and arm in arm, helped her up the steps.

"My husband John is a carpenter and can build whatever you need. But the first thing we need to do is clean this place and make it presentable for the little one you're carrying."

Sophia blinked. No way did she show. "Ridiculous."

"I have the gift of sight. You don't want anyone to know about the baby, do you?" Queenie nodded. "Uh-huh. There is another."

Sophia clutched her. "You must tell no one." How did this woman who'd she'd just met know everything about her?

"Queenie knows how to keep her mouth shut."

Her wide-cheeked ebony face split with a white all-pervading smile. "Each friend is a world in us, a world not born until they arrive, and it is only by this meeting that a new world is born. You and I are going to be lifelong friends. I dreamed of our bond a year ago."

If Queenie hadn't known unusual details about her impending child, then Sophia would have believed everything the woman said was hogwash. Yet a part of Sophia hoped and prayed Queenie's words about their fated friendship were true.

With hands as big a paddles, Queenie yanked the sheets and blankets off the bed and took them outside to shake. Following a cloud of dust, Sophia stared after her, unable to grasp what the woman had told her. Was it some sort of Caribbean sorcery like the gypsies she'd known?

Queenie returned and smoothed the sheets and blankets on the bed. "Don't you worry, I use my gifts for good."

Exhaustion from the long trip took over. Sophia's skepticism melted, shifting into firm belief in the woman's words, the strange eyes that were soft, and filled with an inner glow.

"You come over here. Ol' Queenie's gonna tuck you into bed. I'll clean what I can, and then I'll leave fried plantain I made this morning. Never you mind about chores. I cook and do laundry, too."

Sophia collapsed on the bed. The woman gave her hand a light squeeze and pulled the sheets over her. Despite the wretchedness of her new environment, Sophia felt a tingling warmth in her limbs as she drifted off.

She had a friend.

Chapter Thirty-Four

"Have some more rum," Sophia offered Karl. She poured again, the bottle clinking an icy code of distress against the glasses, her fingers trembling. Two nights of fitful sleep had passed, suffering swarms of mosquitos, and a rat running across their bed.

She must begin a charade to thaw Karl. Needed to focus on the task at hand, needed to make Karl believe he was the father of the baby she carried.

He stared at her for a long time, without a word, studying her with an embittered expression of a man who is being offered a painting with a bogus signature. Something told her the stranger who now lived behind Karl's gaze was too dangerous even for her to handle. Lethal. Suspicious. The scars on the left side of his body were pronounced. The scars inside him were destructive.

Being a German-bred Nazi, Karl was not a man prone to clemency, and hers was a secret that would knock Karl's planet far out of orbit.

"Are you coming to bed?" she asked in a seductive whisper, and then cringed. What a fraud she was. She turned to their bedroom.

As a doctor, he might guess she wasn't a virgin. Prepared for the event, she had procured chicken blood from Queenie and stored the vial in between the mattresses on the side she slept.

Karl entered the room, his cigarette dangled from between his elegant surgeon fingers that swept the air in a negligible gesture. "Get undressed," he snapped.

Her chin trembled ever so slightly as she slipped her dress over her head, and then reached back and unhooked her brassiere, letting it slide to the floor. She pulled her white cotton panties down and stepped out of them. A chill replaced the warmth of her clothing.

Sophia forced herself to look into eyes as electric blue as lightning and made even more sinister because of the features into which they'd been set.

The scar tissue on the right side of his face was thick, wrinkled, making him appear decades older than the left side. The shortest of wounds branched from the light hairline at his temple and interrupted his eyebrow. His blond hair, slicked to the side by his shower did not conceal the drawn and taut webbing from high into his scalp with the longest fissure blazing across a sharp cheekbone to his compressed lips.

Only the heat in his gaze let her know the intensity that flared through his examination.

He'd caught her staring and scanned her critically like Hitler would have done a review of his troops, taking his time flattening his cigarette in a clam shell.

"Don't worry. I'll not add to your mortification by undressing." His voice turned beyond wintry. Grabbing her hand, he gripped her short fingers hard enough to snap them.

"Owww!" Sophia tugged loose her hand.

His hands manacled her arms, and before she could draw a breath of protest, he had her pushed back upon the bed and lay upon her.

"I'll never forget how you looked at the American. How many times did you spread your legs to that barbaric filth?"

Breathing heavy, she calmed herself and wriggled beneath him. His erection was hard against her stomach. Keep to the plan. She lifted her hand and caressed the good side of his face. "I waited for you to return to me, Karl," she soothed.

He was deaf to her calming words.

He reached down, opened his trousers, and yanked her legs apart, thrusting himself into her without preamble. Her body was not prepared. She screamed with the bitter pain. Karl did not care. He was teaching her a lesson. He was the master. His long German bloodlines would rule. It was an act of violence against her body and spirit. Cold indifference and power. He tore into her as if she were less than an animal, simply a thing to bear the brunt of his rage.

His breath turned into panting gasps, sucking the air like it had suddenly become thick and was too difficult to draw in. She stared at his face. The ghoulish way the tissue healed and cracked gave the appearance of melted candle wax, and dropped the right side immobile, ceding facial reactions nonexistent.

He finished and rolled away, his back to her. Sophia waited for his snores, then stretched her arm and reached between the mattresses. With no remorse for her deception, she emptied the vial of chicken blood into the center of the sheets.

Fire. Fire. He was on fire; locked in a cage, metal melting around him. His lungs were full of smoke and his limbs were shackled by fire. He thrashed. He screamed, but only a choking gas. The smoke prevented him from getting precious air.

Men screamed.

From his lips came an explosion of blisters. He lifted his hand and it melted before him, tearing flesh away from bone. Tearing life away from love. And everything he cared about away from him…his Sophia.

He raised his arms, like climbing jagged rocks. After a few seconds, his mind moved to panic. He realized he wasn't facing upwards, and he struggled perpendicular to the surface. His limbs slowed down, trapped in a current of fire. "Get up," his mind screamed. He climbed over the dead soldier next to him. Jump. Jump. His muddled mind told him to jump. His clothes melted from him. The flames licked the soles of his feet, his face, his arms, searing them, peeling the skin. He dove out a shattered window and—

"Karl…wake up…ch-choking me."

It was Sophia, gasping, sobbing. In the moonlight, her face glowed and he saw where his hands were around her neck. He snatched them back. *I'm so sorry, my love. I'm so sorry.*

Karl shook. He might have killed her. His chest pulled in lungfuls of air in great gulps. His hands trembled.

"You had a bad dream," Sophia said, coughing.

He emptied his lungs and dropped his arms. It was just a nightmare. Sophia rose, moved off the bed to light a lantern, and then poured a glass of water. She looked out the window, and beyond.

In the dim shadows, Karl stopped. Blood spotted the sheet. God, how he wanted to believe it was true. He turned and narrowed his eyes on her back. The oldest trick in the book. He was alone. Always alone.

He left the bedroom and swung open the front door. He leaned against the frame with one hand, staring into the coal black night, letting the inhospitable breeze dry the cold sweat that drenched his body.

An old, familiar rage rose inside him, strangling his breath even when awake, drowning him in a hopeless fury. He stretched his arm where the burn scars ached. He'd never be normal again.

Chapter Thirty-Five

Over the past weeks, heartbreak was very hard to live with, yet she hid it well. With Karl, her daily routine was a cruel repetition. In the morning, she longed to bury herself beneath the covers and hide from the sunlight. In the afternoon, while assisting her husband with his patients, she cried inwardly, then would rush to the washbasin to splash cool water on her face. At night, she lay down on the bed without bothering to turn on the light or open the shutters and abandoned herself to the darkness, and the sound of the rain on the tin roof. Her back to Karl, she'd squeeze her pillow, howling inside and yet silent in her agony.

She closed her eyes and tried to conjure up the image of Robert, his touch and smell. She did not blame Robert. She was an adult, and her choices were her responsibility. She wondered if things might have been different if she'd told Robert the truth earlier. Would he have turned his back on her then?

Yet despite the heartbreak, Sophia had grown into her role at the clinic. At first, she'd felt inept and frightened, and told the people she was not the kind of medical doctor they sought. Her husband would have to attend to their needs. But the people refused to listen and insisted on her. After observing Karl, Sophia took on the simpler tasks and found helping the patients rewarding.

Sophia did admire Karl's surgical skills. She saw the strain of his ropy muscles of forearms hardening and relaxing with his rhythmic movements beneath his coat. On the hottest days, even when the wind failed to come off the ocean, he dressed in navy flannel slacks, a white cotton shirt with a dark red tie, with a navy suit jacket. Only when it was unbearably hot and humid did he take off his coat.

Sophia tied off the last suture on an injured man, listening to Queenie's endless chatter on island life. From their meager earnings, they'd hired Queenie to do their washing and ironing, clean house, cook, and at times, assist in the clinic.

The carpentry skills Queenie's husband, John possessed were a godsend. He'd built windows and screens for their shack, as well as simple furniture. He constructed a fence around the perimeter, and Sophia wasted no time establishing a vegetable garden. It was difficult in the rock-laden ground, except for the "potholes" that were randomly scattered and filled with enough soil for her to plant seeds.

Getting accustomed to the lack of running water and the outhouse situated fifty yards away in the bush was a challenge. Before she collapsed into bed that night with complete exhaustion, Sophia begged Queenie if she might make something different for dinner the next night.

"In the store in the next town," said Queenie, rolling bandages, "there's only canned goods. Canned milk, corned beef and salt pork, and then old-fashioned hats. The mailboat comes once a month from Nassau, but lettuce, oranges and apples arrive destroyed by rats. If you want something new, try opening a can of pork and beans from the other end. It might taste different." At her joke, Queenie guffawed, waves of rollicking laughter that Sophia had come to love.

The familiar thump of a cane on the porch heralded Mr. Walnut's arrival. Of course, he'd turn up when Karl had gone to give medical aid to the neighboring settlement.

Sophia held her arm tight across the doorway, making him wait on the porch. Not a chance was she going to enter into a long discussion during which he made lewd suggestions to her. "Have you any word on our refrigerator, our generator, or the jeep's delivery? You can't expect Karl to walk to these far-off places or wait for your truck to be available. Of utmost importance are our medical supplies. Patients have come in large numbers with word of a doctor on the island. Sometimes, sixty to eighty a day."

Mr. Walnut studied the top of his cane, and then let his eyes dip to her bosom, fuller with her pregnancy. Launching into a lecture in his Southern dialect, he said, "You remember how I told you we can be friends here—or how things can be made difficult?"

She wished she could shove the blackmailing cur off her porch.

Despite her husband's ambitions, Sophia thanked God that Karl refused to take part in Mr. Walnut's scheme. Those who became his friend would become very rich. The natives owned beautiful property on the southern coast. He gave them jobs and embezzled timber from the company to build their houses in return for the large portions of their land they signed over to him.

After six weeks of waiting for their dwindling medical supplies to be refurbished, Sophia presumed the order had gone no further than Mr. Walnut's wastebasket. "Do you realize, Mr. Walnut, that Karl has identified numerous diseases with his stethoscope and blood pressure gauge, but cannot offer anything except advice? Do you understand the saddest cases are undernourished babies? There are seven-month-old children weighing only seven pounds. Their stomachs are hard and distended. I run to many huts to boil a brew of condensed milk, syrup, and water to feed them. We can't even dispense an aspirin!"

"That's none of my affair. Can't feed the whole world."

Mr. Walnut had had enough of her haranguing. The man

stepped off the porch to return to his wicker throne. He swung around. "Of course, if you'd like to go to your shack with me while your husband's gone, I can improve things."

Sophia unleashed a torrent of oaths in six different languages. In English, she said, "Pray you don't get sick, Mr. Walnut. A frontal lobotomy would be an improvement."

Sophia glanced at the banana trees growing next to the laundry tubs. The soapy water that was poured on them produced wonderful bananas. Next to the trees was a truck.

"Queenie, whose truck is that?"

"A friend of John's who is visiting."

"Isn't the mailboat due today?"

"I already know what you're thinking, Miss Sophia." Queenie went inside the clinic, finished bandaging the last patient, clapped on her dog-eared straw hat and slammed the door shut. "Let's go."

They drove over dusty potholed, Bahamian pine tree-lined roads, and arrived as the mailboat docked. Karl had given Sophia an explicit command not to get involved in the supply difficulties. She choked on his insistence that Mr. Walnut would provide. How naïve.

Sophia searched for the captain and inquired about the delivery of the items she had requested.

"I'm sorry, Ma'am, but Mr. Walnut said not to deliver the items."

Sophia ground her teeth together, fingering the letter she had addressed to the head of International Paper Company regarding their circumstances. "Please take this letter with you and make sure it gets mailed." She doubted if anything would come of it and prayed Karl would not find out.

Chapter Thirty-Six

Later in the week, Karl had gone to another settlement again. An old black man sat on the edge of the table with the suspicious Queenie giving him a baleful eye. "You don't look sick to me."

"You don't understand," said the man, darting a glance at Sophia. "I get headaches every time, you know, every time I lay with my wife."

Queenie snorted. "I t'ink you just need to move your head back off that headboard. Get out of here. Next."

Sophia suppressed a smile at Queenie's outrageous bedside manner.

It was Friday and, ten yards from the clinic, a lively community church used by different denominations was in full play. Today, the minister from the Holy Rollers shouted his sermon. Tuesdays were reserved for the Baptist minister who doubled as the store manager. Mondays were served by the Anglicans, and Sunday evenings were for the Catholics.

The Holy Rollers had worked themselves into a frenzy, beating the rhythm to their songs on pots and homemade drums. One of the zealous congregants ambled into the clinic with trickles of blood flowing down his head. "I jumped so high, I hit the light bulb above me."

"The boy's cheese done slid of his cracker," Queenie harangued.

Using tweezers, Sophia removed innumerable splinters of glass. She was just finishing up with the Holy Roller when Sophia heard the piercing cries of a banshee. Two men carried a very pregnant, screaming woman into the clinic. Sophia directed them to place her on the examining table. Again, her protests that she was incompetent and possessed a doctorate in zoology and not medicine were useless. No one understood.

"I'm so happy you're here," the woman panted.

Sophia closed her eyes. She'd never even seen a human delivery. To think she was expected to deliver the woman's child? The panic she felt when the Russian soldiers tried to rape her raised its dreadful head. Every memory of helplessness played over and over in her head. She struggled to fight it, calm herself, but the onslaught came in waves, the darkness engulfing and overwhelming her and there was nothing she could do to get out from under it.

The woman writhed on the table. "Help me!" she wailed, clutching at Sophia's arm.

Dear God. Sophia's blood ran cold. She flinched at the screams, her breath bursting in and out to see the woman suffer. Would that be her in the coming months?

The woman's husband hovered near Sophia. "You gotta help her, Doc."

But she wasn't that kind of doctor. Where was Karl at a time like this?

The terror of failing cut deeper than a sword. She turned away, wanting to flee.

Queenie grabbed her arm and shook her. "Get ahold of yourself, Miss Sophia. You've delivered horses. Just a little different, that's all. I understand how overwhelming it is. You must focus on life; it is so full of possibilities. Use your God-given gifts."

Like a vision, she saw the birthing stall in Michigan, Robert, a horse giving birth. Queenie's soft voice gave her strength. Adrenaline surged through Sophia's veins, fight or flight, stand or run, be a hero or a coward. Queenie's message pierced her brain.

"Uh-huh. Believe in yourself, Miss Sophia, and you're halfway there. Courage and determination. Faithful and fearless."

Sophia washed her hands and then gave words of encouragement to the expectant mother. "Breathe deeply, hold your breath, and then bear down." Soon, the head emerged, then a shoulder, followed by the baby's entire compact body, slipping out between the woman's trembling thighs.

"You have a boy," Sophia shouted, and the new mother and father cried out their joy.

Sophia tied off the umbilical cord and cut it. After washing and diapering the infant, she laid the child in the mother's arms. The baby was the woman's first child, and she glowed, examining him carefully.

Suddenly, Karl stood next to Sophia, grinning. "Good job."

Sophia almost cried. It was the first kind thing he'd said to her.

From all the excitement, a sudden cold sweat gathered on Sophia's forehead. She could feel the coffee and the few mouthfuls of beans she'd swallowed rising-up in her throat.

Karl watched her closely. "Are you sure you are all right? Your face looks as pale as a noon beach."

She shook her head and dashed outside, throwing up her breakfast. From a pump, she washed her face in tepid water and rinsed the foul bile from her mouth. Her morning sickness had returned with a vengeance. When she got back to the house, she realized that Karl stood in the doorway, studying her. Half his face was shaded, the burned part illuminated by the harsh and unforgiving noonday sun.

"Better?" he asked.

She nodded.

His burned skin mottled. The flush spread from beneath the collar of his shirt. Little twitches became apparent on his features. She saw in the lips he pulled back from his eyeteeth in the semblance of a snarl. His right eye blinked more violently than the left and a vein she'd never noticed before throbbed at his temple.

All traces of emotions vanished. He was a man, and then seemingly, a pillar of stone. Cold. Remote.

The change terrified her more than any display of temper could have.

He knew she was pregnant. He knew the child was not his.

He stepped off the porch without another word. Palmetto fans crunched loud enough to sound like bones breaking beneath his shoes.

Chapter Thirty-Seven

Alone in his shack, with the darkness surrounding him, Karl poured himself a glass of rum, went to the window and took a deep breath, his chest muscles, half-burned and ridged, tightened against his sweaty long-sleeved shirt. Even in the heat of the Bahamas, he wore a long-sleeved shirt every day to hide the burns on the left side of his body. His face was bad enough without revealing the freak show on the rest of his body.

Though accustomed to the refined fruity-spicy taste of German schnapps, he drank the homemade Caribbean concoction distilled from sugar cane and let it sear down his throat. He grimaced. Diesel fuel. Couldn't even get decent alcohol in this godforsaken tail end of the world. He stepped out onto the edge of the porch. The hot humid night breezes did not cool him. *I'm in hell*, he thought. *No escape.*

Dr. Karl Schneider, top of his class surgeon, receiving accolades for his work with the Third Reich, and from an elite, highly respected German family, scraped by in the Bahamas.

A night hawk swooped by like the first American plane that had bombed his train, an aircraft that had been followed by count-less others—as many as the night stars that mocked him. His train had been loaded with thousands of soldiers, tanks, trucks, and military hardware heading to Saint Lô to quell the massive and formidable Allied invasion tearing across the continent from Normandy. Hitler had ordered a quarter of a million men to the western front and the Germans faced the grim reality of fighting the war on two fronts. Karl's loyalty to Hitler slipped and, unlike his fanatical comrades, he feared the foolishness of the Führer that day. His beloved Germany was doomed.

The explosion had seared the air and the earth, leaving nothing but a void where the life he'd known had been, his torment during those long painful months of rehabilitation in the hospital fearing that his beautiful young wife would never accept him. Now, his German pride had been attacked. She had been unfaithful to him, and he could not accept her infidelity. How he wished he'd taken her in Berlin. Yet he believed the act would be too much for her innocence and he did not wish to leave her with child in case the worst happened to him. How he regretted that decision. To stamp his mark on her.

What made her betrayal hurt so much was the pain, frustration, anger...and that still he loved her.

She hadn't come outright and said the baby was the American's. But he could see it in her eyes. And he was not a man to raise the by-blows of another. Hell. He couldn't have children. He could have sex—but the fires had burned his nuts and the doctors said he'd have no bullets to produce a progeny.

Chapter Thirty-Eight

In the wee hours of Sunday morning and still dark, Sophia rose to answer a knock at the door. Old Ben stood on the porch, shifting from foot to foot. She knew him well as she'd seen him repairing the crooked rails. He bowed his graying head and shuffled his feet, embarrassed.

"Doc, I can't pass no water," he said shyly.

Sophia's stomach clenched. Karl had accompanied a sick patient to Nassau on a chartered seaplane. "I've catheterized women before, but never a man."

"I need help," Ben persisted.

Sophia took a deep breath, tied on her robe over her large belly, and led the way to the clinic. She prepared all the sterile instruments and laid them on the table, and then sat down next to Ben, seated on the examination table. How in the world was she going to do this?

Quietly, he lifted his head. "Doc, don't feel bad, you is a woman and I is a man. Dat's de only difference. We both is people."

"It is a problem for me. You must tell me if I do something wrong because I've never done this before on a man."

Biting her lip, she inserted the catheter, easily at first, then met resistance. Ben groaned. She poked around, trying to find the passage. Suddenly, the catheter slipped in, and to her horror, a cupful of bloody fluid ran into the basin between his thighs.

"I've hurt you."

Ben sighed. His facial features relaxed. "Always a little blood comes first. You did just right. Thank you, Doc."

When Ben left, Sophia returned home and sat on her front porch step. In the mornings, she could not stay in bed and was up early, like the days of her home in Zachwyt, creeping out of the house on tiptoe. Even the incessant sound of the saws could not spoil her morning hours.

An emerald-green hummingbird with vibrating wings took nectar from an opening scarlet hibiscus blossom, while smoke wafted over the native huts. It smelled like the potato fires in East Prussia, with the pigs grunting and squealing, awaiting their feed. The sun rose peacefully above the pine crests. It would be a hot day but at this early hour, the fresh morning breeze felt cool without stirring up the dust that often blanketed the lumber camp like a cloud of fog. Dew had fallen during the night and before it evaporated by the sun, the air smelled spicy and clean.

Queenie joined her with steaming bowls of souse, a Bahamian soup made of chicken wings, broth, and a dash of allspice and hot pepper.

"You should be resting on your day off," Queenie cautioned.

Sophia dipped her spoon into her soup. "I couldn't let Ben suffer."

"Your husband does enough to make you suffer."

Sophia grimaced. With the excessive lime juice, the soup tasted bitter. "Nonsense."

Queenie snorted. "I'm not dead. I see with my own eyes. I see you stare off to the coast and beyond. Those are dreams you hold."

Sophia sighed. "Only dreams. Only choices. I blame Karl's

impassiveness on the infidelity of my thoughts. I cannot be happy."

"You are wrong. He treats you badly."

"I do like Karl and forgive him. He has cared for me. There is nobility in his actions. He is illogical, unreasonable, and self-centered. I like him anyway." She often rekindled the time in Berlin when Karl pursued her and reawakened that gentle Karl in her heart.

"His bedside manner is less than to be desired," Queenie added.

Sophia had tried to soften his outbursts, the way he bullied people, and the fact that he was always right. "I admire him for his great surgical skills. I think he is frustrated because with additional equipment, he could do so much more."

Sophia found herself defending her husband, but perhaps there was another rationale. She shifted her gaze to the sawmill where the saw screamed day and night, piercing like the guilt that slashed at her every day. There was only one reason for telling the truth about the baby, but for lying—the number was infinite. The impending arrival had become a dance of unsaid intimations and ambiguities.

Queenie drank the rest of the contents from the bowl, then set it down. "Forgiving the heel of the shoe that crushes a beautiful orchid? You have a big heart, Miss Sophia. I wouldn't do it."

"We must always forgive, to overlook, to forget. Because if we don't, we are tying rocks to our feet."

"Liking a man is different from loving," Queenie huffed. "You are worthy of so much more."

"There it is! The baby moved." Sophia planted her hand on her belly and grinned from ear to ear. The miracle of life blossoming in her had become real.

Queenie moved her big arm around her and gave Sophia a hug. "You focus on that baby. That is where your real love will come from."

Chapter Thirty-Nine

As the months passed and she had no response from International Paper Company, Sophia began to lose hope that they would ever get the medical supplies that their patients needed. Except for the generosity of a Miami doctor supplying them from time to time, they worked with nothing.

Stirring up a cloud of dust, loaded trucks and a jeep pulled into the community. Sophia followed Karl out onto the porch and watched two men enter Mr. Walnut's home. Slamming his door, the portly manager stormed out of his home, steamed down his steps, and pointed his flaccid finger in Karl's chest. "You got me fired. I had a good arrangement..."

Karl put his hands up. "I have no idea what you are talking about."

Two men flanked Mr. Walnut. "You will leave with us, Walnut, and not hassle these good people. You have no one to blame for your dismissal but yourself. Embezzlement has consequences. You'll be lucky if you don't face jail time."

Walnut was led away.

Another man left the back of his jeep, strode up to Karl and Sophia and said, "The president of International Paper Company,

Mr. Howard Smith, sends his regrets that he's not able to meet you in person, Dr. and Mrs. Schneider. Yet he's sent you with two truckloads of supplies. He is very happy with your work. Can you round up some men to unload?"

Sophia moved in front of Karl, her heart brimming with joy. "Men, unload these trucks!" she commanded.

After all these months? Sophia's heart swelled with joy. She shook the man's hand enthusiastically. "I'm Sophia Schneider. Please tell Mr. Smith how thankful we are. The islanders will be able to get the medical attention they need."

Karl started prying open the unloaded crates and like a kid at Christmas, he said, "See, Sophia, all we had to do was wait and the company provided."

Queenie put her hands on her broad hips. "Yes, sir. All we had to do was lay down and wait for the Almighty to bestow his gifts."

Sophia rolled her eyes, and then continued to unpack the medical supplies, ordering the men from the sawmill to carry the needed items into the clinic. In addition to all the bandages, medicines and medical equipment were canned food items, a crate of wine, refrigerator, generator, fuel, and an x-ray machine.

She planted a fist in her back and massaged. The ache increased daily with her expanding girth. Karl sped off into the clinic to organize their bounty, never knowing the shipment was due to her actions.

"Ma'am," said the gentleman. "Mr. Smith said a jeep will be arriving in a month or two."

Sophia threw her arms around him. "Tell Mr. Smith thank you from the bottom of my heart."

Chapter Forty

Karl swallowed a pang of guilt when he watched Sophia. She was nearly at term and even under the loosely flowing nightgown and robe she was wearing, the bulge was huge and clumsy. She'd always had such a delicate way of walking and now she was forced to balance herself painfully; belly protruding, pace careful, as she went from room to room. Nature had provided women with a kind of necessary lunacy for them to desire to bring children into the world, he thought.

Pregnancy had rounded Sophia's face, and she no longer looked like a schoolgirl. Placid and womanly, her face glowed softly in the sunlight. She was much larger than most pregnant women.

Despite her being near her time, he'd not examined her once during her pregnancy. He could not touch her, knowing the child to be born was someone else's.

She didn't sleep well with the additional load, and he had heard her complain to Queenie that the baby wore paratrooper boots and was at war, stomping on her bladder.

Why wasn't the baby his?

"I'm leaving the island for a few weeks," he said. He saw her quick intake of breath, but she said nothing.

Queenie's snowy white teeth gritted, and her hands folded into tight elephantine balls. "Do you think that is a good idea with your wife being so far gone. She gonna need you, I t'ink."

Queenie would always remind him of what was right. "I believe you two can manage until I come back. I have necessary business in Nassau. I'll be home in time in any event."

Queenie pursed her lips and shook her head with stony hostility. "You don't know if she will have a bad time of it. She's way big. Too long to get back to the island if she's in trouble."

"It is none of your business what is between me and my wife," Karl snapped. His departure was a deliberate act. He didn't want to be around when the child was born. Hopefully, it would be stillborn. Perhaps then, he could start over with Sophia.

Sophia kneaded the middle of her back. Was she having contractions? He resisted the urge to move to her. Better hurry along.

A sudden change took place. Sophia straightened and lifted her head, wreathed in her thoughts which gave her an otherworldly quality. She looked at Queenie, and then straight at him. "I can take care of myself."

Women were supposed to be delicate creatures. Like seashells and flower petals. Easy to shatter and crush and reject. Convenient, pretty. Short-lived.

If this was so, Sophia was a flower made of steel. He admired and hated her for it.

Karl picked up his bag and stepped off the porch. Small barefooted children with shiny black faces, worn shorts and shirts played on sandy lawns, burgeoning with the first frail green of spring. A young woman in a worn dress hoisted a baby on her hip. An old dog dozed on the warm threshold of a plank cabin that was painted white with green shutters. A worker waved at Karl. He didn't wave back. A foreman waited for him in front of the lumber offices. Karl hopped in a truck to be taken to the dock.

A twinge of guilt passed through him. Sophia could die giving birth to a baby that large. Cuckolding him was a filthy slander and an unforgiveable insult. What would the Führer have done? Hitler would never accept the inferior bloodlines of an American scum.

Karl didn't look back.

Chapter Forty-One

Karl's truck vanished, enveloped in a sea of dust.

Against Queenie's protests, Sophia went to the clinic to sterilize gloves, instruments, and syringes, thinking about how much she'd matured. She had stepped into a new and daunting world, far from her realm of experience. She'd taken on midwife duties with Queenie, bandaged wounds, given intravenous and intramuscular injections, and helped Karl extract teeth. This part of her would never be lonely because she'd discovered a purpose in being useful, compassionate, and making a difference by healing people.

Her transformation blossomed like a lotus flower, emerging from the mud, bright and lovely, and reigning supreme. Sophia had lifted herself beyond past pain, clear of fear and vulnerability, rising to beautify the shadows and darkness.

But could she navigate childbirth herself? Didn't every woman experience that nagging uncertainty before delivery? She pressed a trembling hand to her stomach. She was so large.

A short time later, Sophia's water broke, pooling at her feet. Queenie clucked like a mother hen, slamming the door to the clinic, and ushering her to their shack and into bed.

"Queenie, what am I going to do? Karl is not here."

"To the devil with Dr. Karl."

"It's my fault, Queenie," she panted, as Queenie placed a cotton nightgown over her head.

"Alls I gotta say is Dr. Karl is a terrible bully. He's afraid of the world. He's afraid of you."

Pain wracked Sophia's back as if someone had taken an ax and chopped at her spine.

"The way Karl is—" The contractions were getting closer, taking her breath away.

Queenie, her hands, dark on top, pink on bottom, always soft, swept Sophia's hair back. "Don't you worry about nothing except that baby coming into the world. That's all that matters. Dr. Karl is a prideful man and wants to control you with guilt. These old eyes see a lifetime of pain. We are all a mass of vulnerabilities, but not you, Miss Sophia. You are so much smarter and cleverer."

Sophia tried to sort through what Queenie had disclosed but with each contraction came a pain that dominated her entire being. In those moments, for those eternal seconds that stretched into infinity, there was nothing else.

"You can do this," Queenie coaxed.

Sophia screamed with another contraction. "Why is Karl not here?"

"By the time we radio him, and he gets back, you'll be all done. You don't need Dr. Karl. Never did."

"I need a doctor." Sophia pressed her head back into the pillow with another breathtaking contraction.

"You don't need no doctor. Women been giving birth from time until eternity. I have delivered enough babies with you to know what to do."

When the pain passed, it was only for a minute, and she closed her eyes, breathing deep, unwilling to engage with life outside her body. Only the whispered reassurances from Queenie kept her going. Time passed without her keeping track. Her stomach tightened. When would the agony subside? Nothing could be more brutal.

She felt the baby crowning, the hot stretching of her flesh and held her breath.

"Push, Miss Sophia. Push."

Sophia lay exhausted. Faint and sweating, she screamed, "Robert."

When her baby slipped out into Queenie's hands, she heard the baby's lusty cry.

"You have a boy."

The joy of a million angels entered in the room, but the sunshine stopped when her body became wracked with another pain.

"Dear Lord," she heard Queenie say as she lay the squalling infant on the bed next to Sophia. "Push again, Miss Sophia."

The baby slid out. Queenie cut and tied the umbilical cords, and then gave the babies over to their mother.

The instant love Sophia held for her two precious sons made the pain a fleeting memory as their nascent eyes opened and their little mouths rooted for milk.

Queenie cleaned Sophia up, placed a new cotton gown over her, and then tidied up the room. "What are you going to name them?"

Queenie helped her position pillows, helping Sophia so she could nurse both babies at once. While the infants noisily suckled, Sophia said. "Kurt and Michael. What do you think?"

"Alleluia!" Queenie shouted. "They are fine, strong names. Like stars to the sky, your sons will be to the world. Oh, how they will shine in your life."

Chapter Forty-Two

Sophia took a tray of food from Queenie and the newspaper. She had just nursed the boys and they slept in their new cradles that John had made. "You are spoiling me, Queenie. I don't know what I'd do without you."

"Never you mind. You up all night caring for those young ones and need your rest if you're gonna produce enough milk." Queenie padded to the infants. "Those boys of yours sleep like there is no tomorrow except for when they are hungry. Whoo-ee! I've never heard such loud caterwauling."

"No word from Mr. Karl. I checked at the manager's office," Queenie said sourly.

Despite the urgent radio calls to Karl, he'd been gone for a week with no communication. From Karl's desertion, Sophia's emotions swung wildly from anger to disgust to sadness. All she had ever hoped for was a family.

Sophia snapped out the paper to read while Queenie tidied the room and oohed and aahed over the babies. Sophia turned the page and her heart stopped. Robert and his smiling new bride, Cynthia Roessler, were pictured. A bitter agony welled up within her. She wanted to crawl up in a ball and cry. How could Robert have married Cynthia, knowing his contempt for the socialite? Sophia's hands fisted around the paper, finding it incomprehensible that he surrendered to the machinations of his mother.

She folded the paper and tossed it to the foot of the bed.

"What's wrong?" asked Queenie.

"Burn it. I never want to see it again."

Sophia heard Karl's familiar tread coming up the front steps and looked at Queenie. Queenie scooped up the paper and tucked it beneath her arm. "Mr. Karl, good to see you home. Look at your two fine sons."

Karl's icy gaze fixed on the dark hair of the twins. His lip curled in a sneer. "Why has the clinic been closed all this time?"

Queenie placed her hands on her hips. "You can't expect Miss Sophia to run the clinic. Not after delivering twins."

"Get out. This is between me and my wife."

Karl stepped nearer, closing the space between Sophia and him, until he could whisper harshly and be sure to be heard. "I'm not supporting the bastards. You will have to work double hard to earn your keep, and theirs."

She squeezed her eyes shut and swore she heard Karl mutter as he stomped out of the house how he wished they had died.

Chapter Forty-Three

A storm arrived with palm trees swishing every which way. Sophia became the fronds quaking in the whirlwind, with no idea where she was being blown.

Karl with his German temperament, wounded pride—his mercurial character, the alternation of speed and gravity, of fire and melancholy, the intense upswings and the sudden dark moods that followed. In conversations, they both edged around the issue like skillful navigators skirting reefs near the water's surface. Was it the war? His wounds? Her punishment? She must be patient, she told herself.

"Is my company not pleasing? Do you despise me? Tell me." Karl demanded.

"No, no." *No, not at all, you can go right on being the way you are. I can't force myself into this role, to feel at ease. I feel humiliated and insulted, degraded.*

Her gut kicked as her body reacted to the memory of when he came home after she'd delivered the twins. Not once had he shown any love or fatherly instinct to her sons, ignoring them completely. To believe he seemed disappointed they had not died was unthinkable.

Her hands shook with his apathy, but another part of her raged for his continued martyrdom. He was not the only one who had suffered yet had made it plain no one was to speak of the war.

Her laughter came with an edge. Despite Karl being her husband, he so reminded her of the Russians. "You never asked me what I went through during the dark days after the war. You cannot imagine the nightmare of Berlin. There were over a hundred thousand rapes."

Karl abandoned his coffee cup to the table. "You will not speak of such things."

She pointed a finger at him. "Why are women forbidden to mention the subject of rape as if it somehow dishonors men? Are we to bury the subject because our violation offends you?"

"It is not proper."

"No German men helped us when we were attacked. They were too worried about saving their own skins. Cowards. Where were you, Karl, when I needed protection? Yet you coldly stand there and dare to point an accusatory finger at me? I'm forbidden to mention the subject of rape because it dishonors and upsets you? You are just like all the other proud German men preferring to be impotent onlookers when the Russians claimed their spoils of war."

"Say nothing more." The glow from the oil lamp sculpted the angular features of the scarred side of his face in amber and fiery scarlet hues.

Her teeth clenched tight, her jaw aching. "I was attacked. I survived. I survived because a woman helped me to escape. She died at the hands of my attackers. From then on, I survived on my own."

Karl took off his belt and put aside his jacket, all in slow motion, with sideways glances at her. Sophia waited. Her one-year-old boys were asleep in their crib in a new adjoining room. Her palms sweated. *I want to help him. I don't want to help him.*

He asked her something and she didn't hear nor reply. She let another few minutes go by without saying a word, looking at the gray that crossed the lumber yard during the downpour, praying that one of the lumbermen would have a stomach complaint, come in and rescue her from their poisoned silence.

"Give me your hand."

He led her into the bedroom.

Should she call herself a whore? Karl silently did it every day, every night. Trying to prove to her that he was a man, but his arousal—rock hard at first, and then—sometimes petered out.

Sophia traded her body to protect her boys. He could strip her of everything; shelter, food, livelihood. It was likely she deserved it, guilty of the sin of a colossal lie.

Why was she being so moralistic? She might feel as if she were prostituting herself, but hers was not the first marriage without love. Didn't her ancestors have arranged marriages? But this was different—Karl's contempt for her, even as he tried to take her body. The memory of Robert's passionate lovemaking, then his rejection and disgust. No, never would she claim to be a prostitute. But being used this way stood against her nature, wounded her self-esteem—and pride and made her physically miserable.

Chapter Forty-Four

Michigan 1948

For over a year, Sophia's hands had written a curse on Robert's skin that wasn't to be broken. She had stolen his heart, his breath, and his sleep. He'd been haunted by echoes, the color of voices, the rhythm of footsteps. How he wished she'd never stop speaking, that her voice would wrap itself around him forever, that time would turn backward to Berlin and that moment when she belonged to him.

What had Sophia said once? To look forward to the future. What future? He married Cynthia on the rebound. What a tragedy.

After the scandal with Sophia, Robert retreated from the world. Cynthia had been there for him. She'd been sweet, sympathetic, faultless, a real gem in assisting him with his campaign. Robert had dragged his feet popping the question because he wasn't sure what he wanted with Sophia still stuck in his mind. But that chapter was over. With Cynthia's beauty, the benefit of aligning their families to cement his senatorial bid, he partly warmed to the plan.

"Time to move on," everyone said.

A chunk of charred wood fell in the fireplace grate. Cinders flew up the chimney then floated down. He felt dead inside. What was there to life? Why bother? He sat down, hummed a tune from his childhood days. In the distance, he could see Sophia's cottage, the windows boarded up. He had let no one in there.

When he finished the bottle of scotch, he threw the decanter into the fireplace. It shattered, like his life. His shoes snapped across his marble foyer. Outside, it was dark and still raining. The wind had freshened. He kicked an urn and watched it roll down the steps where it crashed in a shadow of dirt and dried ferns.

He limped toward the river.

The river was rough with whitecaps, and made a sucking, rushing sound as it swept past. The wharf was protected by a curling jetty and the water there was calm. He remembered feeding ducks with Sophia there. How a simple activity gave her so much joy.

At the end of the dock, he stopped. Watched the swirling miasma of dark water. It would be so easy to step off. To be caught in the wild rapid current. To freeze to death within minutes. Perhaps his body would be found on the shores of the Detroit River or wash up on Zag Island or maybe as far as Lake Erie.

He pictured the newspaper headlines. Robert Pratt commits suicide. Thirty-one years of age. Genius of Pratt Motors. War hero, celebrated senator hopeful and great philanthropist from Michigan drowns in icy waters. He stood there a long time, the icy rain beating down on his face and inside his collar.

Thoroughly soaked and numb to the cold, he turned and walked back to his empty mansion.

Chapter Forty-Five

Bahamas 1950

With the jeep from the president of International Paper Company, Sophia, Queenie, John, and her eighteen-month-old sons made weekend explorations through pine forests to the coast. The day was magnificent; the skies electric blue, and a crystal breeze carried the cool scent of the sea. She pulled her straw hat down against the high sun, hoping the clouds in the distance would blow this way to give her shade. The incredibly transparent sea with a variety of exquisite colors, ranging from glassy green to light turquoise to the famous Nassau blue normally lifted her spirits.

There were days when Karl had softened like his old self before the war. Today, he jumped in the jeep, and then Sophia saw the darkness return, and he abruptly left without a word. How she wished Karl had come, at least pretended to be a family.

But then, didn't her whole life feel like a lie? She couldn't seem to conjure anything but melancholy, despite the rich scents of briny sea air, pink-sand beach, and jasmine, and the happiness of her sons splashing at the water's edge.

"Mama! Mama!" her boys called, lifting handfuls of sand onto each other.

With every day that passed, they looked more and more like their biological father with the thick dark hair and sea-green eyes. Experiencing them having fun was what she ardently desired yet couldn't bring herself to enjoy. Her melancholy told her she couldn't ask for a hug, reach for the sunshine, or take a walk among the soft hymn of palms, or hear the wind play in the fronds.

She wandered off into the shadows of palm trees and Casuarinas, hauling her shadow like a nun's veil. It was hot and the humidity made the air sweat with damp.

She occupied a world where Robert Pratt existed...and rather than a joy, it was an amplified maze of sadness she couldn't navigate through. A wall of obstacles built by wicked fates.

For a while, she played the "if" game. If only she hadn't married Karl. If only Robert hadn't married Cynthia. If only Judith didn't exist. How Sophia had mastered the art of being alone. How lives of those she loved separated from her own, when the only beating heart on this patch of beach belonged to her. There were days when her brain had become cold fire or panic. She played the "if" game again. If only to possess a magic wand to wave away the loneliness but the intoxicating insanity that let her dream of life with Robert threatened to take her over the edge.

<h1 style="text-align:center">Chapter Forty-Six</h1>

The morning made a rose-colored puzzle out of the Bahamian landscape. A rising sun of brightly glowing pinks and oranges with a strand of indigo scorched the sky and seemed to falter on the horizon. Coconut pollen drifted, sickly sweet on the air. The stone heat of the day spiraled upwards to a sullen torridness as Sophia walked up the steps in the smoldering wind and into the waiting room.

The rum fumes hit her from across the room. Karl had been heavily drinking, the silent reprimand in his bearing shouting volumes. On a desk, a newspaper was spread wide with the headlines, "Robert Pratt. Automotive magnate and war hero won Michigan's senatorial race." Karl tapped his toe, the staccato as deafening as a bass drum. He had left the dreaded newspaper with Robert's smiling picture with his bride, Cynthia, to see her reaction.

Her limbs shook and Sophia managed a weak smile to the patients in the waiting room, sitting on the benches, waving woven palmetto fans to cool their faces. She prayed Karl would not make a scene in front of so many people.

He grabbed her by the arm, dragged her into the examination

room and slammed the door. The burn scars on his neck and face rose thicker and harsher and glowed brilliant white in the shadows.

Sophia's eyelids peeled wide, and she took a step back, tugging against his hold. "I don't understand."

"No?" Karl's visage darkened. He pointed to the examination table.

She glanced at the rough wooden surface. "There are people in the waiting room—"

"I don't give a damn."

"Karl," she whispered, her mind searching for a way out. She struggled against his grip, kicked him.

Karl swore. "You are *my* wife."

He didn't give Sophia a chance to answer as he pushed her face down on the examination table, holding her with the coldness and efficiency of a man accustomed to the task. With a strong hand between her shoulder blades, he pressed her chest against the surface. "Karl, this is not you."

She gasped out a cry of pain as the sharp edge bit into her hip bones.

"Spread your arms," he commanded.

So stunned by the pain, so frightened with the brutality, Sophia complied. The door was unlocked, and she prayed no one would enter. And if she lay quiet enough, no one would know. Closing her eyes, he threw up her skirt, and tore her panties. A whisper of cool air touched her backsides.

He barked gutturally in her ear. "You are my wife and will obey."

"Karl," she whispered. "Please, you don't have to—"

"You're going to remember this."

"No." The rasping protest ripped out of her once again as she reared back and did her best to escape.

His hand clamped on the back of her neck, banging her back over the table with such force that her cheek ground against the wood.

Humiliation stabbed her more than the pain.

Remain calm she told herself. Reason with him. "Please." She struggled to lift her head. "Let me up. You're hurting me."

"Did you squirm beneath your American lover, beg him so prettily." His question was spoken harshly in German, punctuated with hard rasping sounds.

His shadow covered hers, engulfed her.

"Did you? No. You probably lay there like a bitch in heat, spreading your legs for him. How many others did you spread for? You were not a virgin when I married you."

The unwelcomed heat of his breath on her neck nauseated her. He licked her cheek and ear, the rum fumes revolting, the utter degradation unsheathing a fierce response of which she'd not believed herself capable. "Let me go."

He used his bulk to pin her to the table. His body melded over hers. Chest to her upper body, hip to hip.

"Be still," he commanded. "We don't want an interfering patient to come into the room and find you in such dishabille. I will tell the patient you insisted. That you begged for me to be rough. That he can watch if he desires. That they all can watch."

"They won't believe you."

"No? This is a small island. Gossip feeds as fast as fire through a canebrake."

"They will see it as rape."

His drunken laugh filled the room. "A husband raping his wife?"

His logic stilled her.

He reached between them, grappled with his trousers. His cock was hard as he probed her backsides. No way would she allow him to take her. Not like this. Frantic noises emitted from her, swearing at him in several different languages, begging and pleading, anything to break through his drunken rage.

"Fight me all you like," he snarled into her ear.

With a breath pinned in her lungs, she braced for his rigid

entry. She was not prepared. His hard cock probed her backsides. She bucked and reared.

Impatient, he shoved her legs farther apart and, with rough fingers, spread her folds, his fingers poking into her soft tissue.

He made a growling sound in the back of his throat, and with one thrust, he rammed into her, sheathing himself completely. A white-hot bolt of agony pierced her to her womb.

From the searing burn, she bit down on her wrist and to muffle the cries coming from her own throat and the stranger's voice grunting words she couldn't understand. He slammed into her again and again. Starbursts of pain swelled between her legs.

Sophia watched her breath condensate in a white cloud on the polished table in a fading fog, and then completely recede with every agonizing inhale.

If only she just stopped breathing.

Her nails dug into her palms. It would not be long, she told herself. Time meant nothing when losing one's dignity. One's saneness. One's identity.

Her eyes scanned the examination room. How odd the remotest things crammed into her purview. The bottles of medicines haphazardly lined on shelves, a twisted stethoscope like a rubbery snake suspended from a beam, a cracked ceramic water basin, wooden tongue depressors jampacked in a jar, a dented bedpan, the stench of lingering ether and alcohol, and the bitter taste of her own blood on her lips.

Minutes later, he went limp. He backed off, adjusted his pants. She resisted the urge to curl up in a ball, to shriek out her pain. Instead, she rose and pushed her dress down, glaring at him with triumph for predictably as in the past, he could not maintain his erection. She'd not be beaten.

Karl had a sorrowful, resigned look as he picked up her torn panties, evidence of the rage that now left him.

She felt no pity for him, picked up a sharp scalpel and thrust it to his face. "You ever touch me again, I swear, I will leave you."

He backed away. She saw the alarm and sadness in his eyes as her threat registered.

He threw her panties in the waste basket, and then went to the office door and swung it open. His eyes made a sweep of the shocked people who were waiting to see him, like the beam of a lighthouse, sightless, casting shadows.

"Get back to work," he ground out to Sophia.

Were they to continue with the fiction between them? No.

"Remember what I said," she whispered beneath her breath. "If you touch me again, I'll leave you."

With her head held high, she walked out, ignoring the pain between her legs and all the patients' horrified looks. Her hair was askew, and her cheeks burned. No doubt, they had heard his grunts and the banging of the examination table.

She walked onto a forest path, kept on walking for miles. The shadow of a little cloud raced down it, like an animal running. She reached a deserted beach. The sunlight fell through the palms in narrow swaths. She brushed her hair back from her face and lifted her head to a cooling breeze, allowing the roar from the ocean to penetrate her abused body.

Suddenly, with mysterious precision, she felt a different hand burrowing into her hair, the hand of her lover. *Robert.* She felt something swelling, churning, erupting inside her. Tears came streaming out of her eyes. She beat her hands against the rough bark of a Poinciana tree until her hands bled. The flaming scarlet blossoms showered her head and shoulders, creating a blood-red swath on the ground. She howled into the tree.

Her knuckles smarting, she dropped to her knees and dug into the sand. Pain dulled her perceptions. Robert would never again be in her life. Scraping up the Poinciana flowers, she buried them, and with them, she buried Robert.

Chapter Forty-Seven

Bahamas 1953

Sophia listened to Karl's rants, hoping his dark temper would soon subside. He'd brought out the newspaper of Senator Pratt again to torture her.

"I know those boys are Pratt's, not mine."

Sophia slammed the cupboard door. "Hush, Karl! I'm not going to go through this again. The boys are playing outside and may hear you. They are your sons. They love you. You are the only father they have ever known."

"How dare you try to foist them off on me. They are Pratt's brats."

Queenie cleared her throat and appearing beside her was five-year-old, Kurt. "Mama, come outside and see what I made."

Sophia felt the color drain from her face, glancing to Queenie. It was the second time Kurt had been present during an argument. She prayed the boys did not hear their heated quarrels through the thin walls at night.

Sophia smoothed her hand over Kurt's dark head. "Of course. I can't wait to see it."

Once outside, Kurt hauled a clumsily built contraption created out of scrap wood. "What do you think of my wagon?"

Sophia heard Karl follow her and flop in a porch chair behind her. She took a deep breath, so proud of Kurt's endeavor and refusing to let Karl blight her son's enthusiasm. "Fantastic. You built this all by yourself?" she asked searching his young face for any signs of stress.

"Papa, will you help me finish my wagon?"

As usual, Karl replied with an anemic shake of his head. He remained seated on the porch and stared at the boy as if it were painful to him, his eyes lost, and his hands pressed on the arms of his chair.

Michael carried a pot-cake, or mongrel puppy, covered with mange up to Karl. "Papa, can you help the doggie?"

"I'm not interested in the mangy curs you bring home. I've more important things to do."

Michael's green eyes shimmered with tears and he swore, mimicking the language of the lumbermen. It was the first time Sophia had heard him use such language.

"Do not talk like that," Karl snapped. "I forbid it. You will not bring shame on my name."

Sophia sat on the porch step and pulled the puppy into her arms. She always shielded her sons from Karl's belligerent outbursts. "Let me have a look."

She spread a neem ointment over the puppy's skin. "Keep him clean and place this ointment on him every day. Soon, he'll be as good as new." Michael threw his arms about her and hugged her. How she relished those tiny arms around her. A shadow crossed over her and she looked up.

The lumber camp foreman tapped his foot. "Dr. Schneider, I'm sorry, but I must complain about the behavior of your sons. One of the boys was on the very top of the fire tower. That's a big drop to the ground. Other times, they are playing too close to the saw blade. You must talk to them."

Stimulated by the Western films shown outdoors every Saturday night, the boys played cowboys with their friends climbing over the stacked logs or darting between the stacked planks and tractors. Sophia's heart climbed into her throat when she had discovered Kurt atop the eighty-foot fire tower. She had given him a good paddling. Her Kurt, with nine lives and his swashbuckling ways, would be the death of her. It was always Kurt pushing the boundaries, jumping off cliffs before finding the depth of the ocean. Thank God, Michael was more cautious, holding his twin back. Her heart would break if anything happened to either of them.

Karl's brows drew together in a scowl. "You disappoint me, Kurt. I had hoped that time and misfortune would have made you wiser."

Sophia, having enough of Karl's insults toward the boys, rose and faced him. "The fingers of your censure curl back and point to you."

From her rebuke, Karl moved past her, stepping off the porch and into the lumber yard.

Queenie came out of the house with a dustmop and said in her throaty torch-song voice, said, "Tell that husband of yours not to get his bowels in an uproar over those boys. Boys will be boys."

Queenie and John remained childless, but Queenie loved the twins like her own, and would defend and protect them to her dying day.

A well-endowed young black woman, wearing bright red lipstick, raced over to Karl with a plate of cinnamon buns, her hips swaying. She'd been pestering Karl for a while.

Queenie banged the dustmop on the porch railing, dust flying everywhere. "No, sir, you don't want to eat her buns. Even with butter spread on them, they are like limestone rock."

"You don't think he's—"

Queenie snorted like a baby calf. "Nothing could be more laughably tragic."

"Perhaps he has strayed with his thoughts, but not really strayed. Pride is the anchor around his neck."

"That's a pretty big anchor. It clamps him down to the ocean bottom."

Palm up, Sophia spread her hand. "I thought love could mend our relationship. But it's like trying to hold water in splayed fingers."

Queenie sat quietly beside her.

"I'm gutless really," Sophia continued. "I've been cheating Karl by not loving him as a wife should. Love needs honesty and truth, but I can't be honest. I must protect the boys. Most of all, I've cheated myself."

"As far as I'm concerned, the way he talks to those boys, and you, someone should knock that man down and throw lime over him."

"You will not speak of my husband like that." Sophia said.

"You are still a beautiful woman and deserve the love of a good man. Let me ask you a question. What do you think would happen if the boys' real father ever found out he had sons? What then?"

Sophia inhaled sharply. Would Robert take them from her? No. Never would he find them in this remote corner of the world. "Ridiculous. Karl is their father."

Queenie raised a knowing brow. "Life has a way of catching up."

Sophia's mind floated like dust. Her existence depended on her husband.

"You live in denial."

"To prevent my illusion from being destroyed and feeling more guilt, anxiousness and shame? I used to despise ambivalence; now I revere it. Ambivalence is my noblest companion."

"Sometimes men never die when you want them to."

"You must not say such things. Karl is insecure and afraid. Of this, I know."

Queenie scrunched up her black face. "I can't remember his

last spontaneous show of affection."

"I'm going insane. That is what is happening. Insanity." Sophia looked over the camp. A happy couple sat on their porch shelling beans. An innocent teenage girl held hands with her beau. A grandmother rocked a baby. Secure women with the love of their men. *That is not me,* Sophia thought.

Queenie looked at her in silence, gave Sophia an empathetic smile, and then went into the house, returning with plates of bacon, lettuce, and tomato sandwiches on cornbread.

Sophia climbed back up on the porch and sat down on a bench beside Queenie. Everything was made with cornmeal, a cheap staple in the Bahamas; cookies, cakes, cinnamon rolls.

Queenie's face glimmered with concern. "You can care for your husband, but it is foolish to ignore the thieving in his heart."

Sophia took a sip of her Coke. It was fizzy and sweet and stung the back of her mouth in little tart explosions. She drank slowly. "Tears, pain, and fear are a constant and what every woman must pay for her existence. I steer my little ship through the shoals as best as I can." The loneliness was a vise in her heart, squeezing with just enough pressure to be a constant ache. It killed her a little each day, taking inner light and replacing it with a darkness.

Sophia watched her boys play in the dirt, sticks of sugar cane dangling from their mouths. She took a bite of her sandwich, and then returned it to the plate, unable to swallow past the lump of emotion in her throat.

Queenie harrumphed. "You are made of sterner stuff than that. You have conquered the tears, pain, and fear. You've survived the unthinkable. When you go through something like that, it tempers you. It can break you down or forge you. It folds and shapes and sharpens you into something new, a weapon perhaps, and that is no small feat. You are a strong woman. I just hope if the time ever comes you to want and need nurturing, you ask for it. For God knows you deserve it."

Sophia knew she should heed Queenie's gentle suggestion, but her pride rejected it as she watched Karl disappear into the forests with the red-lipped woman following him.

Karl knew the woman was following him. She'd been dogging him for a month. Farther into the forest where no eyes could see them. Karl stopped beneath the shade of a palm tree.

She pressed him back, licked his ear and gave him a hot thrill, then grabbed his groin, massaging him there.

"Let's get you good and hard," she said.

Karl didn't know her name. His nostrils flared. Her breath smelled like tamarind and sour orange.

She stepped back, pulled off her dress. Karl swallowed; she wore nothing beneath. Heavy, pendulous breasts undulated with her movement as she did a sensual dance, toying with him, mesmerizing him. He looked down her lush, rounded brown body, the flare of her wide hips, her soft belly, the black "v" of her curls between her legs, downy, hot, and dripping with dampness. He wanted to touch her, ram his cock into her, spill his seed.

He'd not touched Sophia since the day he'd raped her in the clinic. Not because he didn't want to, but he'd been cursed with impotence. Perhaps he could get it up with the black tart where he was jinxed by his wife. His hands stayed rooted to the tree. He tilted his head up. Huge coconuts swelled above him.

The wild flick of her wide flat tongue laved across his cheek, drawing his attention to her.

"Your balls will be as big as those coconuts with what I'm going to do, and then I'm going to empty them, suck out all your stones," she forewarned.

She took her finger and stuck it in her pussy, drawing in and out, her eyes watching him, deeply aroused with her movements. It seemed to go on forever. Finally, she flicked her clitoris and jerked, then placed her wet finger between his lips.

She grabbed his hands and placed them on her huge bare breasts, pushing herself into him, her heavy musk and wetness rising, luring him like a stallion to a mare in heat. The nipples stuck out, like sandpaper to his touch. They were not soft or rosy like Sophia's. Instead her breasts were heavy, sweaty. She swabbed her tongue across his mouth. He cringed at the bitter taste.

Like a stinging bee, she scattered tiny love bites over his ear and neck. He stopped her when she tried to unbutton his shirt. No way would he reveal his scars.

"Too bad. I've wanted to feel your scars against my breasts."

Was she mocking him?

She clung to him, seizing his hair, continuing her bizarre dance against him, her hips gyrating against him, all the while ruling him.

"I always wanted to touch your soft golden hair. Lived to run my tongue through it."

Breathing hard, she expelled gasps of pleasure. "You are hot and male, and I'm going to make you beg for more." She licked her lips with her promise.

She laughed again, her nails raking down his chest, her finger catching on a button and ripping it off. She unzipped him, massaging his flesh with her practiced fingers, her damp wicked mouth, tonguing him everywhere. He was unable to stop the onslaught, imagining fitting snugly into the fortress of her heavy thighs.

She quirked her brow, moved her hands down on him again, exerting more provocative pressure. She groaned, staring at him, her cat-like eyes unnerving him, a pure, pleasurable Satanic smile lighting her face. She maintained a slow rhythm, letting him know she was in control. A normal man would be as hard as a rock, ready to explode.

He looked at her and, for one moment, her face transformed into Sophia. This was Sophia doing this to him. He shook his head to rid himself of the manifestation. The red-lipped woman appeared again. Laughing.

She increased her speed. He closed his eyes waiting, hot fire went to his cock. Perhaps he'd been cursed with Sophia.

"Ah, there is my stallion. You'll only want me, not that frigid, bitch wife of yours."

At the mention of Sophia, he went limp. What the hell was he doing? Sophia was the woman he loved. Like coming out of a dream, swimming upwards from the bottom of the sea and trying to get air, her incantation lay siege to him, drowning him. Was this Voodoo? He must break the spell.

The red-lipped woman worked harder. She scraped his balls with her fingernails. He held his breath. Nothing happened. His cock drooped.

She sat back on her haunches, looked up at him and cackled. "Ain't gonna get anything out of no rich white doctor. Little bitty thing has no life."

His Nazi hatred skyrocketed to the surface.

"Wait until everyone hear about the proud doctor. His flag got no wind, ain't got no juice." She laughed and laughed, her maniacal laughter spilling over the forest with demonic shrieking and taunting him.

He grabbed her by the throat, pushed hard with his thumbs on her windpipe. She tore at his hands, her eyes bulged. "If I hear of one word, I'll cut your throat."

He dropped her, and she sobbed.

Sophia. What had he done to Sophia? How wonderful Sophia was. She never mocked him. She was only kind. What had he done to her that hideous day in the clinic? He thought of ways to win her back. No matter what the cost. How he hated the impotence of poverty. How he wanted to make her proud of him. How he was going to be rich someday. As rich as Croesus, getting it all back. That was how he'd win Sophia's love. He'd made a small fortune with his outside medical practice. He'd succeed above all else. Yet, he couldn't stop the rage that simmered beneath.

<h1 style="text-align:center">Chapter Forty-Eight</h1>

On the leeward side of Green Turtle Cay, Sophia stood on the deck of the rigged sloop they'd purchased to give medical attention to the out-islanders. "Karl, it isn't safe to travel. The weather report has alerted sailors to hunker down. The Green Turtle Cay residents have warned us."

With the last patient on the cay, Sophia had felt Karl's dark side brewing like a storm. She played the "*if*" game again. If she did the right thing, if she said the right thing, she could prevent an explosion. Despite her doubts of leaving port with the wind kicking up, she didn't want to trigger his temper, which she sensed was building to the breaking point.

"I have an emergency gallbladder cholecystectomy at six o'clock."

Nothing she said could change his mind. A mile out from Green Turtle Cay harbor, a veil of dark red clouds bled across the sky, pierced by splinters of light the color of fallen leaves. "Those clouds look like nighttime, like a bruise. They're the sort that don't wait," Sophia yelled as the sail whipped in the wind.

The channel grew more and more vicious. The uninhabited and barely discernible Manjack Cay lay five miles in the distance.

Karl sat at the rudder, the eerie light playing across his features. Sophia's entire body bloomed with hair-raising gooseflesh.

They were exposed to a five-mile stretch of water, exposed to the ocean and its high waves and tricky currents. Suddenly, the breakers from the open sea pushed into the channel and the outgoing tide made the water churn as if in a boiling pot. The waves towered over them and came from all sides.

"Turn back, Karl," Sophia yelled over the deafening winds.

The "rage" fisherman called it, a tempestuous confluence of violent, uncontrolled bursts where the sea heaved itself in a thundering, whirling frenzy, and devoured ill-fated fishermen. Sophia concentrated on one wave as high as a mountain when another wave slammed from the opposite side. The stern of the boat lifted out of the water, leaving the rudder exposed. Karl was powerless to steer.

The next wave threw her to the deck. The boom broke loose from its tether and swung wildly back and forth. In a valley between two waves, another swell drenched her. Water filled the boat. On her hands and knees, she inched to Karl. Never had she seen such a chilling smile. The boat pushed farther out to sea, passing Manjack Cay, their last refuge before an entire ocean to Africa. The ear-splitting roar of the ocean thundered, a wave jammed her flat into a windlass, pain sharp and jabbing poked in her side. She swept a hand over her forehead to remove gelatinous kelp.

Karl heard Sophia behind him. She touched his shoulder. He shrugged her off. He was numbed to the storm that had blossomed into a full-blown gale.

"I want vengeance," he screamed into the storm. "Vengeance against the Americans who bombed my train. Vengeance against the Nazis who cast me down that wretched rabbit hole. Revenge against you, Sophia, for your unfaithfulness. And most of all, revenge against the American scum who had planted his seed in you."

Rain slashed at different angles from the wind changing direction and blinding him.

"I hate you for cheating on me," he shouted above the clamorous din. "You are a liar. You have broken our lives and everything it has stood for. You are so much worse than a cheater. You killed something and you killed it when my back was turned."

He needed to think of something else—anything else. Until he could really breathe again. Until the rage receded, and the tempest stilled. Until he became himself once more.

Whoever that was.

He needed a distraction from the bleak void that threatened to swallow him night and day. How he had survived believing that if he moved into Sophia's silken arms, she could heal him. How he'd fought the burning pains on his skin for months, crying for her. How he traveled halfway around the world to discover her wicked treachery.

He needed to touch her again, regardless of her duplicity. For something irrevocably told him she was not his. Oh, yes, he'd had had her body when he'd fucked her, but his damned cock rose no more and his inability to perform after the years of abstinence thwarted any claim on her soul.

Nerves rioted up Sophia's spine. Dear God, Karl had steered them into the midst of a squall. He wanted them both dead.

He was talking crazy. His eyes were mad. Water streamed off his face and plastered his hair to his head.

The floor pitched; its oily surface treacherous beneath her feet. She stretched her arms for a handhold and grabbed air. The schooner heaved. Sophia fell, landed on her back. Her fingers clawed a rope coil. She looked up. A giant wall of water crashed over her, an unearthly, malevolent force. Its curled tunnel felt like the inside of a clenched fist as it threw her across the deck and slammed her into the port side. She clung to the gunwale with one hand. The twisting of her body left her free hand flailing. Her fingers clasped a metal cleat embedded in the side. The sloop heaved again, listing deeply to the right. Water washed over the deck and filled the cockpit. The boom was loose and swinging out over the side. One of the front sails, wet and heavy, had ripped loose and was dragging partly in the water.

Another wall of water, the size of a four-story building, swelled on the other side of the trough between waves. The upsurge crushed her like a ton of bricks. The boom swung crazily, knocking Karl overboard, and then swept her up and over. She was drawn down into the steely depths, imprisoning her there.

The sea tumbled her round and round in a revolving motion, sucking her into the belly of the wave. She had no notion what was up or what was down. The strangest perception was that she would drown, and no one would know. In chest-squeezing horror, a sense arose that the ocean held all the authority. Shadows blanketed and clouded at the edges in rhythm with the sea that surged and yawed. No. Her mind screamed. *Swim. Kick. Fight.* You must survive for your sons.

Sophia burst to the surface. She scanned the sea. Nothing. "Karl!" she screamed over the din, and then saw his head. If only she could get to Karl in time.

Sophia cut through the devouring swells with long, sure strokes, and then stopped, treading water. All Karl had put her through. He had almost killed her. Should she leave him to drown? She could swim north and reach the island, save herself for her boys.

No. She had to save him regardless of his anger. A wave rolled over him, carrying him farther away. She fought the top, took a breath of air before another surge slapped seawater down her throat. She choked on the salty brine, keeping sight of Karl.

He swirled in the water. His head disappeared. Sophia dove.

She shot through the murky depths. Her lungs burning for lack of air. She reached out. Her hand settled on hair. She seized the seaweed mass and kicked to the surface. Her lungs burst for air.

Backpaddling, she held Karl tight to her chest, towing him toward Manjack Cay. Her arms ached, the wailing sea screaming around them, hungering for its prey. Fleeting thoughts swirled and echoed then dispersed to nothing, her limbs more exhausted than they'd ever been in her life. If only she had the strength to fight, the urge to go on. She was so weak against the merciless sea. Fatigue settled in.

Keep going.

The waves carried her away, to the island, blessedly washing her into a cove.

Driving rain slashed against them like Satan's own poetry as Sophia dragged Karl's body onto the beach. Thunder roared, lightning slashed close to the ground, the elements growling like wild beasts, the storm refusing to release them from its claws. Wind kicked up the sand on the beach, stinging her eyes. She rolled Karl to his side. Was he alive? Faint beneath her finger, Sophia felt a pulse. She turned him over and pounded his back. Karl retched out half the sea. He was so pale and cold. She dragged him up farther under a tree. Gathering palm fronds and palmettoes, she piled the branches over him to protect him from the freezing rain.

Beneath their crude shelter, Sophia sat very quiet, holding her husband, and giving him her warmth. Karl had blamed her for everything, and like she did when she was frightened of his outbursts, she lifted her chin and squared her shoulders. Never would she admit her love for Robert. No. She would not be provoked by Karl to release her inmost secret.

Karl did not move. Her blood cooled. Chilled. Would he awaken? Her fingers curled and tightened until her nails dug against her palms. What if he died?

"Damn you, Karl. Wake up." She pounded his chest. Nothing.

Sophia watched him for hours. The storm that raged around

her was nothing compared to the furor within her. Should she pray to God to save him when he had tried to kill her and leave her sons, orphans? Did she wish for revenge? Should she had left him for the sea to swallow him? Should she leave him exposed to the elements and let God decide what to do with him? Would her life be better without him?

As the night passed, the storm abated. When the sun rose a great white pearl in the sky, Karl shifted, moaned, and then opened his eyes. The part of her that wished him ill, evaporated, the part that wished him to live, rejoiced.

Sophia smoothed back his hair and smiled. Stunned that she was beside him, he took her hand, intertwining his fingers with hers and bought it to his trembling lips. "I hope you can find it in your heart to forgive me for all my wrongdoings. You saved my worthless life when I didn't deserve to be saved."

"Don't say it, Karl. You were confused...the war..."

"No. I tried to kill you. I tried to kill us both. My selfishness and jealousy have robbed our marriage." He started sobbing and could not stop. "I just wanted the pain to end..."

Sophia held his head in her lap. "I'm so happy you're alive. What would the boys and I do without you?"

"I thought you were dead. It wasn't the boys' fault. It wasn't your fault. It was the damned war. The boys. My greatest travesty. I've been so blind. No more, Sophia. You are my wife and I love you more than anything else in the world."

"Sh-h-h. Save your strength, Karl."

His hand shaky, Karl stroked the side of her face. "From now on, things are going to be different between us. I'm going to be a good husband and father. I'm going to care for you. I'll be a rich man someday. I'll make you proud of me. I will always be there for you. Can you forgive me?"

"Karl—I hope so." She looked off in the distance. After all his other declarations, would he sink back into his rages? She returned her gaze to him. "I just want you to live and be happy. Money means nothing. Right now, I'm worried about being rescued. We're on Manjack Cay and the island, as you know, is completely deserted."

"How is it possible to love someone so deeply, so completely? Just promise me, that you'll never leave me."

Her breath hitched and her arms surrounding him, tightened. "Karl, I've been there for you and will always be there for you. I do love you."

Her husband, a proud man, pleaded with her. The air grew thick with emotions. The storm that had started as a curse ended up a gift. In that instant, it became clear that his anger had been a mask. His greatest fear and vulnerability became suddenly evident...he was frightened of her, terrified she might leave him.

After a while, she built a fire with a lighter tucked in Karl's pocket. She stretched their wet clothes out on twigs, watching the steam rise like a fleeing soul.

She rose, dusted the sand from her knees. "I'm going to search for food."

A tall coconut tree bowed over the white sand beach. She swallowed, so thirsty from the exertion through the salty sea, her mouth raw from brine. How to get the towering coconuts down? Finding a light, withered Casuarina branch, she poked at the dangling coconuts, pushing up with all her might. With several deep thrusts, and a great deal of strength, she dislodged the fruit and they dropped to the sand in a thud.

Pounding the thick fibrous strands of the husk on a rock, she finally broke through and drank thirstily of the sweet liquid, saving a portion for Karl.

The beach had been taken over by a flock of sea gulls but, otherwise, the cove was deserted. She waded in the clear water toward a grassy bed, hunting for conch, and was rewarded with two giant queens. She broke them with another conch, pulled out the snails, skinned them and gave the raw meat to Karl to eat.

Soon, a schooner was seen in the distance. They had seen the smoke from the fire. Old John Sawyer had sailed out to find them.

Kurt and Michael rushed into their arms. "Mama. Papa. We were so worried." They, too, cried, rejoicing that she and Karl were alive.

Sophia saw the tears in Karl's eyes. She was hopeful, yet still not certain. He'd have to prove himself. Yet her gut told her there was a profound difference in him this time—that he was the Karl she'd met in Berlin. No matter the dark road he'd traveled, her patience and love had come with triumph.

Chapter Forty-Nine

Michigan 1953

"What do you want?" Robert asked brusquely. He didn't want to be disturbed. The Detroit Tigers had lost that day. He figured it was a bad day, like all the other days.

"Nothing in particular," Caroline said, shutting the door and ambling through the library like she was seeing it for the first time.

Robert snorted. "I bet. That mind of yours belts out steam all the time. Hurry up. I'm going riding."

"I was thinking of Sophia—"

Robert's hands fisted. "Do not bring her name up in this house. Ever." He'd tried to destroy any emotions about Sophia. To recall her treachery was a betrayal of that effort. He'd shoved people away from him, including his sister.

Caroline browsed the books, running her slender fingers along the spines.

"I often speculated who Sophia really was. Her manners and posture were too perfect."

His little sister was sixteen going on thirty. Since when had she become so sophisticated? "Change the subject or leave," Robert growled. The brat ignored him.

"Her music box was made of gold and silver and, no doubt, priceless gems. At the time I discovered it, I was too naïve to know its value. How would a poor woman from Prussia have something like that in her possession? Then there was the gypsy trick, her knowledge of horses and her talk about the famous stables in Prussia. She always told Liam and me stories of a castle with a lake in front full of swans, about massive and unending forests, her friends, the gypsies, who camped there. My favorite story she told me was a sad tale about a princess who lost her family."

Robert scoffed. "You always like to make fairy tales out of life."

Caroline stuck her tongue out at him. "I've done research. Sophia told us her real name. At least her maiden name. I looked her up at the library and have proved my point." Caroline presented the evidence.

With reluctance, Robert unfolded a newspaper. "I suppose you stole this from the library."

"Not really, since our family's endowment pays for the library."

Caroline pointed to the picture of Princess Sophia, a younger version, perhaps five years before the war with her family. *Sophia.* Her mother was a beauty, too, so like Sophia. Her father, tall and proud. Her lost younger sister and brother showed the same aristocratic bloodlines and light coloring. The article detailed the story of the prominent Prussian noble family.

Robert's chest tightened. What Sophia must have endured during and after the war; a princess reduced to that half-starved woman he fished out of the mud in the rubble of Berlin. The contrast between her life as a princess had been greater than what the Germans had experienced. He had to admit she'd been less prepared for the hardships yet had risen to the challenge.

"Even you cannot deny that is Sophia, Brother. All those stories she told us were real because they were about her. She was royalty."

"Doesn't change anything."

"I don't think you gave her a fair chance. I was there that day, and you were brutal."

"Deservedly so."

"Sophia was in love with you."

"She lied to me."

Caroline harumphed, and then presented another newspaper to him. "Did you give her half a chance to explain? When you get angry, you never listen."

He took it with reluctance. "Another theft? You're incorrigible. Incorrigible girls should be beheaded before they reach marriageable age and perpetuate their dangerous kind on the world."

"This paper was written after the war and tells about her family's heroic efforts to help Jews, gypsies and Poles escape. They were executed by Nazis."

Robert recalled the day in the restaurant with the Polish family. How they had knelt in front of Sophia, paying her homage. The rapid talking, the tears, the exclamations. Sophia had made them rise, embraced them, and then dismissed their exclamations to him without any explanation. Why? Because they were a part of her home. He was going to pay the Grabowski brothers a visit at the plant.

"She's the missing princess that the Nazis did not execute."

"I don't want to hear anything more about Sophia." His sister had been weaned on Nancy Drew mysteries and considered herself a righteous detective.

Caroline tilted her head. "Hm-m. Poor Robert. Even the greatest martyrs don't hold a candle to you." Caroline circled to the front of him. Looked straight at him. "Sophia was not a liar. There had to be more, more that you didn't listen to."

There was a lot he'd thought about over the years. Sophia was married. Yet the woman who gave herself to him in Berlin was a virgin. The marriage had never been consummated.

"I see how unhappy you are with Cynthia."

Robert cut her a sharp look that dared her to argue. "I'm very happy."

Caroline rolled her eyes. "Whatever." His sister paused for a second, and then said, "You were unfair to Liam and me. Sophia was like a mother to us, and we never were able to say goodbye."

Robert strolled through the line of books. He needed a healthier diversion. He pulled out a book and a letter fell out of the pages to the floor.

Caroline scooped it up. "This is addressed to you."

The elegant penmanship was Sophia's. Had the conversation with Caroline summoned a ghost from the past?

"How did the letter get there?" Caroline asked.

Sophia had placed the missive on the table. With dawning realization, he knew who put it there. He had. He had tucked it away, meaning to destroy it, but was unable to.

He remembered Sophia's parting words.

It is not what you think. If you can bring yourself to read my letter, I've explained everything.

He'd been too shattered, too stubborn, and proud to read it. Like a veneration, he passed his thumb over the fine script. Damn his sister for dredging up old emotions. Emotions he'd fought to bury.

In my heart, I wish things were different.

Caroline studied him. He turned, but she tiptoed behind him, placed her hand on his shoulder. He shrugged it off. "This is private."

"Open it."

If his sister was this commanding during her teen years, her future husband would have his hands full. He took the letter opener off a desk, sliced it open.

Dearest Robert,

I was a student in Berlin when I learned about my family's treason and death. Every day, I lived in terror, waiting for soldiers to arrest me. I married Karl in hopes his name would protect me. He came from a respected German family. My only sin is marrying a man I did not love.

Shortly after, I received word that Karl had been killed in a bombing raid. Almost two years passed and then, suddenly, he showed up at Pratt Stable.

I'd never deceive you. Perhaps I should have told you about my past earlier. That I was a widow. But I longed to put that life behind me. Let go of all I lost and embrace the future. In the end, it was not to be. I'm leaving with my husband. I'm honoring my vows. My loyalties and obligations are to him. I apologize for any pain I've caused you. My agony and sorrow are a hundredfold.

From that first day in Berlin, I felt a pull so strongly to you that I couldn't resist it if I wanted to. But fate found its way to rip us apart.

Robert, I will always love you and I leave with a part of you that I will always cherish.

Love,

Sophia

His insides twisted for the woman he loved. He remembered her beautiful, pain-stricken eyes and the horrible way he'd treated her that day.

"Well?" prompted Caroline, who had read over his shoulder.

Robert was silent for a long while.

"I know what part she took," said Caroline.

"For God's sake, she took nothing...not ever her clothes..." Nor the check he'd hurled at her so cruelly.

"I saw her throwing up one morning like Mother did before Liam was born. She said she had a stomach upset and not to tell anyone. She was pregnant—with your child."

Chapter Fifty

*B*ahamas

Near the end of Karl's five-year contract at the lumber camp, Karl kissed her on the cheek. He'd been disappearing in nearby settlements more often of late. "I've a surprise for you."

"What is it?"

"Then it wouldn't be a surprise."

With Karl's sudden dramatic change since the squall debacle, Sophia had come back into herself, like someone returning from a long voyage. Karl had become the wonderful, loving, and adoring man she'd first met in Berlin, and for the first time, she had what she always wanted...a family.

His blue eyes twinkled and in a buoyant mood, he hurried her and the boys into the jeep. After a long drive, they rolled up a private road onto the highest part of a narrow tongue of land where a home was shaded by tall coconut palms bent by the trade winds.

"Who lives here?" Sophia asked, taking in the splendor and beauty of the white clapboard house with charming blue shutters. The boys piled out of the jeep.

"We're off to the beach," said Kurt.

"I don't know," said Sophia.

"They'll be fine," said Karl. "The boys are nearly seven years and eager for adventures."

Sophia worried her lip, looking off to where the pair scrambled through the thick pines and down to the water's edge. Of late, Karl had been their greatest ally, giving into their exploits and allowing escapades she would not.

"Shall we take a tour?" Karl suggested.

Sophia slanted him a sideways look. "Do you think the owners will mind?"

He smiled. "We'll have our own adventure."

How could she resist? From the wraparound porch, one could look out on the vast horizon over green treetops and the shining sea. To the west lay the harbor and to the east across the ocean were several islands, dotting the panorama like a string of pearls. With every breath she took, the ocean seemed to change colors.

"Where else in the world would you find colors and transparent waters like this?" Karl said, looking out across the waves.

Different shapes of coral rocks and reefs, whose depths one could not judge, lay beneath the transparent water in fascinating forms. Sophia held her hand to her heart. "One could only dream to own such a place."

Karl dangled keys. "The house is yours. I saved money tending to patients from other islands, bought the land and had the house built just for you."

Filled with so much joy, she threw her arms around Karl. Then, unable to wait a second longer to explore her new home, she grabbed Karl's hand, stepped over the threshold, and gasped. There were high whitewashed tongue and groove ceilings with rotating fans to cool the house. In the enormous kitchen, sunshine slanted sideways to fall in pools on the shiny pine-planked floor. Every square inch was serviceable, and it hosted a brand-new refrigerator and stove. There were four bedrooms with closets, two large baths, and a spacious living room, boasting a fireplace. Breathtaking views of the seas were visible from almost every room.

Sophia clapped her hands. "After living in a three-room shack, I don't know how I'll become accustomed to all this space."

"I had boatbuilders from one of the outer cays make everything sound. It will last through any hurricane nature may throw at us."

Sophia ran out to the porch again, lifting her head to catch the cooling breezes. Her feet could feel the vibrations of the pounding surf below. She pointed to the landscape stretching out before them. "In the lower areas, I'll plant lemon, lime, orange, and grapefruit trees. There are enough rocks to build a wall around the entire piece of property. I'll plant bougainvillea of scarlet, orange, and purple to veil the barriers."

Karl grinned, and then guided her to the back of the house where a charming guest house had been built. "For Queenie and John with all the modern conveniences."

Sophia threw her arms around him. "Oh, Karl. Everything is lovely."

"I'd do anything for you, Sophia."

In the weeks that followed, they moved into their new home. Enamored with their new residence, the boys dashed about the house, wild with excitement, and then tore down to the beach where they spent hours. Despite having their own rooms, the boys chose to bunk together. Karl gave her free reign to purchase new household furniture. For the time being, they hauled their meager furniture from the lumber camp and used it until the new furnishings could be shipped from the mainland.

Karl surprised her again, closing the clinic at the lumber camp and beginning his practice near their new home in the town of Vane Harbor where a British flag waved happily.

Vane Harbor carried its own ambience. There was hot, humid air where Sophia could hardly breathe, and the people moved in slow motion, grinning, and with the lingual confusion on the scale of Babylon. They turned out in force to help in building the new clinic, happy to have a doctor nearby. The friendly villagers who lived in coral stone homes with thatched roofs enchanted Sophia. Often, they paid fees with quantities of lobster, conch, fish, or fruit from their gardens. Often, she'd see children playing in the shade of huge almond trees or an old man, his shaven head resembling a ripe coconut, sitting by a fire, boiling sugar cane to make syrup, or an old woman husking corn on her porch.

To the boys, Vane Harbor possessed a romantic attachment. Named after Charles Vane, the notorious pirate who had laid anchor there at one time, and as popular myth would have it, had buried treasure there. Soon, she had them enrolled in the local school.

There were other changes in Karl. He dressed different, wearing light khaki slacks and light-colored shirts. He hired a nurse, freeing Sophia from working full-time in the clinic. He came home every night for dinner and made the weekends for family activities.

Working in her gardens, Sophia delighted watching the many colorful butterflies and hummingbirds flitting around her scarlet hibiscus blossoms. How far she had come from her native homelands and the brutality of war. At last, she'd found peace each day.

In a way, she grew to love Karl more and more. She'd been deeply moved by the effort it took to fight his way back from the scars of war. Sometimes, though, she'd have to remember how cruel he'd been to her, then bury it. They were both different people now. The horror Karl had been, the passionate woman she had been with Robert...were gone.

Karl made many sacrifices for the family and had become a real father to the boys. As to being her husband, he had not touched her since that day in the clinic. Because of his impotence, their physical intimacy was nil. But Sophia had discovered kissing, holding hands, and cuddling at night with honest, vulnerable conversation an ample replacement.

Karl spoiled the boys terribly. First, he bought them a red-haired, mulish-tempered donkey named Muriel. The boys galloped freely on Muriel over stony roads, but she resisted the tight girth around her belly to pull the donkey cart. One Sunday, the boys had dressed in their finest and had insisted on driving Muriel to church. Muriel bolted, racing by Sophia like a Roman chariot in Circus Maximus, and dashing into the sea where she stopped suddenly. The boys skyrocketed head over heels into the water. Sophia had found them splashing each other and laughing at the donkey's antics. What surprised her the most was that Karl had enjoyed the boys' escapade, wading into the water, and soaking his good clothes.

On a bright sunny June day, with their glass face masks plastered to their eight-year-old faces, fins on their feet and Hawaiian slings used to spear lobster, they dove into a dream world of sea-spun wonders. Sophia could never get enough of the yellow and amethyst sea fans anchored to orange and green coral ground, swaying with the infinite movement of waves. Swarms of coral fish in brilliant colors and sizes swam between them. Fat groupers moved weightlessly in the dusky depths below, staring at her with bulging eyes, opening and closing their thick-lipped mouths. Kurt pointed to the yellow snappers with radiant turquoise stripes on their sides, darting in and out of the reef. Schools of colorful parrot fish grazed on the sunny cliffs, pulling tiny pieces of algae from the coral heads. Baring its frightening teeth, a greenish-brown moray eel, darted at Sophia from its cave. She reared back and rose to the surface to catch a breath. The boys and Karl rose at the same time, laughing, and then diving back down again, enthused with the same awe.

In the unreal distance, a gray torpedo-shaped body with dark vertical stripes on its flanks steered toward them. Her stomach clenched; a large tiger shark circled closer with undulating movements. Sophia's heartbeat faster. Most sharks left them alone, but a tiger shark would snap out and swallow anything that fell within the range of its powerful jaws. Sophia saw the triangular mouth open, illuminating rows of sharp teeth. Just in front of her, it turned away, its cold lifeless black eyes alarming her.

Karl saw it, too, and motioned for them to surface. "Don't panic and don't splash. If it comes too close, poke at it with your spear."

Watching the large dorsal fin glide through the surface of the water, they swam toward the shore. Again and again, it returned, circling her family like the predator it was. When they all reached shore, she lay down on the fine pink sand, exhausted, but relieved as the sun warmed her trembling body.

"Did you see the size of that shark?" asked Kurt, lifting his spear and heading back in the water. Kurt, her foolhardy son, would take on the devil himself.

"Hold on there," Karl said, putting his arm around their slender son and guided him to shore. "You're not ready to go face-to-face with a predator like that. We must respect nature."

Sophia stood on shaky legs. Michael supported her. "Kurt, don't you think about anyone except yourself? Your foolish stunts will be the death of me."

Kurt hung his head. "I'm sorry, Mama."

Karl looked sharply to her. "Take it easy on the boy. Kurt has an adventuresome spirit that should be admired."

Tears ran down Sophia's cheeks and she clasped her daredevil son to her chest. "I just worry about you. I could never lose you."

Sophia released him. Kurt, the boy growing into manhood,

stood erect, his cheeks reddening by his impulsive behavior. "I'm just me, Mama. I can't change that."

Sophia put her arms around him to reassure him again. Were the devils and angels inside her son the same thing? He was so much like Robert. But the thing that terrified her the most was that she'd lose her sons someday.

~

Michael ran to Sophia with another wounded animal. He exhibited an aptitude and love for all living creatures. Never could he refuse a stray. Michael brought home baby woodpeckers thrown from their nests when the tree was cut down and nursed them to adulthood. Every dog-eared feral cat he fed. One cat had a left eyeball almost out of the socket, blood dripping down, and the poor animal trying to wipe the area with its paws. Michael coaxed him into his arms and took him to Karl in the clinic. Karl put the cat to sleep, removed the eye and put salve into the socket. Michael stood to attention like a soldier marveling everything his father fixed.

The dog he'd found had been ripped open by wild boars.

"We already have six dogs, four cats, two parrots," Sophia said. "One more creature won't make much difference if you care for it. This pup needs your papa's attention."

Karl shook his head. "I don't know, Son, he's hurt pretty bad."

Michael stayed next to his father's side while he performed a surgery, attentive, helpful in handing him instruments and asking questions.

Karl instructed his son, having him stitch up the animal. "I'm proud of you, Michael. You have the talent to be surgeon someday. I know you will take good care of this poor fellow until he heals. You have a gift with animals. That comes from your mother."

Michael carried the dog into their home and carefully laid him in the corner of the living room where he cared for the dog until it fully recovered.

∼

To Sophia, her son's differences were like night and day. Kurt's rare intelligence lay in his gifts for tinkering and creating. The boy talked way above her of his endless theories and postulates, and with awe, she couldn't help falling under his spell. Kurt possessed a gift for all things mechanical and devoted his time to the invention of wonderfully ingenious contraptions, some remarkable and others with dubious practicality.

How he believed she comprehended advanced physics, assailing her with incomprehensible gibberish about alloys of precious metals, enamels from the Far East, and revolutionary theory on pistons and mechanical parts, all of which was part of automotive and aeronautical technology. She regretted he was on an isolated island, far from the type of schooling required to grow his interests and stimulate his great mind. Yet, there was nothing here on the island that stifled him. He was so much like his biological father, in looks, speed, powered by all things machine-driven, but his grades were not good.

Sophia had been happy Karl devoted an inordinate amount of time with Kurt to help grow his talents. But lately, that had fallen apart with Karl's obsession to be rich. Instead, Karl started spending an inordinate amount of time on investments and real estate.

The preoccupation to be wealthy and to recoup everything his illustrious family had lost during the war was unhealthy. A sour taste grew in her mouth with Karl's lack of transparency and what intentional risk might lead them to financial ruin.

"You must realize my dream," Karl said. "It is your dream, too."

"We have worked hard for everything, have saved a little for the boys' college, and are very comfortable," Sophia protested. "Why is it not enough?"

"It is never enough, and we'll not discuss further."

"We will discuss it further. I heard you bought a hefty amount of real estate. How can we afford it?"

"I'm the head of the household and make the decisions. I don't take advice from you on financial issues."

Oh, how Karl fostered his anger against the world. Was his determination to be wealthy from his lack of control? Was it his cold, aloof German father's echoing mantra...*you must never fail, Karl. You must make me proud. Don't be a disappointment*...that hammered through her husband's head?

Karl held her shoulders. "Sophia, I'll be richer than your senator friend someday."

Her throat tightened. How many times during their marriage when she had showed nothing but loyalty to Karl had he thrown Robert up in her face? Her husband was stuck in a poisonous mental prison of jealousy and self-doubt, his pride blinding him. Suddenly, her blood chilled. A premonition arose, warning her with certainty, it'd be a matter of time before his unwavering ambition and green-eyed worm of jealousy would wreak its wicked vocation.

Chapter Fifty-One

Helga Schneider, Karl's sister, had arrived in the Bahamas in Baba Yaga style, lacking the Prussian myth's single chicken-legged hut and broom.

The black smoke of her cigarette coiled around her face. Her lips shone with red lipstick. She held a long black filter between her middle and ring fingers, the skin dry and cracked with marks that looked like bloodstains. There were some people you remember fondly and some you have nightmares about, Sophia thought. Helga made everyone's life a living hell.

She was a shapeless woman with outmoded gray braids pinned fiercely to the sides of her head. She sniffed, and then ran her finger along a fine mahogany table Sophia had ordered from the mainland. A small frown slipped across Helga's face when she couldn't find dust to nitpick about. "Mysterious how neither of your boys look at all like you or Karl."

Both boys possessed heavy heads of dark hair and dazzling green eyes. Exact replicas of their natural father. How spiteful her sister-in-law was to remark on her observation when Karl could walk into the room at any moment.

"Your father had dark hair." Sophia reminded her.

Helga's expression was pure cunning. "There is that. But no one in the family has green eyes like your sons. Always blue."

With one stroke, Sophia chopped a whole chicken in half, ramming the meat in seasoning, and then dropping it in hot oil to fry. Memories flashed about the woman who'd thrown her out on the streets of Berlin to starve, leaving her at the mercy of Russian soldiers. "It is futile to present the facts to people who are enjoying a sense of moral superiority."

"What is that supposed to mean?" Helga snapped.

Sophia unfolded the newspaper, glancing at the headlines. Eisenhower had crushed Stevenson and won the reelection. Rumors circulated that Senator Kennedy's book *Profiles in Courage* might be a shoo-in for the *Pulitzer Prize*. She liked the upcoming young and promising Irishman, Senator John Kennedy who was likely to run for the presidency. "Charm boy," Karl had called him.

Sophia straightened the pile of magazines that Helga had scattered over the sofas and floor. *Vogue, Glamour, Harper's Bazaar, Esquire, House and Garden.*

"Sophia." Karl came in with a bouquet of hibiscus and bougainvillea and kissed her on the cheek. Noting the tight malevolence of Helga's face at Karl's show of affection, Sophia lifted her chin and arranged a centerpiece on the table.

Helga sat at the table waiting to be served. "I see how prosperous you are, Brother. Perhaps you could afford to give me more of a stipend to live on? Inflation has wreaked havoc on Germany."

Sophia looked to Karl. The support of his sister over the years had been taxing on them. "Perhaps you could find a job," Sophia suggested.

"No one wants to hire an old woman."

The woman was perfectly healthy to work. *No one wants to be around you.* Sophia's hand tightened around the platter of fried chicken. She clunked it on the table, adding a bowl of fresh leaf greens with vinaigrette, cold marinated potato salad, and a tureen of lobster chowder. When were the boys going to arrive? She'd told them to be home promptly at five.

The back screen door banged open. "Sorry, Mom about being late." Kurt arrived, his clothes torn and proudly sporting not one but two black eyes. Michael followed on his heels, also sporting a black eye.

Sophia gave Kurt a look. *We'll talk later.* Oh, how that boy loved to fight, and this time he'd dragged in his twin into the melee.

The boys washed up. Michael slid into the chair next to Karl. Kurt gave his brother a dirty look for leaving him to sit next to his contrary aunt. Sophia dabbed her dinner napkin on her lips to hide her smile, thinking of how Kurt complained about his aunt smelling of a mixture of *Evening in Paris*, rubbing alcohol and mothballs.

"Karl," Helga said in her piercing voice. "Look at those boys, coming to the table in such disarray! They're a disgrace. They should be dealt with posthaste."

Sophia straightened and glanced at Karl. He didn't take the bait.

"I was shoeing a mule with Bobby Rosenstein," Kurt jumped in by way of explanation.

"It was a very big mule," added Michael.

Sophia dipped her spoon in the chowder. "Indeed."

"Huge. His name's Henry."

Henry was the island bully, twice the size of Kurt and three times the size of Bobby Rosenstein, the only Jew on the island. Poor Bobby was always bullied by Henry. Despite her distaste for Kurt's fighting, she admired the way he always championed the underdog.

"I hope you were able to get those shoes on that mule," Karl offered.

Half of Kurt's face contorted. No doubt it hurt him to smile. "He got shoed real well."

"I can verify Kurt did a fine job. I caught the tail end of it," said Michael.

"Glad to hear it," commended Karl.

Helga waved her glass of wine. "Rosenstein? You shouldn't have your children associating with...well...Hitler did not finish his job with the Jews."

Sophia inhaled, unable to believe what the woman had said.

"Hush up." Karl commanded. "This is a different time and place. That evil is behind us. It should never have occurred. My best friend, Jules Silverman, was taken away. I can't imagine what he faced. I don't even know if he survived."

Helga lifted a meaty shoulder. "Why you had any compassion for that Jew I'll never know."

"Shut up," Karl snapped. "I'll not having you speak such filth in our home."

Kurt leaned his chair back on two legs and flashed a smart-aleck grin. "I've a riddle for you, Aunt Helga. What do you call a prune-faced old German lady who is as mean as a female boar? A sour kraut." Kurt threw back his head, his laughter echoing through the house, filling the sweet sea air and early evening.

"Sour kraut," Michael repeated, hiccupping, and smacking his knee as he roared with laughter.

Karl struggled to maintain control, finally choking, and then bursting into a full-blown grin as if a flock of flamingos escaped his stomach, lighting up his eyes and spreading into every part of him.

Never had her family been so unruly, yet Sophia felt the corners of her mouth lift, too.

Helga found her voice. "I see what your wicked influence has wrought, Sophia."

"Now see here—" interjected Karl.

"Your sons are filthy, untamed beasts, especially that one," she pointed to Kurt howling, striking his hand up and down almost involuntarily, and barely able to breathe. His laughter flowed over the room and then, suddenly, his chair fell backward. He crashed to the floor, rollicking with more laughter.

"Barbarians!" Helga shrieked, springing from her chair, raining insults upon the family. Like deeply plowed soil, Helga's face possessed a myriad of mottled red furrows, highlighted by a new charcoal-stained mole on her upper lip. "You have created the spawn of Satan."

Sophia stood, heat flooding through her body. "You will remember you are a guest of our family."

Helga turned her wrath on Karl. "If you were like our parents, your boys would have turned out good. Now they are barbarians."

Karl dropped his knife on his plate with a loud clang. "Our parents were too strict, too harsh. I feel our childhood was robbed from us."

Kurt rose. "Sorry, Aunt Helga—"

Helga backhanded him across the face. "Your son has such sloppy and indolent manners."

Sophia advanced around the table, creating an immoveable barrier between her son and her sister-in-law. She drew her hand back and slapped the woman across the face. The smack of flesh striking flesh echoed through the house. Her sons gaped.

"Whoo-ee, Mom's got a great right hook," Kurt crowed.

Between gritted teeth, Sophia clipped out a deadly warning to Helga. "You will never touch my son again. You may hate me if you like. But leave my son out of it. I have put up with your insults long enough and will no longer tolerate it."

Helga glared, rubbing her cheek. "Karl, I insist you punish your wife and make her apologize to me."

Karl met her gaze with a hard glare "I support my wife completely. The minute you thought I was dead, you tossed Sophia out of our family home and onto the streets. I *insist* you apologize to my wife and son."

"You are led by a ring through your nose with Sophia, and she of low birth," Helga spat. "Everyone knows she married you for your status and money."

Sophia laughed in her face, and then pulled herself up, towering over the harridan. "I am Princess Sophia Anna Sonderburg of Prussia. My father is Prince Albert Phillip Konigsberg-Holstein Sonderburg-Beck. When I married Karl, my family's riches and vast estates extended a thousand times farther than the Schneider's. If anything, I married far below my station."

"How nifty is that Michael? We're royalty," crowed Kurt. "What's for dessert?"

Helga's eyes bulged, her mouth opening and closing like a landed grouper. "I-I had no idea."

"It's best you don't say anything," Karl said. "We tire of your company. Pack your bags. You are no longer welcome in this house. I will secure a room for you in town tonight. Tomorrow, you will be sent home on the mailboat. I will give you five hundred dollars and that will be the last of the money you will receive. You will have to get a job to support yourself."

Sophia mouthed, *"Thank you"*. Her eyes softened with an inner glow toward her husband who championed her against his wretched sister. All those years of supporting Helga when they'd scraped by with barely enough money to feed them.

Queenie cleaned up the dishes, and Sophia walked down the path to where the beach swung in a long, lazy crescent, heavily fringed by massive palms.

"You look pensive tonight," said Karl, coming up behind her.

"I have never slapped anyone before," Sophia admitted.

"How did you find the experience?"

"It would have been more satisfying if she'd flown out the window like I imagined." She drew a deep breath, the humidity thick. "I'm thinking of my father, mother, brother, and sister. How I'd like to have one moment with them again."

The horizon was edged with a silver tint and a cormorant flew into the place where the last of the day's sun and the water converged. His wings were a blur of motion and he soon faded from sight.

"Why did you never tell me of your family...your real family? I'm your inferior. Why did you marry me?"

She knelt in the sand and started digging with her hands. "It's complicated and none of it matters anymore. My parents were against the Third Reich and their opinions resulted in their deaths." She couldn't be cruel and tell him the truth. That she hadn't loved him at the time and had only married him for the protection of his name.

"I see."

She quit digging and stood. He needed reassurance. "I love you, Karl."

Karl reached out and smoothed back a swath of hair the Atlantic's salty breeze had whipped across her face. As he tucked the wayward strand behind her ear, she stilled, not seeming to breathe. "I love you, too, Sophia."

Happy tears backed up in her throat. She captured his thumb before it could desert her lips and lingeringly kissed his palm. "Promise me you won't bow and scrape. I couldn't bear it."

He laughed. "Oh, I have something that will make you happy," Karl said and handed her an envelope.

Sophia stood, ripped it open and read. "Gabrielle." She pressed her letter to her breast, and then threw her arms around her husband. "Oh, Karl, she has accepted my invitation and is coming to the Bahamas and bringing a friend. No doubt, she wants my approval of a man she's met. It washes away all the unpleasantness of your sister's visit."

Chapter Fifty-Two

Sophia, Karl, and the boys waited on the dock for the seaplane to propel to shore. Sophia could not wait to see Gabrielle and had prepared two bedrooms, going over the house and property with Queenie to make everything immaculate and perfect for her friend's arrival.

Gabrielle waved to her, jumped out and hugged her.

"This is Kurt and this is Michael." Both boys shook her hand. "Of course, you remember Karl."

"Who is your friend?" Sophia asked, ducking her head around.

A woman instead of a man backed out of the plane, dragging her suitcase. The woman was slender and had light hair like Sophia.

Gabrielle couldn't stop grinning and laughing. Sophia frowned at Gabrielle's odd behavior and was about to remark on it when the woman turned around.

As if ordered to do so, the clouds opened and sky-piercing light haloed the woman. Her dress was white, her hair piled high, adding to the woman's radiance.

Everyone watched Sophia, expecting her to do something, but what?

The strange woman stared at her with amazing blue eyes...the same eyes as hers.

"Sophia, is it really you?" the woman asked.

Sophia quit breathing for a few moments. The ground moved beneath her feet. Her vision blurred. She pushed back tendrils of windblown hair. Her knees started to collapse, but Karl pulled her up.

Was this a cruel joke? No. It couldn't be true.

"Louisa?"

The stranger nodded and Sophia fell into her sister's arms. "I can't believe you're alive. So many years I've thought you dead. Karl, she's alive. My sister!"

They cried and hugged. Never would she let her sister go.

"You survived. I survived. I've prayed for a moment like this for years, begging God to let me see you if only for a moment. To see you, and know you made it. Just once was all that I'd hoped for."

"It took me so long to find you. I thought you were dead... didn't know you had married," said Louisa.

After the joyful meeting at the dock, they all piled in the car. The boys fell in love with Louisa and Gabrielle, grabbing their hands and taking them to show them everything, not giving them a moment's rest. Infected with their enthusiasm, Sophia walked arm in arm with Gabrielle and her sister, exploring the island, beaches, the mangroves, and town.

In the evening, feeling relaxed and peaceful, the whole family sat on the cool veranda of their home, eating dinner, and looking out over the colorful garden toward the sea.

Queenie had outdone herself. There was fried snapper with a creamy coconut lime sauce, peas and rice, macaroni and cheese, and guava duff, a traditional island steamed pudding made from fresh guavas with a sweet rum butter sauce for dessert.

"I could never tire of this view," sighed Louisa.

Flocks of green parrots settled in the peeling bark branches of a Kamalame tree dining on scarlet seeds filched from Christmas palms. Their cries mingled with those of the proud peacocks that seemed to inhabit the bush in clusters.

With the excitement of Louisa's and Gabrielle's arrival, showing them the house and the town, they'd not been able until now to talk.

Louisa clasped her hands together. "There were thousands of refugees desperately waiting to escape. Our parents among the ones who helped them. Who would question a Prussian prince and princess? But after the East Prussian aristocrat, Count Stauffenberg tried to assassinate the Fuehrer, the Gestapo went out in full retaliatory force, rounded up everyone and executing them.

"Our parents had no warning. It was in the middle of the night when the Gestapo raided our castle in Zachwyt. Mama woke Stefan and me up, put on our coats and boots, and handed us out the window. 'Run!' she cried. 'Don't look back!' That was the last time we saw Mother. I could hear the Nazis footsteps thundering up the stairs, the sound of the door splintering and Mother's cries. How scared I was sliding down the roof. We climbed down the branches of the ancient wisteria vine that grew up the south wall and connected us to the broad branches of an oak tree. We were halfway down, hanging like little monkeys from the tree, when I heard our mother's scream.

"We dropped to the arms of awaiting gypsies. In the dark, Mama Zeilinski dragged us away from the castle before German soldiers surrounded it. I heard men yelling inside the house, *Search the timberlands!* We melted in the forests as a barrage of ceaseless gunfire rattled out front. I could hear Mama's pleadings and screams as they killed all the servants, many of the tenants...then Mother and Father."

"My God," Sophia said, trembling from head to foot. "How did you escape?"

"For several days we traveled by foot. It was cold. So terribly cold. Our brother caught a chill. He couldn't eat. A big gypsy man carried him, but Stefan was so slight...he died. We buried him in the forest.

"The gypsies followed a labyrinth of secret trails through the vast woodlands, taking me to a port two hundred miles east of Konigsberg where I was smuggled aboard a ship and taken to Sweden. A lovely old couple adopted me. I begged them to look for you. All their searches via the Swedish government were for naught. Berlin had been badly bombed and there was little hope you had survived.

"Oh, how I wept those first few years. Everything around me seemed dark and petrifying. My family and everything that was familiar to me, gone.

"After a near decade, and my adoptive parents passing, I decided to move to Austria. What had happened to my older sister haunted me. I could not mourn you because, in my heart, I knew you were not dead. This time, I started my own search. I contacted the German Red Cross, extending to the International Committee of the Red Cross since they had located millions of missing people. I also contacted the International Tracing Committee and the Jewish Relief Services, registering my address everywhere. Nothing.

"Finally, I traveled to Berlin and visited your university and your old neighborhood. No one knew of your whereabouts. I covered so much ground searching for you. After a week, I was ready to give up when a wind hurled against me, blowing my hat across the street. Thankfully, a woman on the other side captured it. When I caught up to her...it was Gabrielle. I recognized your friend from the day our family had taken you for your first year at the university. What were the odds?" Louisa beamed. "And so, I am here, after many years and reunited with my older sister."

Sophia grabbed her hand. "I'm ever so grateful. Yet I can't stop thinking about the horror of how Mama and Papa and Stefan died."

Louisa took a ragged breath. "For years, I suffered grief, guilt, and anger like so many of us who survived the horror. Then, small bits of hope peeked through. I discovered Mama Zeliinski and her family had survived.

"My registration at the International Red Cross, and Jewish Relief Services was like pulling a thread on a sweater that unravels it all. I started receiving hundreds of letters from the people our parents had saved, thanking me, telling me how their lives had prospered because of Mama and Papa's sacrifice. I'm so proud of our parents." Louisa handed Sophia a packet of envelopes.

Everyone grew silent. Even the boys' restlessness had stilled as they looked to her. Sophia could not speak, holding the packet secured with a red ribbon. She swiped her eyes with a shaky hand while distant strands of calypso music played at a bar in the harbor. With her sister's declaration, she grew even more to respect her parents for their dedication. Anger she'd felt at what she'd seen as their desertion of her, dissipated like an outgoing tide. "I'll read these letters later in private."

"Well, that's done," said Gabrielle, spooning an extra portion of guava duff onto her plate. "So where will your fine young sons continue their schooling when they are old enough?"

It was a topic Sophia wanted to put off. How lonely her life would be without her boys!

Karl heaped another helping of peas and rice on his plate. "Sophia and I have entertained several options. Perhaps Berlin," said Karl.

Kurt screwed his face. "Michael and I have been talking. Why not the United States? Then we can come home more often."

The next day, Karl promised a deep-sea fishing trip for their guests and the boys. They traveled in their new Chris-Craft cabin cruiser out to the Atlantic ridge where the ocean depth dropped from three hundred to ten thousand feet deep and where the big fish came up to feed on the smaller ones. Magnificent frigate birds skimmed the surface of the glittering ocean, then divebombed, seizing upon flying fish chased by bonito jumping, coming up out, and then dropping back into the water in groups without hardly any disruption of the surface. Her senses alive, Sophia watched the tuna as they emerged, glistening in the sun, and returning, weighty heads down to pass into the water without a splash.

"What a glorious sight," said Louisa, awed by the spectacle.

Kurt clamped his battered straw hat to his head and dished chum from a bucket into the sea. "I hope we catch a big one."

"Big ones, little ones," said Michael. "What does it matter? They are all good eating."

Kurt was barefooted, wore a faded pair of dungarees, and an old striped fisherman's shirt. He fastened his hook onto the line with his own method while Michael made the knot precisely like a skilled surgeon. They cast into the sea, their lines trailing out over the wake of the motor. In three minutes, Kurt had a huge tug on his line.

Sophia gazed over the stern where the wake ran sharply in the unruffled sea and the two baits from the outriggers were lagging, plunging and jumping in the whorl of the waves the wake raised as it slashed through the calm.

Kurt had his rod butt in the gimble and was looking up at the bell on the outrigger line. The line dropped from the outrigger in an elongated, gradual loop that tensed as it struck the water and now was running out at an angle, slicing the water as it set off.

"Hit him," yelled Michael. "Before he spits it out."

"I'm handling him," said Kurt, allowing more line out, his pole bending with the weight.

Karl throttled the motor down.

Kurt braced his feet, tightened the drag down and struck back hard against the great weight. "I've hooked him," Kurt squealed with delight.

"Tighten up on your line," said Karl. "Work him in."

Kurt lifted and reeled, lowering, lifting, bringing in the line on his hungry reel for hours. The great fish jumped above the water's surface, rising, shining silvery white, seeming to come infinitely out of the water. It was mind-boggling as his length and massiveness rocketed out of the sea into the air, seemingly suspended there until he fell with a splash that drove water up high and white.

"It's a marlin!" shouted Michael.

Kurt did not break his concentration, reeling in, and then allowing the marlin to descend several fathoms, his reel spinning hotly.

"Do you think he'll get him?" whispered Louisa, as tense as Sophia, and praying the boy would get the fish.

"Keep working it, Son, the fish will tire," said Karl, steering the boat.

Kurt bent forward and pulling up from the soles of his feet, used all the leverage of his body and all the weight he had on each lift, reeling in fast with his right hand. Sophia wetted his hat and returned it to his head. She worried about his long sun exposure and blisters forming on his soles and hands.

"Maybe we should let him go," she protested.

Behind Kurt, Karl warned her with a sharp shake of his head. "Let him alone. This is man's work."

"I'm not giving up Mama," said Kurt. "What if I don't get him?"

Karl was right. "It is like my mother said. Sometimes, we must suffer the scars of fate and keep going through the erratic surges of misfortune, but always maintain hope." There was no way Kurt would understand or remember the bit of wisdom she shared with him, but she straightened, feeling better for it.

For hours, the boy fought the fish. Sophia gave him drinks of water. The great fish was tiring, and Kurt drew him up steadily, the tip of his pole bending straight down, the marlin thrashing the back of the boat. Sophia took the wheel as Karl and John Sawyer hooked and winched the gigantic fish aboard the boat.

Louisa and Gabrielle clapped their hands, their faces as enthused as the boys.

"I've never seen the like," said, Gabrielle.

"I'm so happy for Kurt and have not had so much excitement in a long while," said Louisa, standing away from the sharp sword of the flapping marlin.

There were numerous fish nesting in the ice hold. A hundred-pound white marlin, six yellowfin tuna, three strawberry snappers, and six Queen trigger fish, their bright blue bands glowing in the sun.

"We'll have good eating for a few nights," said Karl, tousling, Kurt's hair.

Karl cut the motors closer to shore. "Break out the starboard anchor, Michael. It's hot. Let's go in for a swim before we head home. We've earned it."

Flanked by her sister and Gabrielle, Sophia stood watching them on deck, the bow facing into the wind and waves breaking white and green on the reef. Swimming slowly, her sons and husband, two dark heads and one light, swam out in the turquoise blue water, their bodies making shadows over the clear white sand, bodies forging along, silhouettes projected on the sand by the slim angle of the sun, their brown arms elevating and pushing forward, the hands slicing in, seizing hold of the water, and drawing it back, legs beating along steadily, heads rotating for air, inhaling effortlessly and smoothly.

"You and Karl must be so proud of your sons," said Louisa.

Gabrielle shaded her eyes from the sun, leaned over and whispered low and confidingly. "Does Robert know?"

Sophia blinked. "I don't know what you are talking about."

<h1 style="text-align:center">Chapter Fifty-Three</h1>

ashington D.C. 1957

Robert sat in the darkened gloom of his library. Beyond the walls of his upscale brownstone, Georgetown was bustling with the business of government. But even the mad rush of acquiring doners, lobbyists or congressional leaders couldn't hold back the thoughts of Sophia when night came.

He'd wake up in a sweat, patting the bed next to him and finding it empty. How he wanted Sophia by his side, to kiss her, protect her from the invisible barrier that kept her away from him, and from the memories, as if he believed that with a kiss, he could step into the life that should have been.

He sat there facing the rest of the room. Silence came with a myriad of sounds.

The brush of the wind over shingles, the creaking of wood, the hundredfold tapping sounds inside the walls, under the floor, moving from place to place.

The cold and dark wrapped around him. In the time that Sophia had vanished from the face of the earth, he'd been married, miserable and then widowed. Cynthia had been killed in a car crash with one of her lovers. He couldn't blame Cynthia completely. He, too, had become a master of indifference. Perhaps if they'd had children, it might have been different. There would have been something to bind them. But Cynthia didn't want children. Pregnancy might have marred her figure. In that regard, she was as shallow as his mother. `

He liked the idea of having children. A part of an unfilled legacy that had become a huge gaping void for him. A boy to play baseball. A girl to take shopping. He didn't care if it was a boy or girl. To have someone to grow with and see the world through their eyes.

Caroline and Liam were off to school, living their lives. Caroline wrote letters and Liam called once a month. How he missed them.

Van opened and closed the door, and then sat in the chair opposite him.

"I did not invite you here. Don't you have a company to run?" Over the past years, Robert had given most of the reins of running Pratt Motors to Van to free him to be senator.

"I came for two reasons. First, I came to bring my personal condolences over the loss of your mother."

Robert found it hard to feel any grief over his mother's passing. Judith had experienced a debilitating stroke and was placed in a nursing home. Dementia set in. When he visited her, she didn't know him or the fact that she'd piled her mashed potatoes in the drawer. The last six months of her life ended with delusions and suspicion, staring off into space, and compulsive eyebrow plucking, enough that they had to tie her hands to the bed. Eventually, he hoped, he'd be able to learn to pity her.

Van fiddled with a giant globe, spinning it around. "You're still in love with Sophia, aren't you?"

Robert's mouth screwed in a dry smile that was more a scowl. "I plead the fifth."

He was determined to put all thought of her behind him.

Sophia was his greatest failure. His most profound regret. Most of all, he ran from his nature, his choices, and his anger.

Van studied the dizzying globe. "Too long, you've been as gloomy as Prometheus tied to a rock with a bird eating your liver."

"Imagine," Robert said. "Being punished by the gods for an eternity." Van would be the only person he'd admit that to. But the image of Sophia reclining on the bed, her blonde hair spilling across the pillow...the image of her devastation that day in the stables...those two images were burned onto the back of his eyelids.

He'd become hardened, disillusioned, and lost. The war had returned in night terrors. He needed Sophia. Only Sophia had the power to wipe the nightmares away.

"Pay attention to me," Van said. "You've done enough mooning about a woman you'll never find. Pick up some other dame out of the thousands of your adoring fans."

"Out of the thousands that want me for my money or prestige?"

"Throw off those absurd thoughts and get some dame and have kids with her. Delaying is the erosion of the soul."

To think she was alone and possibly had his child? He thought of Caroline's claim...had dismissed it. After all, Caroline had been a child herself. What could she know about pregnancy...and yet...?

But Sophia's cryptic message haunted him. She had taken something from him and promised to cherish it.

No. It couldn't be true.

He couldn't shake that image. "I am absurd to you?"

Van got up and poured a glass of whiskey. "No. You are lonely."

Robert stood, looked out the window at the bare trees. Snow was promised in the wee hours. Oh, to be somewhere warm, with lots of sunshine. "I married Cynthia to punish Sophia. Little did I realize how that revenge would be turned on me with a cheating and cold wife."

Van joined him and tipped his glass. "Ah, revenge, so sweet yet turns bitter so quickly."

"The minute she said, 'I do', her true colors came out. One marriage failure is enough for me. If I have the need, I have any number of women to call upon."

Across the street, an Air Force officer opened a taxi door. A girl exited, wearing a pale-blue dress and the wintry wind twirled it around her legs. His heart panged. She reminded him of Sophia. The old ache spread through his limbs.

"Do you realize every woman you pick is a copy of Sophia?" Van turned and gave the globe a spin again.

Robert had gone out with a myriad of women. Too many. Actresses, models, shopkeepers. Strings of empty relationships.

"Any luck finding where Sophia's gone?"

"No." Robert shrugged, and then collapsed in his chair. "I've spent a fortune on the best detectives over the years. Absolute waste of time and money."

"But still, you search for her?"

"What else is there to do with my life?"

"Do you think she's still alive?"

"She has to be." To think she might be dead before he'd asked for her forgiveness was unbearable. Then, for sure, his life would be over.

"I'm not saying you blew it, but you should have eloped with her."

"There was a problem with that. She already had a husband."

"I remember. She sure fooled me."

"She thought he'd been killed in a bombing. After two years, he showed up from the dead."

"Jesus, Mary and Joseph. No wonder you never talked about it all these years. You were the one going places, the senate seat, owner of the largest automobile company, homes everywhere, the best. You were the one with the great life. In reality..."

"I blew the only thing that mattered," Robert said, rubbing

the heel of his palm against his chest. "What's the second reason you are in Washington?"

Van got up and planted his hands on the desk. "I need you to go to Nassau, Bahamas to meet with Dean Kurland."

Robert frowned. "Why is Kurland so important?"

"It would be beneficial for the people of the United States, especially Texas, and to Pratt Motors. Kurland ran a Ponzi scheme on Gleason Glass, nearly bankrupting the company. That said, we could get another supplier, but Gleason Glass has been a long-time supplier, always on time, and with good product."

"And Hank Gleason is a long-time good friend of my father."

Van straightened. "He built Gleason Glass from the ground up. He attempted suicide the other day."

"God." Robert ran his hand through his hair, thinking of Hank Gleason and the fact that he'd just lost his wife and kids in a boating accident. "What else?"

"I took the liberty of hiring a private detective and he was thorough. Kurland has a chemical plant in Avalon, Texas that is leaking mercury into the town's water supply. Many people are getting sick. No one can prove it is the plant, and the people of the town are without means and the know-how in carrying out a lawsuit that could go on for years in the courts."

Van laid an envelope onto the desk. "Here's a comprehensive dossier. He's also drilling oil on federal lands without a permit."

"Damn. I'll leave tomorrow to take care of the bastard."

Chapter Fifty-Four

Nassau, Bahamas 1957

The Royal Victoria Hotel embodied the charming, graceful atmosphere of Nassau. Away from the noisy street and through an iron gate and into a garden, Sophia had been transported to a lush, tropical, and quiet world. Green and yellow tendrils of large, exotic leaves hung from the slender, shady palm trees. In the thorny scarlet bougainvillea, the mockingbirds burst into song. Turquoise peacocks strutted down coral-lined paths. Colorful little horse-drawn carriages clattered along the driveway bringing tourists with their newly acquired straw hats and bags to the hotel.

To the east was a luxurious pool that the boys had run off to discover nestled in an expansive tropical garden that overlooked the harbor. Built on a former enclave of ruling pirates and vagabonds added to the allure that drew the rich and famous. A major Hollywood film was being made there.

In his standard dark suit with vest, white shirt, somber tie and black shoes, Sophia watched Karl check in at the hotel desk. He was too absorbed with righting his business venture of which he kept secret from Sophia. Oh, how she wanted to trust Karl, but his denial that everything was good broke the last straw. His increased agitation and frenetic phone calls had her pulse racing, and no way could she enjoy the lovely hotel.

"Karl, I looked at our accounts. The real estate venture you have with Dean Kurland has me worried. You have put everything we own into this investment. What do you know about the man you are dealing with?"

"How dare you look at my books."

Her nails bit into her palms. The last thing she wanted was to create a fight in the middle of the hotel lobby. "Tell me, are we on the precipice of losing our home and the boys' education, and everything we've worked for?"

Karl glared at her. "You are not to concern yourself with my business matters."

Her nostrils flared with Karl's obsession to be rich. Despite trying to be a picture of calmness, her brain rioted in panic. She stepped closer and in chilly, precise words, said, "It is my concern because I've worked as hard as you. I will not be pushed aside to lose everything while you make risky investments with an oily business associate."

A finely dressed couple with a thick New York accent haggled with the clerk in front of them for the top floor penthouse that was unavailable.

The desk clerk looked up and said, "Are you Dr. Schneider?"

Karl nodded.

"I have an important message for you."

Karl tore open the missive and read it. "I must go back to Abaco. I'm meeting with Dean Kurland. He wants me to show him the property boundaries. You see, matters are going to be fine."

Sophia's heart sank because she didn't trust the image Karl painted was as rosy as he wanted her to believe. "I thought this was to be a family vacation. What about the boys? They will be so disappointed."

"Business first. Our future depends on it. There was a mix-up in communication. I thought we were to meet in Nassau." He said goodbye and turned. "I'll make it up to you and the boys. Stay here and enjoy the holiday, and then I'll join you in two weeks."

Sophia turned to Queenie, John, and the twins. "I guess we are on our own."

During her dispute with Karl, people had wedged in line ahead of them. She waited, fidgeting with her pocketbook. She took a bracing breath. In the face of their looming financial disaster, she was unable to get over the feeling she was being watched. Listening to the lively sounds of Caribbean music blaring from a side wing of a pirate-themed bar, Sophia counted their luggage, surreptitiously glancing around the lobby. Potted palms, bamboo chairs, huge vases of bird of paradise lined the columns of the lobby where new patrons tapped across the marble tiles, passing antique decor. Long-lashed women with tightly tousled, bleached-blond curls, draped in colorful halter dresses, imitating Marilyn Monroe, decorated the lobby like so many flowers. Businessmen in light tan suits with newspapers rolled under their arms were there, and young teenage girls with *Seventeen Magazines* giggled at college-aged boys.

Robert saw her. *Sophia.* After a decade combing the world for her.

He'd stood stock still beside a column, drinking in the sight of her. The years had not slipped away, they had lessened despite the tragic part of the twentieth century that had fallen on her in a single coup—the Nazis, his unforgiveable treatment of her, and so many years that had cast a shadow without him, searching for her, and now he'd found her. She was older and more classic, an ageless beauty.

Chic in her stylish white suit and matching broad-brimmed hat, she exuded a greater elegance than Princess Grace of Monaco.

With a glaring ache, he remembered his first sight of her in

Berlin. He'd been struck by lightning, his breath stolen, his heart burning as it was now. When she'd sworn at him in six different languages, he'd realized she was the one for him and laughed at the whimsical workings of the gods. Of all the women he'd know, only Sophia had been his match. Was some force reaching through time to reunite them again?

Robert's hands fisted. Karl, her husband told her he was going to a meeting.

She acknowledged him. Always in control. Always prepared. Always well-groomed and well-mannered, delightful, and kind. And always, eternally beautiful.

When her husband hurried through the lobby, Robert stirred from the shadows, everything moving in slow-motion like a hallucinatory blur.

Head tilted, Sophia refastened a tiny diamond stud, one of a pair Karl had given her for her birthday and watched her husband dash through the revolving doors. "Well, I guess that leaves the five of us," she said, pushing aside her resentment at Karl's all-too-familiar-abandonment, and deciding to make the best of their vacation.

Suddenly, a sense she was being watched stole over her, the back of her neck prickling. Wary, she fiddled with her purse again and checked her surroundings. A noise from behind forced her to turn.

She froze, her lungs seizing in her chest and her heart plunging to her stomach.

Robert.

After all these years. He was here. She could no longer hear people busily crossing the lobby floor, children splashing and screaming in the pool, bellboys carrying in luggage. The ceiling fans slowed to a blur. Her heart was thumping so loud she was sure everyone could hear. Time dissolved and everything melted away.

He ate up the whole of the lobby in a few composed strides, stopping in front of her.

Robert was not here, but her logical mind saw the danger. Run. Flee. Her imagination ran wild like a placid ocean transforming into rough waves pounding the shores, pounding her. Cornered. Trapped.

She looked up at the man who stared down at her with a guarded, almost uncertain expression, and she swayed a little only half-believing her eyes. She drank in the sight of him like the condemned might search for a glimpse of the sky, or the faintest hint of kindness.

His features spoke of maturity and self-assurance. His hair was darker than it had been ten years ago, except for a few gray hairs that dared to invade his temples.

He possessed the same engaging smile yet with a hint of melancholy and sorrow.

The proud brow and stubborn jaw, however, were unmistakable. A web of lines fanned out at the corners of his sea-green eyes.

Queenie cleared her throat. Dear God, was Sophia that transparent? She snapped to attention and performed a stiff introduction. "Oh, Senator Pratt. Imagine seeing you here. May I introduce Queenie and her husband, John, this is Senator Pratt from Michigan." The formality fell flat. Her palms sweated. Robert knew she was nervous.

Both boys rushed up to her, pulling on her arms toward a rear veranda. "Mom, wait until you see the pool! It has a high diving board."

Sophia swallowed. What horrid timing.

Robert stiffened, staring wide-eyed at the twins, incredulous. Sophia could almost see his brain stutter for a moment, the mechanisms going on pause as his thoughts grinded to catch up.

A cold, tingling numbness spread across her forehead, into her mouth, into her cheeks. She couldn't speak because her lips were paralyzed. Even if she *could* speak, what would she say?

Her knees shook. Her stomach opened into a sickly empty pit. The boys looked curiously to him, and then to her.

Robert narrowed his eyes on her. "Aren't you going to introduce me to these two fine boys?"

He knew.

The accusing note of his words held her rooted to the spot.

Haunted warnings by Queenie years before hoisted its frightful head. *What if the real father were to find out he had sons? What then?* Sophia had not wanted to think of the consequences.

"This is Queenie and her husband, John," Sophia repeated, trying to draw attention away from her sons.

"I'm Kurt," her son said, stepping forward and shaking Robert's hand. "It's nice to meet you."

Robert held his hand, kept a tight grip as if he'd lose the boy. "I'm Senator Pratt, an old friend of your mother's."

Kurt stared at Robert. What was going on in her son's mind? The boy was ten going on one hundred. Kurt yanked his twin forward. "This is Michael."

Robert shook hands, almost refusing to let go. *Spellbound.* "It's nice to meet you, Michael. Why, you are both two of the finest young men I've ever had the pleasure to meet. Miss Queenie and Mr. John, I bet the boys are chomping at the bit to get in that pool. I'd like to have a word with their mother. Would you mind?"

John scooted the boys out to the pool, leaving Queenie, and Sophia thanked God for her comforting presence. Kurt kept looking behind until John forced him out.

Sophia forced her mouth to work again. "I don't really have anything to say to the man."

"She has a lot to say, and I'd like the privacy." Robert cut her a sharp look that dared her to argue.

He had no right over her. Beneath her breath, she cursed him in six different languages. Years ago, when she was vulnerable, he had discarded her without a thought. And that memory sent a volcano of abandonment and anger rocketing upwards.

Queenie looked him up and down, her strange appraising eyes missing nothing, darting from the boys to Robert, comparing the easily identifiable dark hair and sea-green eyes. The veiled mystery beneath Queenie's one blue eye and one black eye hinted at the shadowy strain of mysticism buried deep in her Caribbean roots. With certainty, Queenie tapped her psychic divination and knew who the man was to Sophia.

"Yes, Senator Pratt, we'll watch the boys. I think this conversation has been long coming. A conversation that might take a couple of weeks."

Sophia narrowed her eyes on the departing black woman. Sophia turned on him. "Senator Pratt, there will be no conversation." She'd fought for years to get over Robert. She'd not fall into that trap again.

Queenie turned, placed her hands on her hips. "Mr. Karl will be gone for a long while—"

Sophia sputtered. "Don't even suggest that I'd spend one moment—"

Robert's features darkened, the shadows pulling around him as if his anger could chase away the light shining through the broad lobby windows. "She will come with me."

"No harm better come to Miss Sophia, or you'll be dealing with me," said Queenie.

"I promise," Robert said curtly. "She'll be returned. And thank you."

"How dare you. I have nothing to say to you." Sophia started to walk away.

Robert grabbed her arm. "Is my directive too difficult for you? Or shall I try to frame an easier one?" Waves of menace rolled from him, emanating with such strength, she was astonished that she wasn't toppled over by the tidal force.

Sophia hesitated. She thought of her boys. Would he reveal they were his sons?

"A scene would be perilous." He angled his head to the growing interest of hotel patrons.

Furious, she nodded her head and, from the lobby, she walked ahead of him, up an elevator to the top floor and ushered into the penthouse suite which entailed the entire top floor. Robert slammed the door.

"What are you doing here?" she asked, breathing as if she'd run a mile.

He just looked at her, his eyes raking down her body in such an inscrutable way she couldn't tell if he was undressing her or sizing her for a coffin.

Shadows lurked in the hollows of his cheeks and smudges darkened the skin beneath his eyes. Eyes that pierced her like the point of a knife, pinning her where she stood. He dropped her arm and then walked to a window, turning his back on her.

She didn't owe him anything. The sooner she put as much distance between them the better. She turned the doorknob.

"Don't even think about it. I'm an important United States Senator and any drama in the hotel would make great fodder for the papers. Do you really want that?"

She whirled. Did he have eyes on the back of his head? "I cannot possibly stay. If you have any shred of decency, you'd let me leave."

"None of those attributes belongs to me."

"At this point, any conversation between us would be irrelevant."

"Are the boys my sons?"

She could see his muscles bunching beneath his suit coat. "They are not yours." Her mind raced with the lie. She thought of how powerful and rich he was. Oh, God, he'd use his power to take away the boys, take them away from her, and destroy all of them if he chose. She tried to calm the nerves rattling up her spine...he couldn't prove that they were his sons.

Robert spun around, piercing her with that incisive intensity that made him so formidable an opponent in the senate, in business. Could he see her mind racing? The lack of honesty nauseated her. How she was still haunted by his smell and the touch of his lips, and the falsehood she'd told.

"Tell me the truth!" He advanced on her, that predatory swagger returning. "They are spitting images of me. You cannot deny that they are mine."

She said nothing.

He stopped only when he towered over her. A smarter woman would have stepped back. Retreated. But Sophia would no longer yield ground. Her eyes blurred from all the years and the angry man in front of her, but she wasn't going to let him get away easily for the humiliation and years of longing and pain.

His eyes were cruel, cold, and hard. Abysmal. "Lies are a scourge, Sophia. They eat away all the good and leave devastation. Now, tell me the truth."

Heat swirled inside her. A conflagration of rage fed by helplessness. Her hand flung out and struck him on the cheek. "Bastard."

His head flinched ever so slightly to the side.

"I deserved that. Do you want to rip our truths open and bleed them all over each other? Is that what we are about?"

They held their gazes. Everything spoken and unspoken filled the spaces between them.

All the hate she had stored up for so many years, the rejection, the denial. She raised her head. "You already know the truth. I will not allow you to take them. You didn't want them any more than you wanted me."

His face softened, and ever so gently, he placed his fingers under her chin and raised her head to look at him. "That's where you are wrong, Sophia. Do you know how many years I searched for you? Thousands of dollars on detectives. You disappeared without a trace. Can you imagine how it feels? To find you after all these years in the last place I'd look?"

"I don't believe you. I left you a letter. You had plenty of time to make amends. You married Cynthia."

Robert nodded. "I was angry. Can you imagine my thoughts in the stables when I discovered you were married? That you had played me for a fool?"

"I was going to tell you everything that day. And then your mother announced your betrothal to someone else. After you had promised to marry me. I was so hurt...I ran. And then...Karl back from the dead...who would have expected...you wouldn't let me explain—"

"I found your letter explaining everything entombed in a book years later."

"I'll never forget that day—"

His gaze grew cold. "My mother was thorough in guiding your husband to you that day, making sure I was present, and achieving the perfect storm. She knew how I'd react. And because of my mother's wicked machinations, I've lived an unhappy life with a shallow woman. Now, I've found you."

"Yes, you've found me, but it doesn't change things. Your mother couldn't force you to marry Cynthia. You did that to yourself to spite me."

"Stop it, Sophia. All these years, my life has been an empty shamble. An unfaithful wife I could barely tolerate. She is gone. Died in an accident with one of her lovers. Because of my pride, I made the biggest mistake of my life in letting you go."

"You are a senator. You have what you sought."

"I'm a senator who has stood on the edge of a river but too cowardly to jump."

Her conscience pricked her. That this beautiful man was so vulnerable and lonely because of her. She looked into his eyes that seemed ancient now, a lifetime of pain. It made her hurt to see his face so ravaged by emotion.

"My boys." She had come so far to mold the perfect family. What about Karl? He had cared for her and the children. And in a way, she loved Karl. What if her honesty with Robert ruined her family? Would Robert be angry enough to expose her publicly? He was that powerful. She should leave now.

Robert put his forehead on hers. "Sophia, Sophia. How many times have I wished to see you? We have two weeks. Your woman will watch the boys."

"I cannot—"

"I would never break up your family. I'd like to spend the day with you or have dinner, whatever you are comfortable with."

The old feelings returned, latent overwhelming feelings. His nearness washed her with such a swath of emotion she feared she might drown in them, opening her soul, releasing pain and fear and sadness and torment like a floodgate.

"Sophia." His voice was deeper than before. *"Please."*

A longing like anything she could ever imagined tugged at her. She wanted to spend time with him, too.

Sophia spent the day with the twins and then left them in the hands of Queenie and John while she went out to dinner with friends—or so she had informed them. A taxi picked her up in front of the hotel. Robert had commandeered a guest house from his friend, wealthy Huntington Hartford, the heir to the A&P fortune who owned Paradise Island. The isolation afforded them privacy from prying eyes and those who might know Karl.

She went to the front of the house where the scent of jasmine wafted from inconspicuous blossoms that opened at night. The metallic singing of cicadas and the occasional plaintive cry of a whippoorwill followed her. There were no neighbors, and a cool ocean breeze swept away her wistful sigh.

The door was open, and she walked through the house into a small courtyard. She heard his chuckle and inclined her head past a palm tree so that she could see better his handsome features. He drew up beside her. His eyes contained the lambent glow of green quicksilver. The way his muscles corded, the sun-browned column of his neck, the way his smile lifted to fill his face, even the heady smell of him...she trembled, her skin suddenly so hot it was like a scorching flame ignited inside her.

Even at forty-one, his body was sculpted of different clay than most, perhaps stolen from some heavenly threshold instead of the pedestrian earth from which others were forged. When the masters brushed onto canvas gods of myths and legends, they might have surveyed his frame.

Feeling a little insecure, she said, "I'm not the woman you knew." She was a decade older, had borne two sons, but had kept her figure. Yet, he lifted her face toward his, and with absolute certainty, she saw her beauty and perceived her own sense of worth reflected back to her in the mirror of Robert's eyes.

He slid his finger beneath her chin, tilted her head up until their gazes met...held. "I love you, Sophia. But I must admit when I first saw the boys, I wanted to throttle you for keeping my sons away from me."

She pulled back, shaping her hand to his jaw. "I never intended to keep anything from you. I was going to tell you I was with child the day of the bar-b-que. But after you...I could not tell you...my shame...how frightened I was...you didn't want me, and I believed there was no way you'd want our child. I went with Karl because I had no choice." She could feel his heartbeat with every breath he took.

He dropped his hand and motioned her ahead. "Let's take a walk down the beach."

A mantle of scarlet and amethyst light slid between the gaps of overhanging palm fronds as they strolled through the surf, side by side.

"I never paused to consider about how a secret of carrying another man's child must have weighed on you year after year, and how distressing and terrifying it would be," he said.

The weight of it bore down on her now, forced her throat shut against any reply.

He seemed to lose a battle with himself, his face completely melted into something she couldn't identify; it was so beautiful. It went beyond gentleness, to a tender, hungering devotion that threatened to turn her into a pool of tears.

"I have lived all these years in a vacuum," Robert said, "pretending not to feel, not to feel the loneliness surrounding me, not to feel your touch, or you lying beside me at night. The years I searched to find you. How many times I wanted to seek your forgiveness and see if you needed anything, and then—that fated second, I saw you in a lobby. To know I might have a chance...that you could forgive me."

She shook her head, wanting to say that she wasn't angry. How did she tell him of the emptiness in her life? How did she tell him of the years of yearning for her one true soulmate? That this powerful man beside her was so vulnerable it broke her.

His face softened as if reading her thoughts. "I've never stopped thinking of that woman in Berlin, that woman I fell in love with. Those cherished times spent together in Michigan. It is impossible to be worthy of such a woman, but I can try. All I know is that I'm a cad, a United States Senator, an inheritor of an automobile industry, but none of it matters. I am no one if I am not yours. And I have nothing if you are not mine."

His hand lingered, tracing the curve of her neck as if it were a delicate thing. A treasure. "Tell me about our sons. You've been so strong to raise them."

She did not want to lose this spell. "Kurt is impulsive and fearless. Fast cars, planes, boats. No one can keep up with him, least of all me. He is so like his father." She looked at Robert with pride. "He is ready to set off for adventures, explore the world, Odysseus-fashion. Life is never dull with Kurt around. He thrives on action, and if there is none around, he creates it. He can be unreliable, foolhardy, and selfish, and I worry about his reckless behavior and how it might affect his twin. He gets in fights readily, which I abhor, but he champions the underdog, and often drags Michael into the fray. Yet he is so capable. If the door lock cannot be picked, he takes the door off its hinges. If a boat motor doesn't work, he'll tear it apart and put it back together. Everything about him is at high speed, as if the world doesn't whirl swift enough for him, taking extreme risks. It is a wonder I've survived his childhood. Yet, he has great compassion."

Robert's eyes shone down at her. Of course, he wanted to know everything about them. They were his flesh and blood. "And Michael?"

She dragged in a deep breath "Ah, Michael. If you have a mystery to be solved, then Michael has all the answers. He takes the time to examine every aspect of an issue. No fast breaks or hurried decisions for him. When he makes a commitment, he invariably follows through, but in his own good time. Unless prompted to protect Kurt. He is an expert in everything, analytical, and a pure academic. He earns high grades and, unlike Kurt, thinks before he acts. He is what you Americans call the 'Real McCoy'. He is genuine. When he gives his heart into something, especially the plight of animals, he is painfully vulnerable.

"Oh, the animals he brings home, heavy with parasites, starving, mange-ridden, broken bones, or wings...no matter what, he cares for them. He has a remarkable gift for healing all living things.

"Unlike his twin, he can be insular, inhibited, and inflexible. Yet Kurt has a way with him, provoking him out of his reclusiveness, and bringing out the warrior in him. Their opposite personalities complement the other."

They stopped for a moment looking at the silvery waves uncurling upon the beach. Robert skipped a stone through the surf. "Do you ever think about the war and its logic?"

"It seems so long ago, forgotten, yet lingers. I believe the prevailing winds that seeded the war are easily buried in mankind's pointless inanities, yet the true import of what happened is there, booming within the faint disguise of a whisper for all who might listen."

"You are stronger than me, Sophia, in many ways. I may be physically stronger, but that doesn't even faze you. You use your grace and skill, your beauty and brilliance. And beyond that, you've managed to do what I never could. Not just survive, but to truly live."

"You humble me."

"You lost your family, endured the war's hardships, the plunder of the Russians, but you have surrounded yourself with enduring love, and you've raised two wonderful sons that any man would be proud of. You've done it through sheer strength of character."

Sophia wanted to turn and melt into his arms. To take in lungfuls of his fine scent and free years of bottled-up sorrow.

He placed his hand on her back, guiding her to his house. "I want to know more about your past years."

Sophia took a deep breath. He wanted to know about Karl. By no means would she confide in Robert the dark side of Karl in those early, bleak years. Despite the shadow of how he was handling their finances, Karl had changed and there was no reason to disparage him. "The truth is, I never got to know Karl before we married. He was a very private person and always kind and our nuptials were done in haste, protection for me, for him, because he was ordered to the front.

"Yet after the war, he was no longer interested in the world outside, or in people. He became locked in the past, a prison of his own design. His father had been a successful banker, a Hitler man and very harsh. I think that part of Karl's past that he tried to leave behind, remained. The words with which a child's heart is poisoned, through malice or through ignorance, remain branded in his memory, and sooner or later they burn his soul."

"You are very forgiving, Sophia. You have a bigger heart than mine."

Robert wasn't stupid. He guessed she'd had a hard time of it. Robert led her into the house. "We are having a late dinner and… well…" She felt Robert cataloging each and every detail of her.

Sophia sat back and watched the waiter laying a table for dinner of rosemary lamb chops, parsleyed new potatoes, buttered string beans, fresh conch salad and a plate of fresh, hot croissants with coconut ice cream for dessert. The waiter removed the silver covers. Priestly hands. A bottle of red wine poked out of a silver ice bucket. A bottle of white wine, uncorked was on the cart.

"Will that be all, sir?"

"Thank you," Robert said and gave him a generous tip.

"Happy to be of service, sir."

When the man left, Sophia said, "Hm-m. Two sirs in thirty seconds."

Robert's windblown hair glistened darkly, and she itched to smooth the bronze waves touched with silver at his temples.

He raised his glass and clicked it with hers. "To us."

He folded his tanned, muscular arms in front of his chest. "Fill me in on your last years."

Sophia teased out a smile. "I'll tell you about Aayla. Aayla was an old woman, smelled like a wet dog and was a terrible neighbor. When we were finishing the build on our home, she would come onto our property at night and steal everything she could get her hands on. Every day, tools, nails, boards were missing, even my grapefruit she harvested. She had added a house to her meager hut. We attempted to buy her property, but it was Crown land. Tried to get rid of her via the authorities, but even a court order to vacate the premises was ignored. An older villager that had suffered from Aayla's stealing his chickens informed me of what to do."

She paused for a moment. "Only Voodoo will work," he said. "Fix a bottle filled with brown fluid and put two dead cockroaches in it. Stick two lily leaves resembling feelers and have them dangle from the opening, then hang it on a spot where Aayla climbs over your garden wall.

"It seemed simple enough. I followed the prescription and hung the vile mess on the path Aayla followed. Within two days, the problem took care of itself. Aayla disappeared with her wooden house, moving three miles away. To think a jar of goo and two dead cockroaches did the trick!"

Robert laughed and Sophia continued to charm him with several anecdotes about idiosyncratic patients and island dwellers.

"Why didn't you tell me you were a Prussian princess?" he asked.

Sophia widened her eyes shocked he'd discovered her history. "Does it really make any difference? From the war, my kingdom is gone like my family. That time and place feels like a million miles away. It is like bringing a dying ember to the winds and reducing it to a cold howl. Dredging up old titles that don't exist makes me sad. So, I didn't tell you. How did you find out?"

"My sister, Caroline, was your greatest ally. She had seen photos of your parents, researched, found old newspaper articles telling of your parents' brave heroics and their deaths. I feel bad you never told me."

"My sister, Louisa, is alive. The gypsies rescued her and helped her escape through the woodlands. She lives in Austria with her husband."

"That's wonderful. Except one thing bothers me. My investigators couldn't find you, but your sister could."

"It was a freak accident. My sister had been adopted and had a Swedish last name. She had traveled to Berlin and ran into Gabrielle. It was pure luck that Gabrielle was visiting the city that week after moving to a small town in southern Switzerland. Otherwise, there would have been no way to trace me."

Sophia smiled and reached for his hand over the table. "I will tell you of my history. Once, I was a princess who lived in a beautiful castle by a forest, and thought it would be my home forever..." And for the rest of the evening, she told him of her castles, vast estates, childhood, and her family.

Sophia was to come to a conclusion soon, and Robert would burn on a thousand crosses for every moment shared with her. Over the following days, the lovely intimacies carried lay unspoken with beach walks, picnics, or swimming in the sea. Bees buzzed outside the screened windows; palm trees silhouetted against the descending sun made a grotto of his cottage.

He thumbed through the *Detroit Tribune* and *New York Times,* papers he had delivered, albeit a day late. The USSR launched Sputnik 1, the first artificial satellite to orbit the earth, precipitating the Americans to enter a space race. He turned the page. Things were heating up in the south. His hands curled around the edges of the paper. Idiots had called up the National Guard to prevent nine African-American students from entering Central High School in Arkansas. Ridiculous. Eisenhower had personally requested Robert to be on the Civil Rights Commission, but he had to defer it for the Ways and Means Committee requirements ate up all his time. He'd fought a damned war, shoulder to shoulder with the best African-American soldiers he'd ever known. Now, he wished he'd taken on the additional responsibility. It irked him that there wasn't equality for all Americans.

Sophia entered the room, and white drapes floated around her like the veils of spirits. "This will be my last evening with you, Robert. My excuse that I'm shopping or dining with friends can only carry so far with my boys. On top of that, Karl is returning this afternoon."

He dropped his newspaper, looked up at her. He'd spent the

past week and a half walking on air, and now his world seemed to be collapsing. He rose, went to the sideboard, uncorked a crystal stopper in the cognac decanter, poured a sniffer, and downed it. "And here I've been hoping that you'd leave with me."

She hesitated for the longest time. "You know I'd never do that, and it is unfair of you to suggest that I'd leave with you."

He, too, was quiet, long fingers wrapped around the glass as he visibly battled emotions both bitter and desperate. Then he set the glass down. "Someone once said that the moment you stop to think about whether you love someone, you've already stopped loving that person forever," he said.

She shook her head. "I cannot leave. I owe Karl that much."

"You don't love him." *Stubborn.* Robert resisted the urge to shake some sense in her. Too afraid to let her out of his sights. Some sort of primitive need to kidnap her and the boys had overtaken all sense of reason.

It was dangerous what she continued to do him.

What she made him capable of.

"But I do," she said, "and that is what is so confusing. He has been a good father and husband. He can be difficult at times, but he loves me deeply."

Robert was barefooted and the wood floors felt cold and uneven against his soles. "I can make your life rich and wonderful, provide for the boys. I love you, Sophia, and you know we should be together."

"How flawed—"

"Our imperfections are the bonds that hold us together. We might as well recognize them. I ask again this one last time."

He was giving her an ultimatum and she pressed her finger to his lips. "Oh, how easy it would be to run away. To live the ideal life with you that I've dreamed for years. I cannot. I would rather fail by honor than succeed by fraud. And a fraud I would be. My life a sham. Tearing Karl apart, tearing our sons apart. No good could come from it. In the wake of so much selfishness, I'd drown beneath an ocean of guilt."

"And me? We've already lost years we should have been together. I don't even know my own sons. Am I supposed to walk away?"

It was the same argument they had had over the past days. She looked at him, saw his pain. "I know underneath you would never expect me to cheat or leave my husband. You have been nothing but honorable, noble, and considerate during our brief sojourn, and I know you'd never forsake your principles. You have too much heart to allow that to happen. Of course, I'll hurt you. But I couldn't bear the thought of making my sons one of those poor forlorn statistics. Children of a broken marriage, permanently homesick, nomads from house to house, preparing for the psychiatrist's couch."

"You always told me you'd protect your children. Like a mother lioness, you are."

She needed a moment longer to bask in his nearness. She swallowed around a lump of sadness and dread, inhaling the warm, masculine scent of him, imagining what it was like to be held by the only person she truly ever loved. Oh, to press her cheek against the heat of his chest. To listen to the sound of his heart. That percussion that had always resonated in her core. Kept her going in the worst possible moments.

She looked at Robert, standing in a triangle of light and searched for words that didn't exist. Every moment spent with him seemed a frozen golden drop of time, like jewels scattered across the sea—as vivid and as precious.

"Robert, in time—whether on earth or in the heavenly realm —we will be together for nothing happens by chance. Deep down, fate has a secret plan, even though we don't understand it. The fact that we met in a remote lobby, that you and I are here now. It's all part of fate that we cannot comprehend, and that fate owns us."

"You will stay the remainder of the morning."

It was a command not a request. They would not lose one second of their idyllic sojourn.

Barefooted, they went through the French doors, sliding between the drifting curtains and onto the terrace, leaving the grounds of the bungalow, the air hot and wet like the bottom of the Congo. Under a bruised sky, they wandered aimlessly down the beach, walking side by side. It would storm later.

Sophia felt waves of impotent frustration well within him.

"I will wait for you," he gritted out.

"You have the patience of a god."

He reached out and drew a knuckle down the curve of her cheek. "No. The patience of a man tormented by the wishes of the woman who belongs to him."

They headed back to the bungalow in a despondent silence. Sorrow ate at her soul.

"There is something else troubling you. What is it?" he asked.

She bit her lip. How Robert could read her mind. "Karl went back to Abaco to do business. All our investments are tied up in real estate. I don't like the man who he's involved with. I fear it is too late. All the hard work over the years for nothing. I'm terrified of losing our home, and any chance for our sons' education. I feel this time we will not recover from Karl's delusional investment schemes."

They walked beneath a knot of swaying palms, the sand warm on their feet. A coconut clunked on the ground.

"I can help."

Sophia shook her head. "I know you would, but your assistance would make matters worse. Karl would never accept your money. We'll just have to figure out something."

His parting kiss surprised her, lightly chafing his shadow-beard across her jaw just enough to still her resistance. In that simple kiss was the sweetness of passion, a million loving thoughts condensed into a moment. Robert took her hand, placed it on his chest, his heart beating hard against her palm, reluctant to let her go. "You will always be mine, Sophia."

She cupped her hand against his cheek. She wanted him more than anything else in the world. "I cannot"

He rested his forehead on hers. "I would never expect...if you ever need anything..."

"I want your assurance to stay away," she said.

He didn't answer.

"You promised me," she persisted. "If you love me, you'll keep that promise."

Robert took a long agonizing breath and straightened. "You will write to me of my sons. I want to hear everything about them."

Outside, the cab honked.

"I will." She swallowed hard and brushed away tears. "The reason it hurts so much to say goodbye is because our souls are connected." Sophia hurried out the door.

Chapter Fifty-Five

The house Dean Kurland resided in was on the crest of a hill, a huge, pink colonial building adorned with slender, white columns. The outside walls hosted a waterfall of colorful bougainvillea. An iron cannon harkening back to the days of pirates stood solitary, its mouth pointing to shore. The edifice was enveloped in terraced gardens and, as best as Robert could define it, resembled a tropical Versailles.

Robert was greeted at the door by Kurland's butler and led to a sprawling courtyard with an exquisite view of a sparkling blue sea where several other people had gathered for an exclusive luncheon.

A waiter appeared and Robert took a glass of Riesling. The high acidity tingled like vinegar, sour on his tongue. He'd journeyed from Washington to investigate Dean Kurland, a crook who was using government funds to build his portfolio in Nassau, Bahamas. Yet the main reason was to break the hold of the notorious swindler who'd pulled off a giant Ponzi scheme that affected a major supply source of Pratt Motors and his late father's good friend, Hank Gleason.

Robert ignored the other guests, walked to the precipice of a balcony, and stared down several feet of sharp limestone rock face.

A tall white crane peered down in the shallow water with his head, neck, and beak poised. A gentle breeze passed, carrying the subtle fragrance of jasmine, reminding him of his time with Sophia.

Just then, the crane rose and flew further up the beach. Braking widely with his great white wings, and then taking a few awkward steps, he landed.

"To what do I owe the honor, Senator Pratt? We expected you a couple of weeks ago." It was a three-martini voice this afternoon. Dean Kurland was a man about fifty, with senatorial white hair and misleading heartiness of manner.

"I had some business to attend." Robert shook hands with Kurland. His handshake was not that of a man with a high cholesterol count. He was a head taller than Robert with a stockier build.

"I work out hard every day. Start by swimming two miles. Then running four miles, and then finishing up with weights." Kurland raised his biceps, Atlas-style, to demonstrate.

Robert trained as a boxer, an enduring exercise to keep in shape. Took his anger out on the bag. He had no time for braggarts.

Robert returned his gaze to the crane. The bird walked along just where the sand was firm from the dampness of the high tide, watching the hermit crabs carrying their shells and the ghost crabs that slipped across the stretch of sand into the water.

"What brings you to the Bahamas?" Kurland probed.

To the crane's right, in the shallow channel, the bird regarded the shadow of a very big barracuda that stalked a school of bonefish. The crane watched the lines of the barracuda, long, pale, and gray, seeming not to move and stalking the bonefish with stealth.

"Maybe vacation. Maybe investment," Robert said, looking Kurland in the eyes. Like the barracuda, Robert hunted the hunter.

When Robert turned his head, the crane was gone, flying with his white wings over the green water.

Kurland laughed. "Isn't everybody hoping to make a quick

buck on investments? Come join us for dinner, Senator Pratt. You are my guest of honor and will sit right by me."

Robert kept his eyes on the crane. The cunning bird landed in the mangrove bay where the sand stopped and the brutal mangroves grew heavy and green into the water, their roots showing like remorseless, tangled brown sticks.

Introductions were made at the table of several notables: the Bahamian Prime Minister, Sir Roland Symonette, Howard Duff, a movie star filming *Flame of the Islands* in Nassau, United States Congressman Ken Keating from New York, Eddie Taylor, a Canadian industrialist, Curtis Turner, a race car driver, and ten other miscellaneous businessmen and politicians. He'd be bored out of his mind if he didn't have this injustice to right. Just a bunch of rich guys who wanted to be seen and known as the who's who.

A waiter brought in bottles of champagne. "Here we are," said Kurland. He nodded and the waiter undid the wire around the cork, his hands working deftly as the wire came away. He twisted the cork gently and, as it came out with a dry popping noise, he poured the foam expertly into the glasses.

The conversation ebbed and flowed over several courses beginning with stone crabs, lobster steamed in a garlic butter sauce, seasoned grilled snapper, and sweetbreads, salads, and other courses that remained tasteless. The banter dribbled from the mundane to pompous drivel—like a pissing contest with men bragging about their achievements.

On a lower terrace, people danced the merengue, the scent of gardenia and the aromatic rum drinks drifting on the breeze. Laughter and flirtation distracted him. How he wished Sophia were there. Maybe they'd dance. Instead, he depressed himself thinking of her in the arms of her husband who had returned. His hands curled into fists.

"Not much to say, Senator Pratt?"

"You are sensitive, Kurland," Robert said with a knife-flick of mockery in his voice, "but there's nothing that has to be hidden between us, is there, Kurland?" The men had drunk enough wine and liquor to loosen their tongues. Robert was ready to mine the information he needed on Kurland's activities, especially his Ponzi schemes.

Kurland signaled to the waiter. Three fingers of rum were poured in Kurland's glass. He downed it in one swig. Robert sized him up. Though drunk, he was not a fool.

"I hear there're some interesting things going on up in Washington."

"There are always interesting things going on in Washington," Robert said.

"More interesting than usual," said Kurland. He sat smoking, squinting through the smoke, watching him with the black eyes of a falcon. "There's a rumor that you're going to step down and return to full management of your automotive industry that is booming. Congratulations by the way."

How Kurland flattered him. An ounce of cajolery to pave the way for something he wanted. A political favor. "I'll never step down," Robert said.

Kurland blew a smoke ring, watching it eddy. "If you do happen to step down from the senate, who's the next in line do you suppose?"

The man calculated his future. "The matter hasn't come up," Robert said.

"Washington means a lot to me," Kurland said, "largely thanks to a few of my favorite senators."

He let Robert know he wasn't in the favorites category. Robert waited for a contrasting clause that would make him included.

"I happen to know what is going on behind the scenes. You have been mentioned to be a presidential contender. Am I right?"

Robert didn't take the bait. He remained silent.

"I thought so," said Kurland, downing another glass of rum. He tapped his glass to be refilled and the waiter responded. "I can make that venture a reality."

Add bribing a United States Senator. "How so?"

"I am not without connections. Sizable donations to your campaign, etc. But to release the Kraken, I need something in return."

Here it comes. Robert waited.

"I need a little help with expanding my oil fields onto government land. You have influence over the interior."

Robert had read the thorough dossier Van Smith had given him that included Kurland drilling on federal lands without permits. He was in big trouble.

Robert said nothing. Just nodded.

"One more thing. I need additional funds and the Feds to back off when it comes to my Avalon, Texas plant."

So, Kurland confirmed he owned the chemical plant that bled mercury into the neighboring town's water supply. Robert curled his fingers around the stem of his champagne glass and smiled. No way in hell was he going to help Kurland. In fact, he was going to have the Feds sent up Kurland's ass and line his colon. Robert was thinking of his father's long-time friend who had fallen prey to Kurland's Ponzi scheme, and on the brink of losing everything had attempted to take his life.

Robert shoved away from the table. "Good evening, gentlemen."

As expected, Kurland got up and followed him, placed his dry hand on Robert's wrist to detain him. "Good boy, Mr. President."

Robert bridled, shrugged him off. No way would Robert become president by taking a handout from a scam artist like Kurland. He'd see the scum in prison first.

Kurland dogged his steps. "How about it, Senator Pratt? Are you willing to do what is best for the American public?"

Are you kidding? The man's hypocrisy was the scourge of the American people. How many seconds would it take to deck this guy?

"Suspend your dislike of me for a few moments, Senator, and listen to what I have to say."

"Dislike? That is an oversimplification."

"I can help you with some great investments. You'd make a killing."

"Not interested."

Kurland dared to swing him around to face him. "They say that more than one person has soiled his pants with bad investments. However, I've got a country bumpkin, a German doctor who I'm ready to take for a good ride. Nazi scum deserves to be fleeced. He's so anxious and stupid. I've been reeling him in over the past months on some real estate holdings he possesses in Abaco. I'll pocket his holdings faster than a Las Vegas dealer."

Robert opened a door to a room. Good. It was empty. He motioned Kurland into the room and slammed the door behind them. "You've got my attention. What's this doctor's name?" With certainty, he had a good idea of the doctor's name. Sophia had never told him who her husband was dealing with, but he knew it was Kurland. The con artist who dared to take everything away from Sophia and his sons. Kurland would feel the warning tap of death on his shoulder.

"I see," said Kurland with smooth aloofness, taking his measure of Robert. "I find your sudden interest stimulating."

Robert's wits were razor-sharp "It's with beneficial optimism you heighten my enthusiasm."

"Dr. Karl Schneider." Kurland smiled widely, showing five thousand dollars of dental work. "But I wouldn't mind having a lay or two with the guy's wife. She's a looker."

Robert used Herculean self-control not to beat the bastard senseless. Robert picked up a book off the table, his lips curved with blatant disdain at Kurland's insult to Sophia. He took his time paging through the novel. Robert had read *The Last Hurrah* by O'Connor, a 1956 *New York Times Bestseller*, detailing the world of a flawed and corrupt governor. Inspiring reading for

Kurland. "I'll tell you what you're going to do, Kurland. You are going to give three million dollars for one-fourth of the land Dr. Schneider possesses. And it must be the worst land. The marls."

"You are a fool to think I'd do anything so stupid. A fool, you hear?"

"I am starting a US Senate investigative committee on your actions, including a Ponzi scheme involving Gleason Glass Corporation."

Kurland looked aghast. "You're bluffing."

"I have plenty of investigators at my disposal, numerous sworn affidavits, and witnesses. You will pay back three times to Gleason Glass what you took from them."

"I don't believe it."

"You are not intelligent at all, Kurland. An idiot, yes. An intelligent man thinks things through. An idiot, however, doesn't stop to reflect or analyze. He acts on impulse, like an ape, satisfied he's forever right, to go around damaging anyone he perceives to be beneath him."

Kurland seethed.

"You have confirmed you own the Avalon, Texas plant that is leaking mercury into the water supply of the neighboring community and making them sick. You will close the plant and make five million dollars in reparations for the people of that town. Do I make myself clear?"

Kurland didn't respond.

"You will also cease your oil drilling on federal land. If none of what I've requested isn't done within three weeks, I will have you thrown into prison for the rest of your life."

"That, that is all of my holdings."

"Your choice." It was better to bankrupt Kurland than to go through lengthy and costly court battles to convict him.

Kurland went to the door. "Men." Two men entered the room, flanking Robert.

"Only two? You can do better than that," Robert said.

Not the smartest anyone could hire, but brawny hired thugs to convince an adversary of Kurland's to come to heel. Except Robert was dying for a fight—agitated by Sophia returning to Karl. Angry at how Kurland maligned Sophia. By how Kurland had nearly bankrupted his friend. Furious enough to lay Kurland and his cronies flat in two minutes.

Nobody spoke.

The guy on Robert's right was more than six feet tall and close to three feet wide. Most of him was packed flesh and bone. The guy on Robert's left was a little smaller in both directions, and more energetic. He was twitchy, moving from foot to foot, twisting at the waist, rotating his shoulders.

"Gentleman," Robert said, "either you need to move right along, or you will need to call a couple of ambulances. Your decision."

The men laughed. The big guy on the right had a tanned wedge of a face concealed in a beard. The smaller guy to his front possessed three days of stubble and fidgety eyes. His mouth hung open like a crocodile.

Robert planned his next moves. Always better to be prepared. He anticipated no major difficulty. He would have preferred the bigger guy to be on his left, because that would have maximized the impact from a right-handed blow by allowing a marginally longer swing, and he always liked to put the larger of the pair down first. But he was geared up to be adaptable. Maybe the fidgety guy should go down first. The bigger guy was likely to be slower, and maybe less engaged.

Kurland stepped forward and pushed the smaller guy in the side.

The smaller guy staggered toward Robert and then stiffened against the movement and whirled back and began to spin a fast one-eighty in the direction of Kurland. Robert seized the guy by the wrist and held on for a split second and then let go again and the guy reeled through the rest of his turn all wobbly and clumsy and unimpressive and finished with a pathetic delayed swing that escaped Kurland completely.

But then he turned right back and aimed a second swing straight at Robert. He stepped left and the incoming fist buzzed by an inch from his chin. The force behind it spun the guy onward and Robert kicked his feet out from under him and dumped the guy's face on the corner of an end table. Robert caught a flash of movement, the big guy charging him with fists like hams.

Easy.

Robert matched the guy's inertia with drive of his own and smashed his elbow flat into the middle of the white space between the guy's beard and his hairline. Like sprinting full tilt into a carbon steel pipe. Entertainment over, except the smaller guy was already up on his knees and clambering for a grip, hands and feet like a runner in the blocks. Robert kicked him hard in the head. They guy's eyes rolled up and he toppled sideways and lay still with his legs folded under him.

Kurland held his hands palms up. He was the one Robert wanted to pound to a bloody pulp. Especially after what he'd said about Sophia.

"Listen up, Kurland. I'll give you two options. We'll settle this now, and you could go on your merry way by adhering to my requests. Option one is agree right now."

"What's option two?"

"I advise you to choose option one."

Kurland rushed him and with a meaty fist, struck Robert in the eye, his head whipped back, blood spraying through the air in a fine crimson mist. His vision blurred and he wiped blood that dripped from his eyebrow and streamed down his temple. He shook his head.

Kurland charged him again like a wild lion freed from a cage, except twice as fast, crashing a right elbow at Robert, like lightning, clubbing down. He wanted Robert gone.

Robert twisted, taking most of the man's force in the meat of his upper arm. Painful. Numbing. But he stayed on his feet, dodged, spun, and kicked Kurland in the groin with enough intensity to break a stable beam. Kurland rolled on the carpet, clutching his crotch, screaming. He wouldn't be using his family jewels for a month. Maybe a year. Maybe he'd have no progeny.

Breathing hard, Robert grabbed Kurland up by the collar. "Are you going to adhere to my requests?" He needed to hear Kurland say what he demanded. He needed to know if Sophia and his sons would be safe.

Kurland staggered, had the audacity to smile. "Yes." He glided his hand in his pocket and slipped out a knife. Before he could lift it, Robert struck a direct punch that drove into the man's mouth, knocking his teeth into his trachea and beyond. Kurland soared through the air, crashing onto the carpet next to his comrades. Robert toed the motionless scam artist. His five-thousand-dollar dental work gone, and his face splattered with blood.

Chapter Fifty-Six

Sophia buttered her toast in the hotel dining room, listening to the twins' chatter and Karl's incessant bragging.

"I'll bet your senator friend isn't as lucky as I am," Karl said. "I received word that Kurland wants only that small hundred and thirty acre parcel of swampland. The marls is the most worthless piece of land on the island. Tell me your husband is the greatest financier."

Yesterday, Karl had been frantic. She'd sworn he mumbled something about losing it all, yet this morning he was dancing on clouds. What had happened to make the turnaround?

Suddenly, Robert entered the hotel dining room, heading right toward them. With a shake of her head, she warned him away, but he ignored her and plunked himself down at their table. She looked helplessly to Queenie.

Karl's eyes narrowed on Sophia and Queenie guessing something meaningful passed between them.

Robert sported a black eye and a laceration above his temple. What on God's earth had happened to him? Sophia glanced at Kurt, wearing the wise smile of an old soul. He'd said nothing about her comings and goings for the last two weeks.

Karl's fists clenched and unclenched. "I don't remember inviting you to dine with us, Senator Pratt. The last time we met, there was an altercation. Perhaps we should have another go of it."

Robert leaned over. "You could try but it wouldn't turn out well for you. Besides, it's not necessary. I'll be leaving in a couple of minutes...if you don't mind."

"I do mind," said Karl, straightening. "But I just made the deal of a lifetime. I suppose I can even tolerate your company—for just two minutes. I made a brilliant land transaction. Try to top that, Senator."

"May I offer my heartiest congratulations," said Robert.

Karl's hard blue eyes locked on Robert, his gloating unmistakable. "I've been maneuvering to make this arrangement for months, and suddenly, the buyer gave in to my demands and paid with an exorbitant amount of money."

Robert lifted a brow. "Hat's off to you, Dr. Schneider. Inspiring, your art of the deal."

"Have no fear, Sophia," Karl said as if he divined the secrets of the universe. She stiffened as he pulled his arm tight around her, an unusual gesture of affection his German pedigree forbade in public. To be between two alpha males ready to tear each other apart.

She saw a vein pulse at the base of Robert's throat. Nervously, she reached for her juice glass, knocked it over, but Robert righted it just in time, his fingers hot across hers. Had Robert had something to do with the sale of the property?

Kurt studied Robert, overlong. "That's an excellent shiner, Senator Pratt. I get those occasionally, too."

"Were you shoeing a mule?" Michael burst into unrestrained laughter. Kurt tittered and, soon his howling laughter had hotel patrons across the dining room looking askance.

Unable to contain great waves of hilarity, Kurt asked, "What's important is how did the other guy look?"

Sophia saw Robert smile. He winced with pain, but, oh, how

he was enjoying the spectacle, and how she wanted to kick him beneath the table. She had made him promise to stay away and he'd broken that promise.

Robert chuckled. "That mule wasn't feeling too good afterwards."

"You must be a busy man," Sophia said, her voice dripping with ire. "I'm sure you have important things to do." He ignored her efforts to remove him from her family.

"I have a proposal to make. A way to celebrate your father's success," Robert said, and Sophia perceived it cost him to call Karl their father. "Boys, what do you say if I send two Spanish thoroughbreds to your home in the Bahamas?"

"Yes, sir!"

"I love animals and always wanted a horse," hooted Michael.

"That won't be necessary," snapped Karl. "There is no need for horses and importing the feed would be astronomical."

As if instructing a child, Robert said, "Of course, I'll make sure feed is sent, lumber to build a small barn and fencing."

Karl rose so quickly it knocked his chair over in a bang. He shook his fist at Robert. "You dare to contradict my authority?"

Robert reclined against the back of his chair; his arms folded in front of him. "Not at all. I need to see how this breed tests out in the tropical heat and you are the only people I know who could see to their proper care. I believe the two lads with the expert advice their mother can give are mature enough to handle the task."

The boys' held their hands in a prayerful pose. "Please Papa. We'll take good care of them."

"You've just made the land deal of the century," said Kurt. "We need to celebrate, too."

Oh, how Kurt could manipulate Karl. Sophia held her breath.

Despite the visible tension in Karl's shoulders, he said, "All right. But you must care for them. Senator Pratt, your two minutes are up."

Chapter Fifty-Seven

Bahamas 1966

The screen door slammed with both her eighteen-year-old strapping boys tripping over each other with excitement. They stopped dead in their tracks. Silent. Not like them at all.

Sophia sprinkled cinnamon, butter, and brown sugar on a rectangle of dough. "Don't be secretive. Don't hold back, you may burgeon with fierce pimples," she teased.

Michael looked at her with a smile that betrayed both enjoyment and concern. "I don't have the foggiest."

Kurt wore his devilish smile.

Sophia rolled up the dough, and then sliced and laid out pieces to raise. "What happened? Don't tell me that you got the jeep stuck in the mud again."

"I'm sorry, Mother," said Kurt, staring at a print of *The Gulf Stream*, a painting of a disabled boat, including a half-naked sailor at the mercy of a hurricane and a school of flailing sharks. The painting reminded her of Diruvert.

"Do you think the sailor made it to shore?"

She gave him a sideways glance. He was distracting her with

Winslow Homer's work. "Your apology doesn't carry much in the way of penitence."

He broke out laughing and Sophia did, too.

"I can never fool you, can I?"

Both boys whipped out letters. "We received full scholarships to the University of Michigan. We came to tell you right away."

Karl strode in from the front porch. "Unheard of. Why would the university give you full scholarships?"

"The university wants to expand the geographical boundaries of its student body to make it more well-rounded. We applied and lucked out."

Sophia's stomach clenched. She was losing her boys. She also knew who had secured those scholarships. Just like the real estate buyout with Dean Kurland.

Over the summer months, preparations had been made for Kurt and his brother to attend the university in the fall. Now they walked to the airport gate with their mother.

"You both look so handsome in your new blazers. Kurt, promise me you'll not get into fights. Michael, make sure you eat. You forget to eat—"

"We're going to be fine, Mom," Kurt said.

This is the day I've dreaded my whole life, Sophia thought.

Michael let her dust a piece of nonexistent lint off his shoulder, and then scrambled off to the plane.

Kurt allowed her to fix his collar and lingered. He'd miss her touch and her voice. His father, Karl, had had an emergency, but Kurt knew Papa was afraid to break down in front of them. He swallowed, finding it hard to part from either of them.

His mother dabbed her handkerchief to her eyes as the floodgates released. His heart panged, and he wrapped his arms around her.

"I'm sorry I've been such a disappointment to you, Kurt."

"Where did you get that ridiculous idea?" Although never said aloud, Kurt knew his mother suspected that he'd guessed Robert was his biological father.

"From your eyes, Son. From your eyes."

Kurt pushed her away, held her shoulders and looked at her. "No. You have it all wrong. I've been a greater disappointment to you since I'm always fighting. I've always wanted to prove myself to you, to make all your dreams come true. I've seen your sadness."

I've been witness to your sacrifice. I know your secrets, he wanted to say but didn't.

He hugged her long and hard. Someday, he'd make it up to her. Michael called to him from the airplane. Kurt picked up his suitcase, slipped through a bevy of passengers and caught up to his brother. He stopped at the top of the stairway of the plane to wave to his mother. She swiped at her eyes, and then turned abruptly, stepping out of sunlight into shadow.

Chapter Fifty-Eight

University of Michigan 1966

Kurt pressed farther into the entrance of the University of Michigan's Board of Trustee's room where a dinner party was hosted, and Senator Pratt was to speak.

"Kurt, old boy," he told himself, "the father-son relationship is based on thousands of little white lies, presents from Santa, the tooth fairy, the Easter bunny, meritocracy, and numerous others."

He'd rehearsed a thousand times what he'd say to his biological father. Since he was five, he'd known Karl wasn't his actual papa. Had heard the arguments his parents had, the heavy silences that ensued, the stony faces. How Karl had always goaded his mother on how he was so much better than Senator Pratt. Kurt shook his head. Even dads who aren't your dad get jealous. When he was ten and they had the meeting in a Nassau hotel lobby, Kurt knew instantly Senator Pratt was his biological father. His mother went missing for two weeks. Despite Queenie telling him she was shopping, Kurt knew nobody went shopping for that long.

He stood in front of the table that acted as a barrier for the VIPs inside, eyeing two big brawny campus police. Would his father accept him? A man of his prestige might be embarrassed with a bastard kid and have him tossed out. Kurt hated to risk public humiliation. He thought of all the bad things that could happen. How he'd get thrown out of school, get arrested, and then have to call his mother from jail, explaining what happened. Hell.

He sweated, but his stubborn side said now or never.

Kurt pulled himself up, stared down his nose, drawing on his heritage as an aristocrat, well, a claim to former royalty through his mother, hoping to kindle a sense of inferiority in the Keystone cops. "I'm here to see Senator Pratt."

"And what for?" said the guard whose name tag said Gary.

"I'm a relative," said Kurt.

"And I'm the pope. Being a student here is no excuse for slow wit, kid. We've heard that excuse a million times before. Get lost."

This came from Gary, who with certainty couldn't make it academically past eighth grade and wore a sign on his face that said *I hate all students*.

"You might be sorry you said that," Kurt threatened. Time was ticking away, and he didn't want to miss the senator with a contest between him and the guards.

The other guard named Greg flashed a smile, sporting a missing tooth. Brothers?

"Why are you going to hit me, kid?" said Greg.

How long would it take him to lay out both guards? Two minutes? Three minutes? Nothing like the island boys he'd grown up scrapping with. Those boys were immense, cool, and determined and, above all, entirely in control of their brains. But this fight held no appeal since it wasn't a nice introduction to his father.

"I'll give you two options," Kurt said.

"He'll give us two options," Gary mocked. The giant's neck swiveled back and forth on powerful shoulders, the kind of shoulders that could easily lift a whaler.

"Option one. I'll forget this conversation ever happened if you let me go in right now."

"What's option two?" Greg's eyes burned like hot coals buried in vanilla pudding and his lower lip hung down his chin as if it had been pulled between here and Kalamazoo, and then snapped back.

"I recommend option one."

Both men looked at each other, and then at Kurt. "You're a raving lunatic. But because you're so polite and entertaining, we'll escort you off campus," said Greg.

Two against one was never a problem. Missing-tooth...he'd take down first. Gary—like chopping down a silkwood tree.

Kurt dropped his mouth open and pointed to the far right. "Look at that girl, she's naked."

When the guards jerked their heads aside, Kurt vaulted over the table and shouted, "That's option two." He raced up front and glanced behind him. He had to pick up speed. The guards dogged his steps, huffing and puffing with their big bellies flopping from weekend beer binging. It was a big risk he was taking in front of the university president, celebrated football coach and a myriad of other dignitaries.

Kurt sprinted past the Dean of the Business School and skidded to a stop in front of the head table, his eyes on Senator Pratt. It was probably one of the boldest things he'd done other than removing Amy Pinkerton's clothing in the basement lab of the chemistry building.

"What is this intrusion for young man?" the university president demanded.

Breathing hard, Kurt said, "I've come to say hello to Senator Pratt, he's a friend of my mother's." The two guards caught up, flanked him.

"Take him away." The university president glared, and then turned to the senator. "I apologize, Robert."

Kurt's heart sank. His own father wasn't going to defend him?

Gary and Greg hooked him under his arms and started to drag him away.

"Wait," said Senator Pratt. "Can we find an extra chair? I'd like to have this fine young man sit next to me."

To the chagrin of the university president, Kurt was placed right in between him and Senator Pratt. Kurt enjoyed the spotlight for the moment. He dared to smirk and wave goodbye to the departing guards.

Before all the speeches were finished, Senator Pratt excused himself and Kurt.

"Takes a lot of guts to stand up to a crowd like that," the Senator said, walking across the campus.

"Almost as bold as leaving before all the speeches are done," Kurt said.

"Touché." Robert laughed. "I try to minimize boring addresses especially when I'd like to get to know my friend's son. Tell me about college life. Living accommodations. Fraternities. Hobbies."

Kurt had the distinct impression Senator Pratt already knew the answers to his questions, but plunged in. "Not much life on campus. Went to a couple of football games. Notre Dame was great, but can't say that unholy word around here. Fraternities? Not for me. Can't get into group think. I can get into enough trouble on my own. Accommodations? The University of Michigan's high priesthood said I couldn't room with my brother, Michael. Besides, my twin studies all the time. He'd be like living with a ghost yet an improvement over my current situation."

"How's that?"

"I room with a guy who weighs three hundred pounds and wears a cat puppet named Oscar on his shoulder that he talks through. He ate a whole tub of my peanut butter in two days, but the cat puppet took the responsibility. Do you know how much peanut butter costs? I was so mad at him. But Oscar the cat told me he ordered a few boxes of peanut butter and he'd repay me. Two days later, fifty boxes of tub peanut butter arrived. I can only sidestep into our room. The cat bit stepped up and became annoying. He'd meow in my face when it was time to get up, or if I returned late from class, he'd say, 'Oscar was wondering where you were.'"

The senator was laughing. "Sounds like you have a full life."

"Yeah, a full life. The guy in the room next door has a dozen parakeets that he taught to hum *The Caissons Go Rolling Along*. It was cute at first but gets old at three o'clock in the morning when you are trying to sleep. Then Oscar starts meowing."

Robert roared with laughter. "How about getting one of the celebrated sodas at the famous Campus Fountain? I haven't been there in years."

The soda fountain lady looked perpetually surprised; her eyebrows plucked into high crescents that gave her a look of lunar astonishment. She took their orders with a jukebox belting out a Beatles' song.

Robert sat and drank his malted milkshake, eyeing a group of young girls entering the soda fountain, their laughter and soprano twitterings halting when they spotted his handsome son. Robert smiled. Isolated on an island all his life, Kurt didn't have much chance to observe or know the flirtations of the opposite sex.

"So, tell me about island life."

The boy lit up with enthusiasm. "There is Old Tom. He doesn't like anyone and lives by himself, living off the sea. He has two thumbs on one hand and has supernatural powers. Many people are afraid and have nothing to do with him because they believe he can stop the flow of blood just by canting a person's name and age. I never believed it and made friends with him. He took me fishing, taught me about motors. I learned a lot from him."

Robert liked that about his son. He wasn't a snob, made friends of old hermits, and seeing a person's value.

Kurt sipped his drink through a straw, sizing Robert up. "Lots of pirates of old and rumrunners. Found a Lucayan arrowhead once. Another time, I found gold doubloons washed up after a hurricane from an old Spanish shipwreck. My brother and I would go sailing and camp overnight on other islands. There's Lusca."

Robert looked around, didn't see anyone new and not sure who the boy was talking about narrowed his eyes on him. "Lusca?"

Kurt's green eyes, so like his, sparkled with amusement. "Lusca is half-shark and half-octopus and lurks in underwater caves. Lusca is notorious for drowning divers."

Robert saw a glint of humor, then the amused twitch of his son's mouth. The boy was all wit and had a wonderful knack for spinning yarns.

Kurt let his gaze pass momentarily over two young ladies, one in a tight plaid miniskirt and a body-hugging shocking pink mohair sweater, the other in a psychedelic green mini dress belted with a gold chain. One had a swirling coiffure that looked as though it had been squeezed from a frosting gun, the other wore her hair long. They arranged themselves on the table beside them.

"Then there are blue holes. Michael and I scoff at most Bahamians who call them devil holes because they have no bottom and won't go near them. We strung a rope high on a tree to swing into the center of a blue hole. One time, Mr. Murphy put his rowboat in one and a great whirlpool took him. Everyone thought he was lost. Three days later, he sent his wife a message, saying he walked for three days underwater and ended up at Miss Emily Blue Bee's Bar in New Plymouth, and for her to send him dry clothes and money."

Robert chuckled, thinking that this was the best time he'd had in years. The boy charmed him with his lazy grin and easy manner. Charmed the college girls who collected at the table next to him, giggling with each one of his tales. With certainty, the show was for the girls' benefit.

"My dad is one of the few doctors that give medical treatment in the islands."

Robert knew that. It still didn't take away the sour taste in his mouth because of Sophia's allegiance to the man. Hot blood coursed through his veins.

Kurt glanced over at the table of girls, caught them gawking, and they all blushed. "One time, my dad treated a fisherman from Cuba. He healed him, but the fisherman had no money. My dad told him to pay him next time. We went on a family fishing trip for a week. Came back, and the next morning woke up to a terrible cacophony of sound. Our maid said a Spanish man came and brought a gift. The maid had tied up a rooster by the leg in the backyard. After three days of being woken up early, my dad ordered the maid to cook him. Fast forward, the Cuban man arrived and asked my dad how he liked his present. My dad said he was tough and chewy. You should have seen the look of horror on the Cuban's face. 'You ate him? He was the grand champion fighting cock of all Cuba.'"

"What about your mother?"

Kurt whispered, aware of the female audience. "I really miss her. Dad too. But I miss my mom the most. She did things for us kids every day. From book learning to learning about everything natural around us. I love my mother. I probably don't tell her enough."

"I'm sure she knows."

"How about you?" Kurt asked. "Do you have a mother?"

It wasn't a topic Robert wanted to discuss. Too many bad feelings. He'd been robbed of years with Sophia and his sons because of his mother's machinations. "She passed away. You didn't tell me about your hobbies."

"Now you're talking. I love cars and you obviously know a lot about cars."

Robert launched into a lengthy conversation involving automobiles, his son a rapt audience. How nice it was to share the same interests.

Robert looked at his watch. Several hours had zipped past. The fountain was empty of customers, the waitress dried glasses, with a "time to go home" scowl on her face. "I should probably get you back to your dorm."

"When are you coming to town again?" Kurt asked.

The boy was encouraging. Robert liked that. "I'm staying overnight. Are you free tomorrow?"

"My classes are done at eleven. Would you go to a car lot with me? I want your opinion."

Robert smiled, thinking what a great job Sophia had done raising him. "Any young man who appreciates cars deserves a look-see."

Robert shifted his new Pratt sportscar down the road with Kurt beside him, chatting excitedly. He couldn't sleep a wink the night before, thinking of spending the day with his son. *Son.* He liked the ring of that. He hoped he could meet with the boy more. Take it slow. Don't scare him off. To Kurt, Robert was just his mother's old friend.

"I like the way you drive fast, passing cars in racing-driver spurts, hands calm on the wheel," Kurt said, and then pointed. "Turn here."

They entered a huge used car lot. The inventory sprawled forlorn, pathetic, and there was no hint of a customer in the lot. A bad sign.

Looking like a rogue from a gothic operetta, a large salesman in an orange plaid suit huffed out. Probably his first customer in a month. Kurt raced on ahead, finding a vehicle to his liking. He waved his arms like a windmill to get their attention.

"Isn't she the greatest?"

Robert rubbed the back of his neck. The car was an antiquated piece of shattered junk, and the lot owner should pay him to tow it to the dump. The sticker price was twice what it was worth. Would it even drive off the lot? "You picked this out?"

Kurt clapped his hands together, his fingertips pointing to heaven. "I've always dreamed of having a car like the ones I see speeding through town. This isn't any old car. This is a 1953 Chevy Corvette, and I want to rebuild her. I want to breathe life into her."

Robert was impressed with the boy's enthusiasm. The same zeal he possessed long ago.

The car salesman preened his chest like a bandy rooster. "It's on special. I'll even throw in a joke. Why did the chicken go to the car dealership? She wanted to trade in her coop for a sedan." Hiccupping with loud heehaws, the salesman slapped the front fender, and Robert feared it would fall off.

"I have twenty dollars saved up, but I don't have any place to keep her," Kurt said.

Robert grinned. He had been given manna from heaven. To guarantee a chance to have his son nearby? By God, he'd pay six times what the piece of junk was worth. "Only if you keep it at my home and let me help you rebuild it. I haven't had my sleeves rolled up and my head under a hood in a long time."

Robert combed his fingers through his hair, struggling to keep his promise to Sophia. He'd always been the responsible one. He was the one who got rid of the scam artist taking advantage of Karl so that Sophia and the boys could live a decent life. He was the one who got the boys into the university and paid their scholarships. He was the one who bequeathed all his assets and holdings to the boys and Sophia in the event of his death. Most significantly, he was the one who painfully backed away when Sophia requested it to preserve her family, agreeing not to have any contact. *Hell.*

There was no way he was going to back away now. He was going to know his adult son regardless of Sophia's wishes.

To see the infectious smile on his son was worth everything in the world. "You'll keep this our secret?"

"To reassure you, I'll swear on a New Testament," Kurt offered.

"Leave the Gospel alone. Your word is enough for me." He put his arm around Kurt's shoulders. "Let's go do some bargaining."

Chapter Fifty-Nine

They finished installing a new carburetor on the corvette, and Robert couldn't have been more gratified with the treasure unearthed from their sweat. Kurt had a good eye. He enjoyed the hours with his son, getting his hands greasy and seeing their work come to fruition. Now the vintage car was completed, boasting a shiny red finish and a new brown leather top. Eye-candy. Low to the ground. Curvy. A toothy-grilled road-ster with rocket-ship taillights and just enough room in the cockpit for two adults and their ear-to-ear grins.

He had bankrolled the expense of attaining a myriad of parts, including a replacement fiberglass body. He told Kurt not to worry about the expense, that he'd purchased the parts at a reduced price through his company. With certainty, he could have bought two brand new cars for the cost.

"What do you think about your handiwork, Kurt?"

Kurt finished polishing the front fender and stepped back, beaming. "She's a beauty."

In the back of his mind, the thought of introducing Kurt to the automotive business had played for weeks. His sister, Caroline, was married and took care of her three kids full-time. Unlike

Judith, she was a great mother determined not to miss out on any of her children's years.

Ever since his brother, Liam, had attended MIT, he'd had been fixated on computers and some sci-fi obsession where processors talked to each other. He never failed to blow his trumpet, claiming his new technology would be the marvel of the future. Neither sibling had any interest in running Pratt Motors and Robert worried about handing over the reins to a nonfamily member. A realm of possibilities opened with meeting his son. Why not?

"What do you think about coming to work at Pratt Motors this summer?"

"Really? Do you mean it? I'd love that. I can earn money and pay you back for all the parts you bought."

The kid was honest and hardworking.

Suddenly, his son looked at him queerly, shifting from foot to foot. He had something on his mind.

"I've gotten to know you...really know you," Kurt said. "It's not that I don't want this, it's that I want it so much. I'm sorry, I'm scared. I've messed everything up."

The boy hesitated, sweat beaded on his upper lip. For whatever reason, Robert felt sorry for him. Had he made a girl pregnant, become involved with criminal activity, acquired a gambling debt? Considering all the boy's spare time was spent renovating the car, how would his son have time to take such risks?

"Whatever it is, Kurt, I'll do everything in my power to help you."

A burning sensation rose in Robert's chest. He could almost see dread pinballing through the boy's mind. Whatever was troubling him, Robert didn't want him to suffer any barrage of intrusive, unwanted, or painful thoughts. He'd done enough of that himself for ten lifetimes.

"So please realize that being cautious can be a great thing—"

Kurt swallowed several times, and then looked all around,

ready to bolt. An instinct stirred in some far-away recess of Robert's brain, significant and gathering strength.

"I know you are not just my mother's friend."

Robert stiffened. Warning bells rang in his head, but for once in his life, he didn't know how to navigate the treacherous waters.

Kurt's hands convulsed around the rag, twisting and twisting, and Robert thought he'd shred it to pieces. Kurt drew a breath and burst out, "I know you are my dad."

Did Robert hear right? Had the boy called him dad? Robert had to jumpstart his brain because it had quit working. Of all the boyish calamities he'd imagined Kurt might be involved in, this was the last.

"I've had questions," Kurt began. "Was I not good enough? Was there something wrong with me?"

"Never, Kurt!" Robert moved to his son but stopped two steps before him, his hands at his sides, unsure as to what to do. "Never, Kurt. Never, ever think that. I didn't know you existed until I met you in Nassau. Your mom thought her husband had died during the war. When he came back from the dead, I had no idea your mom was pregnant. I had to let her go with her husband. After... had I known you and your brother existed, I would have moved heaven and earth to find you."

"Are you telling me the truth?"

He needed confirmation. "Absolutely. Life is complicated, Kurt. When I saw you and Michael, I knew you were mine. I wanted...my God, I wanted you. But that would have turned your lives and your mother's life upside down. She begged me not to destroy the family she'd worked so hard to build. I have always loved your mother and promised to heed her wishes."

Kurt's inner walls began to crack. He fought the tears, then a sob broke free. "I was afraid you'd reject me."

Robert choked back his own tears, unable to hold it together. "Do you realize how many years of loneliness I've had, wanting my sons by my side? You mean everything to me, and I'd do anything for you. Getting to know you these past weeks is a dream I could only imagine. To know I have two fine sons that I could not lay claim to has been agonizing. Now I can quit pretending I'm your mother's friend, and truly be your father. This is a new beginning for both of us."

"Dad. I like the ring of that. Can I call you that?"

"I want nothing more." Robert's voice broke. "Does your mother know that you know?"

"No. You mustn't tell her."

"When did you find out?"

"I've known since I was young. Heard my parents fighting. I kept a picture of you that I found in a newspaper. Later, when I clapped my eyes on you talking to my mother in the hotel in Nassau...I knew."

Robert placed his arms around his son, holding him tight. How many years had he waited to embrace his son? Robert looked heavenward. His prayers had been answered.

Chapter Sixty

For a long time, Robert hadn't believed in miracles, but his greatest wish had come true.

Sitting at his dining room table were his two sons. Every weekend, he'd enjoyed having Kurt, making sure the chef prepared enticing gourmet meals, giving his son a break from tiresome dormitory food.

For the first time, Kurt lured his brother, Michael, away from his seminars and labs to see Robert's stables and have dinner. Seeing the two of them together and how natural they were warmed his heart. He shook his head. How he'd missed this simple pleasure his whole life.

Robert tried to picture them at ten, twelve, sixteen, and held a keen sense of sadness, knowing those times were lost to him. He vowed not to waste another moment, tamping down a bitterness toward Sophia for robbing him of that time.

He sat back, amused, enjoying listening to the two of them chatter endlessly. It was as if they both competed to fill every verbal void, competing to finish each other's sentences. A twin thing?

"Please get to the frigging point," Kurt demanded. "With all your metaphorical spin and flourish, I'm beginning to feel a fiery bowel movement at the gates."

"I'm missing valuable study groups and going to have to make up a lot," Michael complained with the same woe as St. Sebastian tied to the pillars and pierced with a thousand arrows.

"Maestro." Kurt snapped his fingers in the air. "The violins, please."

Michael pointed to his chest. "I'm the genius brother. Fortunately, I have humility, and sadly, there are so few of us left in the world."

Kurt rolled his eyes. "And I walk with a rolling gait and carry a parrot on my shoulder and hit people with my wooden leg."

Michael brandished his spoon. "So, back to what I was saying, without further delay, preambles, or frills."

Michael went on for twenty more minutes with his theory of a new kind of treatment for distemper. Robert blinked, unable to grasp the young man's knowledge, and was proud of his zeal. He would make a fine veterinarian.

Kurt tapped his fork loudly, waiting for the agony to end.

Michael's incredible green eyes burned bright with his fervor. "Listen, if you think my ideas are nonsense, I'll shut up."

Kurt slapped his hand on the table. "On the contrary. Fools talk, cowards are silent, wise men listen."

"Did you sit on the same rock as—"

"Aristotle," Kurt said, completing another sentence. "No. Kevin Monk at the garage in Vane Harbor where we pulled an engine and rebuilt a transmission. He had a great talent for everything automotive and composing witty cliches."

"Boys," Robert laughed. "Before you kill each other enjoy dessert. When you're done, we'll tour the stables."

Robert smiled as Michael's eyes practically popped out of his head when a servant placed an array of desserts on the table. Robert had divined Michael's weakness from his twin. The boy possessed a sweet tooth, and his pastry chef had outdone himself with lemon meringue cheesecake, bananas foster, strawberry gelato, crème brûlée, rich chocolate layered tortes and tons of cookies.

Michael stuffed some cookies in his pockets, and then wolfed down several desserts. "I can't wait to see the stables."

"Can we show Mike the car we rebuilt first, Dad?" Kurt asked.

Michael stilled, his fork arrested halfway between his mouth and plate. He stared at his twin, and then at Robert.

Kurt had let the cat out of the bag. Would Michael resent him?

"Dad?" Michael asked.

Kurt studied the ceiling, his face reddening.

Michael twirled his fork in his hand. "I may be the youngest, but I'm not stupid. I've known for a long time."

Robert coughed.

Kurt slapped down his napkin as if he'd jerked on his gauntlets and raised his sword. "I thought I was the only one that knew. How come you never said anything?"

Michael settled back in his chair with casual exaggeration. "You think you're so smart."

Kurt straightened. "I am. I'm the oldest."

"By one minute," Michael said, indignant.

"You're a moron and Senator Pratt's our dad. Our real dad. Whatever you do, keep this secret from mom."

Chapter Sixty-One

Ann Arbor, Michigan 1970

With Karl at her side, Sophia swallowed an upsurge of sobs and raced down a long narrow dark hallway of an inhospitable hospital. Gurneys moved patients and she had to dodge around them. What was to be the boys' graduation and a joyous day had turned into a terrifying nightmare. Kurt had been in a terrible car accident. Endless slate-green walls and dull beige tile stretched endlessly. The air was stagnant. She gasped for breath, like being shrouded in a mausoleum.

Michael was there. He took a step toward them. Her throat constricted. At least he was safe. He pointed to Robert talking to a throng of doctors.

Robert waved them forward.

"What the hell are you doing here?" Karl demanded, a Caribbean-sized chip on his shoulder.

Sophia placed her hand on Karl's arm, feeling his rage. She was surprised to feel how thin his arm was. "This isn't the time to argue. Our son—"

Karl shrugged off her hand, pushed Robert out of the way,

barging into a circle of doctors. "I'm his father. Tell me what's wrong."

"Your son was in a car accident. He'd been driving fast when he was clipped by a drunk driver."

Karl turned accusatory eyes on Robert. "Where the hell did he get a car?"

"I bought it for him," said Robert. "I take full responsibility."

Sophia gasped. *You promised to stay away from them.* Fury coursed through Sophia's veins. What if Kurt? No. She refused the worst-case scenario.

Karl thrust a fist in Robert's face. "If my son dies"

"Now is not the time for antagonism. We need to focus on Kurt," said Robert, turning to the surgeon.

Remaining professional, the doctor said, "He has many injuries. He has a splenic rupture, broken ribs, a broken arm, has lost a lot of blood and needs a transfusion. Most of all, he needs surgery immediately."

Sophia covered her mouth with her hand. She'd seen such injuries at the lumber camp.

Deadly.

"Yes. Yes. Yes. I'm a surgeon and I want to be present during the surgery," demanded Karl.

Sophia melted. Karl was the finest surgeon she'd ever known. He'd saved many people with terrible injuries. He'd fix her son. Kurt would live, wouldn't he?

Karl disappeared with the doctors. For the first time, Sophia glanced at Robert, his handsome face etched with agony. She wanted to throw herself in his arms and cry. To be comforted. To be told their son would live. But Robert had broken his promise to her.

"Mom, I—" Michael stood there with a guilty expression on his face, wanting her reassurance, but she couldn't provide that to him. If anything happened to Kurt...

Robert angled his head. "The nurses have provided a private waiting room for us."

Sophia followed. One foot dragged after the other. Cheap insipid prints sagged on the drywall. Neglected flowers wilted on the nurse's desk. Her nose twitched with the smell of disinfectant. The nurses looked like they hadn't had a break in the last twenty-four hours. She jumped when the hospital loudspeakers blared, "Calling Dr. Fine, Dr. Howard, Dr. Fine..."

Robert motioned for them to take a seat and closed the door for privacy. It was all in Sophia's eyes, beautiful, pain-stricken eyes. How he wanted to take her in his arms and reassure her. To feel her. To reassure himself. Guilt brought up its hideous head. He'd provided the car for Kurt. If Robert hadn't, Kurt would be walking down the aisle to receive his diploma.

Robert sat down, his elbows on his knees. He ran his fingers through his hair. Thank God, he arrived before Karl. Used his influence to get the best damned doctors and move Kurt to first place in the surgical queue before Karl's pride could complicate things.

Robert wanted the best for his son. He wanted Kurt to live and, by God, he'd do anything to make that possible even if he had to deck Karl.

But Robert was out of his element, drowning in a foreign environment with the medical jargon and diagnoses the doctors pummeled him with. He was a businessman. He wanted answers, solutions, not dialogue. In contrast, Karl plunged in, knew how to navigate that world and he was thankful for that.

"You promised me you'd stay out of my twins' lives. Now look what you have reaped from your deception."

"You've kept me from my sons long enough," Robert argued hotly in his defense.

"Mom, it's my fault, too," Michael said.

Robert heard the agony in Michael's voice, knew how the boy was caught in the middle, and had felt that he'd betrayed his mother.

"You are not to blame, Son."

"Neither is my dad...Robert," he said.

Crouched in uncomfortable chairs, the waiting room was a beast of stress, anxiety, fear and making promises to the Lord Almighty, watching the door in hopes of seeing the smiling face of their surgeon with every turn of the knob.

Sophia and he stared at each other, a silent communion, not needing any words, without the movement of moving lips. To feel the other's pain. It meant everything just to gaze into her eyes, to know their souls had met long before their eyes did, that outpouring of infinite love and forgiveness from Sophia enveloped him like a warm quilt.

I need you. Because I wonder, of all the people in the world, why am I the lucky one who found you, yet am kept so far away.

Sophia's chin trembled ever so slightly, and he read her thoughts.

I have put my heart with your heart.

Michael cleared his throat, breaking their silent communication. "I'm going out for coffee. Anyone want a cup?"

Sophia's face heated in a blush. "No, thank you, Michael. I'll be fine."

"Same here," said Robert.

Michael closed the door. With certainty to give them privacy.

Robert stood. "I want to explain—"

"It's not your fault. Kurt would have found some way to get a car. He could never take 'no' for an answer..." Sophia said. "I've always warned him about the dangerous side of his nature. Too fast."

"I'll do everything in my power to help him."

"I know. You've done so much already. You think I didn't

know about you bailing out Karl? You think I didn't know who procured full scholarships for the boys?"

"I love you, Sophia."

She rose and hugged him. How great her arms felt around him if only for this instant.

The door opened and they drew apart. Karl came in first, yanking off his mask, the surgeon behind him. Karl turned his back on Robert, and then nodded to Sophia. "He's going to be fine."

Sophia's knees buckled, and she collapsed in Karl's arms, crying.

The lead surgeon cleared his throat. "Your husband is one of the finest surgeons I've seen, Mrs. Schneider. He taught me a new technique that I'm certain saved your son's life. Your son will be out of recovery soon, and then you can see him. However, he is going to need weeks of mending in the hospital. Then physical therapy at a facility."

"May I suggest setting up a hospital room in my home with a round the clock doctor and nursing care?" offered Robert. Karl's eyes turned cold and flinty. The stubborn idiot was going to refuse.

"We will accept your generous offer, Senator Pratt," said Sophia. "We don't want our son exposed to staph infection or pneumonia, do we Karl?"

Karl glowered at Robert. "Of course, I want the best there is for *my son.*"

Many hours had slipped by while Robert arranged everything for his son's recovery, allowing Karl and Sophia private time with Kurt. He took a breath and entered Kurt's room. The boy was still sleeping, and Michael had gone for a walk. Robert braced himself, not knowing if Karl would change his mind and fight him.

"I've organized a team of rotating doctors, nursing staff, and procured the best hospital equipment money could buy for Kurt to convalesce in my home, including a state-of-the-art physical therapist." said Robert. "You are welcome to stay at my home as long as you wish. I might add how grateful I am to you Karl for your fine surgical skills in saving Kurt. You worked a miracle."

Karl's voice caught. "I love those boys as if they were my own flesh and blood and would do anything for them. We will take you up on your generous offer." Karl paused. "I also do not hold anything against you. Kurt would have had a car no matter what."

Both men made peace with the past to move forward to heal their son. There was a mutual gain, and they were all changed because of it. The ability to forgive and the capacity to let go of resentments proved their love for the boy, and that love bound them together.

Robert realized the three of them had come full circle in that hospital room. That for all the pain and suffering...that for all the lies and deceptions...that everything was as it should be. That their voyage did not dictate the end. They had. Their choices had determined the shape and path of their lives.

It was late when Karl and Sophia left for their hotel close to the hospital.

Michael sat at Kurt's bedside. Kurt's voice was weak, yet he had the stamina to verbally joust with his twin.

"I didn't want to go to graduation anyway," Michael said. "Dumb awards. Boring speakers, tooting their horns, hauling out the same speeches out of their back pockets with moths flying out every year. You saved me misery, Kurt."

Robert had pulled strings and presented their diplomas. "Looks like you're going to be spending a lot of time with me, Sons."

"That's great," said Kurt. "Thank you, dad. I got the impression you managed to get me into surgery first."

"What makes you think that?"

"Before I went under, I heard a pretty nurse saying how Senator Pratt would increase the funding to the hospital if they took me in first. It was the last thing I heard, and I went to sleep smiling."

Robert laughed. His son would be fine.

Chapter Sixty-Two

baco, Bahamas 1971

Nearly a half a year passed when Sophia was able to get Karl to go for a check-up. He had grown so thin and was tired all the time. The doctor in Miami confirmed the worst of her suspicions. *Cancer.*

Karl had refused all treatments, preferring to live out his days in his home where he could breathe the salt air breezes of his beloved Bahamas. For months, Sophia cared for him. The disease ravaging him and melting his skin to his bones.

For the past two weeks, she'd stayed at his bedside watching him sleep. He'd eaten nothing and was uncommunicative. Large purple spots appeared on his back, his lips were cracked, his skin a pasty white.

Suddenly, his eyes opened, and a spurt of energy seemed to emanate from him. Might he recover?

"I'm going to leave, my sweet Sophia."

"Hush, Karl. You will not leave me now."

"Can you forgive me those years"

She picked up his frail hand and kissed it. He referred to those dark years right after the war, but he was a changed man, and there was no need to bring up the past. "I love you, Karl."

"I love you, too, my sweet Sophia. My princess who I never deserved. Hold me, Sophia. I'm cold."

Sophia repositioned herself to hold Karl's papery body in her arms. She tucked his head in her neck, willing life into him, realizing the endeavor was futile. Tears dripped from her cheeks onto his head in an endless flow of liquid love. "I will never forget you. Go knowing that you will live in everything I do. That you were an amazing father, that you were my best friend, and my love for you is infinite."

In those twilight hours, Karl closed his eyes, his breathing becoming more erratic. Sophia held him close and stared out to the sea. A beautiful boat with bright white sails, sailed on the evening breeze. She watched until the boat faded into the horizon. Karl clenched her hand and breathed his last breath. He was gone.

Night passed into day. Queenie came in to check on them, and then forced Sophia to let him go.

Five months had passed since Karl's funeral with everyone from the island, Nassau and the outer cays paying him tribute. Michael left soon after with summer academic commitments in veterinary school. It had been a year to the day of Kurt's accident with his full recovery thanks to the round the clock care he'd received at Robert's.

Kurt lingered. She was sure Robert ordered him to stay with her despite their son chomping on the bit to get back to work at Pratt Motors where he wanted to make a mark for himself. He leaned against the post, allowing her to let the world drift by in consecrated silence.

In a big wicker chair, Sophia sat on her porch and took a moment to gaze out over the sea. The moon threw its somber light, spilling over trees filled with flowers and spreading gold over orange and tamarind trees; the ocean in its vast magnitude, and breakers rising in their shadowy whiteness, as if to mingle with the fleecy clouds. The waves' deep and perpetual roar, the tide coming in and going out, life ebbing, flowing, forever changing.

Sophia placed the peas she'd shelled on the table. What was bottled-up inside, she suddenly unleashed. "The feeling of Karl dying in my arms won't go away. I prayed his suffering would end quickly. The selfish part of me wanted him to stay forever. We talked a lot in those days, and I grew to love your papa more and more, yet so many things remained unsaid."

Kurt nodded. "I loved him. He cared for all of us. We had so many good times."

Sophia sifted the peas through her fingers. "Memories are what bring us together, Kurt. We make so many mistakes in life, but we only realize this when age creeps up on us. I suppose living in the great conflict broadened and distorted my views on life. The last days of the war were a prelude to the Gates of Hell. Battles, bombardments, and starving. Nothing feeds forgetfulness better than war. We all keep silent and remain persuaded that what we've seen, what we've done, what we've discovered about ourselves and about others, is an illusion, a fleeting nightmare.

"Wars have no recollections, and nobody has the daring to comprehend them until there are no declarations left to voice what transpired, until the moment comes when we no longer identify them and they reappear, with a new face and a new name, to engulf what they left behind.

"When peace finally comes, it leaves in its wake heavily populated cemeteries, shrouds of silence that rots one's soul, and never goes away. There are no innocent hands and those of us who saw firsthand will take the skeletons in the cupboard to our graves.

"When your father returned, he was scarred inside and out. I had enough love to overcome the wounds that devastated him."

She didn't tell Kurt that she didn't love his papa when she

married him, or the years of Karl's anger, nor the reason for his resentment, nor the personal cost of two men and a woman caught in circumstances beyond their control. That part of history she interred in Karl's bones.

"But Mother, you suffered so much more."

"I think being a woman, you are stronger," she said, her voice thickening with emotion.

Kurt moved away from the post and knelt in front of her. "Mother, you have always listened more to your heart. That is why you will always be young."

She ran her hand over his dark hair like she did when he was a boy. "And you will always be a very wise man."

"I remember sage advice from a very smart woman given to me long ago...that we must suffer the scars of fate and keep going through the sporadic bursts of misery, but always maintain hope."

"I told you that when you were ten years old, catching that monstrous fish, never believing you listened." Sophia smiled and took a breath, her heart aching at the earnestness in his brilliant green eyes. She placed her palms on both sides of his face. "All that we love deeply becomes a part of us. I've built a tiny garden in the corner of my heart for Karl. For most, love comes only once in a lifetime. I've been blessed to be loved—" She stopped.

"By two men," Kurt said.

Sophia leaned back in her chair.

"Mother, go to Robert."

"No. He will know where to find me."

Chapter Sixty-Three

Kurt had left six months earlier and despite the void without him, the morning proved a pleasant one. Sophia moved out onto the terrace, drawn to the boundless turquoise waters lost in a vast horizon of greater blue. Her gaze caught in wonder, the sea tumbling in white crescent curls over shallows and sandy flats before swelling over an outcrop, slamming at last into a wild, foamy spray. She breathed deeply of summer air, dew-laden grass, and gardenia flowers opening to the sun. The silence was broken by snowy-white seagulls flying overhead.

She returned inside the house, sat down on the sofa. She picked up three letters, opened the first one from Louisa. As sisters, they had grown close with correspondences going back and forth across the Atlantic. Her sister had married and had two small children. Louisa begged her to come and visit her family in Austria during the summer.

The second letter was from Gabrielle, announcing she was doing well and had been promoted to full professor.

She opened the third letter and shook her head. Kurt's rapid scrawl, barely discernible brought delight. He detailed everything he learned at Pratt Motors, starting from the ground up. Van Smith had been appointed his mentor. Kurt expected Van to marry soon, for the old bachelor had been swept off his feet by the woman of his dreams. "But keep it a secret, Mom."

Sophia exhaled and stared at a wood box she had brought from her closet and ignored for months. She took a deep breath, unfastened it, and pulled out the golden jewel box. She tripped the secret mechanism Caroline Pratt had discovered and held the photos of her mother and father, sister and brother. She wound the box and listened to the familiar melody that reminded her of her Prussia. She placed them beside her and pulled out a parcel swathed in yellowed tissue paper, gingerly unfolding the wrapping. She held the dried bouquet to her nose, drawing in a faint hint of lavender. She smiled. Memories flooded of the day Robert had purchased the floral bouquet for her from the gypsy. She had kept it hidden all these years.

Setting aside the bouquet, she stood and stared out over the horizon again, the ocean breezes lifting the curtains and fluttering about her like angels' wings.

"Sophia."

She swung around. *Robert.*

It was him. His smile. His face. The face she'd dreamed of so many times.

He walked to her, all powerful grace and lean beauty, caught her.

The feel of his strong fingers threading with hers stunned her to stillness. Not just rooting her feet to the ground but weaving something undeniable through the pads of her fingers, threading up the veins in her arm, and pouring into her heart. From there, it pulsed into the rest of her with every beat.

"We are in the winter of our lives," said Robert. "It is our time now. That part that feels complete. I'm asking for you to be mine. In what years we have left, I want you by my side. I'm not going anywhere. I won't leave. I won't give up. And I will be here every single time you need me. You will never need to doubt. I don't care if there are a hundred million reasons...I exist and without you, I am nothing."

"My heart only seems to beat when you are near," Sophia whispered.

He took a step toward her. "When I look back at the way we began, all that we shared, I always dreamed of a future with you. The children you gave me...two handsome sons. They've grown to be extraordinary young men that you've nurtured and cherished and I'm proud of you for it."

"We've lingered long enough, Robert. I've lived a lifetime of waiting. There is a huge part of me who wants to marry the man I fell in love with, the man who stole my heart and soul. Would you be amenable to that?"

His dark brows climbed high on his forehead as he cast her a scandalized look. "Sophia, did you just propose to me?"

He pulled a box from his pocket and opened it, and inside was a ten-carat blue sapphire bordered with dazzling diamonds. "I remembered you telling me once, that it was your favorite color because it matched the lake of your ancestral home."

"Don't make me cry." She studied his face, and what she found there broke open something inside of her that exploded into incandescent sparks of the purest joy. Life with this man.

"You own my heart, Sophia. Always have. I've waited so patiently for you. I have not given up, then or now. Nor ever. For better or worse, you are my fate."

"I was yours the moment we collided in the street."

With a smile brilliant enough to illuminate the heavens, he swept her in his arms and claimed her mouth.

"Come," she urged. Linking her arm with his, she led him to the sea's edge. "What do you propose that we do, live in the Bahamas or Michigan?"

"Why not both? But for now, I've bought a yacht, and we will sail wherever in the world you want."

And like children, beneath bowing palms, they walked hand in hand beside never-ending, sparkling aquamarine water that pearled and foamed at their feet. With the prevailing winds at their backs and under the brilliant sun, they knew that their glorious future was just the beginning.

Author's Notes

This is a novel and to construe it as anything else would be an error. For the sake of storytelling, the timeline of fictionalized events, places and people was compressed.

The Fall of Berlin: On April 20, 1945, Hitler's birthday, Russian artillery began shelling Berlin in conjunction with the United States Air Force Flying Fortresses and Royal Air Force Lancasters and did not cease until the city surrendered. Soon, Soviet tanks smashed their way through German defenses, surrounding the city, and then taking occupation on May 2, 1945.

Then followed what was known as the "Rape of Berlin." The argument that rape has more to do with violence than sex is a victim's definition of the crime, not a full explanation of male motive.

There remain some claims that the over one hundred thousand rapes were in retaliation for the atrocities of the German forces' hostile to Stalingrad. Nevertheless, whispered stories of rapes, pregnancies and suicides against old women, barely pubescent girls—were acts of violence, and an expression of hatred and revenge. Red Army soldiers selected their victims carefully, shining torches in the faces of women in air raid shelters and cellars to find the most attractive.

Rape was to be buried and not to be talked about. When German men returned from prison camps and reasserted their authority, women were forbidden to mention the subject of rape as if it somehow dishonored their men, who were supposed to have defended them.

Women were left to pick up the pieces after the war. They worked with their hands in half-facades of houses, working in grueling bucket brigades to clean the city of ruined edifices. Historians estimate the women cleared seventy-five million cubic meters of rubble in Berlin.

American Automotive Industry in Detroit: After World War II, the American automobile industry transformed itself from a wartime economy juggernaut of building complex war material, i.e., automatic cannons, trucks, aircraft engines, bombers, cargo ships to the anchor of a civilian economy. The Post-World War II era brought an expansive range of technologies to the automotive consumer with innovative designs. The 1950s became the pinnacle of American automotive manufacturing and helped shape the United States into an economic superpower. By 1960, one-sixth of working Americans were employed directly or indirectly by the industry.

Lumber Camps in the Bahamas: During the twentieth century, the resource that spurred transformation was neither turtles, sponges, shark fishing, or crayfish—the islands earlier main sources of income, but the tall, thin hard Bahamian pine. The wilderness of these islands was daunting, having to hack through thick underbrush, and laying railroad tracks to move the lumber to the harbor. Conditions there could be characterized as "primitive", consisting of simple barracks and Quonset huts, and problems with rats and packs of feral potcake dogs.

The Abacos in the Bahamas: By the early 1950s and 60s, The Abacos were discovered by the rich and famous, seeking miles of powder-soft beaches beneath swaying golden-coconut palms and rising limestone cliffs. Today, it remains a place where one could forget every care in the world, watching sea birds scamper, enjoying swimming in endless shallow turquoise waters, reveling in the excitement of top fishing, boating, hiking, and sailing. Throughout the archipelago, people enjoy swimming with wild dolphins, exploring mysterious blue holes, kayaking through lush mangrove forests, or diving or snorkeling through colorful coral gardens. New Plymouth, Green Turtle Cay, Marsh Harbor, Man-O-War Cay, the headquarters of the famous Albury Brothers shipbuilders, Elbow Cay, home of the famous Hopetown lighthouse, and Manjack Cay are all charming islands with a variety of settlements and some of which I've mentioned in the book. All are the loveliest places in the world to visit.

I always say that I'm a storyteller, not a historian, and as a storyteller, I'm more concerned with the what-ifs than the why-nots. I so enjoy taking a bit of artistic license to bring you the most exciting, sensual love story that my what-if imagination can create.

Acknowledgments

Most books wouldn't be written without the help of some special people. I would like to acknowledge my editors, Scott Moreland and Kim Cates. Their insight and expertise were indispensable. Hugs also to my spouse, Edward, my right-hand man because without his support, none of my writing would be possible. Also, hugs to my five children, eight grandchildren, Eugene Dollard, Nancy Crawford, Brenda Kosinski, Paula Ursoy, Patricia King, Joanne M. McKelvey Morgan, Carol Brown, Lynne Denena, and posthumously, Loretta Bysiek—your love and comfort surround me.

Finally, a special note of gratitude to my readers. You will never know how much your enthusiasm and support enrich my work and my life. You are the best!

About the Author

Best-selling author Elizabeth St. Michel has received multiple awards for her work. Her first book, *The Winds of Fate*, was a number-one hit on Amazon's list of best sellers and a quarterfinalist for the Amazon Breakthrough Novel Award.

Surrender the Wind, Elizabeth's second novel, received the Holt Medallion and the Reader's Choice Award and was a finalist of the National RONE Award, which honors literary excellence in romance writing.

Sweet Vengeance: Duke of Rutland Series I won the prestigious International Book Award.

Her fifth book, *Only You: Duke of Rutland Series III*, achieved the American Fiction Award and the "Crowned Heart Award" from *InD'tale Magazine*.

Her sixth book, *Lord of the Wilderness, Duke of Rutland Series IV* achieved the International Book award, *InD'tale Magazine* RONE Award Finalist, *Forward Reviews* Bronze Medallion Book of the Year, New England Readers' Choice Award.

Her seventh book, *Surrender to Honor* received *InD'tale's* RONE Award.

Her eighth book, *Surrender the Storm* was a finalist for the International Chanticleer/Chatelaine Award.

St. Michel lives in New York and the Bahamas.

Dear Readers

It has given me special pleasure to write *On Prevailing Winds* for you, which introduces a World War II love triangle between the last Prussian princess, Sophia Sonderburg, automobile magnate, Colonel Robert Pratt, and ex-Nazi Doctor Karl Schneider.

Due to many reader requests, I'm returning to my Civil War *Surrender Series* to commence Zachary's story, the last of the Rourke brothers.

There is no greater compliment to me as an author than for my readers to become so involved with the characters that you want me to write more.

Although I can't tell you much more, I can promise you this: like my last novels, it is written with one goal in mind—to make you experience the laughter, the love, and all the other myriad of emotions of its characters. And when it's over, to leave you smiling...

Warmly,

Elizabeth St. Michel

P.S. If you would like to receive an emailed newsletter from me, which will keep you informed about my books-in-progress as well as answer some of the questions I'm frequently asked about publishing, please contact me on my Facebook, Twitter or webpage at www.elizabethstmichel.com. I would be thrilled to hear from you!